The Soothsayer & The Changeling

Books by Dennis Danvers

Circuit of Heaven *series*
Circuit of Heaven
End of Days

Novels
The Fourth World
Time and Time Again
The Perfect Stranger
The Soothsayer & The Changeling
The Watch
Wilderness
Bad Angels
The Bright Spot (writing as Robert Sydney)

Coming Soon!
Leaving the Dead

The Soothsayer & The Changeling

Dennis Danvers

SPEAKING VOLUMES, LLC
NAPLES, FLORIDA
2021

The Soothsayer & The Changeling

ISBN 978-1-64540-611-2

A dream you dream alone is only a dream.
A dream you dream together is reality.

—Yoko Ono

In dreams begin responsibilities.

—W. B. Yeats

Prelude

When we marvel at that blue marble in all its delicacy and frailty, and resolve to save the planet, we cast ourselves in a very specific role. The role is of a parent, a parent of the Earth. But the opposite is the case. It is we humans who are fragile and vulnerable and the earth that is hearty and powerful.

—Naomi Klein

I dreamt doom, awoke, and it was no dream, but no one would listen—so busily were they making doom. "What shall I do?" I asked the goddess.

Make them dream, my child, she said. *Make them dream your dream.*

So I did, and here's the story. Forgive me if it's a bit dreamlike. You have to start inside peoples' heads because that's where they live. They don't live on the planet. They live in their desires. The planet, the universe is there to satisfy those desires. If you want to change people, you have to become one of their desires. Absence makes the heart grow fonder. Doom doubles down on that, especially when the absence is everything, for them at least. The Universe soldiers on. Dooms happen all the time. Hence the Fermi Paradox. Does Earth have to join that hit parade of silence?

Who am I? What am I? I've quit trying to explain it, even to myself. You know that story where some human kid is switched at birth with some fairy bastard? A changeling? That theory was big through my adolescence and is still my fave, the one I've come to embrace. Like, yeah, I'll be that. A Changeling. Beats Alien Spy, which I tried on for a while. Not a good time.

I'd rather think I'm a Changeling, here to change things. On a mission for the goddess who put me here, swapped me out for some lucky baby who gets forever in goddessville, while I get a life on Planet Earth. It's on me.

I look nothing like anybody else in the family who all tower over me at Thanksgiving making elf and Munchkin jokes—but everybody has that odd relation, right?

Not like me. I'm only passing as human. That doesn't mean I know what I am. It's easy to overthink these things, best to keep moving and not look back. I follow the magic. Starting at twelve when me and a neighbor friend danced around skyclad and did spells, and mine worked, but hers didn't. Discovered my powers and lost my first friend. Most people spend entirely too much energy revisiting their adolescence, first marriage, whatever cluster of fuckups they're obsessed about, when they ought to be tuned into the here and now where the fuckups of the future are being devised. You can't make the same sausage twice, but you can lose a finger if you're not careful. You can hurt people. I try not to. Despite appearances.

Sometimes it happens you know things nobody wants to know. Unthinkable things. What do you do with that? Nobody wants to know what you know, feel what that horrible knowledge makes you feel. It's not like you can just *tell* them, and they'll suddenly think the unthinkable. People don't work like that. You have to forget what they *think*. Who cares? Not them. What they care about is what they *believe*, or want to bad enough to call it faith. That's how the species operates—the gut, the heart, the spirit of some Lord or other. For that you need a Savior, or in this case, several, to get the job done. I have to bring a few folks into the fold, fold them into the plan. As a polytheist I like the message a team effort sends: *This* is what survival of the fittest looks like.

Meanwhile, the human species is burning the planet to a cinder while denying the existence of fire. It's my job to make them feel the burn and pull together. The first part should be easy. The truth is already lapping at their feet. Coastal real estate prices have been plunging as people sell off like there's no tomorrow, since there probably isn't. It's the pulling together part that worries me, the stepping up, the giving up, the slowing down, sacrifice—survival the destination.

We're talking some extremely serious magic. I'm not without help. The goddess, to put it simply, is on our side, has been from the beginning, as in, the beginning beginning. Or maybe you're not comfortable with the g term. I wasn't at first either—gods of any kind and all their kith and kin. But when you spend your whole life with them showing up on a regular basis, it comes down to goddesses or aliens or monsters or crazy.

Anything but crazy.

Whatever you want to call them, I've had a whole lot of help from beings who were definitely not human, despite their usually looking like ordinary people. Brief encounters but intense. Mostly female when you could tell. They've also shown up as dogs, cats, a raccoon once. That was pee-your-pants scary. It spoke to me in a melodious trill I perfectly understood at the time.

Sometimes she shows up like some shimmering ghost but solid, flesh and bones.

She held me in her arms in the shower once, as if she'd stepped through the tile wall. Scared me half to death. I was thirteen, crying my eyes out over something. Then I realized—*she's trying to comfort me*—my mother wasn't too keen on compassion—and the pain went away, just like that. I let it go. It didn't matter. It was water down the drain. I don't even remember now what had me crying in the first place, probably some boy. It was a trick the goddess left with me: Remember her embrace, and the pain washes away. I take a lot of showers. When things are truly awful, I find a waterfall. Being a freak can be killer lonely.

I say she, singular, because even though she never looks the same, she's somehow the same person. Sometimes she shows up as several people all at once, especially in some of the dreams, but they're all her, all different, from tender to mean, loving, erotic, and wise. Confusing as hell. It's a bumpy ride. You have to hang on, trust them.

They—She—always love me. I can feel it in my bones.

They made me feel differently about myself, about my weirdness, taught me to just go with it. They guided me my whole life, though I didn't always listen, told them to fuck off and bother somebody else at fifteen, but when I finally surrendered to them, my life turned around. She knew I would find my way, that they would guide me, help me, whatever. Life was sweet. Those days they mostly showed up in my dreams, unless I summoned them—got down on my knees and begged. Prayed, you might as well say. They didn't always show right away, but they came, and they always helped me out. They got me out of quite a few self-inflicted messes without judging. They didn't try to talk me out of what I asked for even when maybe they should've.

Then a few days after my doom dream they said it was my turn to give back for all they'd given me, work some magic on their behalf. It was early morning in the aisles of Kroger. Right after opening. There was me, a cashier, and a handful of stockers in the building. They turned to me, these three women stocking pickles and hot sauce and spice blends. Six eyes met mine and said it was time to pay my debt.

"I would be honored," I said. Honored. Not a big word in my vocabulary. Surprised me too, and I meant it. I was grateful beyond words. They'd made me a better changeling. This was the very first time they'd ever asked me for anything. I was thrilled. Then they told me what they wanted me to do, and I couldn't get over how they cared so much, wondered why they should give a fuck about humans at all when they clearly didn't deserve it.

They don't seem to care about *deserving*. Oddly, that's a powerful incentive to *be* deserving. I was determined not to disappoint them. Sometimes I wonder—*why do I think any of this has been* my *idea? Who makes the magic I work, after all?*

Sometimes I think my whole life has been about this moment, that the goddess knew when she laid me in a human cradle just where that life would lead.

And, of course, I like to think that she's my mother, and she had to have an important reason to give up her daughter to a desperate mission: To thwart doom.

For you doubters, true story: Sophomore year I talked a CSI major into using me and my family to learn how to do all those cool DNA things. CSI told me: I'm not related to anyone in my family, and there are some anomalies in some of my sequences that she would *love* to share with her genetics professor—no names, just a subject number, total anonymity. Please, please, please. Some years later, I had a different name and phone number, CSI, now research assistant to the professor, managed to track me down and called begging me to come in out of the cold for a few tests. These aren't the kind of tests one can do well on. They're not pass/fail; they're much, much worse. No thanks. The tip-off? CSI asked me, as part of her sales pitch, *Don't you want to know what you are?*

A *what* not a *who*. That was just from a little DNA. No telling what I would become when they really got to know me.

You too, I suppose, but this story isn't just about me. Everybody needs a little help from their friends, and if you don't have very many, like me, you might have to make some. For me the story starts with

Danny, a fellow lonely freak, cursed—or blessed—by magic. Don't worry. I'll be back from time to time: Kristi Bell, at your service.

PART ONE

Danny Has a Dream

He's back in the hospital in bed, the dead of night. The room is filled with crows. They've come for him. They speak quietly to one another, muted little crow caws that sound like echoes but close. They're all around him, perched on the monitors, the drips, the foot of the bed. One's pacing back and forth on his chest like a weary general, his tread lighter than kitten's paws.

He turns his head and looks Danny in the eye. He's here to save me, Danny realizes. The crows aren't so sure he's worth it.

The door doesn't open. There's not a sound. Nonetheless, someone enters the room, a woman. The crows have gone, as if they've coalesced into this woman. She lies down beside him, strips away the tubes and wires and needles, takes him in her arms and makes passionate love to him. He's completely enthralled. He never sees her face.

In the afterglow, she whispers in his ear, "It's time to wake up," and he opens his eyes. He's wrapped in her enormous wings, high above the Earth. She flings them wide, and he's flying through the air. It's okay. He's been here before. No worries. It's the accident. Once again, he survives.

He wakes up before he hits the tree. Why go through that again?

He dreams about the accident all the time. That doesn't seem odd. What's surprising is that he should dream about falling in love. For that's what it feels like eating his bowl of oatmeal, in the shower, riding the bus to work—that he's fallen in love, with a woman in a dream. Wouldn't it be pretty to think so?

Just when he thought his life couldn't get any weirder.

Chapter One

Head Over Heels In Love

And all should cry, Beware! Beware!
His flashing eyes, his floating hair!
Weave a circle round him thrice,
And close your eyes with holy dread,
For he on honey-dew hath fed,
And drunk the milk of Paradise.

—Samuel Taylor Coleridge, *Kubla Khan*

It's summer in Richmond. The black asphalt shimmers in the heat. Two men with leaf blowers strapped to their backs are blowing around cigarette butts and candy wrappers and trash from the McDonald's on the corner. Their twin clouds of exhaust converge on a third man driving a tiny car with a roaring vacuum waiting to suck up the detritus. The men rev the leaf blowers like two teenagers about to race at a stop light. At the corner the bus idles diesel. The city is in the process of switching to natural gas, but they've run out of money and grants have dried up

This is Danny's stop. He works in the strip mall. He walks through the clouds of dust and carbon monoxide and diesel and burning flesh trying not to breathe too deep. Trying not to breathe at all.

He makes his first appointment just in time, but he's afraid his client is growing uneasy sitting across from him waiting for her answer. Half her half hour's over, and so far she has nothing to show for it since she posed her question some five minutes in. Above her head, on the wall behind her, the clock's second hand sweeps. The clock face is a painted tree—broad, spreading crown, gnarly roots—the store's logo, same as on the t-shirt Danny wears only in this room for his part-time soothsayer job, three afternoons a week at the Tree of Life Book Shoppe. He has other jobs, though not at the moment. Things are slow.

It's been a weird day, the news full of another freak storm barreling up the east coast, though by now you'd think they wouldn't be "freak" anymore. It won't turn out well. A perfect storm. But his client doesn't want to know what he sees about that. You don't have to be a soothsay-er to know that. One of his other clients is right in the middle of it unless she followed his advice a couple of weeks ago on a beautiful, cloudless day to make other plans. He saw her drowning in the lobby of her hotel when the "unprecedented" storm surge hits.

He can see things—in the future. Really. If you're his client, you can believe him now or later. It makes absolutely no difference to him. Here's the thing—he can't always see what you want him to see, or even remotely in the neighborhood. He sees what he sees. Some woman wanted to know about her new boyfriend, for example, but her cat Rudolph was dying. The boyfriend was another loser. Danny couldn't catch a glimpse of his sorry ass past next week, but Rudy adored her. Danny had to tell her the truth, say some sooth: Forget the boyfriend; get thee to a veterinarian.

Clients always want to know how *everything* will turn out—their own personal *everything*—and he can't tell them that. It doesn't work that way. He lays his hand on their forearm usually, touch intensifies the connection, and he sees moments, important moments, though he doesn't always know why or how they're important—when things are still in flux, when things can still be done, when emotions are running high. They're not *his* moments. Not usually. Not in a while. Endings, safe to say, are his least favorite moments. It's taken him awhile to learn

3

to keep his emotions under control. He doesn't just see the moments, he feels them, experiences them. But generally speaking, clients would prefer you not sob or scream or retch, and they're more likely to believe you're a fraud when you do. He never bothers to tell them how tiny their everything is. And how fragile.

Can he change things? Think of it this way: In your future, let's say, you will drive into a brick wall. It *will* happen without question. Does it matter when you see the wall and hit the brakes? Whether you're wearing a seatbelt? How fast you're going in the first place? It's a matter of life or death, wall or rubble, a fireball or a new bumper.

Don't ask him about death—when, how, why. Everybody does it. That's all you need to know about death, and most people act like they don't even know that much. The planet's barreling toward a brick wall, but everybody knows that. They just can't seem to find the will to hit the brakes. He can't imagine what he can do about it. Clients don't want to talk about the planet. They want to talk about their future lives, as if they were going to take place somewhere else. Danny tries to believe their questions matter. That's what they're paying him for.

This client's question isn't that hard: Should I quit my job? Probably, if you're asking, but that isn't the soothsayer talking, just common sense, not what the client really wants to hear—at least the sort of client who looks for her sense in the back of The Tree of Life Book Shoppe. *Quit your mundane jobs, and follow your dreams!* Gwen, the nice Tarot reader, says that stuff all the time. Short-sighted business plan, in Danny's opinion. The unemployed don't waste money on guys like him or Gwen or all the woo-woo merchandise out front, especially if they have to support some dream at the same time.

Anybody can have a dream. It takes guts to live it.

If this client has dreams, he can't see them—just an intense longing to break free smothered by despair like a caged animal who's given up the search for a way out a long time ago. She's hopeless. She hates herself for wasting her life. His heart goes out to her.

He shares the space with a couple of Tarot readers and a palmist on a rotating basis. He doesn't believe in that stuff, but they get more bookings, more repeat customers than he does. He eavesdrops to learn their moves. The Tree of Life owner, Serena, has encouraged him to give his clients a more satisfying paranormal experience; otherwise she might have to give his slot to Terry, a past-life visionary who's been lurking around lately when he's not at the gym bulking out. Perhaps he fancies himself a gladiator in a former life.

If *Consumer Reports* rated soothsayers, Danny would put his sooth up against anyone's when he actually *sees* something. He sees Terry has been satisfying Serena lately, suspects it won't last, having had a glimpse of what seems like a nasty break-up in her tiny little office at the store. He doesn't tell her. She probably already knows. Serena's into lots of side trips along her karmic path. He admires her unwavering ability to make money off the fringy and flaky. She called him up out of the blue about a year ago, asked if he would be interested in coming to work for her, just a few afternoons a week. She'd heard about him, she said.

Like he told her then, he doesn't believe any of the stuff in the books out front—spells, ancient astronauts, numerology, spirit animals, astral projection, crystals. You wouldn't believe what a hunk of quartz sells for. Not just any hunk. These rocks come with instructions. *Step 1: Cleanse Your Spirit.* His dirty little spirit couldn't stop laughing at that one. *Why would I cleanse my spirit for a boxed rock?* He hates that the name of the store has that silly *–pe* dangling off the end like a badge of certified loopiness, refusing to enter the 20th century, much less the 21st—stuck in Ptolemy's universe, leaking phlogiston from every pretentious orifice, venting into the ether. He has no use for the tiniest bit of any of this magickal shoppe crappe. He'd just as soon treat his occasional migraines with leeches.

Yet here he is. He needs this. There has to be *somewhere* it's okay for him to say what he sees, what he knows to be true, and not be crazy. Because it's true. Always.

This place is his only outlet for the sooth. The chance to *say* it straight out to people who might actually want to hear it, because usually people don't. People fear you when you know things about them you shouldn't, even good things, even harmless things. Everybody's got something they don't want anyone finding out. If he knows one inexplicable thing about you, there's no end to what else he might know. It doesn't matter that it doesn't work that way. Nobody knows how it works, including him, but he never knows everything. What he knows, he feels compelled to tell. What possible purpose could it have for him to know if not to tell? These aren't *his* futures we're talking about. It's hard to keep some things to yourself. Sometimes he can't help himself. There are things he sure as hell would want to know if it was his life—like a storm surge hitting your hotel.

Still. At this point, he doesn't go looking. Too much wear and tear on the psyche. He tries not to meet too many new people. He absolutely can't work retail, which is what he used to do before the accident. Commercial transactions amp people up way more than they realize or admit to. No surprise. Consumption is the national religion. He'd rather go to a funeral than Walmart on a Sunday. Mostly he temps in one cubicle after another, converting files or updating records, the quiet guy who manages to avoid everyone if he's lucky.

Sometimes he's not. Like when he told his supervisor his kid was going to fall out of a tree and he was terminated, not thanked, when it happened, as if he was there prying the kid's fingers from the limb. That's an extreme example, but on the whole, when he opens his mouth, it's more likely bad luck than good. Like that's the price for messing with the future.

But here in the back room of The Tree, people *ask* what he sees, care enough to pay for it, though he doesn't care about the money as much as he probably should. Along with all the stuff he dispenses that's just a lot of harmless hot air stolen from his fellow fortunetellers and self-helpers, there's always something real, something true, something he has *seen* and knows to be true. And he gets to say it and be believed.

At least what passes for belief in the back room of The Tree. It's a tricky balance. Clients assume somewhere in the back of their heads, even as they're handing over the credit card, that nobody in this room is going to speak *real* truth. This is cosmic truth, hopeful truth, truth with some kind of entertainment or psychological value. Soothsayer truth, not the real deal. He has no illusions that his clients know the sooth when they hear it, though eventually it catches up with them. They complain to Serena he's too spacey, too random, too creepy. Never that he's wrong. Some have said they found the degree of his knowledge about their personal lives a bit disturbing. He tries to steer clear of disturbing. He wishes only the best for Serena.

He did manage to save Rudolph. He called the client to make sure she had checked on him, and the cat was just coming out of surgery to untangle his intestines. He was going to make it. He wonders if Terry's ever saved a life rewinding through his clients' ancient histories. *Previously on Lost....*

A couple of weeks ago at the store's Summer Solstice Sales Event where all the psychic talent was on display with chips and soda, Terry started talking some blather about Ancient Carthage, and Danny turned and made a beeline to the front door to visit with Gwen's husband Billy. He was having a smoke in the blazing heat, a special organically grown, Native American tobacco that won't kill you like those others will.

Serena sells it, so you know it's good. Shamans bless it or some such. Doesn't seem to help with the smoker's cough though. He's promised Gwen he'll quit. It's a little late for that. Danny likes Billy because he's supportive of Gwen's "calling" to read cards—that's what she calls it. He's even proud of her abilities. Gwen's going to be lost without him. Every nut needs someone to believe in them when no one else will. Unfortunately, Danny's found, there's a shortage of such people. You can't trust a nut to know what he needs anyway. That's what makes him a nut.

Ancient Carthage. What a load. Danny doesn't like looking back. One life's enough. But these glimpses of others' futures? He can't explain it. He gets a charge out of it, like he's seeing over the next rise, what's up ahead. Like it's leading him on, giving him a purpose, even though it's not *his* life. Could be anyone's. Rudolph's life. Doesn't matter. Tomorrow's a precious thing. He doesn't always see bad things, and even bad things can be made better. Sometimes. When he sees the utterly hopeless, he keeps it to himself. He's learned that much, at least, about being a soothsayer. No one needs more hopeless, more despair. Ever. That's one reason he avoids seeing the distant future when he can help it.

He can't shake the feeling that he's this way for a reason, that there's something he's *supposed* to see someday, and he needs to keep an eye out for it. On the other hand, that sounds totally delusional. It's stupid. He's nobody, nobody who was in a car wreck almost four years ago and started seeing things. Things that come true. It would be a whole lot easier to deal with if they didn't, or if they were so vague, like most of Gwen's forecasts, that it pretty much *had* to come true one way or another. "You'll come to see this matter differently," is his favorite of Gwen's, or as Kristi, the not-always-so-nice-but-wickedly-funny Tarot reader, would say, "You'll get over it." Eventually, we're all over it, over everything, over all the tiny little everythings.

No. He sees real stuff. Like some poor cat who hasn't been able to take a shit in days. Like a kid falling out of an apple tree showing off for some cousins. Like Danny's wife Nina leaving him—the last important thing he saw about himself. You can maybe understand why he doesn't go looking for another. That's been a couple of years now. She fled, saying she couldn't take it anymore—living with a man mired in others' futures—left a note on the kitchen counter, took their cat.

Last he heard, eavesdropping on a conversation at the museum where Nina used to work, she's living in Portland. He doesn't know which one. Both are far from here, which is why she's there. "I've become one of them, haven't I?" she asked the week before she left. "You're just waiting for something to happen to me."

He didn't tell her he had seen her leaving. In his vision, she was glad; she was free. It'd been hard, but she'd done the only thing she could do. That's the moment of her life he saw before she lived it, her looking down the highway, heading out of town into a new life. Even back then he kept the hopeless to himself. He's built up a surplus of hopelessness, a hope deficit. When he sees hope, he leaves it alone, lets it be.

Until now. Because this time it's his own.

About his current client's *job*, he hasn't a clue, can't even see what it is she *does*. That whole part of her life is a blur behind a fog bank, as the clock keeps moving. At least it doesn't tick. It would be awful if it ticked. It hums a faint electronic *Om*. Clients complain to Serena about his long silences, like he's off in another world. Tomorrow *is* another world. Isn't that what they're paying for? Do they think it's as simple as going there and reporting back what they want to hear? *Here's just the tomorrow you asked for in a kaleidoscope of colors, with a rich assortment of scents and not a trace of greenhouse gases…*

Elissa. Her name's Elissa Manoli. It's on his appointment list right in front of him, but he knew it the moment he saw her. He's never seen her before today. He's never even seen her around the store, or at the market next door. He'd certainly remember. She's movie-star beautiful. Her entrance into the tiny back room where the sooth is sold, her few short steps, seating herself beneath the clock, completely overwhelmed him. Serena painted the clock face years ago before the store opened. It helped visualize the dream, she said. She's not a very good artist. You only have to be so good to paint a symbolic tree, to visualize what you want to see. Anyone can do that.

He doesn't know what to do about Elissa. Where to begin.

He imagines she's the woman in his dream, the woman he fell in love with. As beautiful as she is, men must fall for her all the time—hopelessly.

There's a 2 o'clock in less than ten minutes—Michael, who will inquire, as always, about his non-existent career as a screenwriter. Danny doesn't know how to make it any clearer to Michael that he's a lazy, no talent poser who will likely never have a career at anything but imagining his own fame. And yet he keeps coming back. Kristi claims she saw him on a red carpet in Hollywood, and he keeps seeking confirmation. Kristi will do shit like that, totally play to the client's fantasies to boost the tip. Good news is more lucrative than bad. It's okay to tip your soothsayer, especially if the sooth soothes. Or in Michael's case, she may just have enjoyed fucking with him. Michael hasn't *written* a screenplay, understand. It's still in the *planning* stages. He just wants to know how everything will turn out before he, you know, like invests too much *effort* in it. Little chance of that.

Michael can wait. Hollywood can sustain the loss.

He can't decide what to do about Elissa, but it's not like he's drawing a total blank. Quite the opposite. He's seen too much. Way too much.

From the moment he touched her bare forearm, briefly, gently.

She doesn't love her husband. He's seen it through her own eyes, felt her loathing as she looks at the man in a few days on a boat in the bay. But she's also here before him. Soft green eyes, reddish blonde hair. Freckles. He doesn't want to speak of this revelation. Or how it makes him feel. He tries to avoid his own feelings, since they can affect what he sees. Not its truth, but its center. People don't come here to find out about *his* life. Trouble is he's seen himself, with her. With Elissa. After her marriage is over. The truth sits in his throat like a big knot, like a fist. He finally asks, to end the long silence, "What does your husband do?"

This takes her by surprise. "My husband? What does my husband have to do with me quitting my job?"

"I sense he's important." You hate him.

"You're assuming I *have* a husband." She cocks a brow with this. A test, teasing him. Of course she has a husband.

"You're wearing a ring." A very expensive ring.

"Lots of women wear rings. It means nothing." Not quite true. This one doesn't mean what she hoped it would.

"This one does. You have a husband. I've seen him in the near future. He has a large sailboat? You'll be part of the crew soon, in a few days. Next weekend? What does he do?" He saw husband Carl through her eyes as he plays captain, ordering his crew about. She tightens a knot in the blistering sun and hates him. *Why don't you love him? Did you ever love him?*

"Can't you see what he does, with your gift or whatever?" She shrugs, smiles. "Understandable, I suppose. He has money: He does nothing. Owns things."

"Does he do it well?"

She laughs.

He saw she would, before he told his little insinuating joke. This, he supposes, is how we'll proceed to our future, the world he's been living in ever since she sat down and asked her question, after the fleeting vision of her loathsome husband's boat sailed over the horizon, leaving Danny and Elissa in its wake:

He's sitting on a mountaintop in brilliant morning sunshine, perched on a rock, looking down into a beautiful autumn valley. He's head over heels in love—whispering her name—the woman he loves nestled in his arms. They've just made love. There's a chill in the air.

In that future. Not now. That's the trouble with seeing the future. It colonizes the present and makes it destiny. She is lovely, however. Her laughter gives him goose bumps. He's perfectly willing to fall in love with her.

It's been a long time.

It's never what you see, but what you don't see.

He didn't see in that moment if she loves him in return. He doesn't know how this everything will turn out. Where's a good soothsayer when you need one? In the future, he couldn't see her face except in his mind's eye—only now in the present where Serena's stupid clock swirls away the time—can he see her incredibly beautiful face.

She asks, "So what about *my* job?"

"Is there a prenup?" he asks. It's a question of ownership, responsibility, accountability. He sees her reading documents, spreadsheets.

She doesn't ask why he asks. She smiles the faintest smile, a ripple in the ether. It has a profound influence on him. Somehow he's managed to free her from her cage. "Yes. There is. Isn't there?"

He tells her to follow her dreams. What he wants to say is follow mine. Still fueled by the passion he felt in his dream, in his vision, he flirts with her, makes her laugh again. She flirts back, idly twisting the big diamond on her finger, as if she means to work it loose. The time slips away. When she stands, and they're face-to-face in the tiny room, he sees she's tall and willowy, as tall as he is, her eyes looking into his, dead level. She takes his breath away. He wants to crush her in his arms. He holds her gaze, and she smiles a little enigmatic smile and turns toward the closed door. He reaches around her and opens it.

It's not until he's escorted her out to her car, past an impatient Michael torturing Serena with one of his many Ideas for a Blockbuster, that Danny sees the connection, as they stand squinting in the sunshine, putting off good-bye.

"You work for one of his companies. You know something illegal that's going to be revealed. If you both own everything, you can't walk away by quitting. Since there's a prenup, you can. It's just a job. There's nothing to connect you to his crimes."

She holds his gaze for a moment. She's standing inside her open car door, about to get in. She's deciding how he possibly knows what he knows. Maybe he works for the detestable sailboat husband, but somehow she doesn't think so. She's deciding if she believes in magic, if she believes in Danny. He can relate. He can't decide that himself. Her face, her eyes, her searching gaze—they're enough magic for him, for now. The last half hour has changed them both, perhaps him more than her.

That's the thing about seeing the future. You can't do it without changing something, even if it's only yourself. He looks at her, reporting back from the future. She doesn't have to be psychic to see something meaningful in his eyes. He will fall in love with her—he's seen it. It will happen. It's already happening. Since he received the gift of seeing the future, he's seen none for himself until now.

"Thanks, Danny," she says. "You've been most helpful."

And then she drives away.

Maybe not tonight, maybe not for a while, but he *will* call her. That's not the soothsayer talking. Just the man. The lonely, fucked-up man, watching another married woman driving away.

The whole thing's impossible. He's never been wrong before, but then he's never wanted to be right so much before. It felt like destiny, that moment in his vision, like he's found his soul mate, not that he believes in that crap. But who doesn't want to?

That night the storm makes landfall. The week is filled with scenes of widespread devastation, even worse than the dire forecasts. Dozens die, drowned in the surge. For a moment, he was one of them.

Chapter Two

Naked In An Icy Landscape

ESTRAGON: We've lost our rights?
VLADIMIR: (distinctly) We got rid of them.
—Samuel Beckett, *Waiting for Godot*

As she's driving away from The Tree of Life in the bright summer sun, Elissa can't believe how she just flirted with the soothsayer, but he's *so* into her. She feels bad because Kris has this thing for him, and Elissa only went to check him out—to finally meet the Incredible Soothsayer Kris goes on and on about in Elissa's half empty mansion she's supposed to be filling with priceless this and that. A showplace. Who's to show? No one ever comes over but Kris who always makes fun of the gaudy opulence. She looks forward to Kris's visits. They split a ridiculously expensive bottle of wine, and Kris does her cards. The soothsayer date was Kris's idea. She practically begged her.

She *did* beg her. "Please, please, please!" They've been friends since freshman year in college. Kris can be relentless when she wants something.

They were out by the pool when Kris came up with the idea of Elissa checking out her soothsayer. Kris had just done her cards, still spread out on the glass top table under the sun looking like ratty bar coasters. Elissa always gets the same cards—Magus, Tower, Star—the same Big Life Change reading despite all evidence to the contrary. She suspects Kris of having a hand in that. It'd be like her. Before she read cards, she did card tricks. Never play poker with Kris.

Elissa was with Kris at a yard sale one seriously hungover morning some years back when she bought the tarot cards, her first and only deck. They looked like shit even then.

"I should learn how to do these," Kris had said. "What do you think? Something to channel my energies."

Try a fire hose, Elissa thought. "I think you should get some new ones that aren't total crap," she said, making it a certainty Kris would *have* to have them.

"They're *experienced*," Kris said. "Maybe there's some of the magic still in them." She fanned them in front of her face, never one to mind a little mold, and peered over the top with her large dark eyes, always up for melodrama. Between the cards and the eyes, she can make you forget they're just cardboard. She stole a couple of books from the library and started doing everybody's cards. She has a knack. At the same yard sale she bought a red silk scarf, stained and ragged, and keeps the cards wrapped up in it till this day. Elissa can never decide whether the whole thing's for real or not, whether she ever sees stuff or is just stringing everybody along. Still, every time anything important is going on in her life, Elissa has Kris do her cards.

She's never been wrong, but she could definitely be more specific.

Poolside, Elissa glared at the Magus, his ridiculously happy face stained with some ancient glass of red wine, the corners of his world crumbling and bent, and said, "You should *seriously* think about getting some new cards."

Kris persisted. "Don't change the subject. C'mon El, just check him out, give me some ideas. It's like I'm invisible. I can't get past pal. I want him."

"Maybe he's gay."

"He's not gay, okay? His wife left him. He still misses her."

"Maybe she left him because he's gay." Elissa didn't really think the guy was gay. She was just fucking with her best friend. That's the kind of relationship they've always had. Elissa's had nicer, warmer, cuddlier friends than Kris, but she never sees those people anymore. Kris is her best friend without question. She's never had many. Kris blames it on her beauty.

"Would you forget the gay thing? I know why his wife left him, okay? And it wasn't because he's gay."

"I know. You told me that story. Makes no sense to me. Did she love him or not? The guy sees what he sees, right? Isn't that what you've been telling me?"

"Doesn't matter. She's gone, and I'm here, but I'm getting nowhere. Just check him out. See what you think. Move things along."

"How am I supposed to do that?"

"I don't know. Guys open up to you. It's the freckles, I think. Make an appointment with him, and he has to talk to you. My treat. C'mon. It'll be fun. A half an hour."

"What am I supposed to ask him about?"

"How about your divorce? That's all you ever talk about."

"What divorce? Get real. I can't ask about that. What's the point? I'm boxed in—you know that. I just wish I could quit before the company goes down, but it would look bad. Carl could make it look like I was deeply involved if it suited him. Technically, I do work for him."

"Ask Danny about *that*. Not Carl's shit, but the job. It's not like you do anything anymore but draw a paycheck. Everybody asks about that career stuff, like that's their whole life. It doesn't *matter* what you ask him. He sees what he sees. I'm telling you, this guy's for real."

Elissa squinted at her, her intense friend. There was a blinding glare off the pool. Kris had been obsessing about this guy for months and months. It was getting seriously weird, even for Kris. "I don't get it.

Do you want to fuck him because he sees the future or because he's so hot?"

"Both. If all else fails you can work into the conversation that the hot tarot reader would very much like to jump his bones. He *will* see something interesting. I promise. He's amazing. Please, please, please!"

Elissa had to admit she was curious.

So she went and checked him out, and he broke the logjam in her mind with just two or three questions. She *can* quit her job, can even seriously think about divorcing Carl without fear of retaliation. She ponders the soothsayer too. That's what his business card says. He made sure she had one, wrote his own phone number on the back. Soothsayer. Sounds silly, but the whole place is silly. If Kris didn't work there, Elissa wouldn't set foot in The Tree.

The truly weird thing is that they *are* going out on the stupid boat this weekend, out on the bay. She couldn't weasel out of it this time. Carl's got friends and their wives he wants to impress, showing off wife and boat both. Nice lines, don't you think? Wouldn't you like to own her?

Is he good at it? the soothsayer asked. She smiles. Not very.

Elissa doesn't know what to say to Kris about Danny. The way he looked at her... Totally Disney, but sweet. And sexy. Like he recognized her from a past life or a dream or something. No man has ever looked at her like that. Like *You're the One.* Certainly not Carl. He's more like, *you'll do.* Elissa didn't get it at first, Kris's thing for Danny, but when he looked at her like that...

What can she tell Kris? It's not like she was trying to steal him. It's not like he's hers anyway. *It's like I'm invisible,* she said. Not exactly his response to Elissa. She turns off her phone. She'll deal with Kris later.

He's not telling her everything. She's sure of that. She wonders if he'll call. She can feel it in her bones that he will, not a bad feeling to have in her current life configuration—married to asshole. A sweet, handsome man likes her. She wants to enjoy it while it lasts.

If Danny calls, he calls, and then she'll see. Why worry now? She's still married to Carl. Doesn't cheat. Hasn't. Not because she's so good and virtuous. She's had no interest in men or sex or much of anything. Then she gets her fortune told by her best friend's crush and wants to make a deal of it. How pathetic, right? *Soothsayer*. C'mon. How flaky can you get?

Besides, she has enough to worry about, an outing with Captain Carl to look forward to. Some men shouldn't own boats. It brings out the worst in them, and Carl's bad enough already. She told Carl that Captain Bligh used to be a nice guy before he became captain, and he asked her who this Bligh guy was. It wasn't worth the trouble to tell him, so she said he was an old boyfriend. "Total prick," she said, picturing Carl at the wheel of the Bounty.

That felt good. The boat is vintage, small and nimble and tricky to sail, a total mismatch with Carl, who bought it at an estate auction. Once Carl bids on something, he will own the thing, whatever it is. He hates to lose.

When Carl proposed, Elissa asked her mom what she should do. Mom had been poor most of her life, had considered all the exits one time or another. She said marry the boss if you want, but remember this is as good as he gets. He won't get nicer. He won't love you more or treat you better. He might get richer, but don't expect things to get any better. Count on them to get worse.

Elissa chose to take that as a yes. Elissa was more afraid of being poor than Mom ever was. Surprise, surprise: Being rich isn't worth Carl.

She had Kris do her cards then too. Her advice—"Go for it if you want. It's a marriage. It's not like it's forever."

The friends on the boat trip turn out not to be friends, of course, but some guys Carl's trying to make a deal with. Like all Carl's deals, it requires discretion, so they speak in clumsy code and look annoyed if you listen too close. Don't worry, guys. Elissa doesn't want to know any more than she already does, wishes she could forget what little she knows.

There were only three people waiting at the dock, the two guys and a woman. Elissa figures one of the wives was smart enough not to get herself trapped on some asshole's fantasy sailboat on a hot summer day with little wind and lots of liquor. The other wife is counting on the liquor to get her through and has a drink in hand before they've left the dock. After a couple of mint juleps, she flirts with Captain Carl in an ever deepening southern accent, lamenting she's *ever* so ignorant of boats, snuggling up beside him at the wheel, and Carl pretends he knows what he's doing.

The men are dressed for a round of golf or a poker game, smoking Cuban cigars, a gift from Captain Carl. Strictly passengers. They're here for the ride and the party. This makes Elissa a crew of one. She's done this a time or two before. She learned to sail in college. She and Kris used to go out on the lake in a boat not much bigger than they were. Kris taught her. Kris says if it's taught in a summer camp somewhere, she knows how to do it. Her folks figured the more time Kris spent away from home, the better. Elissa's seen it for herself. Kris makes her folks nervous.

Captain Carl, who's had plenty of liquor himself, soon has his crew tacking, Dixie Belle's tits up against his arm. The lifejacket buoys up her impressive breasts, like flotation devices. Captain Carl doesn't wear a lifejacket, doesn't fit the swaggering image and his expanding gut. He can always grab hold of Dixie. There must be some serious money in this for Dixie's hubby. Nobody's that clueless. Or maybe she's not his wife. Those certainly aren't her breasts.

Maybe if Danny were here, he could clarify matters. She can't imagine him fitting in with Carl and company, another point in his favor.

She used to try to learn their names, Carl's Associates; now she makes a point not to, to just sort of check out. It helps her resist the urge to speak. Once she speaks, she has to listen, and that's when the trouble begins, because it forces her to think about what sort of man she's married to, and then she hates herself. Mission accomplished. She doesn't have to keep doing that one over and over again. She knows shorter routes to self-hatred, all well trod.

When you hate yourself, you're not expecting some guy out of nowhere to look at you with total adoration. Like he sees past the beauty, like that's only a distraction. He's looking deeper. Maybe she should see Danny again, ask him a few more questions. Steal him from her best friend. *It doesn't matter what you ask him, he sees what he sees,* Kris said going into this. Well Kris, I'm sorry, but he saw me. I sure didn't see that coming. Out of all the things he could've seen, he saw me.

"Would you make an attempt!" Carl growls in her ear in what's supposed to be a whisper. "What's your problem? You're in your own fucking world over here. Have a drink why don't you?" He smells like Bourbon and cigars. He's planted Dixie Belle behind the wheel in his captain's hat, so he could deliver this message. She's hamming it up for the boys with one of the cigars. Pro. Has to be. Carl's not a good enough sailor to take the boat out by himself, and no one who's ever crewed for Carl wants to do it again.

"No thanks. I'm good."

"Makes you seem like a tightass. Like you're too good for every-body."

Too good for you, but let's not go into that. "Oh no. I know I'm to-tally unworthy, Captain Carl."

"Fuck you."

"Since when?"

"Don't push me."

"Or what?"

He stalks back to Dixie Belle and nudges her ass to make room for his, wraps a paw around her and calls to Elissa. "Tighten that line, tightass, if that's not too hard for you." He laughs big, and his buddies join in, and even Dixie Belle has a chuckle.

Elissa grabs the line she's already secured, yanks it hard with all the power of her hatred, imagining it around his neck, his eyes bulging out of his clueless head, his fat, swollen tongue, silenced—pulls a little harder.

She remembers Danny. Not so much what he said, though that's part of it—that she doesn't have to put up with this shit anymore, that she can walk away—but *how* he looked at her, like she was *everything*. She doesn't cut the line, doesn't slip it free, but loosens it, as if whoever secured it didn't know what they were doing—stupid and inept and weak. Like a girl—as Carl would say. Some tightass girl he never should've married no matter how beautiful she is. Some dumb cunt.

The loose line doesn't matter for most of the lurching, pointless voy-age. They're soon becalmed and drunk, and Dixie Belle, who's dropped all pretense of being anyone's wife, has unveiled her pontoons, and is diving off the bow for the boys' amusement.

The wind, the blessed wind, finally picks up, putting an end to the show. Now the plan seems to be that one by one they are to retire below to the tiny cabin with Dixie as they circle the bay. The four of them work this out in giggling, groping whispers. Dixie's below with husband number one when Carl thinks he sees the cops on the horizon headed their way, decides he can outrun them, and unfurls sail like he's in a pirate movie, shouting down to those below to get their clothes on.

The line slips free like a loosely tied scarf in a gust of wind. Elissa watches it snake by, just beyond her reach. She doesn't lunge.

The swinging boom catches Carl on the back of the neck with a bone-cracking thud, his face smacks on the deck, and he bounces into the bay, as the boat heaves up and down like a pony and heels over in a tangled mess. Elissa slides into the water.

That's the last she ever sees of Carl alive. Next thing she knows she's on a police boat. She's the only survivor who passes the sobriety test. Dixie Belle, whose real name is Rhonda, made it out of the cabin below and swam to safety, but husband number one got stuck in the narrow passageway and drowned. Everyone else who wore a lifejacket—Elissa and husband number two—were rescued. Captain Carl doesn't wear a lifejacket. Captain Carl is dead.

Even sitting in the police station knowing the shit she'll have to go through when Carl's dealings come to light, Elissa can't stop saying to herself in a joyous chant, *I'm free! I'm free! I'm free!*

She owes that freedom to Danny. He's changed her life. If she had never been to him, had never had him look at her like that, she wouldn't have acted the same. She would've tied up the line, lunged if it came loose. Stayed the course.

I have no regrets, she thinks. If that makes me a monster, monster's still better than whatever it was I've been since I married Carl.

With everything going on after Carl's death, she's able to avoid the subject of Danny with Kris for quite a while. It all comes out what a crook she was married to. The deal he was making the day he died involved massive amounts of toxic waste dumped into the bay, rendered undetectable by bribes. She could honestly say she had no idea, and somehow none of the fallout came down on her. Since she never stood to profit directly from his dealings and there were no end of crooks who testified how totally clueless she was, she's able to walk away as the grieving clueless widow. Much preferable to jail.

She has her own place, a duplex, living in one apartment and renting out the other to a young couple she envies for their earnest, adoring poverty. There's life insurance and some savings the law didn't seize, thanks to the prenup, and she's doing okay, looking for work, but the economy sucks, and widow-to-Carl isn't exactly a résumé builder. People figure she was either a crook herself or incredibly stupid. Those are the choices. Who wouldn't want to hire that? Before Carl she used to sell Investment Opportunities to horny rich guys, not a career path she's dying to return to. That's how she met Carl. He was a client looking to invest/launder some of his vast wealth. She doesn't know what she's going to do next. That's a whole lot better than never thinking it fucking mattered what she did. Danny gave her back her future.

She's invited Kris over to do her cards, to face the music. They'll get around to the subject of Danny sooner or later. She's ready to tell her. It's been like three months. She wants to clear the air, make her move. She can't stop thinking about him. How many adoring men change your whole life? It's stupid not to *act* on something like that—as soon as she gets her car out of the shop. She sideswiped a sign when she moved in. She's just getting around to getting it fixed. It's unbelievable what body work costs. She hasn't driven herself much in the last few years.

Kris says she's dying to do her cards. Like clockwork, there they are again—Magus, Tower, Star. Major cataclysmic life event, renewed hope. She thought with Carl gone, she might get some fresh cards, thinking that future was behind her at last. She has trouble listening to what Kris tells her about this new spread with the same old cards, in her new kitchen where nothing is new except the paint on the walls. The table, like the cards, came from a yard sale. Kris doesn't say much about the spread. "You're up in the air at the moment," she says, tapping on the familiar trio bunched together in the middle like they're standing at a bus stop, "waiting for your next mistake."

"Waiting for Godot," Elissa says. They did a scene from that as a Senior Project. They got raves.

Kris laughs. "Same difference."

Then sure enough, Kris starts talking about Danny, every bit as obsessed as ever, though she says he's changed—he's going through something. "He's off in another world. I mean, he's always been like that—in and out, you know? Tuned to a distant frequency. But mostly he's a pretty down-to-Earth guy. But now he's somewhere else all the time, like he's seen something in one of his visions he can't let go of, or it won't let go of him. I heard him talking to Gwen about it once—his power—he opens up to her, though he won't let either one of us do his cards. Anyway, he talks about his power like it's a thing, this adversary. Like they're a couple of sumo wrestlers circling around. It's kind of hot, but worrisome, you know? So fucking exhausting. You've got to just fucking go with who you are."

"What did Gwen tell him?"

Kris laughs. "What she always says, that he'll come to see things differently."

"Is that what happened, you think? You think he saw something that changed him?" Or someone, a *certain* someone.

"You tell me. Your guess is as good as mine. You never told me how your session with him went. That's when he started acting weird."

Elissa stares at her cards like they'll tell her what to say. The Tower shows a tower with people falling out of it having a very bad day. There's a big eye in the sky looking down, faded and worn. Kris is always tapping on the eyeball as she explains what a badass big deal card it is. Like husband-dead-in-the-bay big. So what's it still doing here? Maybe she and Kris are a couple of those people falling out of the sky. She hopes not. She doubts that stupid eye can see much anymore. The once red iris is gray and fuzzy.

What the fuck.

Now or never.

She tells Kris everything: Danny saw her and Carl on the boat right before the accident—she hated him, and she loosened the line. Danny gave her that power—he set her free—he's totally into her—she thinks she's into him. She's going for it. Sorry. Really, really sorry, Kris. But this is like—destiny. She *doesn't* say, besides, you had your chance.

Kris is always talking about destiny when she talks about the Star. She's a sinuous and sexy goddess, naked in an icy landscape. You can't quite see her face. Out of her right hand she pours water, out of her left, ice. "Sound familiar?" Kris said of the card the first time it turned up in Elissa's spread. "There you are again," she's said ever since. "Fucking hope springs eternal, doesn't she, El?"

She's not sure what Kris is going to do or say with the information that she's making a play for Danny. There was this guy, years ago, tall and skinny, whatshisname, who Kris stole from her. ("Who's the elf?" he asked Elissa at a party at their place. "My roomy," she said. Roomy fucked him that night). But that was totally different. Donald, that's right. Who cares about Donald? Danny's a different story.

"And here he is," Kris says, "our boy Danny," picking up The Magus and showing him to Elissa, like Kris knew who he was all along, this card Elissa's been getting for forever. She tries to remember what Kris has said about him—a messenger, a catalyst, an agent of change. A Soothsayer. He's juggling a bunch of weird stuff, snakes are coming out of his head, some dreadful monster is climbing up from below, like Carl out of the bay, but The Magus is clueless, serene, looking the other way, like he's seen something wonderful and nothing can stop him now. Elissa looks down at the rest of the spread, trying to remember what Kris said. She'd only half-listened, thinking about what she was going to say. Kris scoops them up with her spidery hands, shuffles them in a flurry, snaps them back down in a fresh spread, a cloud of paper dust hanging over them like a fog.

"Danny," she says and nods at them, as if he were sitting across the table—meaning this is his fortune, his future in battered pictures. Then Kris smiles, the same little snarky fuck-with-your-head smile immortalized in tattoo on her sinewy shoulder, Elissa nestled in her arms, her mouth at Kris's neck. They got wasted and took the photograph, staggered it down to the tattoo artist on the corner. It took two artists all night, and Kris sat for the whole thing. Their old hippy professor in British Romantics allowed Creative Projects in lieu of the traditional paper. The tattoo of El and Kris as Christabel and Geraldine got them both A's, both laid along the way, in a variety of combinations, each more disturbing than the last. They're just friends now, have been for years. Elissa was actually glad at first when she heard about Danny, that Kris was so into a new guy. But it really is time for her to move on, step aside, she thinks. Danny's not Kris's destiny. He's mine.

Kris says, "The cards say you lose, El. Sorry. Give it your best shot. *I want you to.*" She's deadly serious.

"Kris, it doesn't have to be like this."

"Sure it does. If you could see what I see, you'd know. I saw when I did the cards before, that you're my way to him. I didn't know how. I had no idea you'd go for him. Doesn't seem like your type. Practically penniless. Turns out, you're my opening. When you're in a fifty car pileup and you're thrown out the back of a convertible over total carnage into a pine tree half a mile down the road and survive, you get a little taste for melodrama apparently."

Elissa's read all about Danny's accident, watched the news clips. He broke dozens of bones and tore up his insides, but he miraculously survived. Even the doctors were obviously surprised. Then he started seeing things, got himself arrested at the rest area for harassing strangers, and he wasn't inspirational anymore, he was just another weirdo.

Elissa says, "You can't make him fall in love with you." It sounds lame even as she says it. Remember who you're talking to, she reminds herself. That's *exactly* what she can do. You've seen her do it. You helped then too. Kris wears the evidence on her arm.

"Watch me," she says.

"You seem awfully sure of yourself."

"You're not? I thought he was *so* into you. And I'll make this easy for you, El: He *is*. He really *is*." She taps one of the cards. The Lovers. "Very near future. Won't last, but it *does* break the ice."

"What happens?" she asks like Kris would know, like these aren't just junk from a yard sale. You can smell them like a funky thrift store where you never want to buy the clothes because they'll always smell that way, the smell of Elissa's childhood.

"Fuck him and find out. Get your own cards. Better yet, if I'm wrong, you can have my cards, *and* Danny."

"And if you're right?"

"I'm not greedy. Danny's enough. I will tell you one thing though. The time is ripe. The man's dying to hear from you, waiting for your call. How long do you think he's going to wait?"

Kris gathers up the cards and wraps them in their ratty red shroud and stows them away, stands and slides in her chair with her hip. "Kiss.

Kiss. I have somewhere to be." She leaves out the kitchen door and lets the screen door slam. Elissa tries to remember the other cards besides The Lovers at the same time she's telling herself it doesn't fucking matter. They're just a bunch of cards. Danny wasn't even *here*. Kris is just fucking with her. Again. No reason to make this any more complicated than it is: They both want the same guy.

She calls him. He's at work, but he takes the call anyway. She can hear it in his voice, even as he's trying to be all professional, he's practically breathless: He can't wait to see her.

He's on his way.

Chapter Three

Kiss, Kiss

Beginnings, it's said, are apt to be shadowy. So it is with this story, which starts with the emergence of a new species maybe two hundred thousand years ago. The species does not yet have a name—nothing.
— Elizabeth Kolbert, *The Sixth Extinction: An Unnatural History*

When Elissa's call comes in, Danny's in the back room of The Tree with his last client for the day. Michael, *again.* Elissa wants to know, she says, exactly what Danny saw about her husband and his boat. She's trying to sound calm, but even over the phone he can tell she's not, that there's something urgent about her call.

"You knew Carl had a sailboat. You said you saw we were going out on it. I need to know what you saw."

She's not asking for another appointment. She figures she's already paid for any visions he might have had about her, and he agrees. He wants to tell her. Now that she's called, he must see her again, even though he's talked himself out of calling her for weeks now—who could possibly need *him* in her life? Nina made it clear what a joy that was, to share the ride into the not-so-uncertain future. Like picking up the phone on a Sunday afternoon to some screaming father at an emergency room firing your husband for breaking his kid's arm, threatening to sue. What woman doesn't dream of that?

That was then. This is now. They're close to the now in his vision. Danny can feel it. The autumn leaves are turning in the mountains. He tells her the truth, the first part anyway: "It was nothing. You were sailing. He was bossing everybody around, you were securing a line. That was it."

"That wasn't it, was it? That wasn't everything. I saw that look in your eye, like you recognized me from somewhere." Her voice is low and intimate, like maybe she saw what he saw, or maybe every woman knows that look that says, for now at least, *you're the one*. Does he need to tell her she's all he's been thinking about ever since? His heart is slamming inside his chest. The backroom of The Tree seems to slide like a careening automobile.

"From the future. That's where I recognized you from. I saw him through your eyes, your husband…. You hate him." He tries to say this in a neutral fashion, but you can't say something like that without taking sides. He hates him too. Never even seen the man but in a glimpse of a future that's probably in the past by now; he's totally despicable. Time works in mysterious ways, love too—two strangers transformed by what Danny's seen of who they'll become. There seems something not quite right in that, but he's still aching to see her.

She's crying, and for a moment he's not sure whether the tears are now or in the future. She whispers, "We need to talk. I need to see you. Can you come here? Please? I would meet you, but my car's in the shop." She gives him her address. He knows where it is. It's not a rich woman's neighborhood. His bus goes right by there. He sees her door, his future knock. Nothing can keep him away.

"As soon as I'm through here. Twenty minutes." He hangs up. "Sorry about that," he says to Michael, sitting across from him scowling, offended he would take a call in the middle of their session. He's back from a screenwriting workshop in Taos where the food was incredible, and everyone *loved* his ideas. His phone is stuffed with them. He keeps reading them off the little screen to Danny—to see if he can foresee which one, *exactly*, will be his breakthrough hit, so he can like *totally* focus on that particular project and do the others later because they're all too good *not* to be made—like Danny asked for this torture. Danny always turns his phone off, but today he forgot, saw it was Elissa—and answered the call without hesitation. He feels like he's floating above the turning Earth, above time. He's felt this way before. During the wreck.

He can't listen to another moment of Michael's narcissistic chatter.

He imagines Kristi reaching this point when she couldn't stand the thought of reading this man's cards again and again, listen to his preening, his whining. Give the man a fucking red carpet and a blonde if that will get rid of him. If he has to actually sit his ass down and write a screenplay, then he won't be coming to see Danny. There's only one way out of Michael's future. Danny has to lie. He stops the torrent of elevator pitches with a raised palm.

"Let me hear that last idea again," he intones, leaning forward. None of them are any more than a few disjointed phrases, plotless ramblings. This one's about a dog walker. Michael was a dog walker once for a couple of days, but he didn't like picking up shit and got fired. That's what makes it funny, see, is the guy not picking up the shit, but he works with this hot babe who picks up *her* dogs' shit, so he has to or pretends to or—one funny shit thing after another. It's called *Picking Up.* Get it? "That's the one," Danny says. "It will be a huge hit. You on a red carpet. I see the red carpet more in Burbank, but Kristi was close. With a blonde woman?"

Michael nods like he totally knows who that is, whoever he's got in mind to star in his picking-up-dog-shit movie. He plans to hit on that.

"But you must pursue this idea—devote all your energies to writing the screenplay you were destined to write."

"How long do I have?"

"You want a fucking deadline?"

"I find them helpful."

"Six months."

"Then what?"

"Then you send it out to agents, filmmakers, all those people you keep telling me about: Them. Wait. Call me when you have competing offers and you need to decide. I'll be glad to help." When Hell freezes over.

He leaves Michael there soaking in his fantasies and collides with Terry on the way out, bouncing off his muscled chest.

"My, my, Daniel. What's the hurry?"

"Excuse me, Terence. I'm meeting someone."

"Busy, busy. Do you know the difference between the past and the future?"

"No, what? I'm sure you're dying to tell me."

"You can't escape the past." He fixes Danny with his oracular gaze, inspiration with a tinge of indigestion.

"Do you know the difference between you and an asshole?"

"What?"

"Not a thing."

That's another thing that's changed about Danny since the accident. He's not afraid of anyone or anything. Even of death. Don't get the idea just because he doesn't talk about death with clients he's afraid of it. Nothing could be further from the truth. Him and Death have been close for quite some time now.

He leaves Terry huffing back in Carthage, strides across the parking lot toward the bus stop just in time to see his bus rumble off in a cloud of diesel. He stands there like a fool shaking his fists at the indifferent heavens. Kristi rolls up beside him in her car, a faded black Corolla festooned with a generous sampling of abrasive but faded and peeling bumper stickers, like she used to have strong opinions but doesn't anymore. She asks him if he needs a lift somewhere.

Since the accident, Danny doesn't ride in cars if he can help it, preferring the bus where you don't have to watch where you're going, but he gets in anyway. There's something else going on with Kristi, like she was waiting for him to show up. He gives her Elissa's address, and she starts driving, glancing back at The Tree in the rearview and giving it the middle finger salute.

"Did you see?" she says when they're clear of the parking lot. "Terry got me fired. Serena was just looking for an excuse."

He's surprised. Mean as she is, Kristi's always booked up, like clients come to her for a little abuse. Serena usually keeps a better eye on the bottom line. Truth is, if he was going to get advice from anyone at The Tree it would be Kristi. She's no bullshit whether it has anything to do with the cards or not. "So that's what he was doing there? Taking your slot? Unbelievable. I'm surprised Serena didn't give him mine."

"She told me people complained I was too negative. I told her if those spoiled bitches who come in there could manage to get themselves off bullshit and Zoloft for five seconds they might get a life. Didn't help the cause any. I was ready to move on anyway. The cards were getting stale in that room. Don't you feel that sometimes? Like the room just needs a *rest*? Some sort of psychic power wash? Anyway. That's not what I wanted to talk to you about."

The light ahead turns yellow, Kristi floors it, and they shoot through, horns bleating behind them. Danny can't speak for a few moments. She gives him a look. "God, I'm sorry. I forgot. You okay?" She lays a concerned hand on his thigh.

Certain sensations, like a burst of speed, are like scents, triggering memories. He was there again. Defying gravity. Death defying. No fear. It's hard, for a moment, to come back to Earth. But he must. To make things work—to make his life work. Now that he's seen death. He nods. "I'm okay." He remembers to breathe. Kristi gives his thigh a squeeze and returns her hand to the wheel.

He looks over at her. She's in a tank top and shorts. He's used to seeing her at the store where she affects a punk gypsy look, always bare-armed to show off her tattoos. Her right arm, shoulder to wrist, is some scene from a poem by Coleridge she told him. He doesn't remember which one. She designed it herself. It's beautiful, incredibly sensual. Two women entwined, their feet turn into serpents' tails and make a spiral on the back of her hand. If you look closely, it's a maze. In the middle is a tiny heart with a dagger through it. One of the women looks like her. Kristi's small, intense, strong. Like a genie without a bottle. You don't want to rub her the wrong way. Or maybe you do. She has a face like a waif in a Chaplin movie. Pale. Big dark eyes. Today her hair is black.

It's not that far to Elissa's, especially the way Kristi drives. She has to talk fast. "Look. I did your cards, and I saw something and thought you should know, and the store's the only place we ever see each other. So I was waiting for you actually. This is sort of an abduction." She laughs.

Not her usual earthy ironic laugh but nervous to the point of giddiness. He remembers Elissa's tears over the phone. There's some sort of emotional storm swirling around him, despite his efforts to lay low, like Jonah fleeing God. "It works out for me," he says. "I really appreciate the ride. I missed the bus." The other people on a bus are easy to ignore. Not Kristi. He doesn't want to stare at her, but doesn't want to see the world coming at them in a relentless stream either. The face in the tattoo seems to find his dilemma amusing. Okay, maybe he does want to stare at her. Kristi has a delicate, elfin profile, like she's not quite real. He's always been drawn to her but a bit afraid of her at the same time.

"You want to hear? The cards?"

"I guess so."

She nods her head up and down. She knows how he feels about the cards. Both she and Gwen have offered, and he's turned them down as politely as he could. He doesn't see the point, if you don't believe in it. With Gwen, everything is so soft focus and nice, there's probably no harm to it. But with Kristi, he has to ask himself if he's not just afraid of what she might say.

Now, she says, "This place where I'm taking you? Is there a woman there? Reddish-blonde hair? Freckles? Beautiful?"

"If there is?"

"Right. Not 'How did you know! Kristi, you're amazing!' Short version: Not a good idea. A whole lot of heartache, possible danger. No kidding."

"Danger?"

She shrugs her shoulder. Her inked semblance there is still amused. The other woman's face is obscured by the veil of her hair, her face to the first woman's neck, but you can't see what she's doing—weeping, kissing, biting—all three. He imagines peeling back the woman's hair to get a closer look. Kristi goes on—"Definitely danger, betrayal. I had to let you know, only fair. If it was just the heartache, I would've left it alone. Everybody's got that if they're with the wrong person, right?" She gives him a quick, pointed glance, then back to the busy street. "The really, *really* wrong person. But it can work out for you just how you want. I saw that too, if you trust your instincts."

"Why were you doing my cards?"

She makes a face of stunned disbelief at the oncoming traffic as she waits to make a left, dropping her jaw, so that even he can see. "Why do you *think*? Lots of reasons. Mr. Forest, meet Mr. Trees. I'm curious about you, for one thing." She steps on the gas and makes the turn with inches to spare.

She doesn't apologize this time. Perhaps she suspects he likes it. Especially with her tiny foot on the gas. The world slows as they speed along into the future, too fast to think. He wonders if she's for real, if she actually sees things with those battered cards of hers. "Why?"

"Tell me you're joking. *Why?* You see the truth. I've seen you do it. I heard about you before I even met you. You told a friend of mine some shit, at a rest stop or something, *totally* freaked her, but it *all came true*. I'm the one who told Serena she should check you out. Only smart thing she's ever done."

"The rest stop days weren't my best times. I'm doing a lot better now."

"No argument from me. From where I sit, you look better and better all the time. So let's not go see this woman. What do you say? Choose Your Own Adventure. I was into those as a kid. If I didn't like my options, I'd write new ones."

He can't tell if she's serious. Can't see a thing about her future, not the smallest glimpse. It's a little frightening. Why would *her* future be so elusive? Usually when he's around someone a lot, he sees *something*. "You have another destination in mind?"

"We could go to my place. I could do your cards, or we could just have a good time, enjoy each other's company away from The Tree." She gives him a look that's unmistakable.

"Aren't I a little old for you?"

"I'm not a kid; I'm just short. I'm twenty-nine—not twelve. What are you? Forty? I thought you geezers liked young. For a soothsayer you can be fairly dense."

"You're the only one who calls me that."

"That's what it says on your card. I like it."

"It's sort of a joke."

"Duh. That's why I like it. I'm all about jokes. But you're no joke, Danny. I know that. You really see things. There's something special about you. And you're kind of hot too."

They get stuck behind the bus, the one he should've been on, and they miss the light. She has small hands, with long slender fingers. When she reads cards, she uses this huge ancient Crowley deck that looks like the cards might crumble in her spidery hands as they rain down gloom. She wraps her right hand around his left thigh and squeezes. She's strong. Her grip is firm, unequivocal. She's not just fooling around. She leans in close. "C'mon."

His cock stirs in his pants, his heart races, and he's surprised, not because it's Kristi. He's always thought she's incredible, but because since the accident, he's felt pretty much sexually checked out to anyone. Then Elissa came along and changed all that. Now there's a new kink in the maze. At this juncture, destiny trumps lust, since it contains the promise of future lust and more. The future always seems to offer more, has momentum on its side. "Thanks, Kristi. I'm flattered. I really am. I like you a lot, but I'm going to stick with my plans."

He starts to tell her he had a vision of him and Elissa together, but no woman being rejected wants to hear something like that. He realizes Kristi's been coming on to him for a while, but he's been living in a fog for so long, it took a glimpse of the future to get him out of it, like jumping above the clouds, above the dead.

She takes her hand away, and immediately he wonders if he's doing the right thing. But he's vain enough about his prophetic powers to stay the course.

When they start rolling again, he glances over at the sidewalk tables outside a café only a few feet away. There's a young woman there who looks familiar, but he can't place her. She's looking at him like she knows him, an indecipherable smirk on her face. He sees a photo on a phone. Him and Kristi in the car staring into each other's eyes, moments ago, and then it's gone. Sent? Maybe he's losing his mind. Wouldn't be the first time.

Kristi pulls up to the curb in front of Elissa's and shakes her head. "I knew you'd say that. The cards favored Freckles in the immediate future. Can't blame a girl for trying. I thought surely my young flesh would do the trick. She's like really tall and beautiful, right? A real giraffe."

He laughs. "Yeah. Reddish-blonde hair, like you said. Freckles. Thanks for the ride." He gets out.

She leans across the passenger seat, looks up at him. "Pale green eyes?"

"Yes."

"I'm good, right? Tell Serena, when this all plays out, if you get the chance, that Kristi warned you about this woman. Night of bliss, then not so much… If you need a shoulder to cry on, or any other body part, call me. Kiss. Kiss."

She blows him a kiss and drives away, and for a brief moment, he wishes he'd gone with her. They often seem to be in the same head-space, looking down into the abyss and joking about it. She makes him laugh, no easy task since the accident. The thing is, he's had no vision of Kristi. Not ever. She thinks he's the real deal, but she's never once asked him what he sees about her. Nothing. He wonders why that is. It doesn't mean there's nothing there, only that he doesn't see it. She might be right about Elissa. He knows nothing about her but the moment he saw, and in that moment, he was in love. For love, he'll risk danger.

He's seen this moment too. He knows what happens:

He knocks.

Chapter Four

What Do You See in Me Now?

At this early stage in our evolution, now through our infancy and into our childhood and then, with luck, our growing up, what our species needs most of all, right now, is simply a future.

—Lewis Thomas

There are still boxes stacked up in Elissa's living room. It's obvious she hasn't lived here long. That's good—that'll bring up the marriage thing right away. Widow. That's what she is now. Not particularly grieving widow, not for Carl anyway, maybe for the years wasted. She feels like she's gotten her life back, like she gets a second chance to do something she doesn't hate herself for. She didn't know how bad Carl was when she married him, but she did know she didn't love him. Mom was right about that one.

She cleans up the coffee things from Kris's visit and makes fresh, wipes off the kitchen table with a wet paper towel. The cards left a dark grime. She imagines Mom stopping by for a cup of coffee, just to see how she's doing, looking around, liking what she sees. Mom would love this place, except for the living room full of stuff. This was always her dream, a small place of their own, safe and warm.

She takes a quick shower. That whole scene with Kris made her sweat. She's imagined it plenty of times in the last few weeks. It never went as bad as this. Kris'll get over it. Isn't that what she's always telling people? *You'll get over it. Over yourself.* Elissa presses her forehead against the wet tile. Thank God it's over.

She lets the water beat down on her face and remembers once again every detail of the hour or so she actually spent with Danny, the water singing off the tiles as soundtrack. She walked in the room, and his face went through a storm of emotions, but soon came to bliss, adoration, her name escaping his lips in a whisper she doubts he was fully aware of. He babbled a few phrases she can't recall, begging her to sit, to wait, as he looked from her eyes to what she realized was the clock behind her, as if he was waiting on something, some message she found herself desperately wanting to give him. She had the overwhelming sense she was *meant* to be there.

It was easy to see why he had so much trouble speaking. He was completely enchanted by her. He might have thought she was impatient, but she didn't mind that she left him speechless. Carl might be alive today if he'd been a little more speechless. Even as she was driving away, she saw Danny in the rearview, the same look on his face. She wasn't just a client. She was his destiny.

She looks down at the water streaming down her body, down the drain into the bay, and feels beautiful and clean and new. Kris can't be right on this one, she tells herself. Why would he choose Kris and all her weirdness over me? Kris's been after him for forever and gotten nowhere, while I walk into the room, and he positively glows. The only reason he hasn't called is because he knows I'm married. Now I'm not. It's time to let him know that. It's that simple.

Only it's not. On the phone just now, he said he knows she hated Carl. She wonders what else he knows. It doesn't matter. She wants him to know everything about her and love her anyway. She sees her life in the glistening swirls at her feet. *Everything.* Her heart freezes. How can he? She can't even manage that one. But then she hears the whisper of her name escaping his lips at the sight of her—in the future, when he knows everything and loves her *still*—and she believes he can. Maybe it's herself she's worried about.

A song comes to her about it, the way he looked at her. All she's got is a bit of melody and the questioning refrain, *What Do You See in Me Now?* Singer/songwriter, that was her talent in the beauty queen days. Now it's more of a habit. She likes the refrain, where her voice goes on the *me*, making the tiles quiver as Kris used to tease her. Her biggest fan, Kris put her through open mic night a couple of times before letting it go. Elissa got hit on, but no one listened.

Shrieking bus brakes outside the window harmonize with her full-voiced *me* bringing her back to now, standing frozen, water cascading down her body. He'll be here soon. She shuts off the water. There's no clock in the bathroom. She has no idea how long it's been since she got off the phone. She towels off quickly, humming through the scraps of melody to help remember them.

He could be here any minute. She can't seem to decide anything, or even decide what-all she needs to decide. Clothes, words, feelings. She can't sort them out. The place is a mess. She can't find anything. There's no time to straighten up. She wasn't exactly planning for things to happen this way. Kris forced her hand.

Maybe she shouldn't have told Kris everything—*anything*. A bad idea. Getting into some kind of competition or game with her always turns out badly, but that's what they always do. Forget Kris. Danny's on his way right now.

She jumps at his knock. Her heart races with lust, stage fright, fear. And something else. *Fucking hope springs eternal, doesn't she, El?* She runs to the door barefoot, her hair wet. Jeans. She was about to replace them with something softer, but it's too late. It's okay; she looks good in jeans. She grabbed a blouse she'd decided against as too something, but has to go with it anyway, fumbling with the buttons, her forehead pressed against the jamb, totally blanking on what to say.

She opens the door. It's still bright out, the autumn sun low. She ducks into his shadow to avoid the glare.

He's wearing the cheesy t-shirt he was wearing when she saw him at the store. He looks down at it and laughs. "I'm still in uniform, but I'm off the clock. I wanted to get here fast as I could." Like three months ago and every moment since. He still looks at her like she's Venus wading into shore, and he's been shipwrecked for a thousand years.

She takes his hand and pulls him inside, closes the door, and blurts it out, "My husband's dead. A boating accident. The day you saw, it happened then. I—I needed to see you, talk to you." She stops herself there, drops his hand. She starts flailing her other hand about like a wounded bird. A big one. An acting teacher once suggested amputation. She pins them both under crossed arms. She's decided too late, that it might be inappropriate to appear too happy at news of her loss, but she can't help it. She's so glad to see him. He's better looking than she remembered. Maybe he's lost weight. It's been three months. Three lonely months.

He's still trying to adjust to the light. It's dark by the front door. He hasn't taken his eyes off her. "I—I didn't see that. I'm sorry." They smile at each other.

Neither of them is sorry, so they don't have to say anything, don't have to pretend. They both know she hated him. "Would you like some coffee?" The room at the store where they do the readings smells like incense and coffee. Kris's dopey gypsy dresses smell like that. Coffee, in the kitchen.

She's desperate to lead him away from the living room full of boxes into the tidy kitchen. She's been having trouble getting motivated to unpack. It makes it look like no one really lives here. Sometimes she thinks she'd just like to get rid of everything, sell it all, but she doesn't know what she'd want to do with the money. Get new stuff? She's done enough of that for a lifetime. Give it away? Could she do that?

"Sounds great," he says—*a cup of anything from your hands*—still smiling at her like he can't quite believe he's here, like he might burst into absurd laughter at any moment. She's seen that smile somewhere before. Then realizes—The Magus. Fucking Kris and her cards. *Here he is. Tap, tap, tap.*

"Let's go in the kitchen," she says, and he follows her down the narrow hall. The kitchen's bright. There's a window without curtains over the sink. The back door is half glass. He blinks in the light like a hermit coming out of his cave. She motions for him to sit at the table, and he does, looking around, but mostly watching her as she pours his coffee, black, joins him at the table. He's sitting where Kris sat. She sits where Danny would've sat if he'd actually been here for his bogus reading. There are only three chairs. It's a small kitchen. The fourth side's against the wall. She loves her place, her tiny little place. The mansion always felt like a prison; this place feels like freedom.

"You said you needed to speak with me?" he says. He's still not sure why he's here.

She can't remember exactly what she said on the phone. She just wanted to get him over here as soon as she could. She started crying she was so excited. She felt like a schoolgirl. "Not about anything in particular. I just wanted to see you. Is that okay?" His hands are folded before him on the table, the Formica still damp from her cleansing. She covers his hands with hers, looks into his eyes. *Okay?* More than okay. She's never made a man so happy with a mere touch. "I hoped you would call me," she confesses, "but I understand why you didn't." She takes her hands away. "So I called you to let you know things have changed for me." *My husband's dead. I'm free.*

He's deeply serious. Unlike most men, he seems to have no intention of concealing his feelings. Perhaps he can't. How can you deny what you've already seen, already felt? "I wanted to call you—desperately—I've thought of it thousands of times—but I couldn't imagine you'd want to get involved in the life of a crazy man." He doesn't seem to care about Carl, dead or alive. It's himself he's worried about, that somehow he's unworthy. She can relate.

"That's ridiculous. You're not crazy. I've read all about you—that horrible accident. It must be terribly hard to live with something like that."

"You mean surviving when so many died?"

"No. You told that woman on Channel 8 that you got through that. I mean seeing the future." Their eyes meet. His eyes are blue, like a dark sky.

"You believe I can do that?"

"I *know* you can." She remembers what Kris said, that he sees his gift as an adversary. It seems more to her like a burden, an oppressor. You can almost see it weighing him down. She wants to ease his burden, do for him what he's done for her, set him free. "Tell me what makes it so hard. Not being believed?" *Tell me, tell me anything, everything, whatever I want to know—and I will make it better.*

"That's the easy part—*I* wouldn't believe me, how can I expect anyone else to? It's easier in a way that people don't usually believe me. What makes it hard is some of the things I see I have to keep to myself."

"Like what?"

He searches her eyes. He doesn't want to be anyone's freak show—especially hers. "Do you really want to hear about this?"

"You can talk to me Danny. I've thought about this, imagined what it must be like. You sit in that little room and tell people the truth, and nobody probably listens to you. I bet nobody asks *your* troubles." She lays her hands on his again, and this time he takes them. She remembers The Lovers, hands clasped. *Won't last,* Kris said. *Fuck you, Kris.*

Before this moment, perhaps, he may have pursued her out of mere lust and an enticing glimpse of the future, but now she's found the maze to his heart and touched him. His tears well up, his voice trembles. "It's not just the ones who will die, but the suffering I see to come. I have a friend, at the store, Gwen. I don't have many friends. Her husband is dying of cancer. I saw the world through his eyes, just after he's been told it's hopeless, and even Gwen doesn't know yet. The moment I saw—he's on his way to tell her. Any day now. This *will* happen. She'll be so alone."

As he says this, you can see him entering that vision, hear the despair and loss in his voice, as if it were happening to him. He's dying of cancer. He's grieving the loss. Any day now. The tears come, and she holds him, rocks him in her long, comforting arms. Jeez, what a life he must lead. She kisses his cheeks, salty with his tears, his mouth, guides his hand to her breast.

She leads him down the hallway to her bed, a cheap futon, the only new thing in the place, and makes love to him, leading him out of his long loneliness, restoring him. He's incredibly passionate. Starved of touch. Grateful. She feels like a goddess. You must think that happens all the time for her. Not so. She has no trouble attracting men. Adoration, not so much. Some men despise her for her beauty.

They order out, make love some more, trade life stories like lovers do. She leaves out Kris—leaving a big hole like she never had a close friend. He leaves out himself once the accident happened. Since he sees everybody else's future, it's like he doesn't have one of his own. He's kind of sketchy about his marriage, but he makes it sound like everything was okay before the accident, before he started seeing things, and it took over his life. He credits working at the Tree with restoring his sanity, giving him an outlet. His body is criss-crossed with scars like they had to take him apart and put him back together again.

After he falls asleep, she goes to the bathroom with her phone, texts Kris from the can: *U lose.* She softly sings what she has of *What Do You See in Me Now?* into her phone before she forgets it then slips back into bed.

He stays the night. She has a little trouble going to sleep. Whatever else she is, Kris is her best friend, and she doesn't want to lose her. But Danny didn't see *her* in his future, did he? So everything depends upon what the soothsayer saw. It scares her this makes sense to her now. Kris is the one into the weird, though over the years with her Elissa's been forced to believe the impossible more than a time or two. She focuses on his breath and quiets the chatter so she can fall asleep. She can fall fast asleep in the rattiest motel you can imagine, so this crazy day shouldn't be a problem. Mom sat up and worried for both of them, police lights strobing the bed. She imagines her sitting in the shadows doing that now.

Chapter Five

I Don't Need The Cards For This

The violence that exists in the human heart is also manifest in the symptoms of illness that we see in the earth, the water, the air, and in living things.

—Pope Francis, *On Climate Change*

I'm back. So I made all that happen, set it in motion anyway. I don't really have a precise plan as I drive away from El's dumpy little duplex—rather proud of my ad lib performance—more like a next move. I'm more improvisational than tightly scripted. I hadn't planned on doing Danny's cards. It just came to me. El looked severely rattled when I did—the perfect extra creepy little touch, fairly spooky cards too, the ideal outcome—The Fool. I don't plan, plot, scheme so much as imagine. I focus on what it is I want, follow my instincts, reacting to the situation, trusting my hunches, finding my way and usually getting it. El does too but she's always wanting the wrong things. You can't fall in love with what you think you want. You have to feel it.

That's how I read the cards. Totally intuitive. I read some books, but they were useless. Too allegorical. I hate allegory. *The Faery Fucking Queene*? Only Spenser can make sex sound so naughty and so boring at the same time. Allegory saps the life out of everything. Cards and characters and people and gods shouldn't merely *mean* things, not like that anyway.

Imagine instead the cards as seventy-eight distinctive, complicated, quirky, insightful people you know really, really well. If you told them a story, asked them a question, and just watched their faces, listened to their little side comments, watched their body language, how they looked at you when you were done—you'd probably have a pretty good idea what they thought about it before they said a word.

These paper people have one other interesting quality. Like Danny, they're outside of time, so they see the future, see the past, see beneath the present to the way things truly are—cut through the bullshit. I understand them, try to pass along to my mostly clueless clients that things could be different than they imagine. You'd be amazed at the things I see. But you have to know the people—the cards. Get another *deck,* like El's always suggesting? That's like get another pair of eyes, get another mother, another father.

Or in this case, get another friend. Correction: Best friend.

I should've known. Guys fall for El like trees for a paper mill. Half the time El doesn't even notice. When we were roomies I consoled more than one broken-hearted swain mooning after El. I attribute the seductive powers of my Christabel tat to the exquisite depiction of El's perfect backside. You can't watch her walking away without wanting to follow. Following the followers was like following Hansel and Gretel scattering bread crumbs, a fairly reliable food source for the right crow. I'm a great admirer of crows.

Danny's not just some guy though. I'm looking out for him, really care about him. I feel somewhat responsible for the troubles he's been through. Okay, more like totally responsible. Like I'm the reason his wife left him, and that's when he really started falling apart. I told Serena, "You've got to hire this guy," and quietly take credit for rescuing him, though he doesn't know anything about that. I didn't tell Serena I did his wife's cards at one of those stupid street fairs Serena roped me into doing and bewitched her. I don't know what else you'd call it.

I had an attitude about the fair all day long. It was mid-afternoon when I was good and pissy that I talked Danny's wife into leaving him. I have great powers of persuasion sometimes. Some might call it casting a spell.

Some people duck into the little tent because they see you've got a fan going, and it's hot, and they want to get away from the great shuffling herd for just a moment. They'll pay to listen to a fortuneteller's stories about them just to catch a break. Others are hungry for a fortune. This woman was starved. She saw the logo on the tent flap, said she was an occasional Tree customer, had seen Gwen.

"What's your name?" I asked, because I always ask. "Nina," she said. Usually I don't remember names an hour later. Nina was different. She asked whether she should take a job in Oregon, and I'm giving her a big westward heave-ho, because I figure that's what the woman wants to hear—going away is always sexier than staying put—but I sense some other undercurrent, lots of resistance, and ask if there's anything holding her back.

Nina falls apart. Sobbing. It's her husband Danny. He sees things—in the future. It's driving him crazy. Her too. She describes in gruesome detail this horrible accident her husband survived, how he still has nightmares. Sees things. She doesn't know what to do. She doesn't say so, but it's clear she thinks since I'm in the magic biz she can say all this and I'll believe her. And the thing is, I did.

I was definitely not in the mood for some hysterical woman who wanted her problems solved at a street fair for fifteen bucks. Naturally, I did everything I could to persuade her to leave town. Good riddance. Take your whiny ass somewhere else. I told her to visualize it— her crazy husband in the rearview—and rejoice. The more I heard about Danny, the more I figured he'd be better off without Nina holding him back, all that talent going to waste. Nina fought hard, she resisted the idea at first, she wanted to stand by her man, but I was relentless. I can't remember exactly which cards I used to sell the idea, but I sold it hard. By the time I was through, I had a line outside waiting. It was worth it. Crying women annoy me. It had become a battle of wills. I have a way of doing that with my life. I have a strong will. I never thought of it as a problem before, not mine anyway. Other people's maybe.

Then, like a month or two later in the early Fall, I started hearing about Danny—the accident and the powers it seemed to give him, how he fell apart when his wife left him and started riding his bike out to the rest area near where the accident happened, where he said the power was strongest, telling people their futures—absolutely dead-on. I tracked down some of these stories. They were incredible. If I were a journalist, I would've written a book about him, but he'd already had way too much journalism. Nobody seemed to appreciate what he was going through. Not everyone was so happy to have met Danny.

One of them was a state cop who arrested Danny—who then supposedly told the cop something that saved his life. I thought that sounded like a TV movie and said so. So my informant pointed the cop out at a burger joint where a lot of cops eat, and I went over, sat beside him, and asked about it.

Cops are just people. Guys are guys. He was glad to tell me the tale between bites, chewing the whole time. He'd gained a lot of weight recently, unless he liked his shirts two sizes too small. I was itty-bitty beside him. "Told me. Night or two. Somebody's going to take a shot at me. So I ask what happens? Doesn't know that. Just the shot. 'From above,' he says. Points like this. Next night, warehouse. I'm in pursuit. I enter. I look up, right like he showed me. Gun discharged. Couldn't tell where from the sound. Big steel box." He chews, sets his burger down, points. This time his hand is his gun. He sights down the greasy barrel. "The muzzle flash. Saw that and caught him in the chest before he could get off another shot. Kid's fifteen. Gun's a piece of shit. His first shot wasn't even close. If I hadn't known where the shot was coming from, I would've taken cover and waited five minutes for backup." He picked up the burger, bit. "Saved my life? Hard to say. Didn't do much for the kid's though, his mother's. Had to do it over again? Can't say I'd arrest the guy for telling people their futures—so he could tell me mine." His smile was grim and greasy, and I had to notice that though there were several other cops in the place, this one was all by himself.

Then the state closed the rest area because of budget cuts, and nobody seemed to know where Danny was, until he started showing up wherever there were various fortunetellers, as if he was thinking about going into business. He wouldn't actually sit down at the table, but he'd listen to the pitch, eavesdrop if he could. Someone said his wife used to be an occasional customer at The Tree.

By this time, I figured Danny had to be the husband of the woman who lost it when I did her cards. I asked if anyone knew the wife's name. Nina, someone said. She used to work at the museum; now she's in Portland.

Who listens to some cranky bitch at a street fair and changes her life? How did that make me responsible? Still. Who spends more than forty-five minutes trying to convince some poor woman, a total stranger going through some seriously bad shit, to leave her husband because she had the nerve to cry at my card table?

I feel responsible. I can't help it. When Serena balked at the idea of taking on a soothsayer from the rest area, I said I'd absorb the cost until he could build a clientele. I was making good money at the time, which is one of the reasons the street fair thing annoyed me. I'd read cards at one of El's poolside parties and had a steady income from rich bitch soirees thereafter. One night and I could make as much as I made all year at The Tree. You had to be cheeky, speak truth to power and all that—like all fools and jesters know—as long as you totally appeal to their vanity. The rich are like everybody else: They want to be told they're not like everybody else. Once they believe that, they'll believe anything and pay handsomely for it.

I've kept the gig at The Tree because basically you get sick of nothing but rich people and long for some home cooking—Suburban Self-Loathing Stew. It's the dish I grew up on. I almost quit The Tree a million times or leapt across the table to strangle some whiner channeling my mother or my sister or my Jesus-loving closeted brother, but always managed to divert that energy into the cards instead.

Once I got Danny hired on at The Tree, it was my way to get to know him, hang out a little. It's been good for that, but not as good as I hoped. I had some fairly intense hopes, incubating since the day I read Nina's cards.

I finally quit yesterday. It was time. Danny's doing okay outside The Tree, worked his way up to steady temp work in cubicles. Anything that doesn't require human interaction. He'll ride on a bus, but he won't talk to you because the next thing he tells you might not have happened to you yet.

The man doesn't date or even talk to anybody much outside the back room of The Tree. Though I'm not quite invisible like I told El, I haven't gotten much past being his quirky little pal. Tinkerbell. When you're 4-11, you have no fucking use at all for Tinkerbell. Not that Danny's Peter Pan and won't grow up. Not only did he grow up, but now he's outgrown us all, though he doesn't quite know what to do with his new life. He seems to believe time stopped with his accident, but really it started over. At least that's the way I see it. He shies away from the subject. I've gotten as close as I have by never bringing it up.

He talks to Gwen because she's safe. He likes me because I'm not. He wants me, but he's not ready to deal with me.

Most women might not want to come on too strong with a guy like Danny. Might spook him. Fortunately, El's as predictable as a bad porn movie. Competition over a man is a game of plant the flag for her. But rushing a guy like Danny? Bound to make him nervous. Vulnerable. What better time to reach out to him? Warn him? *Danger, Will Robinson!* Didn't this fabulously beautiful mysterious woman you will no doubt fuck tonight if not sooner just drown her husband in the bay? That will only make the sex hotter in the short run, but not so much the morning after.

I know El better than anyone. She'll win him but won't want him for long. There has to be something wrong with any man who would love her, or so she believes, and has the skills to prove herself right.

El's calling Danny right about now. He's working. I know his schedule. I head for The Tree. Quickly. An interesting fact: Although I've repeatedly been stopped for speeding, I've never been given a ticket. I show up at The Tree in no time, right on time.

Sometimes it's easy to believe in destiny, what some call coincidence, when you catch two breaks simultaneously. That's like a sign you're on the right track. The magic is working.

As I pull into the parking lot, I see Terry headed into the store to take my slot. He'll prosper in the little room with all those nervous women. I've worked a couple of parties with him, and he's smooth, though he tends to forget rich wives have rich husbands who might have his neck broken for him. I don't mind him so much. He's just another hustler playing his part. Danny, however, can't stand him, spots him for a phony, and can't believe anybody takes him seriously. That's just it— nobody does. They collide in the doorway, these two, Danny getting his back all up like he does. I had a tiny little cat once named Cleopatra.

Fearless. Danny reminds me of that cat. Cleo got run over, but that was because I wasn't looking after her like I should and left her out New Year's while I partied. I'm here for Danny, looking out for him. El would say obsessed, and she would be right, but it's a good obsessed. The best kind. You'll just have to trust me on that.

Back to destiny: Terry's break number one. Number two is Danny's bus driving off without him. What are the chances? says the spider to the fly. I drive up beside him, and he slides right into the passenger seat, and I weave him a tale about Terry and Serena that's not entirely true, helping him get some closure on his anger at the big galoot, and Serena, who's been riding his ass lately for no good reason. I'm their innocent victim too, I tell him. He's so sweet about it. I should've used this angle before. But bitching about the boss is boring. I hate boring. Truth is, Serena begged me not to quit, and I like Serena, but when it's time, it's time. One of my mantras.

Stuck behind a bus, I make a play. I'm surprised how much he likes the idea, but naturally he doesn't go for it. El must have her hooks in good and deep, or else he wouldn't have taken this ride in the first place. He probably hasn't been in a car, not counting the backs of police cars, for a couple of years. He's doing it to get to El. There's no way I stand a chance in the near future, but I want him to think about what could have been, what he missed, whether he can turn back, or he's lost me forever. Hold those thoughts, caress them. I watch him in the rearview on El's doorstep watching me drive out of his life. *Don't worry, Danny. I'll be waiting just down the road, around the bend, at the next cross-roads. You know you really want to be with me, despite all appearances to the contrary.* I saw him eyeing my tattoo, looking into my magical inked eyes. It's not just about El's ass.

***

U lose.

I get the message in the same burger joint where the cop told me how Danny saved his life. Ungrateful bastard. I gave him an earful. Who cares if the kid's fifteen? Where I grew up, there were plenty of guys younger than that who deserved to be shot. Of course, like me, they all lived in nice suburban neighborhoods. Come to think of it, I was fairly shootable at fifteen myself. There's no useless like bourgeois useless.

The place is practically deserted. The TV's on, but the sound's down—images of the Antarctic ice shelf sliding into the sea, World Leaders promising to do the right thing, coal-fired power plants, raging wildfires, folks wading down the street. They break for commercials: The McRib is back! A big truck that's tough for guys who aren't. Drugs to make it all go away. Poor John Lennon's singing "Imagine" over the sound system.

No cops here tonight, must be busy. This is primetime for crime. I'm here for the red meat. The goddess told me to give it up for the sake of her planet, and mostly I have, but nothing saps the will like self-pity.

With this whole thing with El, I thought I needed a serious burger. Medium rare. Now the dead cow's gone, or rather, it's sitting in my gut, a mass of artery-clogging, planet-destroying, indigestible guilt, and there's this snarky text from El on my phone, sent late enough to send the message that not only has she fucked him repeatedly, but he's staying the night: *U lose.*

Like any of this is news to me. The man's following his dreams. He could've knocked on the door with no hands. Course, I helped with that. I have a sharp eye for details.

I can reply to El with anything. It will have the same effect. Any tug on the rope will do. I go with *Not so fast.* Hope poor Danny doesn't have plans for the day. El won't let him out of her sight, insinuating herself into his life. His extremely private, unfettered life. He found some kind of freedom airborne he's fiercely protective of. He'll follow his heart, but don't push him, or he'll vanish.

I order pie. When your best friend fucks the man you love after you arranged and paid for their meeting, you get burger *and* pie.

I find it useful to gather a few facts here and there to add to the intuitive process of reading cards, grist for the mill. El leaves her life lying around like it's anybody's business. While she made coffee, I skimmed the snarky letter from United Fidelity (love the irony) closing out El's case, apologizing for the delay. A fat check had been attached, paying on an accidental death claim when they had to *know*—sorry El—that she's the sort of woman who would marry a total sleazeball for the money, and that Carl—no apologies—was the kind of guy fatal accidents go looking for. That's got to be hard for them. I may not be the nicest person in the world, but at least I'm not an insurance company.

While I'm waiting for the pie, I find the email address of the investigator from United Fidelity who signed the letter. Proctor Linwood Jr. Ouch. I keep it simple for Proctor Jr.: *Carl Manoli's death was no mere accident.* (which to hear El tell the story is technically true) and hit send when the pie comes.

After an anonymous tip like that, Proctor might develop an interest in El's sleepovers. Danny and El better be careful. But that's not El. Love isn't careful. It's romantic. Heathcliff and Cathy—like she can't remember how that story goes—though she never sticks around long enough to find out. If El's telling the truth, there's no way they can prove Carl was murdered by anyone, certainly not Danny who was on dry land at the time, but would he mind answering a few questions? Oh very much indeed. He's a very private person.

He'll be out of El's arms in no time. Out of danger. Just like I said. I'll comfort him. Somewhere in there—this part's a little sketchy—he falls in love with me. End of story. I get to keep my cards. Of course,

Proctor Jr. might not be the kind of guy who reads all his emails. I'm going to need a backup.

I take out my cards and lay out a spread for myself I study while eating my pie. Purists would be horrified. You're not supposed to do your own, and the cherry(?) pie is kind of a distraction. But I have no use for purity. Life is messy. Magic that requires purity is clearly useless for the living. Something's not quite right with the spread besides the pie, but I'm not sure what it is.

I don't have to pose a question. I only have the one. Clients who have only one question are the only ones worth talking to. If you haven't wrestled with your question enough so that it's the only thing in the room no matter where you are, why are you asking for magic? The ones who say "I can't decide what to ask" catch hell from me: *I see a total lack of direction in your life. Why did you even come here today? Did you get lost on the way to Starbucks?*

Like most everybody whose cards I read regularly, I have my own usual suspects, cards I get all the time. So my cards are no surprise, Moon, Lust, and The Universe—who could ask for anything more? Sounds like a show tune.

To be honest, I've never been particularly fond of The Moon. It's kind of cold and creepy. There's a pair of Egyptian jackal-headed dudes facing each other, with their little jackal dogs at their feet. I always identify a little too much with the two dogs, like they're saying to each other, *What are these two assholes going to get us into tonight?* I know this is childish, that I'm quite good at digging up my own troubles. If you look at the card the right way, the landscape is fairly erotic, like a woman lying back, knees up, thighs open, and once you look at it that way, it's kind of hard to miss. Danny's having some of that right now. I'm just another jackal at the diner eating cow. It's a card about waiting. Wanting. I've been doing that for a while now. Boo-hoo, moving on—

Lust I like a whole lot better. Most decks call this card Strength. I know where my strength comes from. I love this card: Beautiful naked strong woman astride a big-maned lion, a chalice of glowing lava held aloft in her right hand. The lion's several heads have the faces of her lovers. The lion's tail is a serpent raptly gazing at the chalice. In her left hand, she holds the reins, grips the beast between her thighs. Beneath the beast's huge paws, lie past lovers, deep blue and forgotten. One of them, if you look close, is covering his face with his hands, crying his eyes out. Admittedly I'm not so good at the forgetting part, and I've mostly been the one doing the snotty palms thing over somebody who was definitely not worth it. I start out holding the reins, but then find myself tied up in them. But I love the card, the attitude. It's a destiny card for me. Aspirational, you might say.

The Universe. I only started getting the damn thing after Nina showed up asking about Oregon. Another naked faceless goddess, another snake. Snakes everywhere in this deck, which is one of the things I love about it. People seriously respond to snakes. (Out of Lust's lava cauldron's orgasmic glow, for example, scurry—you guessed it—slithering snakes.) This time the snake is big and seems to be uncoiling itself, while the goddess is hanging on like she could become part of the snake if she's not careful. The World, some decks call it. Ever hear that sappy tune "He's Got the Whole World in His Hands"? It kind of limits your options. It's not like you can set it down somewhere. That day in the tent, without either one of them knowing it, Nina handed over that giant snake. *Lots of luck, sister, gone to Oregon.* Fair enough. As long as I get the prize: The Soothsayer—or Sooth, my affectionate nickname—which he allows only because he doesn't know how affectionate it is.

I've fallen in love with him. How stupid is that? It's not essential to the mission—to join magical forces to save the useless planet. But why save the planet if not for love? People don't care about planets. They care about each other. There's all different ways to care. The goddess who put me on this mission has promised me Danny in the end, or at least along the way. The *end* is our mission, only Danny doesn't know it yet. I have to break it to him gently. I'm too weird for most people, so I'm used to opening up a little at a time, but for you I'm making an exception. You get blunt and upfront—I want Danny, but not just for myself. I'm a witch in service to the Triple Goddess, if you want something to put in your notes. We have a deal. And no, we're not taking any questions.

El will fall in love with anybody given half a chance. The other half isn't so sure, gets bored, just never shows up. There was probably a few hours in there somewhere where she even loved Carl. The half-life of El's love is like a day and a half. I'm not like that. I don't take to love easily. I'm all about jokes, like I told Danny. Don't take anything too seriously, or it might hurt you. Danny's different. I believe in him. El never believed in anything but her beautiful self. Not to judge. It's just true. Can't last, obviously, but you can see the attraction of the ride when you look like El. There's a whole lot more to El than her beauty, but just try to tell her that. Her day will come, however. I have total faith in her.

Then I see who's missing in my spread tonight. Danny. Sometimes he's The Hermit, sometimes The Magus. On these lonesome nights he's often The Knight of Cups, angel wings sprouting out his back through his armor, mounted on a white charger, in *love*, leaping into bright nothingness. The horse looks over his shoulder at you like he's not so sure about this, but leap he will, because that's the kind of steed he is. Makes sense Danny doesn't show tonight. He's found a place to land for now. Everyman's dream—El's bed. For a little horseplay.

As Scarlett O'Hara says, Tomorrow is another day.

"You need anything else?" the waitress asks. Twentyish. Nameplate says Courtney. Slightly nervous. Looking awfully good for a dead shift at this place. A little blue. Canceled plans. She's carrying around a question bigger than she is. Since Nina, I've learned to spot my sisters' burdens. Correction. I've always been good at spotting them. Now I give a shit.

"Just the check, thanks."

Courtney's looking at the cards, wide-eyed. The yellowed lighting in here makes them look even creepier than usual, like my great aunt had them in a concentration camp somewhere and smuggled them out. "Those are really interesting cards. Do you read professionally?"

"Indeed. What is it, Courtney? A guy? Works here? Off tonight?"

Courtney draws back. The truth always does that to people. Tell them a lie, and they lean right into it. "He's sick. How'd you know?"

"Like I said, I'm a professional."

"Do you have like a card or anything?"

Poor thing. "You couldn't afford me, but it's barter night. How about I do your cards for the check?" I hold it up, and after a quick glance around to see if anyone's watching, Courtney snatches it back. The only one who would care is the guy who's not here—the sick man she's looking hot for. I've done this one. Teaching Assistant, Assistant Manager—why is it they all have Assistant in their titles? So they can help themselves.

"Looks like you're my last table. I have some side work to do first, do you want some coffee or anything? Five, ten minutes. Is that okay?"

Like I'm doing her a huge favor. "No problem. Coffee with a shot of brandy in it. Don't rush. I've got a phone call to make."

While Courtney gets the coffee, I go to the women's, passing by the bar, making a note of the ABC Managers list required for any booze vending establishment, listing everybody with the authority to do anything, like schedule cute young Courtney for the night shift, so he can cheat on his wife. This shouldn't take long.

There's a Steve who's low man on the list (there's a lower woman) so I ask the cook sitting at the bar where Steve is tonight, and he confirms poor Steve called in sick. The cook doesn't believe Steve's story any more than I do.

"Must've gotten it from his kids. What are their names again?" They're right there on the tip of my bullshit.

"Nick and Stevie."

"Right. Cute kids. Great burger, by the way."

The cook smiles. Everybody likes to be appreciated. All kids are cute.

Back at the table, my coffee's waiting. I'm not that much of a drinker anymore, but I love the sensation of the hot alcohol going up my nostrils. The coffee smell. Jackal girl. I'm a real smell freak. Courtney's troubles have inspired me—I've thought of a backup plan to distract El from Danny: Send in the clown.

I call Terry. It's late. He might be at Serena's. I'll be able to tell when I hear his voice what's going on with him. He answers, "Hello, Kristi. What a pleasant surprise!" He's at home, alone. It's never too late to talk to me, he says. Terry's the Energizer bunny. He's always hitting. Not my type. Though I do admire his ability to craft a scam from pretty much nothing: He took an Ancient Civilizations class in college and has seen every Bible movie ever made. He mashes this together with some reincarnation mumbo jumbo and a radio voice. Despite the math, it seems we were all around for the two or three civilizations he more or less remembers. If something ancient gets a lot of hype because of some new dig or museum exhibit, everybody seems to have once lived there until the next hot culture comes along. He favors concubines, slaves, and queens. All have unfulfilled needs they've carried over into this life where fortunately he accepts cash, credit cards, and/or sexual favors. I've also heard he's a serious disappointment in the sack. Probably the steroids. Could be the narcissism. I passed on my opportunity to find out first hand with a firm refusal.

"So how'd it go at The Tree?" I ask. He loves to talk about his work, as he calls it.

He switches to PR mode and describes his "terrific" experience with a talented young man who writes screenplays.

"Michael?"

"That's the one."

Michael amuses me. Michael should make a movie about Michael. "What did you tell him?" One of the ways you know Terry's a phony is his complete willingness to share the insights revealed during his private sessions. It's all a joke to him. He never seems to notice that I never offer my own clients' secrets in return.

"I told him he'd been a playwright previously, in Herculaneum, a brilliant career in farce cut short by the eruption of Vesuvius. Did you see that exhibit?"

"I did actually, with my friend El. You're shameless, Terry. By the way, did you ever call her? I saw you hitting on her at that River Road party last June."

"I wasn't *hitting* on her. I was merely explaining that her namesake was the queen of Ancient Carthage—some would say a goddess. Besides, I thought you told me she's married to a fairly dangerous man."

Terry never watches any news that's not about the past. "Not anymore. Hubby drowned. She's available. And she sure *thought* you were hitting. Goddess is pretty heavy duty. Girlfriends talk, you know. You want her number? I see her more as concubine material myself. Or Amazon slave girl chained to a wall."

He chuckles. "Sure. Thanks."

"Better act fast. You never know when you'll get another shot at a goddess."

"Ha. Ha."

I send him El's cell, feeling like I just wrote it on a bathroom wall in Ancient Carthage.

"Got it, thanks. When Serena told me you quit The Tree, I was quite surprised."

"Yeah. It was time. I need a break from the legions of the anti-depressed."

"I ran into your boyfriend Danny at the store. He certainly is an un-pleasant fellow."

"Only to people he despises, and he's not my boyfriend." Not yet.

"Serena told me about your little arrangement. We saw you pick him up in the parking lot. I thought he was too crazy to even get into a car. How'd that go? Michael thought he was meeting a woman—took a call in the *middle* of a session. Very unprofessional."

Terry's into gathering useful information too. He's trying to provoke me. Terry's as subtle as a minotaur in a glass labyrinth. "If you must know, we fucked in a church parking lot. He told me I was the Queen of Sheba. I should've held out for goddess, but I guess I'm just easy. Like I'm going to tell you and Serena a *thing*? Don't tell her your secrets, obviously. How's that going, by the way? I can't quite remember my history. Did they have eunuch slaves in Ancient Carthage?"

"Screw you, Kristi."

"Eat shit, Terry. You working Lucinda's party Halloween?"

"Course. You?"

"Outcome uncertain. We'll see what happens. I get enough of her on a regular basis."

"I heard you were being regularly summoned to the mansion."

"That doesn't happen that often. Only when there's a crisis. Mostly, I do her cards over the phone." Meaning I tell Lucinda what to do to deal with being Lucinda. No small task. I charge accordingly. Lucinda's annual Halloween party is a gold mine serving champagne and crab cakes and future clients if you're one of her chosen psychics—those gifted in understanding the special needs of the rich. But when Lucinda crashes on or around November 2nd, she calls me to say her life is unbearable and I must come at once and bring my cards. I would just as soon be gone by then. With Danny. Anyplace but Oregon.

Courtney has shown up, hovering, not wanting to interrupt my conversation. "Gotta go, Terry. A client is waiting." I hang up and motion for Courtney to sit. The cook is idly watching from the bar. He's in his fifties. He's seen lots of assistant managers and lots of Courtney's. Maybe I'm something new. He doesn't believe I know Steve's kids any more than he believes Steve's sick. People lie to each other. It's what people do. Tell stories. Me too. Some stories can change your life.

Courtney looks like she's standing on the high board over a shark tank. I need to put the poor kid back on the many-headed beast, with Steve just another blue dude left behind. "I—I'd like to ask—"

I silence her with a wave of my hand. "Don't tell me. I know. I don't need the cards for this. You're having a thing with Steve, some kind of assistant manager or something. He has you working this shit shift so you can hang around after and get it on in a back room or a car or something, but it's been getting suspiciously late, so tonight he calls in sick so he can take wife and the two kids to the movies because he's never going to leave them for you, even if his wife never does him anymore, and he dreams of blah, blah, blah. They all claim to have dreams. The cook knows his kids' names. Think about it."

Courtney opens her mouth, closes it. Tears are streaming down her face.

"Just nod if I have it right."

Courtney nods.

"How much do you make here in a week?"

Courtney has to repeat it three times, partly because of the gasping snuffles, partly because I can't believe it's so little and figure I must've heard wrong.

I call Lucinda. From now until November, her magnanimity is boundless. What would Halloween be without me zinging one or two of her most special and pretentious friends? Life gets fairly tedious along the river in a big old house. It makes children of them all.

She picks up. "Lucinda, Kristi. You remember last time I did your cards, I told you it wasn't enough to feel guilty about your privileged life, that you had to once in a while lift a pinky finger to do something for somebody else besides writing a check, or you were going to keep on feeling useless? You remember that? I've got someone for you. A terrific waitress. Victim of sexual harassment, needs a job like tomorrow. You and your husband own seven restaurants in town. You must need someone. All she needs to make is…" I name a figure three times what Courtney's making here. Lucinda has lawn ornaments worth more. Good karma for chump change. She's all over it. "Who should she call?"

I write down the information as Lucinda expresses her hope that her people can do enough for this poor unfortunate person. She'll call Sam, the name I've written down, in the morning. "Tell your friend to wait until after ten to call. Will you be joining us Halloween, dear?"

Lucinda calls me dear. "Sure. Why not? It'll be fun." If I say no, Lucinda might forget to call Sam. Lucinda bargains; she can't help herself. So do I. "Did I tell you my rates have gone up?"

"I'm sure whatever they are, dear, you're more than worth it."

"Thanks so much, Lucinda. Bye now. I have to convey the good news." I hang up.

I explain to Courtney twice what the deal is, but she's still stuck with Steve, wallowing in the loss of a cheating loser. There's a reason crying women annoy me, but I figure that's my Karma now, to lend a hand, a kick in the butt. "Courtney, let me ask you, have you two ever done it outside this building?"

Courtney doesn't answer right away. It must be quite the movie running in her head. Shot on a single set. A single camera. Steve's. There's probably even a security camera in here he has to remember to turn off. Or maybe he saves it on his hard drive first. "No," Courtney says. That finally seems to be a tear stopper. The sobs subside, leaving her a little sullen.

"Think about it: Quit tonight. Call Sam at ten, make three times the money, or stay here and be an idiot. Like I said, no cards needed for this one."

A bunch of cops come in and sit down even though it's minutes until closing. Courtney runs to the bathroom to freshen her face and gather her wits. The cook slides from his stool, heads into the kitchen. Courtney will wait on the cops, naturally. After that, who knows? Love makes you do stupid things. Tomorrow will tell.

I leave and drive by El's place—speaking of love making you do stupid things. I imagine Danny inside dreaming. He dreams about the accident almost every night, even after all this time.

How he must long for it to end. I do. With all my aching heart. I've set everything in motion, now I just have to wait. The moon is high, near full. I drive around awhile, knowing if I go home, I won't be able to sleep. I hate lying awake in the dark, hate that more than anything.

Chapter Six

Keys

The world is too much with us; late and soon,
Getting and spending, we lay waste our powers.

—William Wordsworth

When Elissa wakes in the morning, Danny's already awake, looking out the window into an empty sky.

"Regrets?" she asks, snuggling up against him.

He takes her in his arms, pulls her in close. "No. I was just thinking about Gwen."

"Your friend at work and her husband? I think you should tell them. You don't need to carry that around all by yourself. Maybe they might do something differently if they knew."

She can feel him tense all over when she says this. He says, "It also might rob them of the last happy times they have left. There's nothing anyone can do. What good can come of it?"

"If I were her, I'd want to know." She's not entirely sure that's true, but she knows this is a decisive argument for him—what she would want, what she wants from him now. She kisses him on the neck, just a little below the ear. He's very sensitive there. He makes a little noise in his throat, like there's a tiny little animal huddled inside.

He holds her tight. He's strong. Physical therapy after the accident, he told her, more hours in the gym than he'd spent in his whole life. He says, "Maybe I should've told her when I first knew. She'll know soon enough now. I won't see her for a while. The next time we both work is Tuesday."

She starts to suggest calling, but you don't want to call with something like that. "Why don't you go to their place? Do you know where they live?"

"They live kind of far out." His tone is flat and hard.

She takes that as a signal to drop it. She's been pushing it kind of hard for no real reason. She asks instead the question she's been dying to ask, the one she really wanted to ask the whole time they were talking about their pasts, childhood, all of that. "What did you see about me? That day, when you first saw me. It wasn't just the boat was it? You saw me in the future. You *knew* me."

She thought she might have to coax this out of him. Not so. It's like a sin he's been aching to confess, stripped down to the essentials:

Soon. In a certain place, looking into a certain mountain valley, he says, I *will* adore you.

She asks for details of the landscape, the perspective, the view. The rapturous feelings need no clarification or elaboration. They spill out of him as he reports the experience. He's never felt like that before, he says. Talking about it—to her—he's like whitewater. A dam release. What he felt—what he's going to feel—changed his life. Love can do that, she's heard. She wants some of that.

She jumps out of bed and returns with her laptop, racing through photo galleries until she finds the image she's looking for and fills the screen with it. "Is this the place?"

He stares at the screen speechless. He nods his head. "*Exactly*," he whispers. "That's the place exactly." The shot is of Elissa on the rock, looking over her shoulder at the camera, the view behind her. A dreamy smile on her face, her hair blowing in the wind.

"A friend took this shot on some property Carl and I own in the mountains. Did own. The court owns everything now—it's just sitting there—but *I* still have keys." She gives them a dramatic shake, the ring of duplicate keys to all the her-and-Carl things she was supposed to turn in ages ago but forgot, and no one seemed to care. She shows him a picture of the cabin on the property, a mountain getaway—an indulgence for her that bored Carl but gave him a place to park her when he wanted her out of the way. It did give her some peace. Of course, Danny will want to take her to this place he's seen in his vision—this place where he adores her—why else is he here, if not for that? "We can go up there this weekend. What do you say?"

He says yes. Of course, he says yes. A thousand times yes. He doesn't even ask how far a drive it is. They kiss. It's a date. Saturday morning first thing. Perfect.

In three days, he will adore her. It's Thursday.

Before he gets in the shower, she remembers they're cleaning the street this morning, and tells him he needs to move his car if he's parked out front. "They *will* tow you."

"I don't have a car."

"How'd you get here?"

"I would've taken the bus, but I just missed it. Luckily, a friend from the store gave me a ride."

"Gwen?"

"No, the other tarot reader. Kristi."

Won't last... Give it your best shot.... I want you to.... Fuck him and find out.... Watch me.... Kris rolls around in Elissa's brain laughing her ass off in the sheer joy of *I told you so!*

"Are you all right, Elissa?" Danny asks. Concerned, no doubt, that she looks like someone just punched her repeatedly in the gut. Not a good goddess look.

"Fine," she reassures him. "That's why you didn't want to go out to Gwen's, isn't it? You don't have a car."

"That's part of it."

"Guess what? I've got spares." She holds up her fat key ring again. She once believed you were imprisoned by the keys you carried around to lock things in or out. No keys was freedom. She came up with this theory when Mom and her got locked out of some dump they were living in and she was having herself a good cry, like it was some sort of indulgence. She was thirteen? She eventually wrote an essay about her theory in freshman comp. Kris helped her with it a little. She got an A. Whenever Kris helped, she got an A.

Now she's using keys like chips in a card game. She reminds herself never to play poker with Kris, but what choice does she have? Kris gave him a *lift*? C'mon. Now she remembers Kris saying he still doesn't drive, avoids even riding in cars after all this time. She imagines Kris circling like a hawk just waiting for him to set foot outside.

Elissa's sorry. The man needs to drive. Get on with his life, his future. How did he think he was going to get to the mountains this weekend? Fly? He needs to overcome his fears, or Kris will pick him up again, give him another ride. What's he doing taking rides from *Kris* of all people? She drives like the world can't turn fast enough. Maybe Kris isn't as invisible to him as she thinks.

Elissa wraps herself in a robe and leads him out to the garage. He's only in his jeans. "Take your pick," she says. "These were both mine, in addition to the one I'm keeping—like everybody needs three cars, right? Their ownership is in dispute. My lawyer advised me not to relinquish possession. No one's supposed to drive them until everything's settled maybe next year this time, and I can sell them. No one will know or care if you take a drive in the country to see your friend today, bring it back tonight."

He doesn't try to act like this is TV, and he just won the car. He knows what she's doing—that this is sort of a test. A test of his belief in his own vision, in her. Knowing the story of the accident, she's a little surprised when he points at the Mini. It's a convertible. The poor man's still barefoot. He must be terrified, but he'll do it anyway. For her. This must've been some vision.

"Will you go with me?" he asks.

She didn't think of that. "Sure," she says. What else can she say? It was her idea that he tell his friend her husband's going to die, that he face his own worst fears to do so. Maybe she should've stayed out of it, but it's too late now. She hands him the key, and he takes it.

He says, "I always wanted to drive one of these since I saw that movie. I can't remember the name. One of those movies where you're supposed to like the bad guys because some other guys are worse, but it was mostly about the cars."

"Movie?"

"Doesn't matter. I didn't like it." He puts his arms around her. "You want me to drive, because you think it's good for me. Put myself out there."

"Am I right?"

"I don't know, but I think it's good for me that you care what's good for me."

He kisses her. And for a moment she sees it too. She loves him in that future he told her about. It's the both of them. In love.

At least that's what she sees now. She doesn't have this gift like he does. She doesn't *know* anything. She's just guessing, pretending, acting. All she knows about love is what she's seen in the movies—but she's seen lots and lots of movies, excelled in the screenwriting class she took in college. Then she realizes, remembering exactly what he said— he just sees this one moment, nothing after. Anything could happen after. Look at him and his wife. Everything fine, and then a tractor trailer jackknifes into oncoming traffic, and everything changes. They're both alive, but it doesn't matter. They're not the same people anymore. It broke Elissa's heart the first time Kris told her their story. Still does.

She says, "Well, get in the shower, and we'll get going."

He gives her an enigmatic smile. He's different this morning somehow. "I see us both in the shower—the water beating down on the two of us. We have hours. Gwen won't be there until this afternoon."

He's so right.

Poor, poor Kris, she thinks, forgetting in the heat of the moment, as they're fucking in the shower, that every single time she's ever thought that before, things haven't exactly turned out that way. Orgasms can be an impediment to clear-headed thinking and vice versa. Look at them. They could slip and fall, hurt themselves. Scream and no one would hear.

Except you. And you're no help at all. You just like to watch. The world could be ending, and you'd just turn the page.

Chapter Seven

Someone's Died. Someone's Dying

He went like one that hath been stunned,
And is of sense forlorn:
A sadder and a wiser man,
He rose the morrow morn.
    —Samuel Taylor Coleridge, *The Rime of the Ancient Mariner*

Danny dreams about the accident often, or rather he dreams it, the accident itself, like it's happening again. Which makes sense, because when it was happening, it seemed like a dream. He's riding in the backseat of a convertible spread-eagle across a painting to keep it from flying out. The painter's a friend, a neighbor, Lew. He isn't very good in Danny's opinion, but he's been through a midlife crisis and come out the other end thinking he's an artist. He has a show in a coffee shop in Ashland where this will be the last piece to hang. His new girlfriend Melanie is in the passenger seat. The painting, a big thing, is supposed to be a nude of her. It's just colors. She thinks Lew's an artist too. Nina's at a meeting; she's never cared for Lew; she and his ex were friends.   The top of the painting is catching too much wind. Danny unbuckles his seatbelt, so he can turn to reposition it.

 Melanie screams. He flies. There's no seam between the moments, as if her scream ejects him from the car into the sky where he sees the confluence of wreckage below as a pattern of colors, like the painting that flew with him until he lets it go—as if *it* did all this—and it flutters down, canvas scraps among the dead. Fires erupt below him, and become a conflagration, and there's a moment of silence when everything but him has stopped moving. He looks around him, and as far as he can see is devastation, and then he hits the tree.

When he wakes up from the dream, it's usually morning. A new day. When he eventually woke up in the hospital weeks later, they told him Lew and Melanie were dead, but he already knew that—the way her scream stopped in the middle. The weird thing is he remembers it all right up to the moment of impact. That's unusual they tell him. Usually after a trauma like that, some of the memory is lost. And just in case he might forget, he relives it in his dreams almost every night.

This time when he dreams it, he wakes up in a strange car—another convertible—on a familiar road, and he's driving, still dreaming. He hasn't driven in a long, long time, has assumed he never would. He understands this is the future. At first he doesn't remember what's familiar about the road—long, narrow, and dusty, straight to a white farmhouse on the horizon. It's the road he saw in Billy's future, the road Billy's driving when he's on his way to tell Gwen he's going to die. That little square house is where they live.

That's what he's doing, driving that road, to tell Gwen her future, but he doesn't know why he's doing such a thoughtless thing. He looks over to the passenger seat, and there's Elissa. This is her idea. He looks back at the road, and for a moment the two get mixed up, Billy in his truck, Danny in this convertible, barreling down this dusty road, and he wonders if Billy's ahead of him or behind.

Then he wakes up for real.

Elissa is lying beside him asleep. What an incredible night, such a beautiful woman. She must be the reason. He's always thought there must be some reason he got this extraordinary ability, that there's something he's *meant* to see. Dying cats. Broken hearts. Like Kristi said, everyone gets heartache. But nothing remarkable ever happened, nothing that seemed especially important. Until now. This beautiful woman he hardly knows. She walks into The Tree, and he changes her life, and she changes his. Shit like that doesn't happen every day. He doesn't begin to understand it, but he can't ignore it. Now this dream. He looks out the window into the bright blue sky, remembering it, driving a fucking convertible. *Driving* at all. Why on Earth would she want him to tell Gwen Billy's dying? Gwen will be alone by Christmas. It will shatter her. Nothing anyone can do to stop that.

"Regrets?" Elissa asks behind him.

He takes her in his arms, so she won't see he's been crying. "No," he says. He gave up regretting anything when he smacked into that tree. He doesn't need a weatherman to know which way the wind blows. It's blown him here, into the arms of a goddess, dreaming his own future.

It's like magic how it all unfolds: Him behind the wheel again. Just like in his dream. Afternoon. Elissa wanted to leave earlier, but he stuck with his dream. He wanted to prolong his future-inspired good fortune for as long as he could before setting off on this fool's errand. They're still on the Interstate yet. He called Gwen and asked if they might visit—him and Elissa—and Gwen said afternoon would be best.

"Girlfriend?" she asked.

"Yeah, I think so," he said.

"Danny, that's so exciting!"

He didn't know what to say to that. Because he wasn't excited, not like she meant. Something isn't right. *Why am I heading to your door, Gwen, with my think-so girlfriend?* That'll be his first question for the cards even though he knows the answer. Because he fucking dreamed the future, so now he's in it, behind the wheel, Gwen's invited guest, the bearer of bad tidings, the ill wind that blows no good, and she'll greet him with open arms. He feels awful. But he can't shake the feeling that this is all part of something larger than him and Elissa's think-so love affair.

He keeps thinking about Kristi.

He wasn't driving when the accident happened, not that it would have prevented the inevitable crash, but he finds it helps to have the wheel to hold onto, to be the one supposedly in control. The Mini drives like it's glued to the road, heightening this illusion. The wheel in his hands doesn't turn the world. The brakes don't stop it. *Italian Job* is the movie he couldn't think of. Crooks robbing crooks, but some crooks are nicer turns out, or at least better looking with these hot little wheels. Who cares? Nice car though.

Elissa's not sure what to make of his easy compliance. He's not either. Except that having seen himself here with her beside him, it made no sense to argue that he couldn't do it. He clearly could. He clearly would. He clearly can. He's outside of time watching Danny being Danny becoming the Danny he will be. There's a certain thrill to it. *Don't* Choose Your Own Adventure. Just hang on. The events that led him to be here and now feel like cards being dealt.

With Elissa. *Who is Elissa? When is it I fall in love with her? And how? And do I want to?*

Two lesser puzzles haunt him. He too has the fortuneteller's eye for significant details. They're easy to look for when you know where things are going, when you get to see them twice. Before she left the bed to get her laptop, he saw her typing in a password too fast to catch the first time, but not the second, when she actually does it. C-a-r-t-h-a-g-e-Q-u-e-e-n. Then as she's paging through thumbnails, talking a mile-a-minute, totally buzzed to be part of a prophecy (her word), blind to everything but the mountain view she's seeking —he spots Kristi flitting by several times over the years. It's definitely her. There's something unmistakable about her eyes. A bit unnerving. Like they can see inside you.

When he told Elissa Kristi gave him a ride to her place, she practically lost it. He wonders what's going on. He's driving fast, like he used to. He used to like to drive. Kristi would approve of his reckless abandon. *Get over yourself*, she would say of his fears if he let her read his cards. He's making Elissa nervous, so he slows down a little, but he's enjoying the ride while he can.

Elissa probably thought he would be the frightened one on this journey. She's never been up here before. Above the dead. Above yourself. A silent witness—a player in your play. She's wrapped her hair up in a deep blue scarf to weather the convertible ride. He nimbly weaves through moving canyons of eighteen-wheelers as she grips the handle conveniently provided for the nervous passenger, her eyes on the uncertain future.

He's come to believe it's not entirely uncertain. How could he not—having predicted it so many times? But he knows so little, mere scraps of the future, been someone else if only for a moment or two. You don't get over that, no matter how many times it happens.

This visit to Gwen's isn't going to go well, he knows, as he takes the exit into woods and cornfields, but going well's not what it's about. It's got to happen. Going well has nothing to do with it. It's no one's lesson. It just is. Like Billy and Gwen's failed farm, advanced lung cancer, agonizing grief. Is. Is. Is.

It's only when they leave the Interstate that it's quiet enough to make themselves heard, and even then they must project like they're on stage. They know so little about each other, even after a night of telling each other everything.

The road is a two-lane blacktop without much shoulder. He has to keep his eyes on the road, but the trucks are gone. They purr along through a green world, the leaves just starting to turn. "How do you know Kristi?" he asks.

"Kristi? Did she say she knows me?"

He sees her right hand in his peripheral tightening its grip. "No. She pretended she didn't know where she was taking me. Now you're doing the same thing. I saw her in your laptop when you were paging through your photos. Makes me wonder what's going on."

Her knuckles are white. "I thought you could only see the future. Kris is past tense. We used to be friends."

Until yesterday, he's guessing. She's hoping he'll let it go. "Why would she tell me you're dangerous?"

She heaves an angry sigh, shakes her head. "Because she's a bitch. Because she has a thing for you. Because she feels betrayed." She starts out righteous, but guilt overtakes her.

"I'm listening," he says.

So she tells him the story of how they came to meet in the first place. That it was supposed to be about Kris, but he was so into her, and she called him yesterday so desperate to see him because she and Kris had a fight about him, and it had sort of turned into a competition. She tries desperately to be honest, to tell him everything. She still has to practically shout, keep it simple, so her meaning isn't blown away in the wind. There can be no subtlety, no nuance, and therefore no excuses. He's touched by the irony that she should be making this effort on their way to inflict sooth on someone who probably doesn't want or need it, when there's been so much else unspoken.

So Kristi's in love with him. Elissa tries to make it sound as psycho as she can, but even she calls it love. He had no idea—a hermit misses a lot—though now he can see it. The more he thinks about it, the more he remembers little moments he ignored at the time, thinking they didn't mean anything. He's always liked her, her weird sense of humor. What he finds incredible is that she read Nina's cards and has felt responsible for Nina leaving him. She shouldn't feel that way. It just isn't true. She even has Elissa convinced of it. There were a thousand reasons for Nina to go. She used to save fortune cookie fortunes that "spoke" to her. It didn't mean anything. Those voices ended up forgotten in her pockets, drowned in the wash. Nina left because she decided to. She had her own problems to deal with. Kristi probably wasn't very nice, but she gave her good advice. He wishes it hadn't been time for Nina to go, but it was. He was crazy. Maybe he still is, but he doesn't feel crazy anymore. Nina, staying or going, didn't make him whatever he is or used to be.

"Do you hate me?" Elissa asks when she's told him everything.

"No. Don't you remember? I love you. On the mountain in the photo." He has to shout the last over the grinding roar of the gravel under the wheels as they make the final turn onto Gwen's drive. He's still a little angry at all the deceits practiced on him, but he lets it go. It doesn't matter. The straight, dusty road silences their conversation. Up ahead are problems much bigger than theirs. He looks over at her.

This is the moment he saw in his dream.

They come to a stop at the end of the road, and the dust cloud they've raised passes over them and rains grit down on the leather seats and settles into the crevices. A pair of dogs rush out from the porch and run in circles, barking greetings, wagging deliriously. Gwen won't have any mean dogs, she often says. When she says this, Billy always says, "Except me."

Pretty soon she'll hear the silence when he doesn't, when he's not there to speak, then she'll quit saying it. Everyone here will come near to dying of a broken heart. You don't have to tell people about heartache. Everyone has heartache.

Gwen comes out onto the porch to greet them. She's delighted, stunned, to see him, to see him *driving*, to see him with this beautiful woman, Elissa. (She didn't even know he was dating!) Gwen's so sorry Billy's not here. She thought he would be back by now. He's in town, at the doctor's. She's finally talked him into seeing someone about that cough. He probably had to stop at the pharmacy. He should be back any time now. He wouldn't want to miss you two. Billy likes company. He especially likes Danny, and he'll be tickled pink to see he's *driving*. Billy frets about that—a man who doesn't drive.

Gwen bakes, of course. She's made pumpkin bread. Billy likes it with his coffee. She serves them coffee. The house smells like a spice factory, like high end coffee shops wish they could smell. Remind her, Gwen says, and they can pick a pumpkin in the garden before they go to take home. "We have more than we can eat in a lifetime, and there's more every day. They were early this year. I think it's global warming."

He looks at Elissa across Gwen's welcoming, bountiful table. Elissa's terrified he's going to do what they supposedly came here to do, tell this happy, smiling woman that her husband's a dead man driving, that he's not stopping at the pharmacy, because it's too late for anything they have there. Danny smiles at Elissa. *This is your party. I drove. You can do the talking, get a taste of knowing what you're not supposed to.*

"If your husband's not feeling well, maybe we should give you your privacy," Elissa says.

"Don't be silly. You must've driven all the way out here for a reason. Don't tell me. Must be the cards. I can't believe Danny's finally going to consent to having *his* cards read, so it *must* be you. Am I right?"

Gwen offers this with her chin tilted up, like the bright girl in the front of the class who loves knowing the answers. She loves being psychic almost as much as she loves Billy. All the photos in the house from high school on are the two of them and later their son, killed in Iraq.

"Yes," Elissa says. "You guessed it. Danny says you're the best." He said she was the nicest, but he doesn't contradict.

"You have a pressing question? Don't tell me what it is."

Elissa looks right at Danny as if he's the nagging question that's driven her here. "Definitely," she says. It's him. That man across the table.

He smiles confirmation that he's one enigmatic fellow. Gwen's known him a while now. She can see he looks different today. Like he just spent the night wrestling with an angel or a goddess. Or maybe she's just the queen of Carthage. He still hasn't asked her about that. How she knows Terry. He can't picture her as a client of that bozo.

"Oh my," Gwen says. "This sounds like fun. Let me get my cards. Do you need any more coffee? If the dogs bother you, just push them away." Gwen scampers into another room to get her cards. Elissa and Danny are alone for a moment. The dogs, a pair of wild-eyed collies, sisters, have taken to him. He pets a head resting on each thigh as they groan and wag and whimper.

"We can't tell her," Elissa whispers. "I was wrong to make you come here. Do you hate me," she asks again, "now you know what a coward I am?"

"No," he says. This time he looks at her quite lovingly. She told him Kristi doing her cards sometimes felt like being peeled open and examined "like she can lay her hands upon your heart." She must be dreading this.

Meanwhile, they're all listening for Billy's truck on the road, *any time now.*

When Gwen returns with the cards and starts shuffling, Danny thinks for the first time maybe he'd like to have his cards read, after all, not by comforting Gwen, but by Kristi. Peeled open. Her hands on his heart. His thigh. *So let's not go see this woman. What do you say?*

"These are new," Gwen says of the cards. "I just got them. I had an inspiration I should use them for your reading, Elissa. Don't tell Serena, Danny, but I got them from Amazon for half the price, even with my employee discount. Kristi recommended them, sent me the link. You know Kristi, Elissa?"

Elissa nods dumbly as Gwen happily shuffles her fresh Thoth deck, just like Kristi uses, only these haven't been to Hell and back. Not yet. These are new, fresh from Amazon. For Elissa special. "You can help me break them in. No charge. Your money's no good here." She smiles big at Danny. Any friend of his is a friend of hers. She's beaming, delighted by the synchronicity: The cards just came yesterday. UPS. "I've been dying to use them." She fans them and looks at a few of their faces. "My. They are dark, aren't they?"

She closes them and raps them on the table. Three, quick little beats. The dogs lie down under the table, and Gwen laughs. "They always do that when I read. I think they pick up on the energy."

She hands Elissa the cards, has her shuffle the cards several times while thinking about her question. Kristi never lets her clients touch her cards except for a single cut, not that they'd want to without disinfecting after. These are slick and new and stiff, and a couple of times they spray across the table as Elissa tries to shuffle them, and she has to start over again. Concentrate, she's told. On her question.

Her hands are trembling.

Even Gwen notices. She cuts Danny a look. She knows this reading isn't about romance, or that's not all it's about. She has Elissa cut the cards, cuts them herself, then begins. Danny's seen her work enough to know the routine. She usually puts down one card at a time, talks between, like layers of meaning, card, talk, card, talk... like a story unfolding, until the story's done—the answer's revealed along the way, the final outcome of the business, in the upper corner, when the last card is laid.

This time Gwen places a card, starts to speak but decides to see another. Card, silence, card, silence… Layers of meaningful silence. She loses the happy fortuneteller face as the story unfolds. Unspoken heartache. Unspeakable pain. Long after the last card is placed like a blossom on a grave, gently, gently, oh so gently, the first words out of her mouth are "Someone's died. Someone's dying."

Danny looks down on the bright new cards, a pattern of shiny colors, wonders which ones tell her this. Another easy truth. Someone's always died, someone's always dying. Or maybe she could smell it in the dust they blew in. *You will learn to see this matter differently.* This is so horrible, so wrong—her gift turned against her. Gwen knows what they've come to tell her, despite their silence—through Elissa's cards.

"You feel responsible," Gwen continues, her voice shaking. Then she looks up from the table into Elissa's eyes. She can't help keeping the shock out of her voice. "You *are* responsible."

Elissa shrinks back in horror. She looks like someone just hauled her out of the bay dripping guilt, staring at something beyond Gwen, beyond the cards, deep inside.

The dogs jump up simultaneously, eight paws on hardwood, and dash out the dog door, and the three humans hear it moments after. Billy's truck approaching. It's never an easy truth: The next dead man's coming home.

"There's Billy," Gwen says, like she can now count the number of times she has left to say that. Gwen gathers up the cards without another word about them. They're so new they skitter about, and one skates off the table and across the floor.

Elissa stops it with a stamp of her foot and retrieves it, giving it to Gwen as if she can't get rid of it fast enough. The Star. Trying to escape a hopeless situation. Gwen slides it back into the deck like a knife and puts the cards back in the box. Who can say whether she'll ever use them again? Probably not any time soon.

"Look who's here," Gwen says to Billy when he steps into the dining room, the dogs dancing around him. He did stop, but not at the pharmacy. He went for some of the old medicine he hasn't touched in years now, since he promised Gwen he'd quit. He's only a mean dog when he drinks.

His eyes fix on Danny. Two unprecedented events in one day—a death sentence and the soothsayer showing up in a new car. They must be related. Fucking destiny again. "What are you doing here? What's got you out in the light of day? You *knew*, didn't you? You fucking knew. I seen how you look at me. Couldn't wait till I'm gone? Some friend you are."

Elissa grabs Danny's arm and pulls him toward the door. "It's time we were going. Thank you, Gwen. I'm terribly sorry. This was a bad idea. I'm so sorry."

"Bad *idea*?" Billy says to Elissa. "Bad *idea*? Who the hell are you?"

"Billy," Gwen says, laying her hand on his arm gently, oh so gently.

And he stops his bluster. The dogs are still dancing around him. He starts to cry, and Elissa and Danny finally leave, since they never should've come in the first place. They drive in silence, alone with their thoughts.

Concealing them from each other and even from you.

Chapter Eight

The Baby Jesus on the Spice Rack

Away in a manger, no crib for a bed,
The little Lord Jesus lay down his sweet head.
The stars in the sky looked down where he lay,
The little Lord Jesus asleep on the hay.

—traditional carol

They get stuck in traffic going back. A wreck on the Interstate during rush hour has everything crawling in fits and starts through a sea of blue lights and a haze of exhaust. When they reach the wreck, there are shattered pumpkins everywhere. They have to smile. They never picked their pumpkin. His fingers smell like nutmeg and cinnamon.

Elissa checks her messages and sends a couple. He doesn't ask, and she doesn't say. He just wants to go home to his little cell where he doesn't see the future, can imagine there's not one, only the present. Destiny's for suckers.

They finally make it back to Elissa's well after dark and agree they need some time apart. He parks the dusty Mini in the garage. They're still on for Saturday morning. She'll text, she says, work out the details. She has a lot to think about.

Him too.

It's a long wait at the bus stop. He turns to see if her light's still on, but the moaning of a pair of cats, ears back, fangs bared, circling at the threshold of the alley, turn him back around. They finally come together in a short but incredibly vicious fight. The vanquished tuxedo, who wears a reflective collar with tags, obviously has somewhere else to be.

He cedes the alley to his foe and takes his wounds home. Nina kept Danny's cat. He used to pull shit like that when he was young. Serious vet bills. Tristan. He's probably dead by now. He wishes he could have a cat, but his lease doesn't allow pets.

He look back at Elissa's. The lights are off. *How in the world is it I'm supposed to fall in love with her?* Things aren't exactly headed that way.

Back on the bus, he tries to get his bearings, staring at the familiar ads for bail bondsmen and short-term loans and burial insurance and lottery tickets. Ads for people with no futures, willing to pay dearly for the illusion of one. Fortunetellers like him are for people who think they have choices, like tomorrow's just waiting for them to get a fortune they like.

He almost misses his stop, but he doesn't miss what's parked across the street from his building, not this time, the driver barely visible, sound asleep at the wheel. One of her peeling stickers reads I BRAKE FOR NOTHING. Yet here she is. On a stakeout. For him. According to Elissa, this is nothing new. Elissa called her a stalker, knowing where he lived, where he went. Not much to know there. She must've been dedicated in her work to detect the negligible signs of life. Invisible. In a way. Not the way she wanted to be seen. If it hadn't been for Elissa, he never would've gotten into Kristi's car. There was a moment right before he knocked on Elissa's door, when he watched Kristi driving away and wished he was still inside that car, her hand on his thigh. That moment keeps coming back to him.

He walks over to the car now. She has the seat tilted back, the window rolled down. He wonders how long she's been here. Her eyes flutter with dreams. "Hey," he says, rapping on the car door. "What is your piece of shit car doing across from my place in the middle of the night? You trying to get me evicted?"

She opens one eye. "*Sooth*, is that you? Great to see you! How was it? The night of bliss?"

"Great to see you too. Can't complain about the night. Could've done without the day. You were waiting here to see if I came home?"

She has both eyes open now, a drowsy smile. "Sort of. I couldn't sleep at home."

"You seemed to be doing okay just now."

"That's here." She talks through a big yawn. "I had a bet with myself you would only stay one night with freckles. I thought I'd lost. I gave up my vigil, drifted off. The letdown, I guess." She puts her hands behind her head, stretches, tries opening her eyes wide, takes a deep breath. The seat is still tilted back. He feels like he's standing over her bed.

"We got stuck in traffic coming home from a disaster."

"Ah. That will happen." She swishes the cups in the cup holder. Both empty.

Danny leans on the car, his hands on the roof, looking in. "How long have you been here?"

"Parked? I drove by a couple of times. What time is it?"

"Seven."

"About three hours? The *All Things Considered* lullaby was getting underway. I love to fall asleep to those guys. I feel safe. I got zero sleep last night. I'm guessing you didn't sleep much either." She's still smiling up at him, delighted to be waking up to him. He's never seen her looking so happy.

He has the powerful impulse to lean over and kiss her, but he lets it pass, straightens up. Too soon. "Have you had dinner? I'm starved." He's had nothing since the pumpkin bread.

She raises the seatback, looks at him from her new upright position. She's wide awake now. "Let's see. Last food would be yesterday."

He wishes he'd kissed her. "Elissa told me you're in love with me." It just comes out, like one of his prophecies he can't quite keep to himself. He doesn't want her to wonder what he knows and doesn't.

She gives a little nod. "That would be true. You going to tell me to get lost, or are you getting in the car? I promise to drive nicer."

"Neither. I'll cook."

She opens the door and hops out. "Oh boy! I can't believe I'm actually going to see inside your place. Often wondered. Imagined you inside. I'm into visualization. You any good? Cookwise? Not that it matters in the least. Stalkers can't be choosers. Did El call me a stalker?"

He smiles at her excitement. She's bouncing around on her toes in a happy little dance. "Doesn't matter what she called you. How can you tell when I'm home?"

She points. "Bathroom window. Dark, like now, means you're not home. When you're there it's either on, or there's a little night light glow, which is kind of cute. You must not like to pee in the dark."

"How do you know that's my bathroom?"

She makes a what-a-stupid-question face.

He laughs. "Are you a psychic or something?"

"Professional. So what's for dinner?"

They walk across the street and up the front walk to his building as they talk. She's even shorter than he realized. No more than five feet. She's nervous and excited and happy as shit. So is he.

"Best ramen you've ever had."

"No MSG I hope."

"What do you take me for? I have my own secret blend of spices."

"Garlic salt and sriracha?"

"It's hard to keep a good secret."

"Not with friends like El. What else did she tell you?"

"Nothing bad. But you shouldn't blame yourself for Nina leaving me. It's not your fault. You just read her cards."

"El told you about *that*?"

"She thought it made you look bad."

"You *don't*?" They've reached the front door of his building. She stops, apparently wanting to get this settled before they go inside. Her guilt's too heavy to lug across the threshold.

"No. You took responsibility for what you saw, what you said. That's more than most of us do."

"I was just being a bitch."

"So? Life's a bitch, right? Maybe that's what she needed. Sounds like it was effective. Nina was looking for the future you offered her, or she wouldn't have taken it. She needed to escape me. I wasn't about to go anywhere back then—too absorbed by my precious power. Portland was a good move for her—much better than driving her loony husband out to the rest area so he could be closer to the source. I sat blindfolded in the backseat, if you can believe it. So you want the ramen or not?"

"Want. Would you leave town now?"

"If I had a good enough reason."

She likes that bit of news, like she might be hoping to make herself that reason. They go inside. His place is on the third floor, a tiny one room w/ bath & kit. thing at the top of two long flights of stairs, an afterthought of the last rehab, the cheapest solo housing he could find after Nina left.

Kristi says, "I'll go first, so you can see what a nice ass I have."

She does, but he already knew that. He says, "After we eat, I'd like you to read my cards."

She stops and looks over her right shoulder. "Sweet! Then are you going to seduce me?"

He laughs. The sound is strange in the boxy little stairwell, or maybe it's just strange. He doesn't laugh much, and rarely here, climbing the stairs home. "We'll see what the cards say."

"They never lie, but I do, so you're screwed either way."

She loves his place, she says, in constant motion, poking around in the cabinets, delighted there's so little to see. He's usually seen her seated before. That's how they all work at The Tree, planted in that little room. He sees a whole other side of her, watching her move, like a furtive, inquisitive animal. She says, "You are the most totally minimalist guy ever. I love it. I thought you might have like weird little collections of things. Like me, I guess. So what did you do? Sit down? Make a list? 'This is all I need in the whole wide world'?"

He's delighted she likes the place so much. He hasn't had a lot of company. He's not opposed to the idea, has entertained hopes—there are two stools at the bar. (One of his books is *Walden*—to tutor him in solitude.) She lights in one of them, tests the swivel, spins, and stops, looking into his eyes.

My God, what eyes she has. They're disarming, different, like she's not entirely human. "When I moved in I got rid of half my stuff after two or three trips up the stairs. Then I kept getting rid of things I didn't want or need until I'm down to this. Like you say, everything I need in the whole wide world. Except a garlic press. I wouldn't mind one of those."

"What do you do without one?"

"Mince."

She laughs. He could listen to her laughter forever.

Ever since the accident he doesn't care about mementoes. They upset him, as if a moment that was really quite wonderful doesn't know it's dead and keeps hanging around like a ghost. All his connections with people fell apart after the accident. It was easy to get rid of things. Maybe what he needs are new moments he wants to remember. "I like having you here," he says. "It makes me happy."

The thing you should know about Elissa and Danny is this: In spite of the future, the passion, the melodrama, her beauty and his loneliness—he doesn't love her; she doesn't love him. That's Saturday morning supposedly. In a different world. It's only Thursday night, here and now, and he's exactly where he wants to be with the person he wants to be with.

Kristi asks, "You're not just being nice to me because you know I like you, are you?"

"No. I'm being nice to you because I like you. A lot. You're my first dinner guest." He doesn't have to say to her, *since the accident.* She knows the Danny she's talking to didn't exist before the accident. He was happy to hear she loves him, happier still to find her waiting for him when he came home, and he keeps getting happier all the time.

She beams. Her eyes light up. "You can feed me MSG. That would be okay. I'm not feeling picky tonight. Anything."

He was teasing about the ramen. He makes pasta with anchovies and fresh garlic on a tiny little stove. She's easily impressed. The kitchen is a corner with the bar fronting the stove and counter, sink and tiny refrigerator against the wall. She watches as he chops, minces, sautés, seasons, her elbows on the bar, her chin perched on the backs of her long inter-laced fingers like a hammock.

Now that he knows to look for it in her incredible eyes, it's obvious she loves him. It's something of a new sensation, being loved without reservation. He didn't take it personally, but Nina never felt anything without reservations, a shifting constellation of them. Living with him dishing out glimpses of the future, was just too many variables to deal with. Kristi doesn't give a shit about variables. She has her attention focused on something else entirely. Destiny maybe. She uses the word a lot in her readings—mostly blunt, no-nonsense affairs—then Destiny. It kind of jumps out at you, how, in spite of the jokes, she's deadly serious.

"So what do you collect?" he asks.

"Collect?"

"You said, *weird little collections, like me.*"

She dips her head, embarrassed. "Silly stuff."

"Like?"

She sighs. Confesses: "Baby Jesuses. You know, like for a manger?" She holds up her fingers to indicate size—little. She hums a few hurried measures of *Away in a Manger*. "I *loved* that story as a kid, and we always had a nativity scene, a little one. The stable was about the size of a toaster oven, and my mom would put the baby Jesus in it on Christmas Eve, and we'd all sing songs to it and everything. So when I was in the store day after Christmas and saw they had a bin of Jesuses on sale, I bought a bunch with my Christmas money, loaded up the manger with extras, and pretty much put them all over the house, like little good tidings bundles of joy, you know? Mom freaked, and I got my first lesson in theology. You can only deploy one Jesus at a time, unless you want to be some kind of heretic. I was pretty disappointed. Started me down the road to polytheism and worse. You know I'm a witch, right? So you want one? I give a lot away. Like a little bit of Christmas morning. You can think of him as baby Buddha or Cupid or whatever. Not everybody's into the Christ thing. I'm an equal opportunity deployer. You could fit a little god guy on the spice rack over there. He could watch you cook, bless it or whatever. There's a space between the tarragon and thyme. Couldn't help noticing you alphabetize. I think it's interesting you decided you need yet more thyme."

He laughs at her story, her teasing, her silly pun. "That's not really a space. Thyme slid over into turmeric's slot. I'm out. I went on a curry binge. I'd love a little god guy, though, thanks."

"Thyme travel. I like that. I have one. Ta-da!" She pulls a little Jesus out of her bag. Two, three inches long maybe. "I always have a couple with. One stays here in the bag—the bag baby, for general good fortune and guidance and protection. He's charged up with some serious magic. Another, in case, like now, there's a need. I'm into immediate gratification."

He smiles at the tiny beatific child cradled in her hands like it's the real baby Jesus, appearing, tonight only, in his tiny apartment, and looks into her eyes. Time seems to stop for a moment. Like the wreck. The still point. The apogee. Here and now. He says, "I have garlic all over my hands. Why don't you put it on the rack for me? Looks like there's room in the C's."

She comes around the bar and scrambles onto the counter beside him to make the reach, kneeling, arm outstretched, like she's putting an angel on a Christmas tree. "Mustn't disturb the alphabetical order. You want it between the chili powder and cinnamon?" She looks over her right shoulder like she did in the stairwell. Her and the tat both, looking at him, though this time her arm's raised so the women on her arm are reclining. He's stirring the pan furiously with a wooden spoon.

"No. Like you said, not everybody's into that. Why don't you put him between cumin and curry." He tosses the pasta in the pan—patiently, thoroughly.

She smiles at his choice and carefully perches the little god baby on the railing between the two spice bottles. "What do you think? He doesn't have any arrows." She's still kneeling on the counter.

"He doesn't need any more. He's emptied the quiver. It's done." He slides the pasta onto the plates and puts the pan in the sink and washes his hands. When he turns around, she's sitting on the counter.

She holds out her arms. "Help me down?" He puts his hands to her waist to lift her, but she covers them with hers. "I'm sorry I lied to you. I shouldn't have done that."

"When did you lie to me?" Her waist is lean and sinewy like her hands.

"When I acted like I didn't know El, told you she was dangerous, all of that. I was kind of out of control."

"Understandable. Maybe she is dangerous. It doesn't matter. I didn't believe in the cards anyway. You're forgiven."

"I also don't need any help getting down. I just wanted you to touch me—you looked like maybe you wanted to. I did do your cards though. That part was true. They said you're totally into me, and you're dying to kiss me."

"They speak truth." He finally kisses her like he's been wanting to all evening. She wraps her arms and legs around him, and they kiss luxuriously, passionately. That little animal inside him runs free. Released. It's like he's been living in the future, always a few moments ahead of her, looking over his shoulder, longing to stop, be in the moment. And now, she's here, in his arms. He's filled with joy. Joyful. Not exactly what he expected of the day—or any day, for a long time before the accident, leading, as his pal Thoreau would say, a life of quiet desperation.

One of the reasons his near-death experience had such a profound effect on him was he was already dead, plummeting toward the Earth long before it happened. Death gave him a second chance at life. And here she is.

She cradles his face in her hands. "I knew it."

"What did you know? That I'm totally into you—just like the cards said?"

"They didn't really say that. They said it could go either way. I knew that you would taste so nice."

He likes the taste of her too. So they make out some more. After a time, a grumble from one gut, then another, both (it's hard to tell), he mumbles, "We still have a dinner to eat."

"I suppose," she agrees, unwrapping her legs and sliding off the counter. "Bet you're wishing you made ramen now."

She sits at the bar. He wishes he had candles. The overhead's too bright. He tries the light on the stove, over the sink, both, neither. The bathroom light's on, the door open. That's romantic. He considers moving the night light to the kitchen. He's a little weird about light. One of the reasons the place is so cheap is the bathroom's the only window, and the glass is frosted. You have to be a serious hermit to live in a windowless box.

She watches him, amused, laughs when he hovers in the bathroom threshold eyeing the night light. "You could prop open the refrigerator," she suggests, laughing. "If you don't sit down and eat soon, I'll make you kiss me again. I'm not waiting. This is *really* good." Her mouth is stuffed with pasta. "Do you have any wine? I think I need wine."

He has a bottle he's been saving for a special occasion for a long time. None came along. He opens. He pours. So fucking happy. He often wishes he didn't see the future. It's like a stain on his life, but this isn't the future. It's his life. He never saw it coming. He sits down beside her, kisses her greasy, garlic anchovy lips, and digs in. She's right. It's the best meal he's had in years. They toast the Baby Jesus on the spice rack who has showered his blessings upon them.

She says, "I used to dream about stuff like this—you cooking for me."

"You mean like a prophetic dream? You dreamed *this*?" He wants to tell her about the dream that began his day, the crazy scene at Gwen's, but he doesn't want to break the mood.

She laughs. "Not exactly this. Daydreams, fantasies. Nothing prophetic. The cooking wasn't the highlight, you understand, but you cooked. You told me once you cooked yourself dinner, made a point of it. I liked that, went with it. Daydreams aren't magic though. Magic's more like you prepare the soil, create the conditions for something to grow, but you can't control wonderful things, right? That's part of what makes them wonderful. The mystery. Daydreams are too limiting. I don't dream this good."

"The mystery of garlic and anchovies and wine?"

"Exactly."

"How good is your magic? Have you worked any on me?"

"What do you think? We're going on a couple of years now. Believe me, if I could've found a fucking eye of newt, it would've swirled in some cauldron for your ass a long time ago. You've been seriously magicked up one side and down the other. You're not exactly an easy guy to get through to unless you're hanging out in the future with some constipated cat."

He laughs. "Did any of the magic work?"

"I'm here, aren't I? And that's magical, right?"

"Definitely." He kisses her soft, inviting lips. "Enchanting."

She beams.

He clears the dishes and drains the last of the bottle into their glasses. "Would you read my cards now?"

"You've dulled my intuitive powers with spirits."

"I'm guessing it would take more than half a bottle of wine to dull you. I thought you wanted to do them. I sense a certain resistance, as you would say."

"Don't make fun."

"I'm not. I think you're great. I use that line all the time. It's all those sibilants. Seriously, I think you're good. Brutally honest. I like that. So why don't you want to read my cards?"

"I have a few questions first. I thought you didn't want me to. Why now?"

"You afraid of what they'll say?"

"Duh. Afraid of what they'll say, afraid of what you're asking. Who you're asking about. Afraid pretty well covers it. So why you asking for a reading now?"

"My question is of a pressing nature."

"How pressing?"

"Like tonight pressing."

"Sounds like a great question. Can I ask one more question?"

"Anything."

"Listen to you. I wouldn't be so quick with an opening like that with a witch like me. I can ask some pretty weird questions. But this one's obvious. Why is it you're so into El besides the willowy supermodel thing? Is it the freckles? I always figure it's the freckles."

He holds up his hands to stop her. "*Will* be into her. Supposedly."

"You mean?"

He tells her how it is, how his obsession with Elissa got started in the first place—sitting on a future mountaintop he's supposed to visit Saturday. How Elissa showed him a photo. Exact same place—her sitting on the rock. It's his point of view, this future, where he's head-over-heels in love on that very same rock. He's whispering her name, holding her... "I told Elissa the whole story."

"She must've loved that. That's why you didn't come home with me yesterday, isn't it? Just had to have your night of bliss. Fair enough. El is fairly irresistible. I know that place in the mountains. I've been there, probably took the photo. So you love her in the future, scheduled for Saturday. How about now?"

"I sense a certain resistance. A powerful conflicting desire. No. I don't. Definitely not. Can't even imagine it."

"So I guess the question is how that future's looking to you now—whether you still want it more than you want me."

"No contest. I wish I'd never seen it. I don't want to go up there with her. I'm not going."

She presses her fingertips to his lips. "Not so fast: no regrets. They slow you down, make you doubt. If you'd never seen that future, I might not be sitting here now, but enough about El. I don't need the cards for this. You should definitely fuck me, while I'm here and all, and you've gone to all the trouble to wine and dine me with your last can of anchovies, and you find me both witty and desirable."

He kisses her fingertips. They smell like anchovies and garlic. "I find you incredibly wonderful."

She lays her palm against his cheek, her long fingers burrow into his hair, caress the back of his ear. "Really?"

"Really. I didn't see this happening."

She smiles, blossoms. "Then you won't be bored."

He laughs. "That's the last thing I'm afraid of."

"What's the first? The worst?"

"The future."

"Not to worry. You see any future here? Nothing but here and now. You and me."

That's the only thing you need to know about the future. It never, ever happens.

They make love.

Do you want to watch, touch, taste? Go ahead. They won't mind. Imagine away. They're a world unto themselves. Take your time. They have all the time in the world. With or without you.

Sometimes when he dreams the accident, he wakes up in the hospital and Nina's holding him in her arms, but that's not the way it happened in real life. When he woke up, no one *could* hold him. He was being held together with some kind of special mesh with tubes burrowing in and out of him, floating in a ceaseless haze of drugs, wired up to machinery. He probably wanted to be held. He remembers longing. Hunger. Loneliness. Death. By the time Nina could actually take him in her arms and hold him, he was crazy, but everybody was so happy he miraculously survived, they pretended not to notice.

His longing and hunger dissolve in Kristi's arms. She holds him like she loves him, like she'll never let him go, and he holds her like he's finally made it home.

As they're falling asleep in his narrow bed, happily exhausted, she whispers into his ear in the darkness, "Do you want to see it?"

"See what?"

"The place in the mountains. We can drive up in the morning."

"Elissa says it's all locked up."

"We don't have to go into the house. There's just a chain across the road. We can park at the bottom and walk in. It's a mile at most. What do you say? Day trip. Picnic in the mountains. You can ravish me on the big rock." The tip of her tongue explores his ear.

He doesn't see this future. He feels it in her words, the tip of her tongue. It beckons him. He wants it. "I say yes."

She squeezes him. "Have I told you I love you?"

He laughs out loud in the darkness. "You confessed to it. That's not exactly telling me. Close enough, I suppose. You know that feeling I felt in my vision—I'm feeling it now, for you."

"The head-over-heels thing?"

"Yeah."

"So you going to tell me?"

"I love you, Kristi."

"By Jove, I think he's got it! I love you too, Sooth. Damn, I'm good. *Did any of the magic work?* I'll say. It doesn't get any better than this."

"You still haven't read my cards."

"I will. I promise. First things first."

They sleep a long and dreamless sleep in total darkness, the only sound, the mostly empty busses roaming through the night. They've had quite the day. They need to rest up for tomorrow. You never know what tomorrow might bring.

Even you.

PART TWO

Elissa Has a Dream

A solitary crow watches as Elissa sits cross-legged in front of the TV in a dingy motel room on Jeff Davis Highway. She's got the sound way down low so nobody can hear it and know she's inside. Mom's working some shitty job somewhere trying to make rent before they're thrown out. Elissa's alone. She's twelve. If anyone knocks, she's not supposed to answer. She's watching a shopping channel. There's a crow perched on top of the TV. When something comes on Elissa thinks she wants, the bird pecks the screen, and the thing appears in the room. A necklace, knives, a bicycle, a Panini press, Ray-Bans, an aquarium, golf clubs... Since they have almost nothing, she thinks she wants everything, that this is her last chance to have everything she wants.

There's a terrific pounding on the door. The cheap door bows and creaks with each blow. Elissa tries to keep quiet, but the crow lets out a cacophony of caws like maniacal laughter. The pounding grows more frantic. The door splinters and cracks. It's the manager. They haven't paid in a couple of weeks. The pounding stops. The crow lapses into a muted chuckle. Elissa whimpers in fear as the manager jiggles the knob. She hears the jingle of keys. He tries one, then another, and another. The crow pecks furiously at the screen: an enormous teddy bear, a computer, a set of china, a foot bath, a vacuum cleaner, a Segway, a programmable smoker... The room fills up with more and more things until she's surrounded by stuff.

The manager finally finds the right key and the door opens, but it's stopped by the chain. He begins to batter the door with his shoulder, as Elissa curls up into a ball trying to hide behind the stuff. The crow caws louder and louder, taunting him. The manager is shouting, "Open the door bitch! Open the fucking door!"

And then the crow swoops to the doorway and deftly frees the chain with its beak, and the door flies off its hinges, and all the stuff flies out the door, even the cheap motel furniture and the TV and their suitcases, knocking the manager on his ass, a Segway crushing his balls, and she's carried along with the stuff, flying up into the night sky. The crow seizes her by the shoulders. She can feel its talons digging into her, as she watches all the stuff rain down onto the highway, the drive-thrus, the warehouses of more stuff. Somewhere down below, she thinks, is Mom coming home on the bus.

Then she wakes up.

She's been having this dream off and on ever since she met Danny. The manager never gets her. She never falls. Mom never makes it home. She can never decide if it's a good dream or bad.

Chapter Nine

Enjoy Your Journey!

Earth is in peril because of individual actions—by me, by you, by the person sitting next to you, by the person you bump into on the street. The bad news is that when we put all those individual actions together, it becomes one huge number—big enough to change climate, big enough to change how Earth supports life. The good news—the very good news—is that, just as the problem is the sum of what each one of us is doing, so is fixing the problem.

—Anthony D. Barnosky,
Heatstroke: Nature in an Age of Global Warming

Peering through her blinds in the living room, Elissa watches Danny waiting at the bus stop. She should've just told him to forget the whole thing this Saturday after that long, silent ride home. She never wants to ride in that fucking car again. Whenever Carl did something particularly shitty, he would give her a new car. It was like living in a game show. She didn't drive the cars she had.

She saw the look on Danny's face when Gwen read her cards. He probably believes she murdered Carl. Maybe she did. It doesn't matter. She doesn't care if she did or not, okay? Give her one good reason why she should. The man was awful. He stole from everyone he ever dealt with. Those guys on the boat? He was probably stealing from them too, and they didn't even know it, thought he was doing them some kind of favor. Carl drowning in the bay did the *world* a favor. Still. She could've grabbed the line if she'd lunged for it. She didn't move a muscle. She wanted them to go over, to humiliate Captain Carl. She didn't think anyone would die. That's not true: She didn't *think* anything. She just let it happen.

Danny sits there like a stone waiting for the bus. C'mon, turn around. He can't even be bothered to look back at the house? He can't wait to be gone. She gets it. He's not in love with her. Her either. She drops the blinds. Enough about him. She glares at the room full of boxes. Them too. She shuts off the light, heads for the kitchen.

She eats a yogurt, drinks a glass of wine, checks her messages. *Not so fast* from Kris. That gives her a chill. Bluff, she tells herself. Kris has absolutely nothing going for her, following the guy around, watching his apartment—how pathetic is that? Danny didn't seem to mind near as much as she figured he should—somebody basically stalking him. Then she gave him a ride *here,* like Elissa's just part of her magical plan. That's just too fucking much—and you know she made a play for him on the way. But he still came *here*, didn't he? He made his choice. Forget Kris. She can't believe she flashed Kris's picture at him, can't believe he noticed. It's the eyes. You can't miss those fucking eyes.

Forget.

Kris.

The other message of note is from Terry. It takes her a moment: The big guy who told her she's named after the Queen of Carthage, some goddess or other, which she thought was extremely cool. She doubts Mom knew that when she named her. She said she just liked the sound.

He says he has fresh insights about her, wants to see her, so he can share them with her. Insights like that usually show up quicker in her experience, but she remembers the guy as fairly interesting, obviously interested. Kris said he hits on everyone and isn't worth the hassle. What does Kris know?

That's the question, isn't it? On altogether too many levels. What does Kris know? The thing about Kris is—just when you're absolutely certain she's totally bluffing, she's holding all the cards.

She returns to the darkened living room, lifts the blind. Danny's gone. Good. She's tired of thinking about him. She thought Danny's abilities wouldn't be something she had to deal with, that it was just the way he managed to end up at her doorstep, in her arms. She should've known with Kris things are rarely that simple.

She reads in bed, some love story set somewhere else some time ago, several someplace else's, like the story's desperate to find someplace romantic enough. She starts to drift, turns out the light, lies awake in the dark. Paris, Istanbul, the Serengeti. She can't even handle Richmond.

She writes a couple of verses of *What Do You See in Me Now?* The song has taken a darker turn since this morning.

U lose, she said to Kris. *The cards say you lose,* Kris said to her. Who's right? This whole thing isn't right. Maybe they both lose. It was like she went to bed with one Danny and woke up with another, like some weird fatalistic switch went off in his brain, and he was watching things happening like he already knew how they would go, and he was just gliding through, like he's watching himself, but he's not quite real, like nothing is quite real. Especially her. She's from the future, miles from here in goddessville. She gets why his ex left after the day she's had. Even when they were fucking in the shower, it was like he was saying good-bye. To her, to sex, to life—she's not sure, but everything felt like an ending, like it had already happened, like it was meant to be. That's why it was so good, so intense, like a scene in a movie. *Won't last.*

It hasn't even started. Not in her heart. This isn't what she imagined at all. This power he has? It's not his adversary. It's not a burden. It's who he *is*: He's not entirely human. He's not just some guy trying to figure things out. He sees the world differently. He sees the fucking future. When she first met Kris, and she seemed to make things happen, Elissa could always figure someway it wasn't magic like Kris said it was. But she's worn her down. She's seen too much. They've been best friends forever. *Why are we sacrificing that for some guy?*

Because he's magical too. They're two of a kind, him and Kris.

Where does that leave me?

Stop!

She tries to make her mind a blank, like at the end of a good yoga practice. Silence. Peace. It fills up with her stuff, her head stuff and her stuff-stuff. The boxes. When she married Carl, she got rid of everything old, mostly from thrift stores and the like, except for a handful of special things, and bought new, ignoring everything Mom ever taught her, and bought not only new but the most expensive. Everything she owns, just about, she bought with Carl money. If she was going to marry for money, how could she not spend a shit ton of it? It was the measure of her self worth. She boxed it all up and moved it here.

The teapot broke. It slipped in her soapy hands, shattered in the stained porcelain sink. The very first thing she unpacked, intending to brew something soothing. A thousand dollar tea pot. Thousands of dark brown shards. Carl dollars, extracted from the shattered lives of his victims. Everything she owned paid for by the evil shit he did. Carl couldn't help himself. He needed victims. If he wasn't screwing somebody over, he figured they must be screwing him. Enemies, friends, governments, the planet, didn't matter. She just didn't want to be on that list, spending thousands of dollars on boxes and boxes of shattered lives. Now, she can't face them.

She jumps out of bed, throws on some sweats, strides into the living room, and turns on the overhead, a pair of glaring incandescents she hasn't gotten around to changing. Like everything else she hasn't gotten around to in the forty days she's lived here. The boxes are right where the movers left them, all sizes, professionally packed. She has a detailed inventory. She sold all the furniture before she moved, figuring it would all smell like Carl, planned on buying new for her new smaller place. So far she hasn't gotten around to it.

The teapot was the only thing she unpacked, except for a couple of bags she brought with her in the car. The boxes were here waiting for her. They frightened her. That's why she needed the tea. It's still in box 23, a few hundred dollars worth, enough for her and Mom to have survived on for years. Elissa's not much of a tea drinker.

She bought a Mr. Coffee at a yard sale down the block for a buck. Everything else is from the thrift store she used to go to with Mom, totally unchanged, except now there's a designer section. She's well represented. She donated all her hanging off Carl's arm clothes to her childhood haunt, though she felt like burning them.

The stuff in these boxes is worth hundreds of thousands of dollars. Who knows how many lives. A single box of shoes trampled thousands. There wouldn't be enough fine crystal, though she had a shit ton, to hold all the blood. The scheme Carl was working on when he drowned in it would've killed the Chesapeake Bay according to the stories that came out after his death. If you sell yourself, you don't want to sell yourself cheap, and what kind of guy pays top dollar? Carl. Her life with Carl is in these boxes. She doesn't want it here. She doesn't want *her* here, the woman who did this. She doesn't even want to crack open the lids, maybe let it loose. Three thousand dollar boots. Three hundred dollars a toe. One pair. She has several. She looks good in boots. She looks good in everything. She used to say, "I like nice things. Is there anything wrong with that?"

Where do I start?

You are *responsible.*

She shudders, remembering Gwen's reading. It's not like nobody's ever looked at her like that or said something like that to her, but here's this woman who looks like Mrs. Butterworth, her life going to shit, who sees right past the beautiful goddess to the grasping, preening creature inside, gloating over her treasure. It shattered her.

She has to get rid of it. All of it. Now. Nine at night. Not even the Salvation Army will show up at this hour. She grabs a box full of shoes and heads out the back. Tomorrow's trash day. It won't be here long. There's a guy who works these alleys. On her third or fourth trip, a creaking pickup lurches up the alley toward her, catches her in its headlights. She holds up her hands to shield her eyes, and the lights go out as the brakes squeal and the handbrake creaks. The motor grumbles quietly. "You throwing that away?" comes a soft voice from the shadows.

"Yes," she says. "You want it?" She's seen him every week cruising the alleys looking for salvage. Her first real boyfriend's daddy did that, until the truck broke down. They were living in the same motel for a while. "I have more," she says. "Inside."

His name's Vincent. He's fifty or so, black, wiry in a blue jumpsuit that's too short for him. When he sees her living room full of boxes, peeks inside a few, he calls his nephew JJ, who brings a second truck, after some persuasion—"Get your ass over here, *now*! Your Netflix can wait!"

"This is pretty high end stuff," she says. "Do you know what to do with it?"

"How much you want for it?"

"Not a dime. I don't want to make any money off this stuff. It's yours."

That brings a delightful smile. "Alright. Divorce?"

"Something like that."

"Glad we run into one another. You're doing the right thing. Okay if I leave a busted air conditioner behind your place for a bit? To make room? I'll be back for it later on. The metal's worth something."

"Sure."

The two men manage to load it all on the two trucks, piled high. They don't thank her overly. They don't ask her if she'd like a receipt for her taxes. They don't tell her how good and true she is to give this stuff away to those less fortunate than herself. They're perfect. She gives Vincent the itemized inventory. The last column is Estimated Value. It's in Carl dollars.

Vincent smiles for them both. "Enjoy your journey!" he says and drives away.

As she listens to Vincent and Clint recede into the quiet of the night, heading home to celebrate no doubt, she knows Vincent's right. She did the right thing there.

Now what to do about this mountaintop where true love waits? Another grim ride with the dark, silent soothsayer? She winces at the thought. Who can she get to haul away the future? Sounds like a job for Kris. Too bad they're not speaking.

Like Scarlett said in Mom's favorite movie, tomorrow is another day. Elissa never understood why such a good woman as Mom could love a heroine like Scarlett. She starts back into the house, touches her neck, missing her blue scarf. It's one of those few things she saved. From Mom. She wore it when she needed to feel safe. She can't remember wearing it into Gwen's. It must be in the Mini. She opens the garage, looks inside. Sure enough, it's between the seats. She leans over and fishes it out, wraps it around her neck and immediately feels better. She used to wear it when she couldn't sleep in a strange place. Still does sometimes. She suddenly realizes she's wearing it in the weird crow dream.

When she gets out of the car, there's a skinny white guy in a cheap suit standing in the alley watching her. "Nice car," he says. "Looks like you were on a gravel road with the top down. You should watch the grit with those leather seats. It works its way down into the seams and cuts the threads. Mrs. Manoli?"

"Who are you?"

"Proctor Linwood Jr." He hands her a card. United Fidelity Life Insurance. "I've been assigned to your case. You've received correspondence from my office. No reason you should remember my name. Someone sent me an anonymous tip last night suggesting foul play in the death of your husband. I thought you should know. Do you have any idea who would do such a thing?"

"Let me get this straight. You're here because somebody tipped you Carl was murdered?"

"Yes. Not that we take the accusation seriously. The case is closed. My concern is the email was sent to me. Only someone involved with the case would know to contact me. Perhaps a disgruntled relative?"

Or best friend. "I can't think of anyone."

He doesn't look convinced. "Well, call me if anyone should come to mind. We take such matters very seriously. Customer relations are difficult enough without this sort of thing. By the way? FYI? After the vehicles were examined for evidence, the police placed GPS devices on them. Standard procedure. I wouldn't take them anywhere you wouldn't want them to know about." He smiles. Meaning, good thing for me his company doesn't insure these vehicles, that he's not a cop, but in case he should ever need some leverage with her, he knows she was a bad girl. "Good night, Mrs. Manoli."

She needs to think about changing her name. Would that look suspicious? Why? If your name was Mrs. Satan, wouldn't you change it? You can't divorce a dead man or she would. She's not seriously worried about Proctor. Just another creep in the night. So what? Her and Mom dealt with dozens of Proctors. Mom called them weasels and stoats.

She has a second glass of wine, admires the emptiness of her living room, strips down to her underwear and does a little yoga in spite of the alcohol. That first boyfriend gave her a set of yoga CDs his dad had salvaged. She got into it. One morning she was greeting the dawn in another ratty motel they were about to be thrown out of, and Mom asked, "What would you think about entering a beauty contest? This one's got a full scholarship with it."

So much for the empty mind.

She goes back to bed, finally drifts off, imagining all that grit working its way down into the seams of her life and cutting the threads, emptying her heart—nothing but sand.

She sits bolt upright in bed. Something's happened.

Kris.

Elissa checks her messages. Nothing. Silence. A favorite Kris tactic. She, on the other hand, always has to gloat. Like when she had Park Place and Boardwalk and collected the big rents, while Kris quietly cleaned her out with all her slum hotels, railroads, and utilities. Don't play Monopoly with Kris either. Don't arm wrestle. Don't play quarters. Don't doubt her abilities for a second.

That's why she posed for the tattoo—besides being fairly drunk and horny—she never believed it would do what Kris said it would do. And so much more. They both got A's, though Kris would've gotten one anyway, but the professor became totally obsessed, wouldn't quit calling them until Kris threatened to call the cops. He broke up with his wife, lost his job, and dropped out of sight. Total creep. Kris says she still got calls for years, though she hasn't mentioned him in a while except to say they're in touch. Poor guy will likely never be free of her. When Elissa gets these premonitions about Kris, she doesn't doubt their significance for a second. It's that tattoo. Kris said it was magic; Elissa didn't believe her.

Watch me. It was like a challenge. Something's going on. She can't remember hearing the bus when he left. Did he take the bus? Maybe Kris picked him up again, took him for a ride. She likes to fuck out-doors, under the open sky. That Donald guy, she remembers: He kept calling too. For Kris.

Why should I care? Look what I've done for Danny so far. Haven't I messed his life up enough already? She saw how Gwen looked at him, like *what are you doing with this evil slut?*

Still, this shit with Proctor Linwood Jr. is fairly low even for Kris. Elissa can't get her head around whether she actually killed Carl or not, but she has zero worries of the cops coming after her. With what? she really didn't like him? *Nobody* liked him, and the feeling was mutual. As for the cars, she doesn't want them. They can come and get them if they care so much about the fucking upholstery.

She doesn't want anything.

Except Danny maybe. Hope springs eternal. He's nice. She keeps coming back to that moment when he whispered her name. It was like being in a movie. Maybe it'll work out. Love's strange, right? Who doesn't want love, if there's a chance? She doesn't want Kris to have him anyway. The two of them together would be just too weird for words. The perfect couple: He can see the future, and she can fuck it up.

But maybe she should step back. Kris's suburban adolescence was blessed with enriching lessons. She took to karate. Don't let her size fool you. The woman can kick you in the head from across the room. Elissa's seen her do it many times. Not a real head. They had a manne-quin in their old place. Elissa would sucker new guys into bets. It's something to see. Kris can fly, and she doesn't need a broom. They had to retire the mannequin. Her head became so battered no one would take the bet. That head kind of said to any potential suckers, *U lose* before the game got started. Kris still has the mannequin. Her name's Lotus. There was no end to her troubles, though Kris says she has a new head now.

Tomorrow she gets her car out of the shop. Even though she crumpled the fender when she moved in, she's just getting around to having it fixed. She was going to ask Kris to take her to pick it up, but that clearly isn't going to happen. She can take the bus. The body shop is over by the Tree. Kris said Terry's working there now. Maybe she might run into him, see if he's as interesting as she remembers. He's obviously as interested, or he wouldn't be contacting her like months later. Maybe he knows she's free. Carl's death was hardly a secret. That could prompt some fresh insights.

She has a theory about her heart: It's not pretty. No one loves her for her heart. Why should they? It's never been particularly true. She's the Beauty. If they came looking for true, maybe they'd find it.

Does she wish she wasn't pretty? Does Danny wish he didn't see the future—or at least the one with her in it? Does what we wish *matter*? Probably not. If it did, Carl would've died a thousand times before he drowned on Elissa's wishes alone.

She has until Saturday to find out what happens. She has a whole day not to worry about it. Secure in this knowledge, swaddled in Mom's blue scarf, she sleeps better than she has in weeks.

The bus brakes awaken her to a new day. She's looking forward to it. She hasn't ridden a bus since Mom was alive. Mom never owned a car. Not one that Elissa remembers anyway. There was one she spoke of, in her life before her husband left. Elissa was too little to remember. She had a car seat, supposedly, that left with Daddy and the car and anything else they owned of any value. He emptied out their bank account, hadn't paid rent and utilities since October, and it was December 31st. He had somewhere to be for New Year's apparently. Someone.

"You can have my dad," Kris once offered. "He's pretty much a malleable lump. You could probably mold him any way you want, haul him out when you need him for the holidays or whatever."

Elissa's met Kris's dad several times, and she's right. There's all sorts of ways to never know your parents. Elissa could never understand how her father could leave Mom. She knew Mom better than anybody. They were tight, went through a lot together. She always has that—for good or bad—knowing what Mom would think. Mom would like what she did last night—give her old life to somebody working the alleys who could make good use of it. She knows what Mom would say about Danny too. What she always said, *Do you love him?*

Mom loved Dad, until he loved someone else. A Beauty, of course. Look how that worked out. Don't hate your father, Mom told her, but that ship had sailed into a howling storm under heavy bombardment long before Mom thought to offer this advice. She thought Mom was crazy *not* to hate him. Not that she told Mom this. She told Mom most everything, but not that, and nothing at all about how she and her roomie bewitched their British Romantics professor and totally ruined his life with a magic tattoo. She didn't need to add crazy daughter to her troubles.

But Kris worked her magic on El too. Like hating her dad. "Why do you waste your energy on hating some guy you barely remember?" Kris asked her. "You don't have anything going on in the here and now?" And for some reason that took, and she just let her hatred go. She imagined standing on top of a stone tower like the one on the tarot card and pitching it over the side in a bucket—bucket and all. Kris's image. It was a guided meditation, she said, to get her through it.

It did. She was never the same after that. Now she's up here again.

This is The Tower, she imagines—that card she keeps getting. We're all falling out of the sky.

Free.

Chapter Ten

F!Y!I!

Of all the things that are taught in the Lower Trainswitch School for Locomotives, the most important is, of course, Staying on the Rails No Matter What.

—Gertrude Crampton, *Tootle*

Nina hates herself for leaving Danny when he needed her, when he was going through Hell, when he was at the height of his powers. It was bitterly ironic that she was the one who always wanted to believe in all that flaky b.s., as Danny would've called it, but when something magical actually came along, it happened to him, and she didn't have the guts to stick it out.

She was scared. Can you blame her? She felt helpless. He wasn't the same man. He received death threats, more than one. He didn't seem to care, like they were to be expected. They lost all their friends. "You need to get him help," people kept telling her, "professional help," but insurance doesn't cover seeing the future. Psych-o, you can get help. Psych-ic, turns out, you're on your own. Besides, one crazy in the family was enough. The job was filled, all the little orange bottles in the medicine cabinet were hers. They didn't have the shelf space for two crazies in the family. He was supposed to be the smooth-sailing one. That was his job, and he was damn good at it until the accident: The most understanding man on the planet. She's not the easiest woman to understand. Then he started seeing the future, and that just took over everything.

The thing is—he might've been crazy, but he never seemed to be *wrong*. She couldn't tell some shrink that. If he was crazy, it was because he was always right. If he could just screw up *once*, she thought, see something bogus, it would snap him out of this sense of doom, and he could get a grip. It seemed impossible. She was going crazy. She can still hear that guy whose kid fell out of a tree screaming at her: *You keep your fucking husband away from my son!* Something in her wanted to scream back, *You try living with him!* But of course she didn't. She said, "You can't fire my husband."

"Watch me," he said.

There went Danny's insurance. She thought that would be the worst of it. Then, there went Danny too. This double took his place, haunted by the future like really guilty people are haunted by the past. But worse: You can't change the past, but the future might be changed, right? If you could somehow see the right thing, do the right thing. She tried to understand but knew she couldn't possibly.

But she had been doing okay, hanging in there. Maintaining. The Portland job hadn't been something she was seriously considering. It just raised some questions. About the future. *Their* future—her and Danny's—and not everybody else's on the fucking planet. As far as she could tell, Danny didn't seem to give their future much thought. But that was okay. Perfectly understandable with all he was dealing with. They would've gotten past it eventually. Somehow. Someway. What choice did they have? She'll never know: She left.

She blames the tarot reader. What a piece of work she was. Nina immediately had her pegged for one of those lesbian witches who hate men, but she got to her anyway, with those big weird eyes and those funky cards, and she ended up spilling her guts to this cold-hearted woman who clearly did not care. She felt broken down, humiliated, like everything she was holding together just fell apart, and when she tried to pick up the pieces, this bitch just kept knocking them out of her hands and pointing at the cards, going on and on about the Hermit and the Hanged Man and destiny.

Danny's destiny—not Nina's. He was the one, after all, who was special. That's one of the things that kept her in the tent, made her break down crying—from the very beginning the little woman didn't seem to doubt what Nina told her about Danny. *She believed her!* What a relief, not to be walled in by doubt. The only people who believed her were the ones Danny had seen things about, and they tended to have their own issues, and wanted nothing to do with her. It was all about *their* futures.

For this weird little woman in a tent, it was *all* about Danny. You'd think it was him sitting there across from her and not his wife.

She said Nina was holding him back: "Do you think he was given this incredible gift, so he could make your life miserable? He sees the future, and you... *cry*—what's that about? Do you see any semblance of a point in that? Change. You need to make a *change*." She kept tapping on a card with a snake coiled in a figure eight biting its own tail. Two of disks. *Take the job! Set him free!* She left the little tent, vowing to do so. She was doubtful even before she was free of the fair. On the drive home, it seemed crazy. It was like a spell had been cast over her. What was she thinking? She wasn't going to *leave* Danny. The idea was absurd. He needed her. Some day he'd get over this, and they could have a life again. She couldn't just give up on him. Then she got home, and he'd been fired again, and he looked at her for the first time like he saw her leaving, like she was already gone. Not long after, she was. It was all about her future. A bunch of cards in a little tent. It smelled like hot canvas and patchouli.

She's regretted it ever since. Things haven't exactly turned out so great in Portland. Her boss hates her. Her cat's dying; he's been mopey ever since they left Danny. She thought it was supposed to be *Seattle's* weather that sucked. You could die of gloom out there. She hadn't given much thought to where she was going, only that she had to leave. She put a bunch of floodlights on her balcony to trick herself into thinking the sun was shining before she totally gloomed out and jumped off it. The pissy, foggy dreariness seeped into two of the lamps and fried them. One of them blew. The tyrannical little condo prez dressed her down on the elevator about fire codes and global warming and several other issues she can't recall. Her bike was stolen. She has no friends. She hates Portland.

She hates herself. She still has a medicine cabinet filled with orange bottles to prove it.

Now, two years since she left, she's in DC for a conference she's blown off for the day to drive a rent car down the Interstate she hoped to never drive again—to find Danny—*and* his girlfriend. She's a recent unwelcome addition to her plans for this reunion. Naturally, she would think of her here, already feeling a chill. This is the place where the accident happened. The rest area's closed. They said budget cuts, but Nina knows it's haunted, knows dozens of people who would never dream of stopping there again. There was a man handing out glimpses of the future in a steady stream. If you got too close, he would change your life—don't ask for better or worse. The first change is you realize it's a whole lot more complicated than that.

She's haunted, more than a little uncertain about her future. When she first heard about this conference and thought about maybe taking a side trip to see Danny, she made the mistake of floating the idea by her big sister Maria—in case she might've heard something about how he was doing, where he was living. Maria loves gossip. Nina should've known better. Maria thought leaving Danny was the only smart thing Nina ever did. Maria was the first to ban him from her house after Danny tried to warn Nina's niece Lindsey about the snake of a coke snorting stock trader she was dating at the time. All true, naturally, but Lindsey holds a grudge for destroying her happiness. Maria must've told Lindsey her foolish aunt Nina is still feeling bad about leaving Uncle Danny, and Lindsey sent her a photo she opened Wednesday as she was about to board her plane. *FYI. Uncle D likes young!* There he is:

With the little bitch of a tarot reader, the one who started all this.

They're sitting in a car making smoldering looks at each other like she's about to blow him, leaning over close, across the gear shift. You can't see where her hands are, but Nina has a pretty good idea. As for Danny, it's been a long time since he looked at Nina like that. Like she can't remember when. Maybe never. So much for his flagging sexual interest.

All Nina knows about the tarot reader is she worked at The Tree. The logo was on the tent. She was pretty sure she'd seen her there once or twice, breezing in and out like the only use she had for The Tree was a place to do her cards. Nina had been to the other reader and found her comforting but not much help when it came to deciding what to do. She can't remember the woman's name or what her question was. Probably doesn't matter now. This was before the accident, before the fair. It's hard to remember what she worried about then. When she does remember, it's hard to believe she cared about something so stupid and trivial. She hates herself then too. Clueless.

She thought it would be great to know magic is real. It's not.

From the road, once the place is open, she calls The Tree to make an appointment with the little bitch, and Serena tells her that her tarot readers—Kristi and Gwen both—just quit out of the blue, but she can still see a palmist or a soothsayer or a past-lives visionary.

Soothsayer. That's what Danny used to call himself in a mocking tone, like the archaic word would somehow distance him from this thing that took over his life, that if he made fun of it enough, it would just go away. Or maybe that was Nina who just wanted it to stop. Most of the time he talked like that's how he felt too, but there were times it seemed to be what he lived for, the only reason he was still alive, waiting to see a certain future over the horizon. She didn't want to know what he would do if he saw it.

"The soothsayer—what's his name?"

"Danny."

"That's my husband," she blurts out, though he's not anymore. She divorced him. You can't leave a man and not divorce him. "The tarot reader," she asks, "the— the young one. Are they… friends?" Is something going on there?

Serena chuckles her approval at the idea. She wouldn't be surprised, she says: Kristi's been like Danny's guardian angel for a couple of years now, helped him turn his life around. She goes on and on like the little dwarf is Mother Teresa.

Angel. Nina has a different idea. A different image. There it is, on her phone, anytime she wants to drive it through her heart. *F! Y! I!* You see any wings on that little bitch? Little bat wings maybe. *Change. I'll give you change.*

Serena says, "You've been gone a long time, honey. Time's like a river, it just keeps on flowing, you know?"

Sometimes rivers freeze, get dammed up or run dry. Sometimes they overflow their banks, and people die. "When can I see him?"

"You want an appointment?" Serena sounds skeptical.

"Yes. I'll pay for it. I know he's worth it."

"You're not going to make a scene in my store, are you?"

"No. Of course not. When?"

"Tuesday."

"It has to be today. I leave tomorrow. Can you give me his address, phone number?"

"No. Absolutely not. No private information about my employees. Period."

"But I'm his wife."

"Were. I've been there, honey. Take it from me: Let it go, darlin'."

She tried that, didn't work. It slithered inside, coiled around her cowardly heart, tortured her, accused her. What kind of woman abandons her husband when he's going through hell? Like she was afraid of him. There was no *like* about it. She *was* afraid of him. What kind of woman is afraid of a husband who would never lift a finger against her, who rarely even raises his voice? Because he sees things. Because he's not himself anymore.

Now she has a completely different understanding of what happened, what's been going on from the beginning: She's been bewitched. Danny too. Deceived obviously. She see the two of them fucking in her head, the witch on top. Short version: The bitch stole my man. (Short versions always leave out a lot—fyi.) Now, at least, Nina has a name. Kristi. Though don't be surprised if she sticks with bitch.

"Please," she whispers into the phone. The traffic's louder than she is.

"I'm sorry. I can't help you," Serena says.

Serena isn't going to tell her anything. She's the boss. But they must all *know* Kristi. And Danny. Know where at least one of them lives. At this point she's not sure which one of the two she wants to see more, or what she's going to do then, but there's no *way* she's just going to turn this car around and slink back to her hotel room in DC and cry some more. She hates herself when she cries. She wants to stop hating herself. "Who can I see today?"

"You want to see someone *else* now?" Even over the phone, Serena's doubt comes through loud and clear.

Nina finds this fairly annoying. "I need guidance. I don't know what to do. I want to see someone." Isn't that what you sell, *honey*?

"Okay. Terry has several openings."

"Which one's that?"

"Past lives."

"That'll be fine. First available."

"Forty-five minutes from now work for you?"

"Perfect." She pushes her foot down a little harder on the accelerator. That feels like a plan.

"I hope you know what you're doing, honey."

"I don't. I don't have any idea. That's why I need to see Terry, right?"

Serena laughs.

Nina hangs up before she overthinks what's going on with that laugh. She wonders if Terry is a man or a woman. Doesn't matter. She wants to find Danny and Kristi. That's what she came here for. Navigating the city where she and Danny used to live, she expects to see him everywhere, but she doesn't except in her head, in the past, before the accident—her past life. It's like time travel. Makes sense that's who she's ended up with at The Tree—the past lives person—since she's got nothing going on and zero future.

She gets there early, browses the merchandise. Serena doesn't seem to be around. Just as well. One more honey-darlin'-sweetie-pie, and things could've gotten ugly. There's a skinny young guy behind the counter trying to grow a mustache. He ignores her. She buys a Spirit Journey Crystal from the Clearance table.

She buys stuff she doesn't need when she's nervous, restless, like tarot readings at street fairs, but she's been curious about crystals, and she's priced them in Portland, and this is a good size one at a great price. Below cost probably. The box is a little beat up, which is probably what it's doing on the Clearance table, but you don't use the box. The crystal is lovely, shaped like an obelisk. It comes with a little book.

She has a lot of these little books. Danny used to make fun of them, and her for actually reading them. She had become more spiritual, and he hadn't. That was one of their problems. His more than hers. She just wanted him to respect her beliefs is all, at least not mock them. Science can't explain everything. It just can't.

She still can't believe he's working at The Tree. He always made fun of the place. She used to not tell him when she came here to avoid his scorn. Serena said Kristi got him the job. Unbelievable. Clear evidence she's fucked with his head. The Danny Nina knew would *not* work here in a million years.

Terry turns out to be a big handsome hunk of a guy, who's all smiles and dazzling eyes. "You are troubled," he says when he gets her in the back room. Not a bad opener. Hardly a stretch. But he says it in this voice that resonates through eons, like she's *always* been troubled, like she embodies sorrow itself. "In Ancient Egypt," he says with compelling certainty, "you were betrayed by your handmaiden." Hello.

She passed banners on the way here advertising an Egyptian mummy exhibit at the museum. The synchronicity isn't lost on her: She felt curiously drawn to see the exhibit, even though she usually doesn't care about archeological stuff and finds the whole mummy thing fairly grotesque. Grasping after the afterlife. You can have it. She's a fine arts person. Photography. The timeless moment. To each his own immortality.

She's only dabbled in reincarnation stuff, but Terry's voice carries her along like she's floating down the Nile, down the ages. He tells her such a great story about her Egyptian princess past life and her deceitful bitch of a handmaiden she kills with a stone dagger, she almost forgets to ask if he knows Kristi in the here and now. The mention of her name prompts a wicked smile. "I was hoping to have her read my cards again, but I understand she quit?"

Terry tries to look wise and gossipy at the same time, like Buddha as a talk-show host. "Kristi definitely follows her own course through life. She's elemental, that one. A force of nature."

"Which force?"

He laughs. "I wish I knew. Her reading was insightful?"

"Life-changing."

"My. High praise indeed. She does take personal clients. We all like to revisit our successes. I'll wager she left one of her cards." He opens a rickety chaotic drawer in front of him, roots through it, unearths a business card, and gives it to Nina. It's just the name. Kristi Bell. *Readings*, and a number. "You can text her there. Set something up."

Nina can't believe the shabby little card. She made better in middle school for her baby-sitting business. "Not exactly a hard sell."

"She doesn't need it. She's always booked solid. She's quite the phenomenon. She's not cheap, by the way. Don't expect to pay what she charged here. She called this her missionary work." He chuckles. He seems to like Kristi. All the boys must like Kristi.

Nina manages to smile at the joke. "Is that her real name? Kristi Bell?"

"I doubt it. She was a theatre major, I believe. You know how we can be." He smiles.

She does. She smiles back. "Do you happen to know where she lives?"

He quits smiling. "This isn't about getting your cards read, is it?"

"You know that handmaiden you were telling me about who tricked me into betraying my husband and seduced him?—in this life, that would be Kristi Bell."

"Sounds like her. I'm fascinated. Free for lunch? I'm afraid we've run out of time here. Leslie has the next few hours."

"Leslie?"

"The palmist. An ethereal fellow. I would love to do a reading of him—he must have quite the rich past—but alas, he's a very private soul. May I suggest the restaurant at the museum? There's an Egyptian exhibit there that might interest you—in light of what you've discovered about yourself today. It's a pleasant walk though Carytown."

Synchronicity again. But what is it she's discovered exactly? She's not sure. Was Lindsey the faithful servant who ratted out the handmaiden? Doesn't seem likely. But lunch at the museum, her old workplace, with a big, handsome guy? She can handle that. Her husband, after all, is screwing some wunderkind card reader. Visiting the land of the pharaohs with Terry sounds like just the thing. There was some movie, an old one. He sort of reminds her of the actor who was the pharaoh in that. Nice chest. What *was* his name? Doesn't matter. This isn't about him or Terry either.

This is between her and the handmaiden.

The thing you need to know about her is she's a little off the rails. You remember that children's story of the runaway train wandering through meadows? Her absolute favorite when she was a kid. Usually she takes meds to keep her on the rails, has for years, but like lots of people who take meds, she has a love-hate relationship with them. Somehow that gets worst when she needs them most. Like when she opened that photo from Lindsey. There's another piece of work for you. No wonder with a mother like Maria—Mom all over again. The thing is—after crying over the image on her phone for a thousand miles—she flushed her meds over Denver. Roughly 40 hours ago. She wanted to "be herself" for this. Whatever that means. It's been awhile. She's forgotten. She's had professional help, lots of it, in case you're wondering, but none since Danny's accident, none since the little bitch from hell ruined her life.

Walking down the street on Terry's arm, she imagines Lindsey taking her picture, sending it to Uncle D. *FYI— Aunt N likes big.* She asks Terry if he knows Danny, and he says he does. "The man despises me." He shrugs like it's an unfathomable mystery why anyone would ever dislike him.

All the better. She wonders why Danny dislikes him. Jealous maybe. "He's my ex," she says.

He tries to act like this is news to him, but you can tell he already knew. Maybe he talked to Serena, and she clued him in. Doesn't matter. It's worked out. Things always do in the meadow, fresh off the rails—it's like a breath of Spring. She had no use for the think I can, think I can maniac or Thomas the Tedious Tank Engine. Railbound losers.

She loves the completely remodeled museum; lunch is fantastic. Terry spots the Spirit Journey Crystal sticking out of her bag and over dessert gives a testimonial to its amazing powers. He takes it out of the flimsy box, cradles it in his big hands, has her hold it, hot from his touch. "Can you feel the energy?" he asks her.

Definitely.

The cheesy 3-D mummy movie that is the centerpiece of the exhibit, however, totally sucks. The filmmaker has a lot to answer for, in Nina's opinion. She gives Terry lots of her opinions as they tour the artifacts after the movie, and he honors them as one would those of a princess. There is, in fact, among the artifacts on display, a stone knife of the very sort Terry saw in his vision. It doesn't seem to have any handmaiden blood on it. Bit of a disappointment. Nina's favorite artifacts are the depictions of dogs and cats, Anubis and Bast. She likes animals. Cats more than dogs. She hates picking up shit, and dogs are so needy.

There's even a mummified cat. Grotesque. She imagines Tristan wrapped in gauze, and she's drowning in guilt. She couldn't get anybody to look after him, had to board him at the vet. He hates that. He's sitting in a cage while she's admiring his dead ancestor goddesses.

He won't mind as long as she brings back Danny. He was always more Danny's cat than hers. She shouldn't have taken him but couldn't imagine how Danny would've managed to look after him. But Danny would've found a way. He loved that cat. He was probably more upset to see him gone than her. Must've broken his heart. She imagines Danny's loss and tears up. She's getting way too deep and emotional staring at a fucking mummified cat for who the fuck knows how long and wonders if it was such a good idea to flush her meds and drink so much wine, but there's nothing for it now. Don't look back. She loved that movie. Young Genius Kind of an Asshole Dylan's one of her favorite Dylans. She loves Dylan. Danny too. She and Danny screwed to a whole lot of Dylan, but that was in another lifetime, before the wreck. He's with the pixie bitch now.

Once they get away from all the guilt-inducing cats, the rest of their museum tour makes up for the disappointing headliner. It's a great museum. Jeffrey in Educational Outreach spots her and Terry as they're looking at the big white whale and makes a fuss, interrupting her incoherent babble about Dylan and *Moby Dick*. Like Ahab, she'd lost the thread.

Jeffrey claims he'll tell everyone how wonderful she's doing. How well the rail-free life suits her. She's moved on from being the fucked up wife of the nutjob at the rest stop. She maybe goes on a little long with Jeffrey about how *horrible* the mummy movie is, but he doesn't disagree with her. Maybe he senses she's a little wound up. The acoustics seem a little screechy in here, or is that her? He has a meeting to go to, and he's gone.

That was strange. Everything seems just a little bit strange. She usually doesn't drink because of her meds. They don't mix. Or this is where they mix it up. She's never felt quite this way before. Different. Altered. Exciting and scary. She hates horror movies, but she feels like she's in one. Like she's under a spell.

Turns out Terry's place is two blocks away. His car's parked there. He could drive her back to The Tree where her rental's parked. She could see his place first. He could show her how to use her new crystal. All of these sound like great ideas to Nina as Terry rattles them off in his lush baritone, all of which she takes to mean they're going to his place to fuck.

Next to the crystal is her return ticket to Portland. Would it be the end of the world if she missed her flight? That would give her more time to track down Danny and his fucking angel. Or maybe she should just send them a photo from Terry's bed. Not that the bitch was the one who sent Nina the photo of Danny hot for her two years after Nina left him.

Maybe *she's* it, the future Danny's been waiting for, like all those mummies waiting on the afterlife. You can't live with something like that without it creeping into your life, into the way you look at things. Could this be it? Could this be the sign? Sign of what? Who the fuck knows? You start looking for meaning in everything. Doesn't matter if you believe, only if the believer you love believes, so that maybe you can move on, move past it into what you used to have. Maybe Terry's right, and the pixie's the inescapable past Danny's been waiting for—a reunion with his hot handmaiden. Terry didn't mention what became of the pharaoh who fucked the handmaiden. A chariot wreck, she's guessing. She'll ask when they get to his place. It's a sunny day. The maple leaves are brilliant. She wouldn't mind if she never saw Portland again.

It's raining there. She just checked on her phone. The six weeks of summer are long gone. Sorry Tristan, you're going to have to stay another night. She texts the vet to tell her and request Tristan get his catnip toy tonight.

Chapter Eleven

Yeah. Ain't I Something?

Two crows, Hugin and Munin—"Thought" and "Memory"—were the
constant companions of Odin, the Nordic Hermes. They flew far and
wide throughout the nine worlds clustered about the world tree, gathering information from living and dead ... which they would then whisper
in their master's ear as they perched on his shoulder.
> —Paul Huson, *The Devil's Picturebook*

So I've made a mess, stirred the cauldron, and fallen in love. Trust
me—it's all for a good cause. Change is messy. Some disassembly
required. Part of me wishes I didn't know about the photo of El on the
rock—the direct link to my magic. Sometimes I just throw it out there to
see what sticks, never quite sure in the end what worked and what didn't.
I did a whole set of shots at the mountain place—calling out goddess
names, El striking a pose—an actor's exercise. El enjoys being beautiful—who wouldn't? The goddesses were into it too: Even they want to
look like her. The image in question, the best of the best, was Circe.
Perfect, right?—the irresistible stopover on the way home to your true
love? I sent El a copy, only slightly tinkered with photographically, but
with some serious magic worked on it and the rock in question.

While anybody can enchant a rock on a mountaintop, I had no idea
whether magic would work on a digital image sent from an iPhone. You
never know till you try, right? Magic in the palm of your hand. Perfect.

Half the time I have no idea what I'm doing. It's not like I went to
witches school. I can't watch those movies, read those books. Boarding
schools seriously creep me out. Battles between Good and Evil bore the

fuck out of me in direct proportion to how Epic they become. I don't know where my talents come from, but I do have the knack. I definitely make things happen. With a little help from the cards and the goddesses.

That my magic showed up in Danny's vision makes it pretty clear what got him here with me. It would be lovely to think Destiny. When most people say they want magic, what they really want is destiny—*meant* to be, right? Meant by whom? There's the question. One of the many advantages of polytheism is you have a choice in the matter. Thousands of tributaries into an ocean of Magic. It's worked out, don't you think?

That Danny spotted my eyes peeking out of perfectly ordinary images in his zip through El's photo gallery is like an added bonus. The magic ever since I set my heart on Danny can only be described as wildly enthusiastic, always finding new ways to work, like tendrils reaching out, taking root, like it wants him too, feels my desire. Together we can take it to the next level. He's already been to the apex, soaring over all that death and destruction, time freezing. That's where his power comes from. It's a genuine gift from the goddesses. Magic. They have a use for him. They don't grant such a gift for nothing. Prophets have their uses once in a while, though it's the riskiest of callings.

Danny seems totally happy with the plan, smiling at the wheel, asking about me, getting to know me better. He wanted to drive, and not just because I drive like a bat out of Hell. He's into it. He doesn't even complain about my crappy car. I hope it makes it to the mountains and back. Magic, I'm good at. Auto repair and maintenance not so much. If it runs, that's magic enough for me. Cars have no future anyway, and they've done far too much to fuck up ours already. If all goes according to plan, a big if, they'll all be parked soon.

He's asked me which kind of witch I am. You don't work at the Tree for a year without knowing they come in different flavors. He even says wiccan like it's a regular part of his vocabulary. He's sweet, Danny is, one of his many endearing qualities.

I'm goofy in love with him. The cards kept insisting that would happen, but I never quite believed that part till it happened. His feelings for me, like I told him, were more uncertain—the cards waffled—but *I* would most definitely adore him. Didn't take long either: First time to actually speak was at The Tree, first time to meet face-to-face. I asked him what he called himself, and he handed me his card. *Soothsayer.* Cracked me up, our eyes met, and he had this crooked little half smile— nothing like the despairing seer who haunted the stories of the spooky dude who rode the bus—like he was peeking out of his cave just for me. My heart went *thump-a-thump*: *That's him. That's my man.* That silly card's been through so many rituals it's got a soft and fuzzy feel and smells like an explosion in an incense factory. It's in my bag now if you want to see. I'm going to need all the magic I can muster.

I try to answer his question. "I'm sort of a blend—neopagan mix-and-match—though I lean toward the Greco-Roman classics. Solo Loco. I'm not much of a joiner. The coven thing: Too fragile in my experience. People move away, get jealous, etc. Suburban soap operas with nice parties. Not that much real magic. It's helpful though, to have a guide sometimes. We witches do visualizations. There was this one moon. Years ago. A drummer came to the circle, and this old woman talked us through this whole finding-your-spirit-animal thing. Changed my life. I was an osprey, dove right into the James, seized this big fish in my talons. Course, I'd smoked some serious weed beforehand. Otherwise, I might have found my spirit crow. I'm more into crows than raptors, actually. Though ever since, visualizations have been my thing."

"Crows are probably smarter than osprey. I see you more as a crow."

"Thanks. What about you, Sooth? You a seeker?"

"Not so much. I'm more a science guy. I can work up a serious sense of wonder, but that's as mystical as I get. I know a good crow science story though."

He tells me about a researcher who rigged a corn vending machine for crows. At first he supplied corn and coins. Then he cut off the coin supply, and the crows had to find their own. Turns out they were more than up to the challenge. The scientist had trouble keeping the thing filled, making constant trips to the feed store with bags of change. Danny's into his story, relaxed telling the tale, driving the car. He happily imagines all the places an enterprising flock of crows might gather money in a university neighborhood. A cash drawer left open at a sidewalk café could look "like a scene out of Hitchcock," he says. Science guy indeed, evoking Hitchcock. I prefer the Du Maurier short story myself, but it's Danny's tale, his imagination playing with the crows, borrowing from the masters. I did this, opened the cage door, flushed him out. It's too cramped in there for the two of us. Why not fly the friendly skies? You never know who you might run into, what might happen. Isn't life better that way?

I shake my head skeptically at the end of his tale. He likes my teasing, my rebellious spirit. "You call that science? So where do you think this science guy got the idea to buy all that corn for the crows in the first place? Do all that shopping basically for nothing? Not counting tenure, of course."

He laughs. "The crows, I suppose?"

"You got it. When crows fly though your dreams, they're there to tell you something you need to know. Don't see why it can't be Feed Me, Professor Sucker." He thinks I'm joking. He's charmed. He's as in love with me as I am with him. Only difference is, nobody worked any magic on me. Just happened. I wanted to share the glorious feeling. Is that wrong?

He doesn't seem to recall right at the moment that crows have been showing up in his dreams a lot since he met me.

He's as into the mountains as I am, so the higher we go, the less we talk, and just point, all agog at the scenery. I've been up here to El's place maybe a couple dozen times, and it still takes my breath away every time. We roll down the windows to breathe it in, to hear the rushing stream beside the road. I stick my head out the window and suck in the woods like a dog. So fucking glad to be here! With Danny. Dreamed of this moment doesn't begin to cover it.

When we get to El's place, we park at the chain across the narrow twisting road in. I know the combination to the lock, but I'd rather walk. It's more romantic, and the car might get stuck at the badly drained curve about halfway. I helped El find this place. We drove all over these mountains looking for just the right energy. In the Mini. Carl gave it to El after her mother died so she would quit moping around so damn much—it was getting on his nerves. Sensitive guy, that Carl. Did Elissa kill Carl? Might as well blame Danny, or me. I did send Elissa to Danny. I did sneak onto Carl's boat and spend some serious time with the line that eluded Elissa's grasp, making sure if she lunged she'd miss. So yes, blame me for freeing a friend by stepping on a roach.

Sure enough, a flock of crows follow me and Danny up the overgrown road into El's mountain retreat, gossiping about the human goings-on. Crows find us amusing, as well they should.

No one seems to be here. Looks like nothing's been on the road in a while but deer and the occasional bear. The damp morning woods glisten. Shafts of light that look like you could hold them in your hand break through the golden canopy and find the forest floor. It's another world, my favorite. Whenever I'm up here "elf" leads the list of what the fuck I might be, that this is where I belong. Danny thanks me for bringing him here, forgetting, it seems, all about his date with El tomorrow—the supposed reason we're here.

I must admit I'm delighted he's forgetting the unforgettable El.

The cabin itself is modest by El standards, only a few thousand square feet, probably because Carl didn't really want it, or maybe he knew she wouldn't spend that much time up here. I explain it all to Danny: El grew up in the gritty city. The big bad woods scare her a little. While I, the suburbanite, camped and hiked and biked the wilderness into submission in numerous organized assaults during my adolescent enrichment years when some sadistic counselor advised my parents years too late to see to my socialization/assimilation pronto lest I be lost forever. The diagnoses were all over the place, but the message was clear: *This is one seriously weird kid you got. Watch yourselves!* Made for a cozy homelife, as we all adjusted to each new acronym of who I was supposed to be. I sold all the drugs that came my way, in case you're wondering, after taking each one for a test drive. It was like trying out being different animals. Sloth one week, gerbil the next. Is that what it's like to be human? Seems exhausting.

As an adult, I discovered the bliss of woodland solitude, roaming the mountains, bathing in icy creeks. Being out in nature gives me a charge like nothing else, but I wouldn't want to do the hermit cabin thing and never see people. I like city life—like people—in general. The specifics can get iffy. Not everybody takes to me, you might say. Frankly, I scare the shit out of most people. Once they get to know me. It usually starts with the eyes, and then it spreads. The things I say. The things I do. The way I smell? I've quit trying to figure it out, but the question still comes in spells: *What the fuck am I?*

I tell him all this as we sit on the porch of the locked house and wolf down the sandwiches we brought for lunch, though it's only ten. We aren't really here to picnic.

I know where a key to the house is hidden too, but we won't need the house, the bed. We have a blanket, a rock, the morning sky, and a prophecy. I risk a little premature eruption of joy. I can't stop smiling—not a common problem for me. I've got some facial muscles that are going to have to get used to this. They won't be alone. Neglected bits of me abound. When you're working serious magic to enamor someone—ever since I read Nina's cards—it makes no sense to fuck whoever, like giving up on the Grail for a coffee mug at the Family Dollar. Absolutely worth it in the long run. Goddesses eat up sacrifice like dessert. Makes you feel sometimes like you're a piece in some divine board game where sacrifice is worth triple points. But I speak blasphemy. Fluently. They like it, the goddesses do. They have a sense of humor, quirky as you might expect. But just because I make them smile doesn't mean they don't do what they do or always tell me why. Living, learning, evolving—that's three more things they like. I do my best, balancing changing the world and changing myself.

I could still lose him, but I refuse to think it. Witches need faith too. If you don't believe in your magic, nobody else will. Even so, I'm moderately terrified. We've sort of reached a crossroads. Hecate's the goddess of crossroads. Always tricky territory. Fortunately, me and Hecate are tight. We have a deal. If my board game theory is correct, the points must be monumental—like Isaac sacrificed, no ram in the thicket, like Noah's Ark striking a drowning mastodon's tusk and sinking, all hands, hooves, wings, etc. lost, except fins, I imagine. Tough to drown those fish. God, I love the Bible.

Danny and me amble around, hand in hand, around the clearing, up the creek, past the babbling falls choked with crimson leaves, mossy green rocks, mountain laurel, hollies thick with berries. He loves the place, the day, loves me most of all. We can't keep our hands off each other. By the time we reach the enchanted rock with the lovely view, warmed by the late morning sun, he's more than ready to ravish me and spreads a blanket right where El posed, and I have to say, once again, *not so fast*. I wish I could share the irony with him, but he's maybe not ready for that just yet. We have to get to the magic first. It's time.

If you want things to turn out the way you want, you have to do them in the right order, because they only happen once—if they happen at all. If I'd told him everything up front, we wouldn't be here now. About to fuck, to work some magic, to save the world. Because only love for each other, for life can do that. Because we all have to sacrifice to keep the planet going so that love can survive.

I dive in: "I have a confession to make. It's about when I read Nina's cards. I didn't tell you everything exactly. I—I wanted you then. I wasn't *just* being a bitch. It wasn't just that Nina was seriously annoying. I decided I wanted you for myself—*from the beginning*. Then I did everything I could to make it happen. Magic things."

"But you didn't even know me, had never even seen me, right?"

"True. But lonely's always on the lookout. When I began to get an inkling of who you were, listening to Nina, I did another pass of the cards just for me. Between the cards and Nina's stories about you—she was talking warp speed—totally manic—I got a pretty clear picture, maybe not as clear as you get sometimes, more of a broad stroke thing, but it's been pretty accurate so far: Socially disabled weirdo cut off from ordinary life by his extraordinary abilities, trying hard to do the right thing, when the ordinary rules don't seem to apply—I saw us as kindred spirits. Fellow freaks. Possible soul mates. But that makes it sounds too intellectual. It was more like *zing!* I *want* this guy. I will do whatever it takes to get him. Insane, right? In my defense, you didn't seem to be in a very good situation at the time—a vale of tears with waders, actually. Even if you didn't need *me*? I figured you didn't need *that*. I've tried to help you any way I can, but basically I've been *after* you. Still am. If you want me. Still will be if you don't, but it'll be too bad, I guess." I tear up, can't help it. Terror tears. *Please, please, please!*

"What are you *talking* about? Of course, I still *want* you. I'm crazy about you. I've never—"

"Weren't you *listening*? I worked some serious magic to get you. I *made* this happen. I made a deal with the goddesses. It's not like we just met, and you fell in love with me because I'm so cute and hot like in the movies or something."

"Then thanks. I should have. Sometimes a kindred spirit's got to do what a spirit's got to do, right?" He lies back on the blanket, looks up at the sky. "Do you have any idea in the *world* how happy I am?"

Didn't I say enthusiastic magic? Maybe the Cupid was overkill. "Maybe I do. You don't believe me, do you?"

"Sure I do. *You* make me feel this way. It *is* magic, believe me. Allow me to demonstrate. Come here." He beckons.

I crawl on top of him, nestle on his hard cock. Perhaps there's more to this than just magic. "You're not listening."

He presses against me. Just right. Just so. He's been paying attention the three times we've made love, is applying what he's learned. "I'm listening. I believe you. I just don't care. I'm glad to be here no matter how I got here. You're the one who put the ravishing idea on the table, the rock, whatever. I most definitely *want* you."

Now that that's settled, I move in a tiny circle. There's more to tell, but surely it can wait. "No matter what you think, I drove Nina away from you. I threw El at you to get you. My best friend. Like staking out a goat to get a lion."

I rise and fall on the wave of his deepening breath, as he moves with me. "I thought she was a giraffe. Now she's a goat. You need to get your story straight. You made an appointment for her. We spent the night together. Like you say, lonely's always on the lookout. We'll both survive. I still love you and fully intend to ravish you because when I'm with you I don't feel lonely anymore. I want to *live*. Before I met you, all I knew was I didn't want to die."

I kiss him for that. He's not making this easy. I have to tell him everything. He has to believe me. That's part of the deal. "You left out a dead husband, but that's El's problem. What about tomorrow?" I hate to bring it up, but that's the elephant on the rock.

That stops him. "You mean me and Elissa—here? What about it? It won't happen. I'm not coming here with her. No way."

"But you *saw* it. It must've been important. It must *mean* something. You've been obsessed with it for weeks, right? Can you remember it? Visualize it? Maybe you missed something. Visualizations can be very powerful."

He groans. He's squeezing my ass, nibbling my ear lobe, his cock between us is like the tree that saved his life. This is our apex, back down to Earth, grounded on this rock. It's taken me two years to get us here. "I'll make you a deal," he pleads. "Ravish first, visualize later."

"Deal."

We fuck on the rock.

We do it incredibly well. It's exquisite. Primal. The valley echoes with our cries of passion. He shouts to the skies how much he adores me, and I'm one joyful little witch. Did I say I was good? I had no idea in the universe I was *this* good. We fall asleep together. Crows fly through our dreams, bless us, and wish us well.

The goddesses smile upon us.

Still, I can't control the weather— you need everyone for that—and the wind changes direction and intensity, and the temperature begins to drop way too much to be lying in a naked sweaty heap together. I've ended up on top. The wind blows across my bare back, gusts, and I shiver. The woods are filled with the sound of cascading leaves. I can't stop shivering. "I'm getting a little cold," I say at last, when I'm almost frozen, scramble off him and start pulling on clothes as fast as I can. He does the same, helps me with mine. He's not as chilled as me. Maybe part of it's fear of what happens next; there are no guarantees. He holds me in his arms and wraps the blanket around our shoulders, so we're shielded from the wind.

"You're still shivering," he says, rubbing my arms and legs to warm me. "You must've been freezing."

"I didn't wa-a-nt to spoil the m-moment. Ready t-to visualize?" My teeth have *mostly* quit chattering.

"Now?" He tries to be gentle in his incredulity.

"T-timing is everything. N-nothing like a good f-fuck to clear the mind. Come *on*. It will t-take my mind off how fucking cold I am." I burrow up against him, as he rubs my back.

"Okay. What do I do?"

"Give me a thumbnail of the vision again?"

"I looked into the valley, right out there, picturing Elissa in my mind, sort of replaying our time together. I was feeling this incredible wave of passion and love, like I'd found the love of my life, and I was holding her in my arms. That was it. It was intense. An epiphany. I was whispering her name—that's how I knew it when she showed up at The Tree."

"By time together, you mean fucking?"

"Mostly. There were some tender moments as well. She comforted me."

"You didn't tell me about that part."

"We talked about Gwen and Billy. I broke down."

"Poor thing." I kiss his heart. He told me about the Gwen fiasco. I knew El would fuck up, but had no idea it would be so spectacular, or that the magic would reach out even to Gwen's timid cards. Those new Crowley's I suggested could've come a day late, and me and Danny wouldn't be here now. Some twisted part of me wishes I could've been there for the reading, the spider on the wall. Sounds like it was pretty rough for Gwen. I feel bad about that, will have to try to make it up to her somehow. "So it was mostly visual, right? Any other senses? Touch? Smell? Sounds, beside you whispering her name?"

"Not that I recall."

"How was the weather?"

"Sunny. Like today. Like the forecast for tomorrow. Colder."

"No jumping ahead. Not yet anyway. Okay. Empty your mind of everything. Look out into the valley where you were looking in your vision and pick a point. A particular tree. A rock. Found one? Stay focused on it: It's *in* the future you saw. Understand? It's your anchor there, in that future. If you should feel the future slipping away, concentrate on that spot. Breathe deeply, steadily. With each inhale, let in the memory of your vision; with each exhale, empty your conscious mind of all distractions. You are your senses, and they are timeless in your mind. You are there again, in your vision. In the future. Do you see her face in your mind's eye as you did then?"

"Yes."

"Is she beautiful?"

"Yes."

"Say her name."

"Elissa."

"Say it like you said it in your vision. Repeat it until you have it right."

He whispers in a steady murmur of growing passion, "Elissa… Elissa… Elissa…"

"Come *on*," I whisper, "let those feelings *out*. That epiphanous passion, that this-is-the-love-of-my-life feeling. Now slow it down. Remember to *breathe*."

His voice takes on a fresh intensity, as he continues to whisper, trying to match the adoration in his remembered vision.

"Now I want you to open up those other senses, open yourself to the possibility of remembering your forgotten senses. Touch. Taste. Smell. You are *there* again. In that future. Remember. *Everything*."

I slip my finger into my vagina, dab the tip of his nose with the wetness, his lips, the tip of his tongue, his throat, kiss him there. He crushes me in his arms.

"…Elissa!" he whispers and shudders with realization, clinging to me. "Oh my God! *This* is the future I saw!" He looks into my eyes. "It was you I was with all along."

"Yeah. Ain't I something?"

We're both crying, kissing each other's tears. It's been a long journey, a winding difficult road. We take a moment to admire the view together, buffeted by the gusting winds, the sky alive with swirling leaves stripped from a thousand branches.

He laughs.

"What?"

"The tree I was focused on—the one in the future—I can't find it anywhere."

The future has happened. What now? The one scheduled for tomorrow is no longer relevant or real—we're free of the wheel we've been turning on. Perhaps it comes as no surprise that I have a few ideas about where we go from here. Some of them are not original with me. Magic like this comes with a price.

He's the one with more to process, so I take the wheel on the drive back to town. When he first rode with me, I felt like he looked at me to avoid looking at the road. Now the road's not a worry. He's looking at me because he wants to, likes to. He's in love with me. Even I can't doubt it.

I look into his eyes, back to the road. "What would you think of you and me running off together? Fresh start, new beginning, somewhere we don't have so much difficult history?"

"By difficult you mean crazy? The Rest Area Prophet?"

"And a total witch bitch like me. What do you say?"

"Sounds great. I especially like the together part. When do you have in mind?"

"Soon, I guess. There's a Halloween party I'm dying to miss. It sort of represents everything I don't want to do with my life."

"I'll have to pack all my stuff."

I laugh. "In that case, we could leave tonight. I've got a couple of shopping bags you can use. You haven't even asked where. Don't you care?"

"You've seen my place. I figure anyplace will be branching out for me. What I'm saying is, it doesn't matter where. I'd follow you any-where."

"Me too, Sooth. Obviously, I guess. I was thinking DC. There would be lots of interesting work there for me. You too. We could partner up. I see broad strokes, while you have the laser-vision-from-the-inside-out thing." There's also the magic, but I don't mention that. He's not quite a believer yet.

He considers the life I've suggested. There's lots of angles to consider. It's not just a crossroads. It's a fucking roundabout. Have you ever driven in DC? It's a wormhole. He looks down the road. Right here and now, it's a mountain valley, a pretty farm. "It's never going to end, is it? It doesn't matter where I go or what I do. That's why you keep putting off doing my cards, isn't it? You don't want to break the news. There's no normal life for me ever again. I'm always going to be the Soothsayer."

"We all *end*, Sooth, sooner or later. Normal life mostly blows. Might as well make use of your weirdnesses while you can, right? Not be in such a big hurry to exit the stage just because it turns out you're the monster. Ever read *Frankenstein*? The Creature is my all-time favorite character. I have to say, Sooth, if Mary Shelley was still around, you might have some serious competition. Seriously though, we could do some good. Work some magic. Think of it as an alternative fuel to money, which currently makes things happen, or stops them from happening, as the case may be."

"Is this what you had in mind all along?"

"No. Like I said, I'm more attuned to my baser, hubba-hubba instincts. I had to have you. The saving the planet from the assholes idea synched up with it as I thought about how we were going to spend our lives together—two freaks in love. If that's how it went. Goes. Whatever."

"Whatever. What did the cards say? What is it I decide?"

"I saw yes."

"Is that because that's what you wanted to see?"

"Duh. What about you, Sooth? You and me?"

"You and me."

I bounce up and down in my seat. Not an everyday move since fifth grade. "You know how you were asking me if I know how happy you are? I do. I most definitely do. Let's celebrate. I'm starving. Do you mind if we stop somewhere and have a bite? There's nothing at my place, though that has to be our next stop. I have to feed my cat."

"You have a cat? I love cats. I'm dying to see your place."

"Few are so fortunate as thou to step into my lair and live to tell the tale."

He grins at me. "You don't scare me one little bit."

"I know. It's great. You crazy fool. That's how you came up in the cards, by the way, last time I did them—The Fool. Great card: Beginner's Mind. Is this place okay?" It's one of Lucinda's. The one where Sam works. He works the Halloween parties too. I've done most of the help's cards for free one time or another, changed a few lives. For the better, I hope. Sam's a pal.

"I don't know. It looks a little pricey."

"Obscenely so. Not to worry. The owner's a client. I get a discount here."

"How much?"

"100%. The food's great too."

He laughs. "Sounds good."

The lunch rush is over. The dining room is sparsely populated. Sam himself takes our order. We both have fish. It's a last fling for that as well. Case you haven't heard, the oceans are about fished out unless you're fishing for plastic. If you want to piss off a goddess, just mention the oceans. They hate it when humans act like they're helpless when all they have to do to help is quit fucking up.

Courtney's training. She's *still* making more than she was. She looks adorable in her posh server garb, like an earnest penguin. She shows up tableside to thank me profusely—Sam said it would be okay. Courtney lays it on so thick it gets a little embarrassing, like a feel-good news story they tack on at the end of a disastrous day, real heart-warmy stuff. I can hardly listen, but Danny takes it all in.

"…you *really* changed my life. If I can *ever* do anything for you, let me know. Are you her boyfriend?" she asks Danny, suddenly turning to him, her rapt audience. I didn't bewitch the kid, honest. She could believe me or not. This Steve must be one piece of work.

Danny smiles. "Most definitely, proud to say."

"You are one lucky man," she says.

"I'm beginning to see that." When she leaves, he asks, "What was that all about? Did you just read her cards?"

"I thought about it. That was enough." I tell him the story.

"You're nicer than you generally let on."

"Not really. Just trying to restore the balance. I screwed over Nina. It won't kill me to help out the occasional Courtney. It's just a job. Sam won't hit on her because he's devoted to Frank. She'll probably hate it in a few months, but she won't be so broke, and she might have a few more options, a little more self respect. I helped her out at a crossroads. The next one, she's on her own. So you ready to meet my cat? He must be starving by now. His name's Scratch, but don't let it scare you. He's sweet, like you."

I've saved half my fish for Scratch—the reason I ordered it. Sam's wrapped it in a little foil swan. Scratch will go ballistic when he sees that. When he sees Danny finally coming through their door at long last. I couldn't have done it without Scratchie's help.

Chapter Twelve

The Last Surviving Members Of A Species Of Two

PUCK: Up and down, up and down,
I will lead them up and down:
I am fear'd in field and town:
Goblin, lead them up and down.

—Shakespeare, *A Midsummer Night's Dream*

Elissa stares dreamily out the bus window, still feeling high over her empty living room. Before she left the house she took a few minutes to just sit in the middle of the emptiness, and let all the *stuff* leave her. It wasn't just the stuff. It was the woman who thought she wanted all that stuff, thought she needed it, ransom for her life. She's feeling hopeful. About Danny. About everything. Maybe she won't go by The Tree. She found the place depressingly dopey the two or three times Kris dragged her inside.   Besides, the last thing she needs is another Terry in her life. Mom, who's riding beside her on this journey, says Amen to that.

So she's only half in the moment, lost in this pleasant reverie, look-ing at her reflection in the glass where she can see Mom beside her, more than what's right on the other side in the early morning sun, when it hits her what she sees: Kris's car. Her ugly little car. It takes her a second to process what that means. She looks around. There's Danny's place. Kris has pointed it out a dozen times when they've driven by. *He's home*, she'll say inexplicably. Showing off her psychic abilities or bullshitting. You never know with Kris.

The bus lurches into motion. She twists around to look inside the car as the bus rolls past. No Kris. She must be inside with Danny, must've spent the fucking night. This prompts a slight change in plans: Elissa nuts out.

Give it your best shot. I want you to.

He must've gone straight to her fucking arms.

Just like Kris knew he would.

By the time she finally pries her car loose from the body shop guy who has to explain every little thing he's done before he'll turn over the fucking key, she's lost all her calm, all her perspective. If she has any trouble, he tells her, she should bring it right back. No chance. You *leave* trouble, hopefully unseen, then hope like hell it doesn't follow you, but it always does—that's what she learned at Mom's knee.

Watch me.

Fucking Kris.

Racing back to Kris's car, Mom advises her she's going way too fast, asking for a ticket, weaving through morning traffic. Mom's right, but Elissa doesn't listen, never listened when it came to matters of the heart. What the fuck did Mom know? Stuck with a kid on the street. Elissa glances over to the passenger seat. Mom's gone. Just as well. Mom hates it when Elissa gets her back up.

Kris's car's still there. Elissa's circling, looking for a place to park, when Danny and Kris emerge into the morning sun, arm-in-arm, ambling all lovey-dovey to Kris's shitty car. He throws a day pack in the back, gets behind the wheel. This is too much. He made Elissa feel like she'd tortured him to make him drive, but for Kris's junker, it's not a problem. He looks at her like she's the center of the universe. Kris is so fucking happy, you just want to smack her. Not that Elissa would risk it. Sometimes big guys grab Kris's ass because she's little. Sometimes Kris likes to slam them to the ground. She's scary strong, though she never works out. *I'm an ant*, she says to explain it.

She tells herself it's fucking stupid to follow them, but does it anyway. She has a bad feeling about where they're going. The happy couple are both dressed for a walk in the woods. Kris is sporting what she calls her flannel pixie look, big (on her) black and white tablecloth plaid shirt over black yoga pants. Cowboy boots. She keeps clothes in her trunk, so she can change on the fly. She never takes guys home. The place is always a total wreck, and since it's Kris, a disturbingly weird total wreck. *I'm working on something, okay?* she says to justify the mess. *Don't look at it.* Her and her weird cat and the cat box. It's been awhile since Elissa's been there. Too spooky. While you're there you believe every crazy thing she says. But that's anywhere. She's always saying, "You know, deep down, you believe me." And fuck if she isn't right. El's in the middle of some Kris craziness. She's been here before, when Kris works her magic.

It's easy to follow them. Danny doesn't seem to know he has a rear-view mirror. He's talking, gesturing, having a great time. They're headed steadily west, out of the city. Kris avoids Interstates and prefers the more picturesque Hwy. 60. She'll switch once they get past the sprawl in an exit or two. Elissa slips past them while it's still three lanes by zipping around an 18-wheeler, then sticks with the quicker Interstate. Kris's ugly little car shrinks and vanishes in the rearview.

With any luck, Elissa will beat them to her mountain place by twenty minutes at least, more the way she's driving. Sometimes she thinks she's turning into Kris.

She replays their friendship in her head. Her first real friend of any duration. She and Mom moved around a lot. Didn't always have an address. Nothing lasted. Then she's in a dorm room with Kris because they're both theatre majors—total strangers. Elissa thought she was being pretty cool dealing with the huge University. First night, Kris said, *You're not from Kansas, are you, El? Not to worry. I'll be your guide. The Emerald City takes some getting used to. Fortunately for you, you're rooming with a Munchkin.*

More like the Wizard. Their room was the center of things, until they soon slipped away into a city apartment and took the center with them. Kris took El home Thanksgiving, Christmas, took her along on summer vacations. After graduation they worked shitty jobs and partied too much, stayed mostly roommates for years unless one of them was living with some handsome mistake for a while. Then she met Carl and moved into the mansion, set Mom up in a nice place of her own. When Mom went in the hospital a month after the wedding, Kris was the one who stayed with her in the ICU until the end, even though Mom had never been sure about Kris. *Do you ever feel like she's taken over your life?* Mom asked once. El thought she was just jealous back then.

Now? Totally, Mom. Totally. The thing is, El wanted her to. In the worst way. She blurs past the scenic beauty, whips around the mountain roads like she knows what she's doing, like Kris advised: *Don't think about it. Just drive.*

El had Carl buy the place more for Kris than for herself. She knew Kris would be into it, that it might be something she did with her new-found wealth Kris would respect—as much as you can respect someone whoring herself out to a pig because she'd given up on anything better, given up on herself. Looking around it seemed to her she had plenty of company selling out for immediate gratification.

When Danny described the *moment* to her—the two of them on that rock totally in love—it was like something she'd always dreamed of but doubted would ever happen for her. She hasn't had that kind of life. When she realized it was supposed to happen *here—her* place—that made it seem more real, made it easier to believe in, for a while at least. For Kris to mess with it like this just isn't right.

Then she remembers how she hooked up with Danny in the first place, supposedly helping her lovesick best friend but going after the guy instead, and she can only be but so righteous. The thing is, she hasn't totally, a hundred percent, given up on that *moment*. Everybody thinks the Beauty finds true love. Not even close. The Beauty finds men—women too, but El's only been with one. Men soon find another Beauty. She supposes women are the same. You can't love beauty. Beauty's just a thing. Like a busted air conditioner in the alley. Worth something, but not so much as what it takes to haul it around.

Watching El apply her beauty contest makeup the first night they went out looking to meet guys, Kris took charge of her beauty too. *You cover up those freckles, and you're a fucking idiot. Just saying.* Kris never tires of being right. That's okay. El can't imagine who she'd be without her. She didn't have a life before Kris except some version of her and Mom hanging by a thread.

She doesn't want Kris to see her car, so she parks in the drive of the place next to hers, still for sale, and hikes in from their place through the woods. She sets up a good vantage point inside the house, bolts all the doors.

There's yet more of her stuff here in the same legal Limbo where her two extra cars are parked, more Carl dollars at work. It's ridiculous. Four families could live in this place and never want for anything except an excuse for all this fucking stuff. There are eight crystal champagne flutes. For example. Mimosa brunch in the mountains, anyone?

If I was Kris, I'd hate me, but I still wouldn't do this.

He must have told Kris about the beautiful moment he saw with Elissa, and now she intends to steal it.

She always gets cold up here, but she can't start a fire without giving herself away. She pulls on a couple of smoky sweaters and a wool stocking cap. There's no food in the obvious places, but rifling through pockets in the mud room she unearths a couple of energy bars and a baggie of stale trail mix, Kris's special blend. El never learned to cook. Growing up, it was hard enough to find food, much less a kitchen. She'll devour anything. Kris loves to feed her.

It's a good forty-five minutes before Kris and Danny show up, all over each other like two lovesick beasts in a nature show, all grab-assy and playful. They don't even bother to walk in a straight line. You wouldn't think the man was with El yesterday, would you? She's not the least bit surprised. She was a scene in a movie—*A Night With the Beauty*. What she's watching now is more like mating season.

It's not looking so good for her magical moment tomorrow.

When Danny and Kris plop down on the porch and talk, El sits with her back against the door and listens to Kris completely charm her prince charming while making El sound like a cowardly woos afraid of the big bad woods. Not exactly fair. She's slept outside way more than Kris ever has, and the predators were way worse than anything up here. She knows that. In her head. But she does get scared in the woods. It just gets so dark up here. You feel so small. Like one star in a billion. She's always hated that feeling. Even when she was a big deal—The Beauty Queen—it made her feel small in the end. Only Kris ever made her feel like she was somebody special, and now listen to her. El feels totally betrayed.

She moves to the window and watches them through the curtains as they eat together, feed off each other's looks, like they want to gobble each other up. They finally move on, slowly, sashaying up alongside the creek.

El knows where they're going. It's a loop trail up the creek to the rock with the view, then back down the ridge line where it meets up with a switchback down to the road a few hundred yards from the house. She doesn't have to hurry. They'll take their sweet time getting to the rock. Foreplay. El will take the switchback.

She finds a stained brown coat with big pockets. She remembers the combination to the gun safe (999, selected for panicky recall). Carl insisted if she had to have a place out here among the hillbilly meth heads, she had to have a gun. Kris sided with Carl, which never happened, though Kris tossed snakes into the discussion. Copperheads. Rattlers. Kris suggested a rifle, taught her how to shoot, another one of those female-empowering summer camp skills Kris shared with her less fortunate friend even after she had become the poor little rich girl.

Now recently widowed. Suspected of murder. Shit happens. Amen. *Do you have any idea who would do such a thing?* Proctor Linwood Jr. asked her. Krystal clear.

There's ammunition. She loads, takes her time, munching on trail mix. Tries to recover a little of that lost serenity she left on the bus, though Mom's pretty much bailed on this mission. That's okay. There's a bear at the door, but she's got it under control. That was a bedtime game she and Mom played. They didn't always have books. They made stories up, took turns. Mom took a creative writing class once before Elissa was born and used writing prompts she remembered from that. Elissa's favorite began *There's a bear at the door...*

This one begins, *There's a bear at the door, and she's trying to steal my future.*

That was another fear both Carl and Kris evoked—bears. There are black bears up here, but El's not afraid of them. Neither Kris nor Carl knew she has a long history with bears, one of those Mom things she's managed to keep to herself, like the blue scarf. Mom's bears tended to be nice—enchanted princes and the like—bought off with potions or magical incantations, hardly bears at all. Sweethearts in bear suits. Elissa's were relentless monsters she eventually slaughtered with an enchanted sword or lance or arrow. Mom didn't allow her to play with guns, and she only made the weapon enchanted for Mom's benefit. Any old sword would do. Any old arrow. Through the heart preferably. Then buckets of blood until Mom cried *Enough!* Then she'd hug her like she was actually in danger from her made up bear, and Elissa felt Mom's love pouring into her.

She hikes up the hillside to a bend in the trail with a clear view of the rock. She's been here before, knows the perfect place—where Kris set up the camera to shoot El on the rock. She hunkers down out of sight beneath the low-hanging limbs of an old cedar. The smell is intoxicating, like she's becoming some beast in the woods.

There's a scope on the rifle. Kris, who helped her pick it out, told her she'd want one of those. When Kris showed her how to use it, they came up here and played Assassinate the Evil Dictator with Lotus the mannequin whose battered plaster head finally exploded into powder. For the game, to help El feel better about the whole thing, they called her Carla—the Evil Dictator in one of his many clever disguises. El felt bad about Lotus, they'd been through a lot together, but supposedly Kris has since replaced her head, saying she would never let Lotus go headless. If you look closely you can still see plaster dust in the crevices of the rock. That's Lotus.

It's a glorious morning, and there they are, walking out into the sun maybe fifty yards from her, the happy couple. He spreads a blanket, and they plop down on the rock like they own it, their own personal Eden. Who owns it isn't exactly clear, but El's certain it's not them. Not Kris.

Not this. This *moment*. Kris couldn't leave her that? She couldn't leave it alone? She had to have everything that mattered?

Assassinate the Evil Dictator. Kris explained it this way: You never know when you may have to change the course of human history by taking out someone Truly Evil for the good of humankind. It was like preparing for zombies. They imagined *Pride and Prejudice and the Evil Dictator*. They had a pretty good laugh over that one. Lotus's head was totally falling apart anyway. She needed a new one. Kris asked Lotus as they were setting her up on the rock, overlooking the land Evil Carla enslaved, *Ever hear of a scapegoat, Lotus? Do you know the story of Abraham and Isaac?* El laughed in spite of herself. She was really drunk a lot of the times Kris kicked Lotus's head off, but she remembers each and every time. It gave her a weird thrill. How sick is that? She was stone cold sober, however, the day she pulled the trigger and blew her head off. Carla's head. Carl in disguise. Was she practicing for Carl's death, or for today? Knowing Kris, maybe both, plus a whole bunch of other shit she doesn't even know about. And don't want to. Not now. Don't ask her to fucking *understand* right now. She's in this shit now, wherever it takes her.

She watches Danny and Kris through the scope. She knows Kris: She will be on top. An easy head shot. Danny is all over her—she's thinking *this won't take long*—and then he stops.

Kris stops him. She has something to say. El can't make out the words, but knows the look. She's telling Danny some kind of story. It might be true. Might not be. That part doesn't seem to matter as much as you might think. But it *will* be effective. Whatever Kris wants it to do, in El's experience, it will likely accomplish. Men take one look at El and follow but soon wander off. They *listen* to Kris. She's always got some story to tell them—and they're in it, and they're into it. They don't forget her. They call her in the middle of the night, their voices filled with longing, waiting for a denouement that never comes.

She watches Danny's face through the scope as she weaves her story, with her weird, fluttering gestures. Whatever he's hearing from her, and it doesn't look good—she keeps pointing at herself like she's the Evil Dictator on trial, totally guilty of slaughtering innocents and innocence—nothing shakes his lustful adoration. Do you shoot a man for that? Kris is the sexiest creature El's ever met.

Then, eventually, just like El thought would happen, they're fucking on the rock. They've stripped, using their clothes and a blanket as a makeshift bed. Kris insists on totally naked. They go at it so intensely, you think they might fall off the rock into the valley, not that they'd notice if they did.

El watches. Their intimacy is almost unbearable. Kris used to say Danny was maybe, finally, the one guy who might actually get her. That whatever she was, he might be one too. El never paid too much attention to all her crazy ideas about what she was. She was Kris, and that was enough. She didn't want to think about it. Now she thinks, watching them, Kris may be right, or maybe all true lovers look like that—the last surviving members of a species of two.

When Kris comes, bolt upright on his cock, hollering like the whole planet's got to hear the good news, she has her head in the crosshairs just like Lotus's. El knew it was Lotus, not Evil Carla, but she pulled the trigger anyway—one more kick in the head—dust on the wind. This may look like her best friend Kris—she always looks like El's best friend—but she's not. Not anymore. All El has to do is squeeze. Like Kris taught her. Just squeeze, firm but gentle. *Like it's a cock*, she said, making El laugh.

He cries out: "I love you! I love you! I love you!" Kris laughs her earthy, infectious laugh, like *of course you do!*

And El can't do it, can't take that away from him. Them. She just can't. Besides. She doesn't want *Danny*, not like Kris does. El wanted that moment. It never was hers. And now it's over. She'll live. That's what you got to do. No matter what. Live.

And besides. She can't kill Kris. She loves her too.

***

She doesn't return to the house but goes straight to her car, so she's halfway home before she realizes she's in a dumpy brown coat with a box of shells in the pocket, a loaded rifle in the backseat, making her feel a whole lot crazier than she probably is. You remember the story about the woman astronaut who drove across country in diapers over some man? El totally understand her. The mind just gets swept away in the motion. Then you're there. Then what? Change the diapers? Change the man?

Change your mind?

You think? Try it sometime. Harder than it looks. She's trying. Kris keeps telling El her life's going to change in a big way, change so much she'll hardly know herself. Anytime, Universe. Anytime.

When she gets home, she's reassured by her empty living room—like it might have filled up again in her absence. Just her and her loaded rifle. This can't be good. She puts the coat and gun in the gritty backseat of the Mini, puts the top up now that the damage is done. Maybe she should call her lawyer, ask if she can just surrender. *Here are my terms: I want nothing. Ever again.* That's what the yogis say—if you want to be happy, want nothing.

She almost shot her best friend through the head for a man she doesn't even love because she thought he was "hers." How fucked up is that?

Then it hits her: Kris *wanted* her there, wanted her to see. It's always about what Kris wants, even when you think it's not. *Go ahead. I want you to.* Kris hates Eastwood. She'd only quote him if she meant it. One thing El's learned, never assume Kris is being ironic or metaphoric or whatever. She speaks truth. Her version. What about the gun? Was that part of the plan? What was El supposed to do? Join them? Shoot them? Walk away? She considered all three, chose the last. Like a crossroads. Kris is always on about crossroads, like we're all, the whole planet, standing at one, and we're totally blind.

Was all of that what Kris *wanted*? How can El be the Tall Fetching Beauty, as Kris calls her, and always live in the elf's shadow?

Kris was into technical theatre, stagecraft. El was the actor. One of the few times they shared a stage is when Kris played Puck and El was Titania. Kris stole the show. El's Titania was reviewed as *more lumbering beast than magical creature—the giraffe queen.* Kris's Puck—*an other-worldly androgynous delight!*

Maybe Terry's not such a bad idea after all. Don't say anything, Mom. Nobody's asking you. *How much do I hate myself?*—Still obsessing over bad reviews in college. Get over it, as Kris would say. The other-worldly one—they got that part right.

El finds The Tree even more depressing than she remembers. Last time she was here, she only had eyes for Danny. Serena spots her and remembers her from a party at Lucinda's. "Kristi's friend, right?"

"Right."

"Hated to see her go. Extremely talented. But I understand. You have to explore new horizons. She can always come back, right? Visit. It's not so far."

"Wait a minute. Where's she going? You talk like she's moving."

Serena lays horrified palms over her heart. "I'm so *sorry*. I just assumed you knew. When she gave notice, she told me she's moving to DC. I know it's just up the road, but it seems so far away."

Like the Emerald City, just the other side of that field of poppies. "She hinted she has big plans. She'll let me know when she's ready, I suppose. Do you know if she's going alone?"

Serena smiles. "That's what I was going to ask you. I'm dying to know."

El too. "It's hard to believe she'd leave without Danny. She's been after him for so long."

Serena bobs her head up and down. "That's what I'm thinking. I hope not. I've always thought those two were made for each other."

Of course you did. Kris had you under her spell the first time you ever met her. Kris told El about it. *What do you mean interview? I just did her cards. I'm the difficult adolescent daughter she never had. She adores me. I'm always right.*

Why did I ever come here? The scene of the crime. *Please, please, please!* Oh yeah, Terry. Still seems like a bad idea, but she might as well ask while she's here, about the man even Kris, always Ms. Go For It, warned her away from. Right now that makes him even more attractive. "I understand Terry works here now? I met him at Lucinda's too. I can't remember what he does exactly? Something with past lives?"

"That's right. He just started. To tell you the truth, he should be here now. He had an appointment he was running late for, so I called, and it had slipped his mind apparently. I'm a little concerned. Fortunately, Leslie offered to stay and see the client who was kind enough to accept that arrangement. Oh here's Terry…"

As Serena looks out in the parking lot, her face darkens. El follows her gaze. Terry's not alone. The woman he's with looks familiar. It looks like Terry's trying to get rid of her, ditch her at her car, but she's not having any of it and latches onto his arm and points them toward The Tree. El remembers who the woman is. She was in the clips about Danny Kris showed her when her obsession was just getting started.

This woman was hanging onto Danny's arm trying to get him away from reporters. It's Danny's ex. Nina.

Nina and Danny and Kris have been the stars in Kris's year-long mini-series. El's heard her name a million times by now. Now El's a late addition to the cast. What in the world is Nina doing here? Doesn't she live in Maine or someplace?

Chapter Thirteen

The Deepest Jungles Are In Our Heads

These days every wild place has, to one degree or another, been cut into and cut off.
— Elizabeth Kolbert, *The Sixth Extinction: An Unnatural History*

Danny likes *Frankenstein* too. He's identified with the Creature since the accident, stitched together from broken parts, frightening the villagers. As he remembers it, Frankenstein promised the Creature he'd make him a mate, even undertook the project, then tore her apart right before the Creature's horrified eyes. So much for a merciful maker.

Kristi stepping out of the shadows, professing love—a fellow Creature—is that good? It is if you're the Creature. No question.

It's not entirely true that he's not afraid of her, but not so much as of ordinary people, who, frightened of him, do frightful things.

Her place is a little white forties cottage close to the river. It looks perfectly ordinary. Green shutters. "It's sort of a rental," she says. "Otherwise I would've painted and freaked the neighbors. I used to have a lawn lion, but I gave him to a good home, when I decided to move."

"Let me guess. The landlord's a client, and you get a deep discount on the rent."

"Something like that. Everybody likes to help out a struggling young girl."

"So why are they helping a capable woman like you? Because you're short?"

She makes a face. "Ha-ha. I feared prolonged exposure to me would make you mean."

"You'll have to punish me."

"Nasty too."

"I thought we'd already established that."

"Mmm. I'll say. Time to meet the family." They kiss.

He feels so free and easy with her. That's not how things go since the accident. He gets close to someone, starts having glimpses of their future, and pretty soon he's not in it. He doesn't see Kristi's future. Not a flicker. He's quit trying. "How come I don't see your future?" he asks, nose to nose.

"Because we're together, Sooth, like hydrogen and oxygen. We're a fucking force of nature. You can't see me without seeing yourself, and as we've already demonstrated once already, that shit will fuck with your head. I usually don't employ such extreme measures."

"Like masquerading as your best friend, hanging out in the future like a constipated cat?"

"You say the sweetest things."

When they get out of the car, he's startled at how loud the river is. "Is it always this loud?" he shouts.

She laughs, shouting herself. "Isn't it great? Like living next to an artery. Gives me hope that the planet's not dead yet."

She plucks her mail out of the mailbox without looking at it and drops it in a recycling bin on the porch, steps into the house, and flips on a light. "Oh shit! Scratch!"

Danny steps in behind her. There's blood everywhere. Not everywhere, but enough to give that first impression. Stripes and dribbles and smears of it. It's the cat. He runs to Kristi, meowing his distress. The blood's his, copiously streaming from his torn ear. He leaps into her open arms, and she catches him in one arm, thrusting the bag with the swan inside at arm's length with the other, and Danny plucks it from her hand before Scratch can catch a whiff, holding it behind him, stepping

164

back to give them a little breathing room, as she coos to the cat. "My brave boy," she says. "I know you did. I *know*."

What the cat's claiming, Danny has no idea, but he'd sure like to know. He knows that cat. Knows cats. Same collar, same cat. It's the little tuxedo at the bus stop by Elissa's. Nowhere near here.

"Sorry about this," Kristi says.

"I saw this happen when I was waiting for the bus at Elissa's. But that's like a couple of miles from here at least. On the other side of the freeway."

"More like three miles and a couple of freeways. I know. Scratch gets around. Don't you, boy? Do you mind seeing to yourself for a bit while I tend to him? It looks worse than it is. I just need to stop the bleeding. Would you put the bag in the fridge? Whatever you do, don't let him see the foil water fowl—or say the word or think about it too loud. Come on, boy, let's tend your brave wounds."

She takes Scratch down the hall into the bathroom and closes the door, talking to him the whole time, but he can't make out the words, only the occasional plaintive meow. The water starts running. He puts the bag in a spotless, empty-but-for-a-box-of-soda fridge, finds a roll of paper towels sitting on the counter, and starts cleaning the blood smears from the floor, the counters, around the cat door in the kitchen. He returns to the living room following the trail on hands and knees. It leads to what is apparently Scratch's house. Not just the usual pillar of carpet, it's like a little elevated temple, the hardwood columns all scratched and polished from his attentions. He mops up the blood from the temple floor. That seems to be the worst of it.

Beside Scratch's house are Kristi's set models from her theatre days, all inhabited by baby deities in a variety of costumes that make Danny smile. He identifies *Streetcar* (baby Stanley in the street in a tiny torn undershirt), *Midsummer Night's Dream* (featuring a baby with an ass's head), some musical with a dancing ballroom full of babies he can't remember the name of though he remembers the movie—Audrey Hepburn and Rex Harrison?—*One Flew Over the Cuckoo's Nest* (a circle of babies in group session in a ward that looks like a missile silo). One stumps him, cobbled together from bits and pieces of franchise architecture—McDonald's, Toys R Us, Best Buy, Walgreens—in the usual garish colors, festooned with designs that look like corporate logos but aren't quite. When she emerges from the bathroom with a bandaged Scratch purring in her arms, he asks her.

"*The Trial*," she says. "A fave." All the babies are wearing suits but one, naked on the witness stand/manger/checkout stand/scanner. "El played K. She was incredible."

"Is she a good actress?"

"The best. Too beautiful maybe. No one takes her seriously."

"Except you."

She shrugs. "Yeah. That's my job, taking people seriously."

He studies the sets, filled with Baby Jesus and has to smile. Everything is spotless. "You must dust all the time."

"Not really. I cleaned up for you. Usually the place would be a wreck. A serious cobweb collection. Thought you might like the sets though."

"You knew I was coming?"

"I knew it was possible. Likely. Hoped for. Whatever the outcome, it's always good to have a clean place, right?"

"It's practically empty."

"I had the mother of all yard sales. There was something of a traffic jam actually. I almost called one of the many cops of my acquaintance."

"When did you find time to do that?"

"When El called last week and invited me over to read her cards and see her place."

"That was your plan?"

"No. That was a sign. She was ready."

He nods like he understands. "How's the patient doing?" He points at Scratch, still lying in her arms. The front of her shirt is covered with his blood.

"Blissed out. He's delighted you're here—at long last. He kind of throws himself into things. Like me."

"Did you give him something? He seems awfully mellow."

"Drug my kitty? What do you take me for?"

"A witch."

"Point. Just a few herbs to calm him. Otherwise he'll tear the bandage off and bleed all over the place again before the topical coagulant has a chance to work. If I feed him now, he'll just barf it up. Battle gets him a little too charged I'm afraid. He's more a lover than a fighter, aren't you, Scratchie?" His purr is strong and steady. He's one happy cat.

Danny scritches the top of his head with his fingertips, careful to avoid the wounded ear. The rumble deepens. "How did he end up on the other side of town?"

"He lives to serve."

"You?"

"The goddess. Like me." She slides him into his little house, and he curls into a contented ball. "Want to see my work room?"

She looks like a nubile victim in a slasher movie in that blood-soaked shirt. "You should probably soak that in cold water," he suggests.

"Are you *kidding*? My brave warrior's blood? *This* shirt? We fucked all over this shirt—all the way to the future. Wash away *this* day? No way. I may never take it off again—except for you, of course. Come on. I want to show you where the magic is imagined."

He follows her down the short hall.

He's not sure what he'll see when she opens the door and turns on the lights. Bird entrails. Seething cauldrons. It's mostly empty space, a clean wood floor. For a split second, he thinks someone's already in the room on a high stool by a work bench on the far wall, a tall, leggy woman—with a bear's head. That gives him a jolt. It's a mannequin with the head of a large teddy bear stuck on top. The body is clad in a ragged brown Tree of Life t-shirt. The *pe* has been X'd off the *Shoppe* with a Sharpie.

Kristi explains, "Danny, meet Lotus. She's already heard all about you. She lost her old head, but you can't get this kind of mannequin anymore. The fittings don't fit. I didn't want her to be all headless for your visit. I needed something I could just glue on. I started to get a doll's head, but that seemed way creepier. Too *Chucky*, if you know what I mean. I kind of like the bear. She could like change out every month or something, gain fresh insights. I saw a terrific elephant where I got the bear."

"Learn all the secret stuffed animal ways?"

"Exactly. Go ahead. Make fun, Sooth. The deepest jungles are in our heads. Nobody knows that better than Lotus." She lays her hand on the mannequin's thigh, and for a moment, he can almost believe the damn thing's alive. Kristi turns, looks up at him, stands on tip-toe. "Kiss me."

He picks her up in his arms and kisses her. She wraps her arms around his shoulders, her legs around his waist. When they break the kiss, she looks into his eyes. "Is this okay? Am I too heavy? I like being eye-to-eye without getting a crick in my neck. Four-eleven, and you're a sweetheart not to ask."

"You're fine. Perfect. You're going to tell me something, aren't you? Give me another piece of the puzzle? I'm beginning to recognize the look, the need for eye contact. There's only one thing I really want to know. In the end, are we together?"

"That'll be up to you. Your choice. I promise."

"Then we'll be together. I promise. I already made my choice. So tell me your worst, if you think I'm ready." He likes holding her like this, his feet rooted to the ground, holding her up. He's felt dead since the accident—like Frankenstein's Creature before the lightning, just sewn together but not really alive—until she woke him. But this is bigger than him. That's what Kris has been trying to tell him all along: It's not about the two of them but what comes next.

She's quiet and serious. The effect is like that river outside he can still hear through the walls, suddenly becoming a still, deep lagoon. "You know, I told you I worked magic to get you? Had help? I had to make a deal to do that."

"Deal?"

"Ever hear of the triple-goddess? Doesn't matter. Goddess is enough, right? She basically said she'd help us hook up, give us her blessing, but only if I was willing to lay my life on the line, that she wasn't going to be a part of messing with two women's lives, if it wasn't truly life or death for me."

"You're scaring me."

"Finally! It's about *time*. I'm a scary person. Let me finish. The women I've wronged have to have a chance to stop me. It's only fair. I think I've made it past El, but we're not out of the woods yet. Literally, we are. Not so much figuratively. Nobody in the woods loathes me like this woman does for stealing her man."

"By stop, you mean *kill*? Elissa and *Nina*? You can't be serious."

"You're a stubborn son of a bitch, you know that? What does it take with you? I'm deadly serious. I'm the most serious thing that's ever happened in your whole life that isn't just some random accident. We weren't alone in the mountains, Danny. El had me in her sights, and for whatever reason, decided not to blow my head off. I can't say I'm surprised. El and I go way back. Nina, on the other hand, *knows* I am her worst nightmare bitch from Hell—because I pretty much am." She takes a deep breath, holds it a moment, then has her say: "Just so you know. So you know what's going on if something happens. I'm just saying. No regrets. I love you, Sooth. So much." Her huge eyes brim with tears. Her lips are trembling.

"*Wait* a minute. Would you slow down? You think you saw Elissa in the mountains?"

"I *know* I saw her. I knew where to look—giraffe with a rifle's hard to miss. Saw the sun glancing off the scope. That's how Lotus lost her head. Practicing for today. Sort of a ritual, I guess you might call it. *Kapow*. First shot. El's good. Had a good instructor." She snuffles, and a tear rolls down her cheek. She dabs at it with the collar of her shirt, rests her forehead on his shoulder, and they sway back and forth.

She's not joking. He felt the fear in her body as she recalled the moment, a brush with death, feels her trembling with her tears, like a sparrow in the palms of his hands. He's never loved anyone so much. He would die for her. "It's okay. Okay. Let's say that happened, didn't happen, we're *here* now. Together. But *Nina*? She's like a thousand miles from here. She has no idea I even know you."

Kristi raises her head from his shoulder. "I wouldn't count on it."

He looks into her red, tear-swollen eyes. "You're just being paranoid. How many times do I have to tell you? Nina left because she was ready to leave."

She cradles his face in her hands, snuffles, smiles at him like he's the sweetest fool in the world. "Right. And you love me because you like my tattoo, and you fucked my best friend, and you have a thing for short girls. Yeah. It all makes sense. Happens every day. You remember when I took you to El's, and we were stopped behind the bus, and there was a woman looking at us? I saw you struggling to place her. Granted, you were a little distracted."

He shakes his head. "Vaguely." What does that have to do with anything?"

"You remember me coming on to you?"

"Vividly."

"*Then*."

He thinks back, feeling the arousal even the memory stirs. He can scarcely believe he turned her down. "Okay. I remember now."

"You sure I'm not too heavy?"

"No, no. You're fine."

"Lindsey. Did her cards at a revelry once. Told her coke would destroy her pretty little sinuses. Ring any bells?"

"Oh shit. Nina's niece. Her— her hair's all different. She's gained a lot of weight. She looked so angry…"

As that sinks in, Kristi slides off of him, but keeps talking. "She snapped our picture with her phone and sent it to someone, I'm guessing her auntie. We talked about Nina when I did Lindsey's cards. About you. I was kind of on the lookout for anything about you. Truth? She had a girlish crush on you until you had to go be an asshole and tell her the truth about her cokehead boyfriend. I told her she would have a chance to be a messenger. Gossip Girl. Shake things up in return. She loved it. You can imagine her reaction when she saw *us* together. So naughty. Who would *you* send it to? I checked by the way, according to Nina's workplace, she's attending a conference in DC, though she still hasn't picked up on a message I left at her hotel this morning."

"You're saying she might be in town?"

"If I were a gambling woman, and I obviously am, I would bet everything on it."

"Why don't we just go now? Go to DC, like you said—if you're sure Nina's not there—Philadelphia, New York. It doesn't matter to me. I'll help you pack. There's nothing I need at my place."

"You'd do that?"

"Absolutely."

She searches his eyes for certainty. He's certain it's there to find.

He says, "You're going to get a crick in your neck. Am I going to have to pick you up again?"

"Okay. Okay. We can do this. You are *so* wonderful! We have to stop by The Tree first. I promised Serena I wouldn't leave town without saying good-bye. She's eat-up to know how things are going with us anyway. She's been rooting for you. She's a total romantic, case you hadn't noticed."

"I thought she fired you."

Kristi winces. "Sorry. I kind of lied about that too, trying to buy some cheap sympathy—downtrodden coworker. Not to judge, but you kind of like downtrodden I've noticed. Mostly I didn't want to get bogged down. If I'd told you I quit, you would've asked me why, and I didn't want to get into all that right then. Had to keep things moving. The cards said it was time. "

"Time?"

"That the magic had started working. Everything was falling into place. El was ready to make her move."

"Is there anything else you haven't told me?"

"You mad?"

"No. Curiously not. I keep waiting to be, but I'm too happy to be mad. Did you give *me* any herbal remedies?"

She laughs. "No. Want some?" She points to shelves of jars over the workbench. "I've got more than catnip here. I have a fungus from the Amazon that will take you to another world."

"Is that where you make these deals with goddesses?"

"Sometimes."

"Maybe later. This world's just getting interesting. Back to my question. What else you got? I'm betting you haven't told me everything."

"I haven't shown you the magic bus. That's one of the things I wanted to show you in here."

She turns on a shop light over the workbench, and there's a model bus about eighteen inches long, painted to look like a city bus—if they hired Kristi to paint one. It's his route number on the front. There's a sullen little baby hunched inside, wrapped in a dark cloak, his back turned on all the other passengers. Beside the bus, tacked to the cork wall above the workbench, are photos of The Tree of Life Book Shoppe, Elissa's duplex, and Danny's big hulk of a building. Three stops on the line.

Kristi points to them. "Like beads on a string, you see? I worked with that, that connection. It made things happen. I used to ride the real bus with you sometimes, and you didn't even know. It was easy. You didn't want to know anybody else was there. It was like you were in the manger, and the shepherds and the wise men and the fucking pope himself showed up to adore you and tell you how you were sent to save the world, but you weren't having any of it, knowing what happens next. The guys with torches and crosses, right? There was a lot of your energy on those busses, like your life in miniature. I'd ride in your seat after you got off, still warm from you. I couldn't keep riding with you all the time, or sooner or later you'd notice, so I made the magic bus here. Witches ride free after midnight, when they can't sleep."

He looks down the aisle of the tiny bus, imagines her imagining herself inside, beside him, following him deeper and deeper into his tiny life, headed nowhere, seeking a still point. After the accident he thought he would live his life differently. He hadn't counted on *being* different, on being the monster like she said. But he doesn't have to be the Incredible Shrinking Man, vanishing into nothing. "Do you need help packing? Let's go. I'm ready."

"It's mostly done."

"You're leaving this stuff?"

"Except for Lotus and some of the irreplaceable herbs and some other witchy stuff. Lotus likes the HOV lanes. The bus has done its work."

"What about your set models?"

"I think I've hung onto those long enough. I have everything I need in the whole wide world."

"As long as you have your bloody shirt and me?"

"I knew you'd understand."

"Is that part of the deal? That you give up everything?"

"Yeah." She gives me a look. "For somebody new at this, you're getting pretty good at understanding how it works."

"Thanks. This place isn't really a rental, is it?"

"No. A guy gave it to me—he used to rent it out, years ago—a professor who was obsessed with me. He had in mind we'd meet here, but that only happened a few times. I went through a phase where I thought I owed him somehow since I ruined his life, but it just made things worse. I'm giving the house back. It's worth a whole lot more now than it was then. I'm leaving the set models for him too. He saw all the plays. Front row. El was in all of them. Poor bastard. People talked. I'm not a very nice person, Danny."

"Nobody's a very nice person, Kristi. Mostly we just fuck up, right? I got a fifteen year old kid killed, shot through the heart."

"I know that story, and that was *not* your fault."

She's fierce and immediate in his defense. He shouldn't be surprised. She loves him. He'd do the same for her. "This professor. He was of unblemished character before you came along, I suppose, never dreamt of hitting on students until you enchanted him?"

"You're a fool, you know that?"

"Yeah. It feels good."

"You *know* the professor—as well as anyone knows him anymore, except me. He's not a professor anymore. Not so much a creep. Leslie."

"You're kidding. Weird Leslie?"

"Be nice. You should talk. He's been through a lot. It'll be better for him if I'm not around him for a while. I didn't know what I was doing. I didn't know how to undo it."

"How do you know you did anything?"

"C'mon. How do you know you *see* anything?"

"Okay. What's he doing at The Tree?"

"Reading palms. You're right about him hitting on students. I went to his office because in class he was always talking about his interest in the occult, and I thought maybe he might be like me. He used the palm thing as a come on, you know, but I'd studied palmistry a little and could tell he was a phony, and that pissed me off because I was so disappointed in him, you know, and I started fucking with him, and one thing led to another. It took me awhile to learn that. One thing leads to another. And another. He's really quite good now. As a palmist. Not so much of a lech. It's some sort of a penance thing for him. He's a big Coleridge fan too. His fave's *Ancient Mariner*. I'm his albatross, I guess. I'm more into *Christabel*. Coleridge never finished it, so I sort of keep it alive—there's no ending to tie you down. I'm into rewriting endings."

She drops the bloody flannel shirt off her right shoulder to reveal the Christabel tat. "This was a 'special project' for Leslie's class. Try not to stare."

"So I've noticed. You did that for him?"

"No. That's where I was wrong. I did it for the magic, to see if I could do it. I didn't do it for him. If you just enchant somebody and give them nothing, that's not enchantment, that's a curse. He was a creep, but I was too."

"When did all this happen? When did you get the tattoo?"

"Ten years ago this Halloween."

"You were just a kid."

"I was way worse than that."

"A nineteen-year-old monster. I still love you—even though I thought you were a virgin. I'm kind of crushed. Anything else?"

"There's just *one* more thing—"

"Jeez." I roll my eyes.

She laughs. "No, no. This is a technicality. You'll like this. It's Scratch. I'm supposed to leave him, since he's definitely part of 'everything,' but you're under no such obligation, and I thought you might be willing to adopt him."

"You think your goddess will go for this obvious dodge?"

"Oh yeah. She's flexible, definitely where kitties are concerned."

"I would be honored to adopt him."

"Great! He should be ready to eat by now. Why don't you wake him up and bond over the swan while I put a few necessities in a bag, and then we can blow this town." She jumps up and kisses him and bounds into her bedroom across the hall. She leaves the door open. It's practically empty.

He goes to the fridge, take out the bag and put it on the counter. He pulls out the swan and turns to find Scratch, his head swaddled in bandages, sitting in the middle of the floor, smiling. Danny pries the swan open, sets it before him, and Scratch feeds on the bounty his wicked mistress has provided, rumbling like a motorboat. This is one lucky cat. Chefs cook for him.

Danny guesses his next meal is up to him. The thought makes him smile. It's good to have a cat again. He'd like a dog too. Nina wasn't a dog person. He hollers down the hall. "How do you feel about dogs?"

"I love dogs!" she hollers back.

He knew she would. He takes a deep breath. *Remember to breathe.* Fish and garlic. He listens to Scratch's contented rumble and the river's roar, and he's the happiest monster on Earth.

He has found his mate.

Chapter Fourteen

The Three Magickal Stones

"Red flags," muttered Tootle. "This meadow is full of red flags! How can I have any fun? Whenever I start, I have to stop. Why did I think this meadow was such a fine place? Why don't I ever see a *green* flag?"
—Gertrude Crampton, *Tootle*

Nina learns the rest of the ancient Egypt story goes something like this: The princess takes her troubles to the priest who renounces his sacred vows of chastity for her, and they know a passion like no other beneath the towering pyramids under a full moon...

Terry must have cast all his seed upon the Nile. Nothing much was fervently happening in his king-size bed. *This never happens*, he tells her. What every woman wants to hear. Now he's sulking in the bathroom.

She hates his place. It doesn't look like anybody lives here. *I have someone come in and clean*, he told her. Looks like he had someone pick out the furniture, the dull prints on the walls. He told her over lunch he inherited some money—a great grandfather amassed a fortune selling burial insurance to poor folks, really quite deplorable, he admitted, but you can't escape the past. He says that a lot. He wasn't cut out for graduate work, he lamented. Fortunately, he's found his life's work helping others with his uncanny ability to unearth their buried lives, their hidden fears and frustrations, hopes and dreams, giving them a new direction for the future. He had his hand on her thigh for that little speech. She didn't need a new direction to know where that was going.

What was she thinking? Coming back here to Richmond? It just keeps getting worse. Not only is Danny fucking the goth pixie who chased Nina out of town, but she has to suffer through a muscle-bound faux priest who can't get it up. Did Egyptian priests even take vows like that? What a load, as Danny would say. She remembers the actor Terry sort of looks like, the movie. *Ten Commandments*. Yul Brynner, kind of beefed up. Just like her to pick the losing side. Why did Nina's hateful boss even suggest the DC conference in the first place? Now she's missed all the sessions related to her work. She'll look like an idiot when her boss grills her. She can't stay here. She has to fly back to Portland to get Tristan out of the vet.

She rolls over in bed, rolling over the Spirit Journey Crystal, gouging into her back. It's still wet, Terry's desperate impromptu stand-in for his limp cock, a seriously bad idea. Sharp point, chiseled edges. Cold as ice. She slammed her head into the headboard, and that was pretty much the end of that. He made a speech, grabbed his clothes, and hit the john without pausing to consider she might have a need herself after her close encounter with a crystal dick. She wipes it off on his sheets and puts it back in the box, which is starting to come apart at the seams. She looks around for the little book and finds it in the bedclothes. It looks like it might've taken a knee. When you're that big, why in the world insist on being on top? She feels like roadkill. Like this little book. She tries to flatten it out as best she can and returns it to the box. Another smart purchase.

Another reason to hate herself. It's like she's on a quest, one of those dopey stories where the heroine has to find the three magickal stones and learn their powers to discover her true destiny and save the realm! This one's clearly The Rock Of Total Humiliation. She sticks it in her bag. She kept the receipt, thank God. She starts putting on her clothes, shed in a flurry of passion, soon over. No significant accumulation. There's a print of some erotic art buried by Vesuvius above the bed to show the living how it's done. The people there are having a way better time than Nina.

His phone on the night table starts buzzing on a scattering of change. Is there any sound more annoying? She hollers, "You've got a call. Would you hurry up in there? I need to pee."

He comes bursting out of the bathroom. "Don't answer it!" he says, like she would dream of it, and snatches up the phone. Change goes flying. He's fully dressed. He's been in the bathroom doing what? Gazing in the mirror? Talking things over with his disappointing member?

She makes a beeline for the toilet and only hears enough of his end of the conversation to hear he's terribly sorry. Time got away from him. Is that what happened? She doubts Terry knows anything about time, how it really works. Time always gets away from you, but you can't escape it. You just have to get through it. Sort of numb down and let it happen. That's how it works when you're off the rails. After a while the wheels won't turn, things shut down, seize up. Too much to process. The heart grows cold and hard, another stone on her quest. The Rock Of Perfect Pointlessness. *Do you see any semblance of a point in that?* pixie bitch asked her. None. Nina's default setting.

There's one more stone—there's always three, right? It seems to be growing in her gut. Like that thing in *Alien*.

The bathroom is seriously annoying, little ancient statues from the museum gift shop, travel posters of ruins on the wall. One of these ancient piles is probably the handmaiden's hometown. The handmaidens who clean this place make everything gleam. What is that trick? You smear it with baby oil. Nina touches the golden faucet. Oily. He's like a giant baby, living in the cradle of civilization. Maybe he just keeps this place because it's close to the museum and actually lives somewhere else. This is just a place to bring women and seduce them with the rise and fall of some empire or other.

When she comes out of the bathroom, he scarcely makes eye contact. "You ready? I'm afraid I have an appointment that slipped my mind completely, and we really must hurry."

Hurry, hurry, hurry. That's how they got nowhere so quickly. She nods. She's ready to be rid of him. He acts like she should be comforting him for the calamity that has befallen his dick. Try my life, she wants to say. One of the side effects of her meds is the suppression of sexual appetite, as the fine print in the package insert so delicately puts it. Suppressed, as in obliterated. Crazy or cold? Take your pick. She hates her meds. Her life without them, she's beginning to recall, is no day at the beach either. She inevitably starts thinking about swimming out to meet the riptide.

He drives a Land Rover laden with amenities for the luxurious adventurer. She wonders if the car ever actually roves, or whether it's just for show like his muscles. He says, on the way, "I'm afraid I have to rush right in. My client is waiting. You don't have to bother coming inside."

In other words, *I don't want you coming in.* She's beginning to see why Danny doesn't like this guy. As sensitive as a rock. "I *want* to come in," she says and looks out the window at her hometown gliding by. Case closed. She has a fucking rock to return.

They're passing the polished marble bunker of the United Daughters of the Confederacy headquarters, a cannon pointed at her. Welcome home. Just the name of the place gives Nina the creeps. Dead for 150 years and still spitting out *daughters*? *What am I* doing *here?* For Danny? When she and Danny were married, it wasn't so great. Ever. One long endless perfectly ordinary Instagram moment, like one of those shots everyone takes of the same things from the same angles for the same reasons, same feelings. Look! I'm ordinary! Is that what she wants out of life? Another United Daughter of Redundancy? Same as it ever was, same as David Byrne ever said it was. Everybody she knows knows what David Byrne says, like he's hanging on the walls in the museum.

Now this big stupid jerk. For someone who's supposedly in a hurry, he drives like an old lady. He's still acting like his limp dick was the end of the world, like he had no idea it could do such a thing—his own personal Lost Cause. Nina hates Richmond. The Confederate Daddies torched the town when they left. Too bad they didn't burn down the whole place, and she could've been born somewhere else where she might have had the tiniest chance of fitting in.

She wonders where Terry's from. You can't tell from his accent, like a voice over the radio. "Do you *really* see anything, or do you just make up bullshit?"

He bites his lip, chooses to ignore that insult. Theatre major. He says, "If you catch up with her, I wouldn't mess with Kristi if I were you."

"We're not talking about Kristi at the moment."

He has an annoying little blinky thing he does, meaning he's as over her as she is over him. "I know, but this is about Danny, isn't it? Him and Kristi. Whatever's going on there, it's serious. Listen to me: She paid his salary at The Tree for a *year*, so Serena would keep him on. I talked to her best friend a while back, and she confirmed what Serena and I suspected—Kristi's totally obsessed with him. She's not someone who takes things lying down. I'm only trying to give you good advice. Take it or leave it." He purses his lips, weaseling his way back to his own story. "Look. About when we get to the store—The thing is, I'm not supposed to get personally involved with clients, so it might be better if you didn't come *in* with me exactly. Maybe you could—"

"God, you are such a coward. Answer my question. Do you see things or not?"

"Why does it matter?"

"It doesn't. Maybe I'd prefer to think you were just trying to screw me than to believe anything you say."

He's wounded, though she's not sure why. "Okay. Total bullshit. All of it."

"Thanks for being honest. You're lucky. The stuff Danny sees is real. He changes people's lives. He has to live with that."

Terry smirks. "Real is what people believe is real, and it doesn't have to be real to change your life. People change their lives for lies every day. Danny thinks he's special because he sees the truth? There's nothing special about the truth, especially when there are so many other choices. Danny needs to lighten up. But none of that matters in deciding what to do here. Seriously, I'd back away from this. I don't know if Kristi's for real—she *can* read your fucking mind, with or without her damn cards—but more importantly, I saw her drop a guy bigger than me to the ground once because he got the tiniest bit out of line—and he didn't get up right away either."

She has to wonder what his idea of the tiniest bit out of line is. As much as she hates to admit it, she'd probably side with the bitch on this one. He's just trying to scare her off with all this melodrama anyway. So a big drunk guy fell down one night making a pass—so what? She's never been afraid of a fight. Quite the opposite. That's how the meds got started in the first place, part of her anger management program, a condition of her continued enrollment at a school her parents paid dearly for her to attend. Twenty-some years ago. The program lasted six months. The other girl's parents didn't sue. She's still on the meds, with a few lapses now and then. It's like time travel to go off them: *So this is me. Way back then.* The last time was when she fled to Portland, left a note on the kitchen table like some kid running away from home. When she panicked in Portland, the young doctor at the doc-in-a-box lectured her about withdrawal and wrote her a scrip she's been riding on for a couple of years now.

When they pull into the parking lot, Terry peers through the store windows to see who's there, swaying back and forth to adjust to the glare. "I don't see my client. I hope he didn't leave." There's someone Nina guesses is Serena behind the counter talking to a tall slender woman. "Oh shit," Terry mutters.

"What is it?" Nina asks.

"It's Elissa. The woman I was telling you about. Kristi's friend."

"Why should you care?"

He bites his lip again. This time with a little head tilt. He doesn't have to draw her a picture. The only question is whether he's hitting on one or both of them. She wonders if Terry's the big guy Kristi dropped to the ground—somewhat smaller since. She can see where he might have it coming.

Nina says, "I want to meet the friend. Come on."

Reluctantly, he hauls his big frame out of the car, and she takes his arm. Resistance is futile. She wants best friend to report back to the little bitch that Nina's doing just fine, thank you very much. And then she'd like an address for Kristi. Terry's just trying to scare her. The woman's tiny. Nina has twenty pounds on her at least.

When they walk through the door, Serena's glaring at Terry like there's definitely more than psychic-client etiquette to her anger. Elissa gapes at Nina like she's seeing a ghost.

This is one weird place anyway, and it seems to have gotten even weirder in the few hours since Nina was here, or maybe that's her. Everything has bright edges. It's fairly busy with several meditative browsers moving up and down the aisles being pretentious, like buying things is some new form of Tai Chi. (Nina hated Tai Chi). The color scheme of most of the merchandise is your basic kaleidoscope of metallic intensity and enlightenment and transcendent razzmatazz. There's probably enough nasty heavy metals in the packaging, Danny once pointed out, to contaminate the city's water supply if the place flooded. The music is some impossibly nasal chant in a language nobody understands with drums and flutes and bells and so on, with something like an electric kazoo looking for the lost key. She hates it.

"Terry," Serena says icily, tossing her head toward her office. "A moment. Excuse us, please," to Nina and Elissa. Serena exits trailing Terry behind. The office door closes with a sharp click. Waves of negative energy slosh around the place, and you can almost hear everyone struggling to regain their center. The dweebie little guy is stocking the incense. Nina takes out the Spirit Journey Crystal and puts it down a little harder than she intended, the exposed corner of the crystal making contact with the glass counter, and everyone in the store jumps. "I want to return this," she says.

She looks up at Elissa who's still staring at her like she just landed. "You're a friend of Kristi's, right?"

"Yes." She doesn't look so sure. Cautious, like she's walking on ice.

"Do you know my husband, Danny?"

Elissa looks off into the distance, like she's trying to decide. She's like a swan with her long graceful neck. "Yes." She turns back to look Nina in the eye. "I know him." The swan neck sways, and Nina feels something turn over in her gut.

The dweeb has finally managed to get behind the counter. Nina turns to him, slides the receipt across the counter. "You can't return this," he says. "It's a Clearance item. All sales are final." He points at the sign. He opens the battered box, takes out the crystal, looking like he can tell where it's been, and he's inspecting for pubic hairs. He picks up the crumpled book. The spine is cracked. "Besides, it's damaged."

"That's bullshit. I just bought this stupid rock a few hours ago."

Customers start drifting out the door. There's a soft bong somewhere to mark the door's opening and closing, like the tolling of temple bells. *Bong... bong... bong...* What a load. She hates this place. "I'll—I'll get the manager," dweeb says and slinks away toward the office, where the volume of Serena's rage has been growing, though no one can quite make out the exact words. Sounds like the last few hours have caught up with Terry. Time slipped away and got his ass fired, dumped, both. She almost feels sorry for him.

"You do that," Nina says to the clerk loud enough for everyone to hear and turns back to Elissa, in no mood for any more bullshit. *Bong... bong... bong...* "So how do you know my husband?" It comes out kind of loud and brittle. She wishes someone would shut off the fucking music. Who pretends to like this stuff?

The swan grows taller, more elegant, more beautiful. "It was my understanding you were no longer married."

"Answer my question."

She doesn't answer right away. She seems to find the whole thing weirdly amusing, like everybody knows what's going on but Nina. "We were lovers. He saw me in his future. It was beautiful. I thought it meant something. Kris set me straight on that. You think you want Danny back? I'm not the one you need to worry about. He's totally into Kris. I'd give it up if I were you. It's over."

Everybody's always trying to give Nina advice. *Do I look like I'm asking for advice?* "You're *not* me, okay? You're nothing *like* me." *Bong... bong...*

Long comforting arms snake toward Nina, and she knocks them away, shoves her palms hard into the swan's chest, trying to split it open, knock her down, this beautiful creature who fucked her husband, and devour her heart. Elissa staggers back into a display of aromatherapy supplies, thousands of little vials, and the place explodes in scent and broken glass. Nina stands over her. Blood streams from Elissa's hands. Nina's heart's racing. The fucking music goes on and on. *I may have seriously fucked up here.*

"Leave her alone," comes a shout behind her. "I'm the one you want."

Everything starts to happen real slow. Nina turns to see Kristi coming toward her in a fighting stance. Danny's out in the parking lot charging at a dead run, like he knows what's about to go down. The little bitch is looking right at her. Nina remembers those fucking eyes. *Come on*, Kristi seems to be saying, *Make a move, bitch!* She remembers Terry's warning. She picks up the Spirit Journey Crystal, holding it like a dagger. "Don't come near me," she says.

"You haven't got the guts," the little bitch says.

That's it. That's what one of her shrinks called a trigger for her, so she's supposed to understand that and deal with it. So she deals: She puts everything she's got into the blow to Kristi's heart. The little bitch doesn't do anything to stop her. All that badass talk was just bluff. She spreads her arms and takes it, like that's what she wanted all along. The force of the blow carries them both to the ground, and Nina lands hard on top of her, driving the stone in. Blood is everywhere. Danny's screaming, wailing for her to stop, but he can't get to her in time. Nina raises her arms for another blow.

Terry yanks her off before she can drive it in again, and she's thrashing like crazy in his hard, unyielding arms, and then it just vanishes—all that rage. The desire to kill the bitch is gone. *I've really done it now.* She lets the crystal go. It falls to the carpeted floor with a quiet thump. Danny's holding Kristi cradled in his arms, begging her to live, and there's the faintest little smile on the bitch's face, like everything has turned out just perfect, even as the paramedics and the cops come crashing through the door. Then they haul Nina away in handcuffs, reading her her rights. *What a laugh. I have no rights. I'm cursed. Same as it ever was.*

Chapter Fifteen

There Is No Kansas

It may be said that natural selection is daily and hourly scrutinizing, throughout the world, every variation, even the slightest; rejecting that which is bad, preserving and adding up all that is good; silently and insensibly working, whenever and wherever opportunity offers.
— Elizabeth Kolbert, *The Sixth Extinction: An Unnatural History*

Elissa can't believe Kris is in the same ICU where Mom died. She and Kris went back there together then, through those double doors, when they turned off the life support. It had to be done. The doctor let Kris go in, even though she wasn't family, probably figuring without her there El would just shatter.

One moment, Mom was there, some tiny bit of her anyway, and the next she wasn't. Elissa will never forget that moment, that absence. She never believed in anything like a soul until Mom died, and she was gone.

Kris got El through that, never once telling her to get over it, move on, any of that. She just waited, like a friend, and held her sometimes when she cried. That's when they went looking for the mountain place, taking long drives in the country, helping her heal.

And now Kris is here, and she might die, and there's nobody to get El through this but herself. This is some crazy Kris shit she's gotten El into once again, and she better not die before El has a chance to give her some serious shit about it.

They all have to get through it alone, sitting in the waiting room together. Nina's in the psychiatric ward under heavy sedation, but Danny, Terry, Serena, even Leslie, are here.

And Michael. He's beside Elissa, holding her bandaged hands. Kind of an airhead, but sweet. He was the first one to get to her, helping her to her feet, wrapping her bloody hands in his shirt. He told her about his screenplays to distract her while they waited for the EMT. One called *Picking Up* sounded great to her, but she told him the woman should be the lead since women know way more about shit than men. She's been trying to distract herself with how it might work ever since. The unfortunate clerk, after being told to fuck off at the office door by a screaming Serena dressing down Terry, fled out the back and is still being sought. He was long gone by the time the real craziness started.

They're witnesses, though only Elissa and Danny actually witnessed the *blow,* the attempted murder. Like a dagger of ice. Even knocked on her ass, looking through Nina's legs, El saw what Nina saw: Kris wanted it. El knows Kris, knows what she can do. If she'd wanted it that way, it would be Nina in the ICU with a rock sticking out of her chest.

They're supposed to wait in the waiting room where a fat cop watches over them waiting for another cop who will take their statements. They're not supposed to discuss the case with each other. Nobody's particularly coherent anyway, all a little crazy with Kris on death's door. They're like a bunch of moons who've lost their planet.

No surprise El seems to be the calmest one. She's an old hand at ERs. They were the family doctor. The last few days have prepared her for this moment. *Enjoy your journey!* Kris says one of the things she liked about the old religions was the idea that any random stranger could be a god or goddess taking on somebody's appearance. *It's happened to me,* she claimed, and maybe it's true. Maybe Vincent in his pickup is an itinerant deity. Looking like she does, El's been goddess material for more than a few guys, though she can't say she's ever lived up to the title or wanted to. For Kris she would, if she could save her.

After three hours in surgery, the doctor said it's touch and go, that most women Kris's size wouldn't have survived the blow that shattered ribs and punctured a lung but just missed her heart, and she has a re-markable constitution, so we can only hope. For now, she's stable, a tricky word at the best of times. Time will tell. The next few hours are critical. It's like all the doctors watch the same TV shows. Fortunately, there's more than hope and platitudes. El has faith: If it missed her heart, Kris will live. No doubt about it. She broke her arm once in a bike wreck, ignored the doctors and took off the cast in three days. It was fine.

In case you're harboring some notion that Kris is weird but still an ordinary human, let El disabuse you of that notion immediately: El knows her better than anyone, and she's seen too much to doubt her anymore, doubt the things she can do. She's not one of us. She's better.

The only change in this waiting room since Mom died is now the TV is permanently tuned to a medical advice channel where TV doctors tell you how not to end up here. At El's pantomimed pleading, Michael found a way to mute the volume. She still finds herself staring at the smiling faces cajoling people into at least making an attempt to stay alive. She wonders if they have one of these down in the ER. They might have to tailor the message. *Avoid poverty and eat wisely!* Sound easy? Try it some time. The lesson up here should be *Don't mess with magick!*

Serena has been going on and on like a frantic mother, incredulous that anyone would do such a thing to her beloved one, who had her faults, sure, but always meant well. Did she? El wonders, has always wondered, probably will always wonder. Doesn't matter. Meant well—who knows what that means? Kris is her friend.

The cop puts a finger to his lips and gives Serena a pleading look. Could you *please* put a lid on it?

Terry is surprisingly tender comforting Serena, like one of Mom's big gentle bears. Kris's blood is all over his shirt from when he pulled Nina off, saving Kris's life. The doctor said a second blow would have definitely proven fatal. Not too many guys would've been strong enough to hold onto Nina in her blind rage.

Lucky Kris. *Luck belongs to the lucky*, she would say, an expression El never quite understood until now.

Leslie, like the ghost he is, sits in the corner and tries to remain invisible. He looks like a different person ten years on. She might not have recognized him if they passed on the street. He's lost the substantial paunch, the smiley rakish charm, the professorial swagger. His hair's gone white. His sunken eyes stay fixed on the double doors. You can tell those eyes don't see the same world they used to. She can't imagine what he's thinking, what he's feeling, but it's intense. She remembers he was a good teacher. No matter what else he was, he lit up when he talked about poetry, especially *The Rime of the Ancient Mariner*. This isn't exactly a wedding feast, and it looks like only the cops will hear his tale, but he's definitely been lugging an albatross around his neck. Now she's in the ICU. "Hello Elissa," was all he said to her at the Tree like he was just her former professor, now reclusive palmist in a fringy bookshoppe. Happens every day in the Kris universe. She wonders how often he relives the moment he made a play for an earnest young sophomore looking for a little understanding, shattering her illusions. That was the only time El ever remembers Kris really crying her eyes out, when she came back from that conference with him and holed up in her room for days, finally emerging with a sketch of a tattoo and a plan. Now, El suspects, her plans have gotten bigger.

Nobody really got Kris. Ever. Even El. Until Danny. Because they're the same.

Danny paces up and down. He can't contain his anxiety and fear. She wishes she could lend him some of her faith, but figures he may not want to talk to her, even though all her jealousy and rage seem to have been purged on the mountain. But the minute the fat cop goes into the Men's, Danny sits down beside her.

He hands her a familiar silk scarf—Kris's cards inside. "She told me to give you these for safekeeping. She had them stashed in the glove compartment."

She takes them and slips them into her bag. "Told you?" Like him, she's speaking just above a whisper for matters pertaining to Kris, cop or no cop. It's like she's laid out in the middle of the room, monitors bleating, tubes snaking in and out of her.

"She asked me to stay in the car with Scratch while she went in the store, said she wouldn't be but a moment. She slipped a note in my shirt pocket when she got out of the car. I didn't find it until she was inside the store." He shakes his head, recalling that freakout moment. "I ran as fast as I could, but I couldn't stop it."

"It wasn't your fault," she says.

"She did it because of me."

"Nina?"

"No, Kristi. There's not time to explain. The note begins, *Be my false witnesses.* She says no matter what happens, it wasn't Nina's fault. She says, *El will know what to do.*"

That's Kris all right. "Meaning what exactly?"

"She wants us to say it was nobody's fault but her own. It's part of a deal she made, I think. Just say everybody fell. It was all a big accident. Nobody tried to kill anybody." He glances toward the bathroom. "She also told me you were up in the mountains this morning—that that was part of the deal too."

El doesn't want to talk about what could've happened in the mountains this morning. Did nobody try to kill anybody? She's not sure. Nobody did. That's all that matters. Nobody's dead yet except Carl, and she's already covered that territory. If she decides to feel guilty about it, she'll let you know. She feels way worse about this morning. She's beginning to wonder if there wasn't something in the funky trail mix. Kris is into the occasional botanical adventure. *It's an elf thing,* she jokes. *You wouldn't understand.* "I was there. She wanted me there—I don't know—to judge, I guess. Kris is kind of obsessed with balance. I don't pretend to understand. That's over. This too. She's going to make it, Danny. Don't worry. I know she's going to make it."

"God, I hope so. I can't see a thing about her. It's driving me crazy." He shakes his head at his fickle gift—just like an adversary not to show up when you think you need him. "I also need to see to Scratch. He's still out in the car in the parking garage, but I can't leave her until we know something." He looks, with a grimace to the double doors. *Her* is Kris. Will always be Kris. He's torn apart with her in there. "She sort of gave him to me, before we showed up at The Tree. I didn't think it really meant anything. She knew, didn't she? Jeez." He takes a deep, shuddering breath. El knows the feeling. He's beginning to understand: We're not in Kansas anymore. Even when we thought we were in Kansas, come to find out, we weren't. There is no Kansas.

El knows Scratch. Kris got him not long after the tattoo from a guy who used him in TV commercials. One seriously spooky cat. He must be ancient by now. She hasn't seen him in a while. He had a habit of riding around on Kris's shoulders, wrapped around her neck. When Kris looked at you, Scratch did too, along with the tattoo. Six eyes, all mysterious, you never knew where to look. Kris has a way with animals. They take to her from the get-go. She scares most people once they get to know her. In a weird way El always liked that. It made her feel brave.

"I can go," Michael says. "I love cats. I know where the car is."

El and Danny have both forgotten he's sitting there on the other side of her. They came in two cars, parked them side by side. Danny and Leslie in Kris's car, everybody else in Terry's Land Rover, following Kris's ambulance, cops following them.

The cop comes out of the bathroom and gives them a look, so El speaks up, like Kris would do. "Officer, we were just discussing the victim's cat. Someone needs to see to him. He's in a car in the parking garage."

The cop rolls his eyes.

"I'll go." Michael says. "I was in the back room having my palms read the whole time. I didn't see anything anyway except the mess when it was over." He shows the cop his palms, like they'll corroborate his story. He has a goofy, irresistible smile.

Michael came right to her and helped her up. *Are you all right?* He was more scared than she was. It was the blood. None of the cuts were that deep. The doctor said her hands will be fine except for a few tiny scars on her palms. Most of the blood was Kris's. She presses her bandaged hands together and pleads to the cop, "Please, please, please!" She still reeks of aromatic essential oils.

"Oh all right, but be quick about it."

Danny hands Michael the keys. "Scratch is in his carrier in the back seat. The cat box is in the trunk. The back seat's folded down. You just need to open the carrier door. He'll figure out the rest. Check his water bottle. He should be okay on food."

"Come *right* back," the cop says.

"No problem," Michael says, with a lingering look at El that lingers all the way to the elevator and beyond. He smacks into the wall. She smiles. Slapstick. No one's ever tried slapstick on her before.

She imagines Kris's deadpan comment, *Another smitten swain.*

Her reply, *Maybe this one's different.* She asks Danny, "So what's his story?"

"Michael? He's The Tree's most regular customer. He thinks he's a screenwriter."

"You two," the cop says. "If you would refrain from discussion, *please?*"

They bridle at being told they can't talk, but since they both intend to lie about what happened, they make nice, and Danny returns to his pacing.

Leslie seemingly ignores all this. She wonders what Danny and Leslie talked about on the ride over. She catches Danny's eye and points toward Leslie, makes a little book of her hands. *Anything in that note about him?* Danny nods. He takes out his keys and points to one, slips them back in his pocket. Kris left him a key? To what? She furrows her brow in perplexity.

He traces a shape in the air. A house. Kris's place, her river house. El always assumed Kris's parents bought it for her. Now that she thinks about it, Kris would never accept a gift like that from her parents in a million years. *Money grows tentacles*, Kris told El once. *Parents come with more than enough tentacles already. Look at your father—a fucking giant squid sucking the life out of you, and he never gave you a dime. Just think if he sent you a check every month: You'd be nothing but squid shit by now.* You can't be thin-skinned and be Kris's friend.

Across from her, Terry still holds Serena. Her head rests on his shoulder, weary from crying. She drifts in and out of snuffly sleep. He coos comfort. They make a nice couple.

The cop sits down beside El. He keeps his eye on the elevator. "You're her best friend, right?"

"Right."

"The doctors don't tell us nothing, but I know serious when I see it. When her name came up on the call, I hauled ass to get here. I said some things to her last year about this time—I was kind of harsh—about her boyfriend over there, poor bastard. He don't even recognize me. Fair enough. I don't look the same as when we met. I was about to get myself kicked off the force when I met your friend in there. Real heartbreak story I spilled to her. She says to me, 'Get over it,' like it was nothing. Pissed me off, I can tell you. This little slip of a girl telling me to get over something really awful, like she would know. But it stayed in my head. *She* stayed in my head. 'Get over it. Let it go.' Cause what choice do you have, you know? 'Who the fuck are you?' she said to me, if you can imagine. She was right. If she pulls through this, you tell her thanks, okay? There's something different about her. I never met nobody like her before."

"Me neither," I say. The tears roll down. She doesn't try to stop them.

The cop nods his head thoughtfully. His shirt's a little big, heavy as he is, so his neck jostles around in the collar. His nameplate says Ferguson. The elevator doors come open, and he springs to his feet.

It's another cop, young. He says, "You're not going to like this. Your boy just drove off in the victim's car at a high rate of speed. He seemed to be in hot pursuit of a cat."

"Jesus Christ!" Danny says in disgust. "Leave it to Michael to turn a simple task into a fucking car chase."

"Amen," Ferguson says, pinching the bridge of his nose. Mom used to do that. Never helped then either. "What can I tell you? Find him.

Bring him back. The cat too if you can manage it, and if the detective can get his ass here before next week it would be helpful."

"You want me to tell him that?"

"If you think it would help. A lady nuts out in a psycho shop and attacks a nice young girl. I don't think this is too complicated. No reason to disrupt these good people's lives."

Danny says, "No one attacked anyone."

"What?" Ferguson exclaims. "That friggin' thing went damn near *through* her."

"She fell," El says. "She stumbled against me, and I fell, tripping her. Her weight drove the thing into Kris's chest." El stands, demonstrates what never happened, like an actor's exercise, a yoga practice, defying truth and elementary physics.

"Kristi ran right into her—trying to keep Elissa from falling," Danny chimes in, leaning into his lie. "The force—"

"Enough," Ferguson says quietly. "Please."

Just enough, as it turns out. The elevator opens a second time, and there's the detective at last. The only two witnesses to the alleged crime agree completely: It was a freak accident. Everybody fell down. They stick to their story. Terry has a chance to cast doubt on it. He did pull Nina off Kris, apparently ready to deliver the deathblow, but for whatever reason, he goes along. Nina was crazy, hysterical, but who wouldn't be? It was all that blood.

Danny says, "She takes medication. Travel can be especially stressful."

The detective nods like that explains everything.

When the cops finally clear out, convinced there's been no crime, Serena, who's wide awake now, tells El she has something to tell her, and they huddle at a little table down the hall by the vending machines. Serena eats a pack of chocolate covered donuts and drinks a diet Coke as she narrates in a low voice. She has to stop whenever anyone uses one of the machines.

"They showed me the crystal that Nina used, asked me about it. I explained it wasn't a weapon. They showed me the receipt and said some customers thought Nina was trying to return it. I explained our return policy on Clearance items, and they were happy, but I have to tell you: That crystal wasn't supposed to be there on the Clearance table, and the last person I saw handling it was Kristi. She took it out, making fun of it. You know how she is, making me laugh. We were the only two in the store. She was making like it was a light saber or laser or something, holding it in both hands, pointing it at things and making zapping noises, joking around. I told her to put it away. Next time I see it, the detective is showing it to me in a plastic bag with her blood on it. And there's something else. One of the reasons the cops wanted to talk to you and Danny so bad is the security cameras quit working for the whole thing. That's what Kristi was zapping with that crystal. I have four cameras in that store. I've had a serious shoplifting problem in the past. I have a lot of small merchandise. Not everybody's particularly evolved. She aimed that crystal at them all. The cameras stop when you show up. They come back up when they're wheeling Kristi out to the ambulance. This is all about Danny, isn't it?"

"Of course."

"Has she ever gone crazy over another guy like this?"

"Never."

"Well, I sure as Hell hope he's worth it, don't you?"

Mom used to say there's a lid for every pot. With Kris, El had begun to doubt it. Until Danny came along. "He is."

Terry takes Serena home to get some rest. El promises to call the minute they hear anything. Danny and El stand vigil. Leslie seems to have vanished in the night.

The doctor wakes them in the morning when the sky is still gray to say Kris is awake and wants to see them.

He says it's truly miraculous. He has one bit of bad news, however. When she fell in the glass, her right arm was badly lacerated and required aggressive treatment to prevent scarring and possible infection. As a result, her rather spectacular tattoo had to be removed. If all goes well, however, she can someday have another.

Danny and El burst out laughing, and the doctor's not too sure what to make of them. Kris always makes doctors nervous. El's so happy Kris is alive, happy for us all. She feels like she could do anything, like she's starting over.

Chapter Sixteen

Follow The Cat And Open The Doors

When [The Devil] appears in a tarot spread he is said to symbolize something totally inexorable, an occurrence which there is absolutely no possibility of ignoring...How you can react or adapt yourself to it is, of course, another situation altogether.

—Paul Huson, *The Devil's Picturebook*

Michael gets a chill right down his spine when Danny and Elissa start talking about the cat. Everything else has been *exactly* like Kristi said it would be—a catastrophe, an incredibly beautiful damsel in distress, someone's life hanging in the balance (she didn't tell him it would be her own!)—and now the cat. He doesn't know why the cat is such a big deal, but it is. It's like *his* part begins. The cat's on him. Kristi drilled that into him. *Follow the cat.* All these weeks, he's been waiting for Scratch to show.

Anything bad happens to my cat, and the deal's off, Kristi said a dozen times if she said it once.

Everyone told him not to bother with the rest of them at The Tree—Kristi's the one you want to see. He wanted to know about his career, of course. It's not about money. He has an income. He won the lottery. Not one of those millions and millions things, but he clears a couple of thousand a month, enough to live on, so he has a great deal of freedom. Too much, maybe. He wanted to pursue his dreams, but there were so many. He's a pretty dreamy guy. Which is sort of like movies, isn't it? Virtual dreams. He read that somewhere in a book he mostly didn't understand in a film class he barely squeaked a D in. How does anybody fail movies? In his defense, many of the films were subtitled, and he's not a quick reader, and it makes him drowsy reading off a screen in a dark room at ten o'clock in the morning. He slept through all the French films and most of the Italian. In spite of the film class, he wants to make movies. He's seen lots and lots of movies. That's one thing Kristi told him about the damsel—that she's totally into movies just like him.

Kristi sees all that about him immediately. (Not the whole film class thing, but who knows? She told him all sorts of stuff about himself, all dead on. She can be fairly insulting, but he'd been warned about that.)

She says: "Some guys don't want it enough. That's not your problem. You have no talent, and you're spoiled and lazy and clueless." She points randomly here and there at his cards, like they're dead soldiers on a battlefield, and she's saying the stupid things they did to get themselves killed in the worthless cause of his life. "You have a good heart, however." She doesn't point that one out on the battlefield. Maybe she's just being nice (doubtful) or maybe it's bled out. She's looking right at him.

He objects, sticks up for his dreams. If you don't, nobody else will. (He read that somewhere too). "I have talent: I have a million ideas." He picks up his phone to show her. It's just easier that way. There're so many he can't remember them all.

She lays her spidery hand on his forearm to stop him. "Ah! I see the problem. Listen carefully, Michael: Ideas aren't talent."

He almost drops his phone. "They aren't?"

"No. Don't let it trouble you. Fortunately, you can collaborate with someone who has talent, someone who will know what to do with your ideas."

He searches the cards. "Am I going to meet somebody like that?" This sounds like a pretty good idea, someone else doing the work who knows what they're doing.

"Better. I'm going to hook you up. You and she will be standing on a red carpet together—the most beautiful woman you've ever seen, a brilliant comic actress/writer/director, an indie sensation, the next big star." She touches The Star card, a naked blue woman, strokes the back of the woman on the card like it was some tiny little person, and he feels this weird combo of horny and scared shitless, but he doesn't feel foolish and wonders why. He usually does—feel foolish. That's why he never shuts up.

"Why would a woman like that have anything to do with me?"

"Good question. A little self-knowledge can go a long way. Mostly magic, but I'll give you an insider's tip, so you don't totally screw it up: Be funny. Make her laugh. Don't tell her she's beautiful and desirable. Believe me: She already knows that *way* better than you. You have ideas, but you need to turn them completely over to her because she has something you totally lack."

"What is that?"

"Substance. Experience. An understanding of how life works. Otherwise you wouldn't be in the back room of a store front with some weird little elf in a gypsy outfit looking for guidance from a bunch of cards created by a pair of notoriously weird Brits, now would you? What you've got is dreams. Don't underestimate them. They've led you to me. They just need a little shaping, a little guidance. This woman can definitely use some dreams. She'll show you what to do with them. Here's the deal..." Then she lays it out for him, crazy as shit, but he believes her, every word, even the saving the planet part. Something about those eyes.

And here he is, chasing a cat in what occurs to him is a stolen car in defiance of a direct order from an officer of the law. On the whole, it feels pretty good, though he does wish he was a better driver. The cat likes the alleys. Kristi's car is small, but the clearances are tight, and a cat can run faster than you might think. Fortunately the big super cans he occasionally knocks out of the way are plastic and don't hurt the car that bad, even when he gets stuck between two of them, and it's half a block before one of them busts loose and spews pizza boxes and wing buckets and a million pop bottles everywhere. The other goes airborne when he hits the cross street, terrifying a woman and her furiously barking beagle, crazed by a flying can.

That's the constant soundtrack behind his reckless passage through the alleys: Dogs Barking. Out of control, like postmen are parachuting out of the sky to take over and put the cats and squirrels in charge.

His presence hasn't gone unnoticed in the neighborhood.

The car smells like cat shit. Scratch was already out of his carrier by the time Michael showed up with the keys, had already taken a dump or two to get into running shape. The cat carrier's riding in the lap of the mannequin with the teddy bear head, sharing a seat belt. The mannequin's hand is resting on the door of the carrier like *it* freed the cat. Michael's asked himself a million times just who or what he's hooked up with here, but it doesn't matter at this point. He's in for the whole ride. Fulfilling his destiny, like Kristi said. Everybody's a sucker for that, right? Hook your wagon to a star and all that—but *first*, he has to catch this cat.

He flies across a side street with inches to spare to avoid getting hit by a honking, screeching panel truck filled with painters. He's totally blind coming out of these alleys. Zero peripheral. He could hit a nun. Well, a deaf nun maybe. The exhaust system sustained heavy damage on that last curb cut. He glances in the rearview to see if the guys in the truck are following and forgets to keep his eye on the cat and loses him. He slows, searches every trashy nook and cranny. The dog thing's totally out of control. They're flinging themselves against chain link like this is a dog prison movie, and this is their big chance to bust out.

Maybe it's the cat shit smell. He remembers they like that, like a fucking delicacy. He might have his problems, but he doesn't eat cat shit.

Then he finally spots Scratch *way* down the next block—standing there, waiting for him to catch up, twitching his tail like *I haven't got all day*. This is no ordinary cat. This is a devil cat. That was one of Michael's cards, The Devil. He was thinking the goat in the middle of the card looked fairly stupid. Naturally, the next words out of Kristi's mouth, tapping a finger on the goat? "That's you, Michael: You make things happen; you don't know when to quit; you lower your head and charge." He floors it, tires squeal, the sound of action, though it's a little hard to hear over the barking and the hole in the muffler and his own cries of terror.

He again barely misses the panel truck, which has circled the block to catch up with his sorry ass. The driver has to hang his head out the window to see because the inside of the windshield is splattered with a large coffee, looks like two creams, steaming hot. This time one of their ladders breaks free of old bungies and goes flying overhead, but Michael has his own problems with physics. He hits the alley entrance with too much front bumper—shitty shocks—and goes airborne, pancakes, fishtails, slaloms through a gauntlet of super cans and almost doesn't see the heap of a pickup truck stopped in the alley, a black man wrestling an old air conditioner into the back. He slams on the brakes and skids to a stop a couple of feet short of his tailgate. The cat box and its contents slam into the back of the driver's seat. There's cat litter all over the dashboard. There's cat litter in Michael's hair. Now it *really* smells like cat shit and cat piss and whatever the chemical crap is they put in kitty litter so that the shit doesn't stink. Doesn't work, whatever it is. Piney cat shit. Woodsy cat piss. Cats stink way worse than dogs. Male cats worst of all. Male devil cats have made a practice of it. What is that? *Garlic*?

He shuts off the ignition, and it gets a lot quieter (except for the barking dogs). He lost the last of the muffler back there somewhere. Don't look back, right? The rearview's caked with pissy cat litter anyway.

He rolls down his window and sticks his head out, takes a deep breath. The black man is leaning over, looking into the car. He has a faint smile on his face, like he's reconstructing why there's a cat turd stuck to the inside of the windshield, and he's trying not to laugh. "Damn!" he says laughing, "When I seen you coming, I thought you had a *bear* in the car!" He laughs some more. Leans in to get a better look at the mannequin with a teddy bear head sitting in the back seat. *Don't ask me what it's doing there. It's not a cat. It's not my future.*

The windshield turd loses its grip, its adhesive powers, whatever, and falls in Michael's lap. He ignores it. "Did you see a black and white cat come through here?"

The man manages to stifle his laughter and points at the garage Michael's stopped in front of. "The cat, he ran in there." The garage door isn't quite closed, stopped in its descent by a brick in the corner. The man laughs again. "I coulda *sworn* you had a bear in there. Good luck with the cat. Lady that lives here, she's real nice. She'll help you out. Enjoy your journey!" He gets in his truck and drives down the alley, giving him a friendly wave out the window as he lets his laughter loose.

Enjoy his *journey*? Right. He's having a rollicking good time. He gets out of the car and wiggles the front of his pants, shakes and shimmies trying to get the cat turd to fall off. They're nice pants. Neverwrinkle khakis. He'd just bought them before he went to the Tree, changed out of his bloody ones while they were still there waiting for the paramedics to load Kristi up.

He stuck by Elissa as the paramedic bandaged up her hands, thinking, hoping it's *her*, the woman Kristi told him about. The beautiful woman with freckles he'll remember he's seen before. That day Danny kept him waiting last summer, right after Kristi read his cards. Danny walked her out to her car. Kristi told Michael, "Keep bugging the Soothsayer till he gives you an answer. That will get things moving. Listen carefully to what he says. Cause even though he won't believe it himself, it will come true."

Kitty litter rains down from his hair, but the pants turd hangs tight. He jumps up and down. It slides. He leaps higher, shakes his trousers furiously, keeps hopping, the turd falls free—he's triumphant!—and he lands on it. New running shoes. Now he's got a waffle sole full of cat shit, and he just can't deal with it right now. He has to deal with the shitter. On his own. He doubts the lady who lives here would even talk to someone who looks and smells like him. Besides. Kristi was clear on this point. The cat's on him. His mission. How hard can that be? he thought.

He gets on his hands and knees. How careful do you have to be with khakis that have a shit stripe down the front? He tries to see under the garage door, but all he can see are two sets of tires, two parked cars, no cat. He gets his hands under the door and lifts, but it won't budge. There's a side door with a window, which is why he can see anything. He opens the high wooden gate and goes to the door, presses his face against the glass, and he can just make out in the gloom, the object of his quest—Scratch on the hood of a Mini licking his ass.

Kristi's instructions were minimal. She wanted to keep things simple, she explained, for a simple guy like him: "When you get to a door, open it. If you have the key, fine, if you don't, open it anyway. The last door, you'll need the help of the woman I told you about. Think you can remember that? Follow the cat. Open the doors." She made him repeat it. He felt like an idiot, like a child. "There's a reason for that," Kristi told him.

He tries the knob. Locked. He starts to return to the alley to find something to use as a tool, though he's not very good with tools, when he hears the rattling sound of a rapidly approaching vehicle bearing ladders, and freezes in his tracks. It's the panel truck full of painters. He can't return to the alley.

He's only wearing a Tree of Life t-shirt because he gave his other one to Elissa who *has* to be the woman Kristi told him about. Not just because she's so beautiful. He would've never had the nerve to speak to her if it hadn't been for his cards. She's so together. She inspires confidence. For all his ideas, he really doesn't have a whole lot of confidence. What the hell?

He takes off his t-shirt, wraps it around his fist and slugs the glass. Only it's not glass. It's some kind of plastic, and his fist just bounces off and turns him around so he steps back into the hole left in the brick walkway when the brick jamming the garage door was pried loose by person or elf unknown. He falls on his butt and bangs his head against the stockade fence on the other side of the walk. It's a big garage, the walkway narrow.

The panel truck has stopped. There are several voices speaking Spanish, sounding about as happy with Michael as the dogs.

He picks himself up, dusts himself off, put his shirt back on, aims his shoulder (that's spent *some* time at the gym) at the door, and charges, bounces, charges, bounces, charges, pops through the plastic window and flies into the garage, skidding across the hood of the Mini and flopping over onto his back onto a Saab, and for a moment he sees stars. The world is upside down. He's breathless. That was the title of one of those movies he slept through. Then he tried to watch it before the midterm and watched the wrong one. The professor read his essay answer to the class, and not in a good way.

He hears a meow, but he can't tell where it's coming from. He rolls over, falls off the hood of the Saab onto concrete. Another meow. He stumbles to his feet, goes back to the door, finds the light switch and turns it on. The doorframe and the deadbolt are completely intact. The window is still in one piece. The hood of the Mini doesn't look so good.

Another meow.

The cat's inside the Mini. The window's open a little. It doesn't look like enough—Michael's arm won't fit—but there's the devil cat, sitting inside. He's almost afraid to try the door, knows what will happen. The door will be locked, and he'll have to blow it up or cut the top off or something, and the cat will run out anyway, and who knows what fuck-all else. Fine. He opens the driver door. He gets in. The cat just sits there in the passenger seat. Smiling at him.

No keys, just the car. He looks in the tiny backseat, and there's a rifle and a funky old coat with a box of bullets in the pocket. This can't be good. Every breath he takes smells like cat shit. He shakes his head in frustration. Cat litter rains down on the nice leather upholstery. He tries to think it through. He obviously needs to get the cat back into his carrier if he's to have any hope of returning him to the hospital. Maybe wrap him in the funky coat? He starts to pick him up but gets a warning low moan and backs off.

"Don't think," Kristi said. "Just follow the cat and open the doors." Okay, he's followed the fucking cat. Now what? He opens the Mini door again. Nothing. Reaches across Scratch to open the passenger door. Scratch watches him with amusement. Michael gets out of the Mini and opens the Saab's doors. Its alarm starts going off. Of course. He spots the manual controls for the garage door opener in the corner where the brick is still wedged. Does he feel like an idiot? Not a good time to ask. He strides purposefully to the open button and pushes it.

His hands reach for the sky as the door rises without even being told. It's all those guns pointed at him, the flashing blue lights. The guys in the panel truck must've vanished when the cops showed up. *Habla español* to cops was not a good idea these days, even if you were in the right. The cat was in the Mini, Michael explains as they cuff him. He was just trying to get the cat. "He's my responsibility!"

Cat? What cat?

He's not surprised. The cat can obviously take care of himself.

He took Spanish in school—you had to—but he wasn't very good at it. All the way to the jail, he tries to remember a word the guys in the alley kept using besides all the words they never used in Spanish class. He's sure he's heard it before. While he's waiting in a cell with a bunch of other guys who mostly look Mexican or whatever, he asks what the word means.

"*¿Bruja?*" he asks.

"Means witch," he's told.

Jail is one door after another. He figures the one out is the one he's going to need help with. At first he's fairly terrified, but everyone gives him his space. He's not sure if that's because he was asking about *brujas* or because of the way, even after they took away his shoes and clothes and he showered, he still smells like a cat box. He wonders if there's such a thing as kitty litter lung. He's never spent a night in jail before, though he's probably seen way too many prison movies. He reassure himself with Kristi's words, *Some guys don't want it bad enough. That's not your problem.*

He's suffering for his art. That's got to pay off, right? He's waiting for Elissa to show up and set him free, so he can tell her his ideas and change both their lives forever. At least according to his *bruja* Kristi who hasn't been wrong about anything yet, though they never discussed cat box.

Except maybe getting stabbed by Danny's ex, finding herself at death's door. Did she plan on that?

He pictures it as a long shot, a simple door, Kristi in the threshold looking good, except for the wound. *Death's Door*. It could be like a whole series. *Six Feet Under* with magic.

Starring Elissa.

Chapter Seventeen

Because **I'm Not Like Everybody Else**

Farewell, farewell! but this I tell
To thee, thou Wedding-Guest!
He prayeth well, who loveth well
Both man and bird and beast.

He prayeth best, who loveth best
All things both great and small;
For the dear God who loveth us,
He made and loveth all.
—Samuel Taylor Coleridge, *The Rime of the Ancient Mariner*

I'm not dead. I'm standing at a crossroads, all directions dissolving into mist. Kind of a tip-off that not everything's what it seems, because I'm not standing anywhere. The only crossroads are corridors. The end of the road. There are dying people everywhere. Some are trying not to. That would include me. I'm over there lying in bed hooked up to all that beeping, blinking apparatus. I dated a hardware geek for a while until I started to feel like a sexbot, but these guys make him look like a Luddite.

Stable for the moment, I heard the cute young doctor say. There's a first time for everything, right? As you can see, I haven't lost my sense of humor. I've lost a lot of blood and mind, but I'm so full of joy juice the universe is fairly hilarious. Same as it ever was.

"This is where I died," El's mom Cindy says, standing beside me. El must get it from the dad who split, because Cindy isn't much taller than me—no more than four or five inches. She looks good except for that finished look the dead get. Meeting ghosts isn't particularly scary, but it doesn't make you eager to be one either. All the longing's gone, the story done. In Cindy's case, that story would be El—beginning, middle, end. It was as if, when her husband left, everything up till then became a fatalistic flashback—the exposition of her personal doom.

At least that's what me and El came up with one night stoned as shit supposedly studying for a narrative theory class I'd talked El into taking with me. I can't remember which one started using Cindy as an example of something. Pathos maybe. There was no happily-ever-after for Cindy—except through El—her beautiful girl, fairy princess, beauty queen, college girl—a Whole New Life ahead of her.

Back then we didn't know how it ended: El marries the evil Carl troll, and Cindy dies as fast as she can of what sure looked like a broken heart, whatever spin the doctors put on it. What a load for El to bear. The Tragedy of Mom. She had to let it go. Least I thought so. Or maybe I'm a selfish little bitch, and nothing's worth what I just put El through. It's hard to know the truth, and working magic makes it even harder. I hope El doesn't hate me. I hope she's okay. I hope she's fantastic. I love El. I really do, despite any appearances to the contrary.

Cindy is inspecting the paraphernalia surrounding the unconscious me, like she's trying to figure it out, whether to make sure it's working okay or to fuck it up is hard to say. I always liked El's mom, wanted her to like me back. Didn't happen. That's what happens when your kid makes friends with a monster, but maybe she feels different now that she's a ghost. "Why are you here?" I ask.

Cindy doesn't bother looking away from her examination of the dying patient. "The goddess sent me. She says to tell you you're done— you've pleased her. You can move on. I guess that means you can quit fucking with my little girl now."

"She's not a little girl. She's six-one." We measured in the dorm room. Fourteen inches separated us. I stood on a chair, made the mark, told her, standing in front of her before the mirror. *Between us, we control a lot of critical airspace.* We had a great laugh, which didn't make it any less true.

Cindy turns and glares at me. "Five-eleven." Six or over was too tall in Cindy's book. The beauty contestant was five-eleven, if anyone asked. Don't say the word basketball. Then she nagged the poor girl not to slump. Which is it? How tall was she supposed to be?

"Six. She's going to be okay. I promise."

"So I hear. Do you think you had to put her through all this to lend a hand?"

"That was the deal."

"You and your deals."

"Yeah." I study the form in the corner, *me*, the patient etherized upon a table, though they don't use ether anymore, and with this stuff I'm on mermaids will call to you 24/7 if that's where your mind goes. I can't tell which is breathing—the machine or me. "Me and my deals. Am I dead? Is that why you're here?"

"No. You're supposedly going to wake up soon. Dawn." She sounds disappointed, the waste of a perfectly good sunrise. She runs her ghostly fingers along my gauze-swaddled arm, looks me in the eye, just like she used to the few times we met, like *You don't scare me*, like that's what I wanted, somebody else afraid of me. Like my own mom. "The surgeons stripped away that wretched tattoo, flayed your flesh. I watched them do it." Ghosts don't have fun, but this was close for Cindy, a peak experience in a featureless plain, perhaps worth her journey here to where her own life ended.

"It was the only way to release Leslie."

214

"Good riddance to both." Cindy knew all about Leslie. He called her up when he was at his craziest, looking for me, to whom he later confessed the call to demonstrate his pitiable desperation, as if I would somehow find that attractive. Leslie told Cindy the whole story of the tattoo and the magic, like Cindy could give a fuck about *Christabel*. The man was loony, made so by the weird runt who claimed to be her little girl's best friend. Cindy never told El she knew about Leslie, waiting to see if El would tell her. Things were so much simpler between me and my mom. I never told her anything, and Mom didn't want to know, always wished she could forget what she did know. She totally freaked when I tried to talk to her about feeling different from the family, from everybody. *What are you suggesting!* she said and stalked off to her bedroom. I wasn't suggesting anything. I was looking for suggestions.

But Cindy's not like that. Cindy, in my book, is a great mom. She loves her girl like nobody's business. "I'll miss the tat," I tell her. "I loved having a poem on my arm—the British Romantics changed my life, best class I ever took despite the bad ending. Leslie's okay. He's changed."

"Nobody changes."

"Everybody does."

This exchange of certainties, delivered with equal certainty on both sides, makes Cindy smile, like that says it all. "Was Leslie the start of all this?" She passes her hand though my shattered chest to touch my heart, to caress it, to hold it beating in her palm like a wounded dove, gentle but firm. Even dead, she's got strong hands from cleaning other peoples' houses, from holding her daughter's hand tight at every hard luck crossroads.

"No. That would be me. I should've just kicked his ass, dropped the class. Instead I had to curse him, teach him a lesson. I didn't exactly have a lesson plan. Ten years on, lesson to self: A curse is a two-way street—No—it's more like a one-way street, and you're going the wrong way, like Captain Ahab chasing after his lost dick. I always wanted to say to him: 'It's just a fucking *leg*. You've still got your heart. Get over it, dude.'" Cindy knows her *Moby*, the Gregory Peck movie anyway.

Right answer apparently. Cindy releases my heart. "I just want to know one thing," she says. "For myself. Since I've come all this way— on a *thankless* errand."

She wouldn't be here, she wants me to know, if the goddess hadn't sent her. Not to watch me *live* anyway, when it could have been other-wise. "Anything."

"Anything? I'm surprised to hear that from you. Always so careful, in your reckless way."

Cindy had my number alright, but every warning she ever gave El about me only seemed to make us closer, like any friend that rattled Mom so bad must be the friend for her. "I figure I owe you." *I stole your child. Someone had to. You would've loved each other to death.*

"Did you make her marry that wretched man?"

"God, no!"

"But you *could* have stopped her. She listens to you for some rea-son. I know she went to you for advice."

So that was it, what was stuck in Cindy's craw. She blames me for Carl. Some decisions you have to stick by if you're going to move on, make the next decision without it being all about how you fucked up the last time you made a tough call. "I read her cards on the Carl question. They were clear as day. They said it would be awful, that she would hate herself, *but* that she would come out the other side this whole new wonderful person who would live a life beyond her wildest dreams— because face it, El's dreams weren't for shit. You want to tell me what I was supposed to do with that knowledge, *Mom*? Sure, I could've talked her out of it. But here's the deal: She wanted it—to cash in her chips. That's the only way she was going to find out what they were worth."

"Did you tell her all this?"

"Of course not. Untold suffering and heartache? What do you think she would've done? She'd be living with you, looking after you, watching reruns on a motel TV. How could I deny her?"

"She trusted you."

"To decide for her."

There's nothing finished about Cindy's anger. There's nothing ghostly about her fierce glare. "Just who do you think you are to make decisions like that?"

"That's what I keep asking, but nobody's got a straight answer. The Girl from Brazil, Mars, or Faeryland—nobody's saying. How about Elf? That's simple. I like the organization. Go Gaia all the way. *Changeling*, okay? Which means I don't fucking know, and I got tired of figuring it out a long time ago, but I know—freakshow that I am—I can do better than Halloween parties on the James for the living dead. I thought I'd spread my cards on the banks of the Potomac. The place can use a little changeling you can believe in, don't you think? Because let me tell you something, when you know what's coming, you have decisions to make whether you want them or not. Not every Carl's nice enough to drown himself in the bay."

"I figured you were responsible for that."

"I can't take complete credit for that one. I don't kill people."

"Against your principles?"

"No. So far I haven't needed to. I'd kill all the Carls if it would save the world."

She snorts, quite a display of emotion for the dead. "Is that what you're doing—saving the world?"

"Trying. It's not easy to save a suicide."

"I understand why Elissa likes you so much."

"That's the nicest thing you've ever said to me."

"I meant that Elissa always went for the crazy ones, cracking jokes, telling lies."

"Somebody has to. Don't they?"

A ghostly smile. Maybe she does like me just a little tiny bit, just enough, to let me live. I didn't tell Danny about Cindy, that I had three chances to die—everything's in threes with the triple goddess—duh. It's a deity thing. You wouldn't understand. No use putting Danny through that weirdness—knowing a ghost killed his true love might not be a comfort graveside or a big help moving on.

Even monsters and ghosts have to move on.

But he doesn't have to grieve for me just yet, because I'm alive and plan to stay that way for the foreseeable future, which between me and Danny is fairly fantastically foreseeable. As foreseeable as it needs to be. Here and now will be love and bliss. In a few moments, zonked as I am, Danny and El—the two people I love most in the whole chaotic universe—will come to my bedside and forgive me, will be glad I'm alive. Not everybody can say that at the end of the day. I'm not an easy changeling to love. But these two love me like I'm away in a manger, no crib for a bed. I love the baby Jesus. I really do. Not everybody's into him the same way. But we have this in common, besides our mysterious origins: I love everybody—even if I'm not like everybody—*because* I'm not like everybody.

I don't regret that choice, nor where I've ended up. As for all the shit I put the world through in between, it was no picnic for me either. Doesn't matter *what* I am. Today I feel like an alien, but that's probably just because a hospital is sort of like a spaceship on TV. Some days are mutation days. I liked android for a while. Whatever. The Changeling motto: love everyone, be whoever you are, don't expect that not to change. Not that I'm perfect, but I'm getting pretty good at Changeling.

I even love crazy Nina. And she is crazy. She really is. It's the meds. She's been on them *way* too long, and the abrupt withdrawal combined with lots of caffeine and alcohol has produced a neurological train wreck of monumental proportions. Did Nina mention she was shit-faced when she flushed her meds? Add the wine at the museum. A flagon of heartache.

Soon—the timing's fuzzy, six months or so—there will be a big nasty scandal about the long term effects of this class of drugs, systematically suppressed by some pharmaceutical giants—congressmen and regulators in every pocket—for years and years. I have this from a big pharma wife with a lovely place on the James just downstream from Lucinda. But even a couple of months will be too late for Nina. She needs to get off that shit *now*, before she goes totally around the bend.

This being a hospital, the place is full of ghosts, but none of them but Cindy pay me any mind, figuring I'm one of them. I've never been that good at the astral projection thing, but it's sort of like riding a bicycle. Once you're outside your body, even at death's door, you get the feel of how it's done. My body's not such a great place to be at the moment anyway. Nina had a lifetime of rage to uncork. She didn't hold back. She missed my heart. Luck or second thoughts, I don't need to know. Thank you, goddess. For what it's worth, the girl Nina slugged in 8th grade? Totally had it coming. Punched Nina in the stomach and called her a cunt. Nina forgot about her braces, forgot the girl was the bishop's daughter. If you look real close you can see the scars on Nina's knuckles. She must've had a mean right hook.

Nina's in a stupor, in restraints, with nothing but an acoustical tile ceiling to stare at. Given her current state of mind, that's like wrapping her up in duct tape with an amphetamine drip. More bound and helpless, the woman doesn't need. She's still mad as hell. Who wouldn't be? Anger's the toxic waste of the endocrine system. It takes awhile to recover. But she *will* recover. She sees me floating above her but doesn't speak right away, hoping the bitch is just a hallucination.

"Does this mean I killed you?" she finally asks when it becomes apparent I'm not going anywhere. Nina's voice is a blurry croak.

"No. This means you didn't."

"Tha's good. 'Cause I'm not a murd'rer. Don't know what came over me."

"The perfect storm. You're going to feel better. I promise. They're going to retire your meds, recommend some dietary changes. You won't hate everything anymore—even yourself."

"Can I still hate you?"

"Of course."

Nina smiles or tries to. The sedatives she's on don't care for those muscles. "Sounds like a goo' deal."

Nina may or may not remember this conversation. The cop in the corridor hears her babble but doesn't care. Nobody's told him Nina's no longer a suspect in a possible homicide, though one of the nurses says she heard it on the radio. Typical, the cop says. How do you like your coffee? the nurse asks.

Nina's thinking about being alive—whether it's worth it or not. The sedatives don't like those muscles either. "Does Danny hate me?"

"Of course not. He's concerned about you."

Nina snorts. "Know what's worse than hated? Concerned about. Poor sick Nina."

I would explain that poor sick Nina is going away once the balance is restored to her system, but Nina's not ready to hear that, and she's drifting back to oblivion anyway. Instead I check out the iPad with the results of Nina's blood work, left behind by a sleep-deprived resident who's searching for it on the wrong floor, when she should be getting some sleep. She'll find it soon. She's usually not forgetful, very conscientious. She'll check it and act accordingly.

Turns out when you're ethereal, digital's a breeze. A few numbers do the trick. Little red flags to say it's time for Nina to manage her own anger, thank you very much, before organs start failing and psychoses take permanent root.

Nina should be in great shape in time for the class-action lawsuit. There are some serious suing lawyers in Richmond. I know a bunch. They like Halloween too. Parties. Fortunetellers. Remember tobacco? Chump change. Watergate? Just another burglary. Don't ask your doctor, call your lawyer. I wouldn't leave Richmond if she didn't have to. I love Richmond, but I'm needed elsewhere.

I think about visiting Michael in jail—I have high confidence he's there by now—but the Richmond jail's a shithole, and I need to get back to my body anyway. Nobody will get more mileage out of a little suffering than Michael. He'll get more than one movie out of this night and the glorious morning when El releases him from his cell, and they spend the next several days together. Actually, El will make the ideas into movies. To Michael's credit, he doesn't ask for one—a writing credit. To El's credit, she'll give him one anyway.

I find Danny and El asleep in the waiting room, waiting for me to awake, and I'm incredibly moved. Perhaps that's the spark that will keep my heart beating, that they should love me so. I don't wake them yet. I sit down next to Leslie and waits for him to notice me.

You can go now, I tell him, *I'll be fine.*

"What about me? Will I be fine?"

"The curse is lifted. You have your life back." For now at least. I'm not entirely sure Leslie can handle freedom. It's like those drugs Nina's been on. He may have passed the point of no return.

"Thanks for everything," he says in a whisper and rises to his feet, throws back his shoulders and quietly walks away. I watch him disappear down the long corridor and hope I've finally done the right thing by him.

Then I return to my body. When she awakens, it seems to bring the whole place to life in a flurry of activity. It's nice to feel wanted. "Nothing short of a miracle," the surgeon says, and I wonder about the short and long of miracles and magic, how one can tell the difference.

As Danny suspects, there's more to the deal I made than just me and Danny. The goddess wants her planet back, and Danny and I have a role in that. As usual the goddess was sketchy with details. Things are always in flux with her.

But she made it clear: If I could make him fall in love with me, the two of us could change the world. True love was mere prelude. If I could pull that off, I'd have a shot at the species killing the planet—to see if I could make them love it instead. An offer I couldn't refuse, since I was already in love with Danny, and saving the world would finally give me a good enough reason for being born such a freak.

I have a lot to attend to before you see me again. Until then, much love.

PART THREE

Gwen Has a Dream

Gwen's sitting at a card table out by the road. The world is big and flat and dusty, and the road is choked with refugees, all headed one way. She can't see where they're coming from, or where they're going to. None of them look like Gwen. They speak languages she can't understand. They're down to nothing but the strange clothes on their backs. Some carry children. Some of the children are dead. Gwen doesn't know what catastrophe they're refugees from exactly. Does it matter? It's something truly awful. Folks don't live their lives for the big things, it's the little things, some tiny bit of love we'll fight for.

There's them on the road and her in her nice clean clothes at her card table and a big flock of crows perched shoulder to shoulder on the power lines watching, and that's it. It's all on Gwen to help these people.

She sets out cups of water on the table, but no one takes them. She looks in her bag for snacks. She always carries snacks, but there's only the cards, still in the box—the stolen ones living in the back of her underwear drawer for a couple of years before she finally used them. Phyllis, at their high school reunion, did Billy's cards and flirted with him the whole time at a silly carnival party where she was supposed to be the fortuneteller, and he flirted back. Gwen was jealous. Jealousy's an awful thing. She slipped the cards into her bag when Phyllis and Billy were having themselves a big long good-bye hug. Even then Gwen knew Phyllis didn't know what she was doing, that she was just making stuff up for Billy's big blue eyes.

Now she finally takes the cards out of the box and starts shuffling them, and folks start sitting down, and she reads their cards for them. She doesn't know where it comes from. She just knows how to do it. She looks at the pictures and knows what they're saying, talking to the people on this long, hard road. She feels their trouble like it was her own.

They all ask the same thing, and now somehow she understand what they're saying even though she doesn't speak the language, just like she understands what the cards are saying when they were just pictures before. Everyone asks the same question. They want to know how they can keep on, leaving everything they've ever known behind, headed toward what may be nothing but false hope.

Hope is never false, she tells them. It's her one message: Set everything else down you have to, but hold that one close. They move on. That's why she's here by the side of the road, to give the hopeless hope, because going back is not an option. There's here, now, and hope. That's it. The rest is up to the Lord.

Gwen woke from that dream knowing her life's purpose is to read the cards, and she got them out of her dresser drawer and spread them out on the kitchen table till they covered the whole thing, and it's like they were talking to her from the very beginning, showing her the way, leading her out of her misery into some hope of her own, helping other people, working at The Tree. Maybe she needed something after her boy died. She doesn't deny it. Maybe it was all in her head. People didn't complain though—*That crazy woman gave me hope!* She felt good about herself and her calling. Billy too. He was always telling her how proud she made him. She told him the story of stealing Phyllis's cards, and he laughed himself silly. The family was none too happy to have a fortuneteller in their midst, and things were said at Thanksgiving and whatnot, but Billy was always there telling whoever how proud she made him, actually helping folks stead a just talking about it like most folks do. There was always one or two young men in the family calling themselves preachers, and he'd give them the eye. She's not ashamed to say that gave her joy. She loves Jesus, but she never had much use for smug little preacher boys. Her life was grand, and the cards had shown her the way out of the Valley of the Shadow, and she was grateful for the dream that had changed her life.

Then Elissa and Danny showed up, and Gwen excitedly read her cards with her new deck—and her life seemed to shatter. She turned her back on her cards, her calling, cause she didn't like what they had to say. She shunned them, wouldn't have a thing to do with them, and her life ground to a halt. There's only so much wallow in your sorrow a girl can do before even she's tired of it. More alone than ever. Except for Jesus. But the Lord's not exactly what you'd call company.

Now she's been having that dream again. Only this time when she looks in the bag, her old cards aren't there. She listens to the weary tread of the refugees, the crows scolding her to use the new ones. She can't keep the crows out of her head. Seems like there's more than usual hanging around the place, watching what she'll do.

Make Billy proud.

When the Lord gives you work to do, you can't just up and quit.

That's what the dream's telling her this time. She knows it in her bones.

Chapter Eighteen

Surrender To The Magic

All are but parts of one stupendous whole,
Whose body nature is, and God the soul.
> —Alexander Pope, *Essay on Man*

Billy's gone, a couple of years now. It was a blessing by the time he went. There's no reason a good man like that should suffer so. Not that the Lord tells you His business, and Billy was far from perfect, but no one is. It's not their fault. Billy smoked like a house afire. All the boys did. Not all of them are dead before they're sixty. She should've made him quit. He quit drinking for her. Went to those meetings he used to make fun of. Every day was hard for him, but he never broke that promise, even when the soldiers came to the house to tell them David was dead at twenty. Is there any fair in that? For what? Saddam Hussein. Remember him? Man must be chuckling in his grave.

That's when she had the dream and took up the cards. It says somewhere in the Bible that cards are wrong, all kinds of fortunetellers are an "abomination." It says all sorts of things in the Bible. There's no sense chasing after each and every one, when it's a question of whether you believe or you don't. Gwen believes. Like Billy believed in his promise. Even when it was hard, standing around drinking coffee, smoking cigarettes. *You* tell him to quit, if it's so easy, like he hadn't done enough for her, like they hadn't been through Hell together. Always broke, always trying, always there for each other.

Now he's gone. Nothing changes the past. It just goes away. Leaves you changed, like hurricanes tearing up the shorelines, busting up houses like kindling. She probably watches a little too much Weather Channel for her own good. Today it's wildfires in Colorado; she watches all these rich folks' houses burn to the ground. Last week it was tornados where they never had tornados before, Greenland melting into the ocean, choked with plastic and rising. Don't ask about tomorrow. You don't really want to know.

It's just her and Genevieve, twelve, arthritis in her hips and going blind. She and Gertrude moped around on the porch once Billy was gone, started snapping at each other all the time. Gertie got hit by a car out on the highway that never slowed down. Clint, one of the neighbor boys, carried her up the drive, helped Gwen bury her. Gennie mopes around like she can't wait to join her, though she perks up when Clint comes round.

Gwen knows how she feels. This is a lonely life they're living here, but she doesn't know of no place else to go.

She made it through the second Christmas since Billy died okay, when she didn't think she possibly could. Billy loved Christmas, and she loved Billy, they had lots of good times. Then two peculiar things happened right together, though they didn't happen so much as Gwen discovered them. They'd been happening all along. She just wasn't paying attention.

She and Gennie watch a whole lot of TV, too much probably. They were watching *Entertainment Tonight* when the woman who showed up that day with Danny, Elissa Fenice, is on the TV, but she's with some other young man who's very handsome but lets her do all the talking. Next day, they're on *Ellen*—Gwen likes her—and they show a couple of scenes from their movie. One's a silly car chase through an alley after a cat, but the other one's really good. Elissa is standing in front of some fancy place picking up dog shit, telling off her useless coworker—the handsome guy—that it's bad enough picking up rich people's dogs' shit for them without picking up her shit and his shit too. She must be holding a five-pound bag in each hand. He doesn't dare backtalk her unless he wants a bag of shit upside the head. Naturally, he falls in love with her. She's terrific.

Gwen can't stop laughing, and then she's crying too. Cause that's her and Billy and everybody really—that's what we do. We pick up shit and try to love each other, even those who don't. She finally lets it all go and cries her eyes out until Genny starts whimpering and licking on her. But she's okay. She's a whole lot better. She was crying over the love she lost, remembering all the love she had. She might never of had that. People go their whole lives without that kind of love. Everybody told her Billy was no good, that he'd let her down. Turns out, everybody but Billy let her down—or that's what she'd been thinking at the end of this road, feeling sorry for herself. Boo-hoo, as Kristi would say.

The second thing was when she discovered after all this time that the reason she didn't lose her house wasn't some insurance Billy supposedly had—which never did sound like Billy in the least. It was Kristi. Serena told her. She and Terry drove out, showed her pictures of their honeymoon on their iPad like that was supposed to cheer her up, which it did in a way, having folks care like that. They went to Thailand, rode on elephants. She never thought much of Terry, but something had changed about him. He didn't seem so useless anymore. He was awful good to Serena.

She asked how Danny was doing, since she'd just seen that same scene on *Ellen* and a few times since on *Good Morning America* and *The Daily Show*. They did a big long story about her on *60 Minutes*. Elissa's a star. She's going to be on *Today* day after tomorrow for another new movie. Gwen saw something like that in the woman's cards, but that had been kind of overshadowed by what else she saw—Elissa's husband dead, Gwen's husband dying—nothing about Danny who brought her to the house, who was pretending to be her boyfriend, but any fool could see his heart wasn't in it no matter how beautiful she was—so Gwen was curious what became of Danny in all that. She never could figure out why he'd driven out here in the first place. It was so unlike him.

Serena said it was complicated. She tried to explain. It was all about Kristi. That's when she let it slip that Kristi had stopped the foreclosure on Gwen's place, paid off the note. Kristi told her about it when Serena was worried about Gwen keeping a roof over her head with Billy gone. The letter from the insurance company that came with the cashier's check, she told Gwen, had to be a phony. She looked it up after Serena left. There's no such company. Serena told her Kristi and Danny call themselves "Consultants" in Washington. Kristi's retired the gypsy dresses. She's completely recovered from the accident, and the happiest she's ever seen her. Danny too. They adore each other.

Gwen laughed out loud at that notion. "Danny happy? Imagine that. I'm so glad. I always liked him." Like everybody else but Danny, she knew Kristi was crazy about him but never could see them together. Danny's so nice, and Kristi could be awful mean sometimes. Clients came crying to Gwen over something Kristi told them more than once, even if she did end up being mostly right most of the time. Now to find out she was responsible for Gwen having a home these last few years is a lot to take in. She doesn't know what to make of Kristi's kindness because she's never known what to make of Kristi.

She's different.

Once, when it was just the two of them at some street fair or other, Gwen started asking a whole lot of questions because she was curious. Kristi's pretty strange, not the hair or clothes or anything or even that tattoo. All sorts of girls have tattoos. There's something in the way she moves, the way she thinks. She's not like anyone Gwen ever met before. Kristi answered her questions for a while, joking around with her, contradicting herself. Finally, she said, "I'm not who you think I am, Gwen—or maybe I am. I don't really know. I'm open to suggestions."

Kristi always sounds like she's just joking around, but you can tell pretty quick when she's serious. She doesn't always let that side of her show. Gwen was touched and flattered. Then Kristi gave her a little Baby Jesus no bigger than your thumb she still carries with her to this day.

But she was still afraid of her. Though she knew Kristi would never hurt her. When angels show up in the Bible, folks are generally afraid. Maybe it's like that. She's not saying Kristi's an angel, and she's not saying she's not. But she's not just another person either.

Finding out she's done Gwen this great kindness has her thinking back, thinking ahead. *Thinking* again. She's been living in a fog. She's got to move on. Folks aren't nice to you just so you can sit down in the road and give up. The Lord helps those who help themselves.

It's not always easy to know what that *is*—the helpful thing.

When she had the dream that got her started, it was to give the hopeless hope.

She took that to be her calling until Elissa came here and changed all that. Gwen told all those folks all those times to have hope, so she could have hers snatched away? No thank you. Hasn't touched the cards since. Just up and quit on Serena, but Serena understood even if she did worry. That's okay. Gwen didn't worry near enough. Just grieved.

Now here she is, rooting around in her bedroom, trying to restore some order to things, because she's let things slide entirely too long, that old dream replaying in her head in an endless loop, when she discovers buried beneath newspapers and laundry, the deck she used to read Elissa's fortune, the one and only time they've ever been used.

An angel climbing through the window couldn't have startled her more. It all comes back, that day—like a burning city over the horizon she's left behind. Her old life.

She takes them out of the box and knows she's been called again to read them. *These* cards. The ones Kristi guided her to. The ones who never lied to her, just broke her heart. She cuts them. They divide at the point where she inserted the card Elissa stamped with her big feet. The Star. She smiles. Of course. You can still see her footprint, like at that Chinese theatre in Hollywood, or is that their hands? She can't remember. Doesn't matter. It's a sign.

She makes coffee and banana bread. The bananas are ripe and ready. She lights a few candles. Gennie curls up under the table at her feet with a contented groan. She leaves the TV going with the sound down, gets inspiration from it. There's a terrible flood somewhere. Folks are helping each other out like they usually do. Kristi said she liked to read cards in the park at rush hour with all the traffic and chaos, that it helped her see more clearly how everything fit together. Gwen's out here in the country. It's almost never silent out here. Tonight it's the cicadas and Gennie snoring and crows cawing back and forth in the field out back.

She practices with the cards until they lose their slickery feel. She predicts an Oscar sweep for *Picking Up* even though all the people on TV who pretend to know about everything say a comedy hasn't got much chance for best actress and best movie, but she might get original screenplay or director or best song—"What Do You See in Me Now?" She wrote and sung it herself. Haunting, one fellow called it. That's about right. You hear it all the time. Gwen hums it to herself. Just lovely. But she's going to win it all according to the cards.

Clint watches the Oscars with Gwen. She's told him what the cards say. When Elissa's accepting like her third Oscar, this one for directing—the darkest of dark horses, a Sundance sensation winning for a comedy—Clint asks how she knew when nobody'd even heard of her. The media has been going nuts about her ever since the Golden Globes. When she wins Best Picture, she has to stand there and weep waiting for the applause to die down before she can speak.

Gwen tells Clint, "I know her. I read her cards at that very table. This was all in her cards."

Clint doesn't believe her, of course. He knows her to be crazy, everyone around here does, but he likes her anyway. Maybe he even likes her because she's crazy, different from anyone else around here, like she's somebody out of a story. She does make the best cookies he's ever had. She showed him how to make them himself. He told his mother he saw it on TV.

Gwen talks to him about her son, how he was killed in the war. Clint doesn't remember him, barely remembers Billy. She's pretty mad about the war and all the wars since. She says things Clint knows not to repeat to anyone. He figures if she's crazy, what does it matter anyway if she says crazy things?

Clint's folks would rather he not spend so much time hanging around her house and ask him embarrassing questions like she's going to molest him or something. It's not like that. The boy helped her bury her dog. She cried so hard. They both did. He doesn't care if she's crazy, and she believes the Lord sent him to her in her time of need. Whenever she thinks of just giving up altogether, she thinks of Clint carrying Gertie up the drive, and she keeps on.

Now she's asking him to help with a little carpentry project. She wants to make a sign for down by the road at the entrance to her long driveway. She's already painted it. Big piece of plywood with a big red hand on it. Eyeball in the middle. He's not sure how he's going to explain this to his parents. He hasn't told them about the cards—and how she can tell the future and knows things. So many things he can't help but believe.

When he saw the lumber being delivered, he thought it was for a pen for the stray he brought her. Someone dumped her by the road, a brindle mutt maybe six months old with a sweet face, scrawny and scared. She's playing with Gennie in the yard. Gennie seems like a new dog, like she doesn't hurt anymore. If Clint were allowed to dream, which up till the time he met Gwen, he hadn't done much of, he might just become a veterinarian. He has a special connection with animals.

Gwen asks him what he thinks of Isabel as a name for the brindle, and he says he likes it fine, but he doesn't know if he can help her with the sign.

"Why not?" she asks.

"What does it mean?" he asks, scrunching up his face, preparing for the worst.

"I saw it in a dream, then looked it up on the internet. It means someone lives here who can see the future."

"Nobody sees the future." He says this, even though he's seen her do it, knows she knows stuff going on in his life nobody knows but him. Maybe she's just smart, pays attention. She listens to him when he talks. Folks don't usually do that, definitely not his parents.

She says, "Everyone sees the future, dozens of them. The trick is knowing which one's true. Though mostly it doesn't matter."

"But it matters sometimes?"

"Yes. That's why I need to put the sign down by the road."

"Nobody comes down this road."

"*Exactly* the sort of person who might be glad they come upon me, out here in the middle of nowhere, no direction home. If you find something out here in the middle of nowhere, must mean something. Amazon didn't just bring it to your door."

"My parents think you're peculiar."

"I *am* peculiar, don't you think? Believe me—it takes some serious getting used to on this end too. That's why I have responsibilities others don't have."

"Like this weird sign you saw in a dream?"

"Exactly. Somebody out there's looking for it. Maybe a whole lot of somebodies. Don't want them getting lost, wandering around the countryside like a bunch of drunk hunters, do you?" He can't help but smile at that.

The long and short of it is Clint helps her set the posts in the ground and screw the sign to them when they set. Then he never comes back because he's strictly forbidden, once his folks catch a look at that sign, but she has glimpses of him in her dreams. He always notices whenever a car slows and turns down her road—some nobody looking for somebody like Gwen to give them hope. Sometimes they stay for hours. He sees their headlights coming out and wonders how the world looks different to them now that they've talked to her, because he knows *his* world is nothing like it was before. And he wonders every time if he'll walk down that road again himself, and knows he will. They have a connection—him and Gwen.

The thing is, when she read his cards—which she must've done a dozen times at least, practicing with the new deck—she told him he was different, special somehow. Gifted is how she put it. Special talents and abilities—magical abilities—but she didn't tell him that, didn't think he was ready for that information. She also saw their fates intertwined, but she didn't tell him that either. Sounds way too creepy to say such a thing to a child. Sometimes in the woods near her place, he'll come across Isabel and Genevieve and walk with them awhile, and it's like they're telling him everything's okay with her. Everything will be okay with him too. Sometimes at night after one of these walks, crows fly through his dreams and call to him. "Welcome," they say. "Welcome." Just like they did not so long ago, to Gwen.

Tonight, he'll be awakened by a small caravan of limousines coming down the road bearing a famous movie star for her second reading at this dining room table. It's easy to imagine that this is why she's returned to the cards, why she's still using those same cards, to read again for Elissa—not the movie star but Kristi's best friend. She's gone to the trouble to learn a bit about her past and the husband who drowned. Gwen was too hard on her, had no right to judge. She took out her rage on the messenger, because it was in her cards she first saw Billy's death. Her killing a husband she didn't want, while Gwen was losing one she adored was just too much for her. Gwen hated God. Hated everyone. She's made her peace with God. She's different now. You got to keep moving on—back to what God put her on this Earth for, which certainly isn't feeling sorry for herself. When she found these cards everything started to change, come back to life.

She sees Elissa on TV a lot. Gwen loves her movies. Likes her. She seems like a genuinely nice person. When she won all those awards, Gwen cried for her like she was her own daughter.

So when she called and said she wanted to have her cards read again, Gwen said yes without really giving it much thought. She liked her on the phone. She was real genuine. But she's almost cancelled a dozen times since. That was the worst day of her life—the last time she was here—and Gwen didn't want to sit across the table from *that* Elissa ever again.

She was worried over nothing. Elissa's as nice as she is on television, a different woman from when she was here before—confident, not beaten down, real positive. Michael, who Gwen saw on the Oscars, is with her, and he's just as nice as she is. They're a sweet couple. The other cars are security they tell her. There have been death threats.

"Is that why you wanted your cards read?" Gwen asks.

Elissa laughs off the idea. "Oh no. There are always death threats and love letters—sometimes from the same people. I want to know what Kris is up to. It's something big. I know her. You don't almost get yourself killed just to get a guy. There's something more at stake. She pretty much made my dreams come true, Michael's too. And Leslie's. The surgeons stripped off her tat, setting him free. I know Kris. She doesn't pay a price like that, work all this incredible magic, just to be nice."

Gwen is silent.

"I was surprised to hear you've started reading cards again. You're getting quite a reputation: Michael and I heard about you at a party in LA. How did that happen? How's it going? Do you have abilities you didn't know you had before? Do they possibly have anything at all to do with Kris?"

Gwen hasn't wanted to believe it, wanting to believe in her old powers, but they were nothing compared to what she sees now—with these cards Kristi practically placed in her hands, under this roof, courtesy of Kristi, along with the baby Jesus Gwen keeps with the cards. What *doesn't* have to do with her? "You're saying Kristi worked magic on me."

"On you, for you, for a higher purpose—I don't know, but when people on the other side of the country are sharing the GPS coordinates of a plywood sign by a gravel road, I smell Kris all over it. Not just you, all of us—me, Danny, Michael."

"Who's this handsome young rascal?" Michael asks, nodding toward the threshold where Clint stands transfixed by Elissa in Gwen's parlor. Gwen's a fan; Clint worships. Elissa gives him a big smile.

236

Gwen says, "Come on in, Clint. This is Elissa and Michael. I was just about to do a reading. Maybe you'd like to sit down over there next to Elissa?"

She doesn't have to ask twice. She doesn't ask if his parents know he's here. They don't. Now that he's witnessed Gwen's most outlandish claim to be true—that she has indeed read the cards of a goddess—then the whole crazy business might be too, including the parts about himself. No telling how long he was standing in that doorway before Michael thought to announce him.

"So your question is about Kristi's future? Her intentions?" Gwen asks Elissa.

She nods her head. "As her best friend."

"Has she been in touch?"

"Sporadically, pithy texts and Instagram and so on, but nothing real. We're both busy all the time and difficult to get ahold of for long stretches. But Kris and I, we're practically joined at the hip. Something's up. I know it."

"What about you?" Gwen asks Michael. "Do you have a stake in this question?"

Michael doesn't hesitate. "She straightened me out and changed my life on so many levels I can't begin to comprehend them yet, so I'd have to say yes. She has powers. Serious powers. Basically, I'm in it strictly for the action movie ideas." He cracks a smile, and Gwen realizes he's joking, about the movie ideas anyway.

"He's awful," Elissa says, laughing, giving him a playful nudge with her shoulder. They remind Gwen of her and Billy when they were young. She's so glad.

"Who shall shuffle?" Gwen looks from Elissa to Michael and back again. The idea of doing Kristi's cards is a bit intimidating, presumptuous even. They hesitate.

Clint pipes up, "I will," even though he has only a vague idea of who Kristi is—some weird woman Gwen used to work with. He's been tuned into the conversation like he's trying to memorize every word. Lord knows what he heard of what Elissa was saying. He helped plant the sign in question at an obscure crossroads, and it shook his world hard, and maybe he'd like some answers himself. She couldn't have raised the sign without him. He showed up out of nowhere with her dead dog in his arms and saved her life. The magic happens for a reason. Maybe he's beginning to think so too.

Gwen hands him the cards.

He smiles, squares his shoulders, and concentrates on his shuffle, as if the truth depends upon it, feeling the power in his hands. A certain taut, little wrought up way he has about him loosens and drops away like a shriveled up skin. He's finally surrendered to the magic. It's been tugging at him since he could crawl, chasing the old dog around the kitchen, sleeping with the kittens. He shuffles three times.

He hands the deck over solemnly. They're ready. Gwen can't imagine a better channel for the truth in all the world than Clint. He'll meet Kristi before too long. She's in the air. Behind everything. It's like she's summoned them together.

Gwen lays the cards down and studies them a moment. They all are in a tight circle around the table. The dogs thump their tails on the floor, and Gwen sees the whole thing: "Three men are going to visit her. One of them's already on his way. That'll start the ball rolling for a cascading series of events, profound change." She points out the three cards she sees as three men. One of them, Prince of Wands, is Clint himself. He'll meet with Kristi in a forest and work magic, but Gwen doesn't tell him just yet. It's a ways off.

Elissa leans forward, points at The Hierophant, the one in transit, and says, "I know who that is from Kris's readings of herself where he shows up all the time. That's Leslie." She looks up at Gwen. "Isn't it?"

"It is. I would say she's expecting him."

"I thought he was free," Michael says. Elissa told Michael the story, poor miserable fuck. Be careful what you wish for, though wishing's done all right by Michael.

Clint speaks up again. He's been studying the card with great care. "He's faithful," he says. "To her." The card shows a priestly figure. In the foreground stands the object of his devotion, a diminutive goddess, Clint's finger pointing from above. *Her.* They all know who she is, though not, as she would say, what she is.

"What else do you see?" Gwen asks Clint.

"That's you," he says to Gwen, pointing to the Empress at the crossroads of the spread.

"So it is," she says. "I believe Kristi wanted this reading to happen, for us all to meet, because we're all a part of it, for what comes next."

"What's that?" Elissa asks.

"I know," Michael says, sounding surprised that he should know something they don't. "It's what she said all along, what she told me it was all about. Saving the planet. She called it a Hail Mary, whatever that is." He points at the spread. "Do you see me in there?" he asks wistfully, glancing back and forth between Clint and Gwen.

Gwen smiles. He wants to be included, poor dear. It must be hard to be married to a star like Elissa. "Right here," Gwen assures him, pointing to the Knight of Disks. "In the near future. On business."

"But I make movies. Or think them up anyway."

"Then perhaps Kristi has an idea for a movie." As Gwen says this, she knows it's true and something more. She looks at Elissa. "She wants you to write it, star in it."

Elissa laughs out loud. "That's Kris! She can't just ask? She want songs too?"

"I do!" Clint says, and they all laugh, the dogs thumping their tails on the floor, and they all know they're part of something as big as the world—and as wonderful and fragile.

Chapter Nineteen

Two. Fucking. Seconds.

Alone, alone, all, all alone,
Alone on a wide wide sea!
And never a saint took pity on
My soul in agony.
> — Samuel Taylor Coleridge, *The Rime of the Ancient Mariner*

Riding up to DC on the Greyhound, gives Leslie the chance to reflect on his life since Kristi, since his magical transformation. How many people can say that, contenting themselves with reading stories about it or self-help books on how to transform yourself "as if by magic." Magic isn't an "as if" kind of thing turns out. They're not the same at all. Like a Christian reading and rereading the Gospels, he delights in it, the gruesome and all, it's not like looking at before photos thinking *I did that*. It's more like *She did that—and I'll never be the same*. And that inevitably leads to the same question that must've haunted the disciples, Paul, the whole crazy bunch of original Christians, *Why me? What purpose does she have for me?*

Kristi talks as if he had this wonderful life before he met her and Elissa, when really, nothing could be further from the truth. He was dead and embalmed when he met them, a burned out Romantics Professor in a dwindling marriage. Is there anything more pathetic? The literature was just as magical as it had ever been; of that he never doubted. He'd lost the ability to respond, the eyes to see, the ears to hear, the heart to feel. He didn't give a fuck. Kids gone hither and yon, wife who didn't give a fuck either. Nothing to keep him going but habit and conditioning. How had he become so foolish and ordinary? He even imagined himself becoming a dean, one of that bloated tribe he was fond of loathing. While he lived in fear that one of the young women he'd preyed upon over the years might come forward and destroy him as had happened recently to two of his former colleagues. Pathetic.

And then there they were—the two of them—sitting side by side in a seminar Leslie had fully intended to teach once again on autopilot. Nowadays, he could just put the jokes up on Blackboard along with a few hapless great poems and let them screen babble about it and be done with it. This was face-to-face in a small seminar room fashioned from a century old posh rowhouse, like something out of the poems they would be reading. This would've been the dining room. There was an electrified chandelier hanging above them, thirteen counting himself in swivel chairs crammed around a plastic wood-grained slab, totally out of character with the room's aesthetic. The rich who used to live here took their fine furniture with them, and now it was furnished by the state. Still, it was effective when Leslie read from Mary Shelley's introduction to *Frankenstein* with the lights dimmed down to a buzzing hum. The carpet smelled a bit like a graveyard.

Elissa, the stunning beauty, grabbed Leslie's attention first. She sat next to the empty chair at the head of the table students always leave vacant for the professor, so she was sitting at his right hand. He would've had to swivel his back to her not to have her in his peripheral vision as he tried to call the roll without seeming to notice anything special, but everyone knew the Beauty's beauty was not lost on the prof.

And then when he began talking to the class, looking around, making eye contact with each one—not always easy around a conference table— there was Kristi beside Elissa, looking at him with her incredible eyes and disarming intensity, demanding he make this class worth her precious time, her voracious curiosity, and her agile intelligence—all without speaking a word. He'd never had a student look back at him quite like that, and he'd looked into countless students' eyes by then. None after. He didn't know it at the time, but this class was to be his last, that he was going to be alone. *Alone, alone, all, all alone, /Alone on a wide wide sea!*

Except for her.

He felt himself right then, that very first night, coming back to life, stirring out of the self-involved torpor he'd been wallowing in, accumulating pounds and emptiness—a poor starving swine lamenting that pearls have no flavor.

Kristi was right. Her eyes told the story: He had to make this class good for her. She was someone special, something extraordinary. He knew that, very first day. She soon spoke, of course, smartest person in the room including himself, and he was completely enthralled. He's told her all this, but she insists the magic came later. "You just thought I was hot," she says.

But she's wrong. Tattoo or no tattoo he would've made a fool of himself over her. Over Kristi. It was always about Kristi. Everyone assumes he wrecked his life, as they call it, for a mere Beauty, not that there's a thing about El that's "mere." She attracted him, no denying, but Kristi fascinated him from the moment their eyes met. She credits magic entirely—her enchanting tattoo—completely dismissing her enticing beauty and brilliant mind.

The magic just pushed him over the edge. Gave him what he thought he wanted when he came onto her in his musty office. He lost his mind and most of what he called his so-called life. Then Kristi rebuilt it, piece by piece, into something better. He has faith that this journey too is part of that process. She likes to make you think it's all about revenge, but she already had that. She didn't have to put me back together again. She could have left me lying there, a shattered man. *O Felix Culpa!* His fortunate fall.

He's never doubted her magic—*he* didn't do this—but the ink is gone, the spell supposedly broken, and yet here he is riding the Greyhound to DC. He has an excuse, a rationale, the enthralled always do: The Tree has finally toppled. Serena decided to pack it in after she and Terry married, and Leslie can hardly blame her. He wouldn't have endured so long catering to a finicky, mostly privileged clientele if he'd had to run the place too, herd her passel of clairvoyant cats. But now he's looking for work. He's heard through the grapevine that Kristi and Danny have done quite well for themselves the last couple of years in the psychic trade. Their clients win awards, champion causes, spend a lot of money, and want the best.

He suspects she's doing more than handing out fortunes. If so, maybe he can help. The pen is mightier than the sword, but the hands hold both.

Leslie can hear Kristi dressing them down now, telling them they need to write some checks a whole lot bigger than they write her to restore the dying planet. She can't wait to tax the rich. She funnels it straight into her causes. Mostly environmental. She wasn't a fan of space travel and its promise of some other Earth to go to when we've murdered this one, a new mistress waiting in the wings. There's only one Earth, Kristi says. Don't run out on her. She might not let you come back. She might die, and you could never go back. You think Mars gives a fuck about you?

The Professor is dead. She's taught him everything he knows about his new vocation. To seduce her, he pretended to be a palmist, so she made him what he is today, a palmist extraordinaire. Open your palms, and he will look into your soul, and what he sees there will be, as Kristi likes to say, the real deal. You—as you are right this very moment. The reality of *that,* he'll leave for you to decide. Now is always the most difficult for people. The past and the future distract them, and they have no end of theories about them, built upon little understanding of the present. How could that possibly go wrong?

Before all the craziness with Nina, Leslie read Terry's palms. They were easy. Leslie told Terry who he was, and it was as if he'd unearthed one of his mysterious past lives he trades in—only it was the very one he was living. The man was totally clueless. Something changed in him when he pulled Nina off Kristi, saving her life. The damage has done him good. Leslie knows the feeling. Sometimes having your life ruined isn't such a bad thing.

Kristi will not abide a phony but always gave Terry a pass, she said, because he's so obviously full of shit that only the willfully deceived would ever believe in him. But Leslie suspects Kristi transformed him when he saved her life. "I use people," she admits, "but I always pay them back threefold. It's a goddess thing." Of Terry, she added in his defense, "You *want* to believe him, and that's what most folks are paying for. The Truth just pisses people off. The Truth talks too much."

"I'm putting my money on Love and Terror," she says. "Love for obvious reasons. What else is there to live for? Terror changes folks bigtime. As long as you have Hope. You need that just to take a breath."

She understands people, knows our limitations, forgives us all our fuckups. She gives it off like a radiance or scent—we might all be fools, but she forgives us every one. You can feel it. In the early days, Leslie used to think, *Who are you, you little pixie, to forgive me* my *sins?* It didn't take him long to figure it out.

She's not one of us. She's something else. He knows how that sounds.

Such creatures are a favorite theme of the Romantics—sexy magical monsters of all sorts from mermaids to vampires, lamia and so on—they all pale in comparison to Kristi. It's because she's not one of us that she understands us so well. She loves us, looks after us. No one cares more about the human species than Kristi, but Leslie has no idea why. She's not out to merely forgive us—sin is our problem—but she does think we could use some help evolving before we fuck the planet up beyond repair.

She confided in him early on, one of the few nights they spent together at the river place, that she didn't know what she was, but she *wasn't* one of us, and they had a long talk about all the possibilities from android to angel to alien. She said she had grown rather fond of *Changeling*, and asked him what he thought, and he said it sounded perfect. Of course she could have called herself Grendel's Mother, and he still would have adored her.

The worrisome thing about her being a changeling, swapped for a human child? In most stories of that sort the fairies or elves or whatever prize the human child for various weird and gruesome reasons, but care little about the elf child stand-in left behind. They're left to fend for themselves in a human world where they are thought to be demons, monsters, and worse.

When he told her this Kristi replied, "This time maybe, my mother has something else in mind. Maybe I'm like a magical secret agent."

"What about the human child?"

"Good question. You humans should ask it more often. Maybe she wanted to be a goddess. Live forever, no hassles."

Kristi said she didn't see her parents, grandparents, the older generation in her family. "I weird them out," she said. "*You* are my older generation, Les." Then, that was tragic news. Now, he's more at peace with it. Age does that. Living well. Except for the emptiness Kristi's leaving has left behind, his life is full. The Tree was getting stale, and his lease was up. It's time. Kristi has a job for him, he imagines, hopes. The reason she saved his sorry, pompous ass.

She showed him how to read palms—not the silly business you see in books, like detailed maps of the canals of Mars—but how to wait for the lines to weave a story, to let it coalesce into a vision, a window into the subject's very soul. He thought she was spouting poetic bullshit, and then she read his palms, *showed* him on his fucking palms who he was and who he could become if he'd let go of his stupid ego "for *two fucking seconds*."

"Say it," she coaxed him.

"Say what?"

She rolled her eyes. "Two. Fucking. Seconds."

He did.

That's all it took to change him forever. A lot fell away in those two seconds. And for years to come. Pounds, bullshit—he had a lot to shed.

She left him this gift, this ability. While others see the future, he offers something much more difficult and rare: He sees you in the moment you're in. Open your palms to him, and he knows you as well as you do, probably better, because he looks squarely at what you don't want to see. Usually some part of you cries out to be revealed, and Leslie's the go-between. People thank him. People hate him. It all depends on how you feel about yourself and your purpose on the planet besides arguing about the past and the future.

He's harmless, truly. He never *does* anything with the knowledge, never judges. It just piles up with all the other things he hasn't forgotten but doesn't think about much, like most of his life before Kristi. Every day then was a fresh misery of his own creation. Sometimes he misses teaching, but now he reads the poems he used to merely teach—orate them, let them do their tricks, mean something meaningful, spawning discussions of Negative Capability and Willing Suspension and Spots of Time, and whatever else came to hand to illuminate the *text*. The poems. Now he submits to them, lets them work their magic like a sunrise, a summer breeze. He likes reading palms. It's not unlike teaching. He always taught self-knowledge along the way even when he totally lacked it, one of his many affinities with the Romantics.

He's been living off reading palms and Social Security. He's renting out the river place Kristi gave back to him to an intense young man with writerly ambitions. Leslie couldn't bear to live there. It smells like her. It's filled with her crazy sets. He can't throw them away. They're magical. He put them in the metal shed out back. It's teeming with black widows. Maybe they'll know what to do with all those haunted babies Jesus. If he knows Kristi the widows will be weaving mandalas. If Leslie's tenant can't write poetry in that place, perhaps he should take refuge in an ad agency and make his parents happy.

In DC he's hoping for wealthier palms. All those guys who'd like to do away with Social Security if they could, even they have souls to look after, whatever's left of them, though in his business, it's more often their wives who have time for the likes of Leslie. He's comforting: The white-haired grandpa they never had who understands them, though in his case it's true, but that won't matter if they don't believe in him just a bit, just enough to ponder, to nudge their course in a more honest compassionate direction.

As Kristi taught him, more important than anything he tells them is how he cradles their hands. "You've got their fucking *lives* in your hands, right? Hold their hands like that, and they'll listen to you, otherwise they're already putting together the story they're going to tell their friends about the funny little palmist and the bullshit he fed them, which they will totally ignore. They won't be back and neither will their friends, so whatever infinitesimal chance you had of doing some good is down the drain. You hold their lives in your hands, like little Baby Jesuses."

Sound advice. Often people don't want to believe Leslie, a phony old man. He sometimes wishes he were a phony. Lies are easier to live with than the truth. Learning to live with the truth, however, is learning to live—which is effortless once you get the hang of it. Takes two fucking seconds.

Kristi was only wrong about one thing: She apologized for what she did to him and his once-wonderful life when not a day goes by he doesn't thank the universe he's *not* the man he used to be. He'd have died in his wallow of a heart attack years ago, fat and unhappy, rambling on about Keats' "Ode to Melancholy," leaving a trail of nubile prey behind him, if it hadn't been for her.

Fortunately, Kristi doesn't look out for him just because of guilt, but because no matter who else came along, or whatever happened later, he was the first to believe her, to believe *in* her, to accept her tutelage. That last part was the hardest. What could he, the extinguished professor, possibly have to learn from this pipsqueak less than half his age? Everything turns out.

All of this is to explain why he feels like he can show up on her doorstep unannounced. They have a long history. It's not over yet. He's guessing she already knows he's coming, don't you?

She does. Greets him at the door of her Georgetown row house she shares with Danny with a big hug and "Took you long enough to get here." And before he can shed his coat, says, "Tell me when you *first* had the feeling you just *had* to come to DC." At this point Scratch joins them and drapes himself across her shoulders like he does. Even he seems glad to see Leslie. He's brought along a newcomer, a black-and-white mutt furiously wagging for Leslie's attention, weaving back and forth between them. Kristi introduces her as Cassandra. Leslie kneels and showers her with pets. "C'mon, Les, when did you know?"

He continues to pet the wildly wagging Cassandra. He knows she's asking to check up on the precise timing of her magic. Timing is everything, she says. She can be terribly vain about her powers for one so wise.

He foils her question with the truth: "The moment you left town I knew I would follow." His coat and bag are whisked away by Courtney, a pretty young woman, introduced as "My most able assistant." He's never known Kristi to want assistance before. Enchanting people into doing your bidding isn't *assistance*, is it?

"Come on, Les. You know what I *mean*. When did you *know* you were coming and make your move?"

"Thursday. Around noon. I was eating a whole wheat bagel. Without even thinking about why, I opened my Greyhound app."

"Sweet."

Cassandra trots after Courtney down the hall, and Leslie follows. "I like your dog. You going to tell me what's going on? I'm incredibly glad to see you, by the way." Bit of an understatement. His feelings for her are stronger than ever. His stomach's in knots. He's tingling all over. It's almost like being a young man in love again, but without the hope. He rejoices in it, the feeling itself. He has no doubt she intended to free him from his curse, but maybe you can't break a curse if the victim sees it as a blessing.

She looks into his eyes and smiles in such a way to let him know her feelings haven't changed either. It's not going to happen for them, not that way anyway. She says, "I'm glad to see you too, Les. Always. But you know what's going on: Work. Meaningful, magical, work. You're looking for work, right? This is the *New* Tree. We call it the Tree of Knowledge, the one papa god shewed us away from. We don't have a shoppe. We don't sell shit. We make things happen. Your first client will be coming here this evening. Danny got you clothes. They're in the guest bedroom. End of the hall. That's where Courtney put your things."

"Where did you find Courtney?"

"One of my lost kittens. She was tired of food service—who isn't?—about the time I needed some help."

"Where's Danny? I was hoping to see him."

"Out saving the world, of course. That's what we do here, Les. Welcome aboard."

"Is there a salary?"

"Saviors don't get a salary. Martyrdom's a much more common outcome. Don't be a chicken shit, Les. I've got a vast vision."

"That's what I'm afraid of."

"The money's good, believe me. These people wouldn't listen to you if the price wasn't slightly ridiculous. Seventy-five percent goes back into the enterprise. Magic can't make everything happen; for that you need money. That twenty-five percent will be plenty, I should think. You're a man of simple needs."

It's true. And standing here with her, the most fundamental is fulfilled. "And what is the enterprise again?"

"Saving the world. I told you, silly. Pay attention, or your grade will suffer. It's everything we've talked about—Love and Terror. It's time."

"And Hope."

"Yeah, and that too."

"You know I'm your best and most devoted pupil."

She smiles. "I know. Now go make yourself devastatingly handsome. Important palms tonight, Les, very important palms. We do all the sessions in the dining room, the room with the cameras. Don't worry about blind spots. There aren't any. Don't worry about speaking up. We can record a gnat whispering its secrets in there." He gives her a loving kiss on the cheek, Scratch purring in his ear, and heads off to dress for the part of world changer.

Still relishing the hug and kiss, the ready familiarity, he ponders what a gnat might whisper as he dresses in front of a mirrored closet in the nicest clothes he's ever worn or thought himself ever likely to wear even if he'd committed a deanship, a vice-presidency, or some other such redundant atrocity. These are celebrity threads. Everything fits perfectly.

Kristi is wearing nice jeans and a cashmere sweater that covers her arms. Are they scarred? Did she suffer that to free him? Then why is he not free? Is there a new tattoo? A new spell?

A gnat whispers in his ear, *Does it really matter? You're here, with her.*

He wishes Danny was here. He wanted to see them together, witness the happiness Serena goes on and on about. He wants that for her. Not with him, of course. How could he wish such a fate on someone he loves?

There's no possibility, however, that he'll say no to living and working with her. He feels like a knot that's bound his heart since she left has finally loosened, that he has his true life back. He looks great in the mirrored doors, a foxy old man. Whose palms will he cradle tonight? What soul will bare itself to him? He's humbled by that responsibility. When he took the sophomore Kristi's hands in his, it was in hopes of seducing her. He wanted to underestimate her, trivialize his fascination with her by screwing her. It was all about power. So he never saw anything in her open palms but his desire and his ego. She taught him how to read palms, he believes, so he would know how terribly wrong that was.

***

His client is a woman with desperate palms. She's not sure what to do with them when they can no longer hide in her coat pockets. She lays her nicely manicured hands on her chest, feels slightly ridiculous, then sticks them under her folded arms as she watches Courtney disappear with her coat. She's suited importantly but not fastidiously. Nice shoes. Short fashionably cut hair, glasses—she's an important person, an executive or public official. He gestures for her to take her seat, and she does, across the narrow table. It's a little lower than a standard table as well, for Kristi's benefit he assumes. There's no room to hide her hands in her lap, so his client lays them palms down on the polished walnut. She glances from one to the other as if she's standing guard over a pair of captured enemy combatants. Lots of palms come to him as fists— which makes perfect sense. Hers are already cowering in the trenches hoping to weather this latest barrage unscathed. There's something she very badly doesn't want to know. Which means, deep down, she already knows it.

It's hard not to smile at her predicament, impossible not to sympathize. "Tell me about yourself," he says.

She laughs. "Isn't that supposed to be your job?"

"You're not ready for that part just yet. I'm trying to get a sense of who you *think* you are first, so I can see how you're lying to yourself when I know. If you aren't self-deceived, my dear, why would you come to see me?"

This silences her, the smirking smile vanishes. She's fifty or so, not so young to be "my dear," but she oozes guilt and denial. He might as

253

well play Daddy, the kindly white-haired gent who understands. Rather like God without the judgment. He never judges, never acts either. That's Kristi's province. His client's hands are now pressed flat across her chest. They fled the table when she saw he intended to speak the truth.

"Your hands, like this." He spreads his palms before her in the space between them like an open book.

Slowly they descend, opening before him, spilling forth catastrophes she doesn't want to see, doesn't want to deal with—but she must. Fear and denial and despair have her hemmed in. She's on the edge. She's terrified. That's why she's come to Leslie, in the hope he'll aid her in her blindness and show her an easier path forward free of suffering and sacrifice and conflict. He'll prove to be a disappointment. There's no easy way.

He focuses on the crossroads of lines at the center of her right palm, the center of her life. Her hands are trembling. She's stuck in the past, hiding from the future, reliving a few moments over and over again. She can't let them go. They won't let her be. She's seated in a room, people gathered around a table, at the head is a familiar figure. "You are in the President's Cabinet?"

"Yes."

She's not impressed. She assumes Kristi has told him, or he recognizes her. The President is new, his cabinet is news, but Leslie pays little attention to the news. The Cabinet has been assembled to discuss a report. It's her meeting. The spin is in her hands. She's frozen, but the right choice is easy. It's the hard one, but she chokes, begs for more time to dig a little deeper. She hasn't a single ally in the room. Leslie reads the title of the report. It's on every laptop screen.

She has to go back and set that moment right. Too much is at stake… "You must persuade the President of the truth of the…" Being a Coleridge fan he has to laugh at what he sees. "Something called *The Xanadu Report*? It requires decisions of overwhelming significance. Tell me. How do you feel about it?"

Aghast, she yanks her hands from his. "How did you know?"

"It's all you can think about."

"Who told you about it?"

"You did. Just now."

She gasps like a fish out of water and flees the room. If she had bothered to cite a reason, it would be National Security, but he felt it too. She was overwhelmed. She didn't need to dig deeper. She was in too deep already, and she was afraid, not only of what was in the report. Afraid someone means to kill her. Or several someones. Timing is everything. For some folks the proper timing for this news is never. Eventually this will be impossible—it's hard to keep an apocalypse secret—but they're not in it for the long game—because there is none for them.

Kristi stops her at the door. He can't hear what Kristi's saying. She keeps her voice to a murmuring purr, but the client's voice echoes down the hall. "This was a mistake. I should never have come. I have no business being here."

Leslie would say, rather, her business is now concluded: Kristi has the information she wanted, and the client will likely never be the same again. Welcome to the club, my dear. Kristi's in the transformation business. Prolonged exposure, and you could end up like Leslie. That's the hope, anyway.

Kristi can film the session but not what Leslie saw. For that, she needs him to tell her. It's not always easy to put into words—the state of a sinuous train of thought at a given moment, imagining outcomes, remembering mistakes, regrets. Seeing things. This client's visions coalesced around a common theme. Floods, plagues, famines, wildfires, die-offs, widespread panic, the usual apocalyptic stuff. No zombies, however. We can all be thankful for that. Zombies are just the lazy attempt to personify the enemy so we can bludgeon it to death, when we should be bludgeoning ourselves for the mess we've made. One of the reasons the report is entitled Xanadu is that it begins with X, and extinction is one of the most frequently occurring words in the document.

Kristi isn't kidding about saving the world. Us humans, at least. Thousands of other species haven't been so lucky, thanks to us. That's what Deborah—his client—is carrying around with her. He always gets their names. It's an early piece of the puzzle for our wondering *who am I?* It becomes a receptacle of sorts. The possible and conflicting answers pile up there like wadded up drafts. Most of his clients lug that around with them, just like he did most of his life, until he tossed it away. Kristi calls him Les. No one else ever has. He's always insisted on Leslie. They have a joke between them. He can't remember who said it first. Les is more, they say.

So far the way to deal with Xanadu has been silence. Deborah's certain that won't last. And here she is blurting it out to Les. Pretty soon everybody will know, and nobody's ready.

That's what this is all about. Kristi's stepping up. She intends to save the world.

When they had their changeling conversation, he suggested superhero, and she groaned. "I hate fucking superheroes. Anything but that."

And here she is doing everything but the spandex and the cape. He guesses that makes him her sidekick. He can always hope.

Chapter Twenty

We Have A Deal!

Consciousness is so much a total mystery for our own species that we cannot begin to guess about its existence in others.

—Lewis Thomas

So here I am, back again. The magic spilling over into Leslie's hands, the terrible truth like a quivering sparrow. That only sets the stage. I figured out early on it's not enough to *tell* the future, you've got to give people the experience, the *personal* experience of the end. Whatever it is you cling to, gone. That's why I needed Danny in the first place—before I fell in love with him. With me as midwife he could deliver that experience; I was certain.

Here's how the goddess had it figured, I imagine: If you want to motivate a changeling girl to save the world, you got to give her the boy of her dreams to share it with—a real True Love story. You've got to give the changeling freak a chance not to feel lonely and unloved, or what's to keep her from throwing up her hands and going, *fuck it!*

Now she has incredible motivation to save the world. The boy-of-her-dreams plan has turned out to be some powerful juju. Maybe a little too powerful, fueled by our mutual loneliness. When Danny and me first hit DC we didn't know what the fuck we were doing. We found a little place, took a long honeymoon of museums and picnics and fucking. We were like one of those montages I hate in movies but without a hit song playing in the background, not counting me. I'm a noisy lover. I loved it. Who wouldn't? But what about *The Universe*? Isn't that why we're here—crossroads of the empire—instead of somewhere else? The whole world is fucking off, however, so why should we be left out of the fun?

We'd talk about our mission over croissants and espresso like college kids talking earnestly about the Third World, (don't you love that term—like there's more than one?) then go to a movie, fuck, wake up, fuck, repeat. In these discussions, our perpetually post orgasmic minds decided that the only way to do this thing was to aim for the top dogs, sure, because they can always squelch you, but for this kind of change we really needed to reach out to *everyone*, all the Worlds, first to last. The whole enchilada. We had no idea how, of course. Even Twitter et. al. wouldn't get the job done. So far we had mostly been reaching for each other. Naturally, just as I was thinking that, the goddess showed up.

Me and Danny were doing the zoo, wending our way through school groups for a little panda porn. There's survival value in cuteness, no denying. Most species headed for extinction don't get this celebrity treatment with the cute names and the breeding program while their habitat's being gobbled up like popcorn. Danny needed a bathroom, and the one close by was out of service, so I took a bench beside the panda walk and waited for him to go pee. The man drinks way too much coffee, but then he does have to keep up with me.

So there I was on the bench, people watching, when a black girl in pigtails wearing a blouse and skirt that had to be a school uniform, sat down beside me. She looked ten or twelve. It was hard to tell, because she was looking at me like she was older than the planet.

She said, "What do you think you're doing, child? You wanted him. You have him. An advantageous union, you said, and we agreed. The two of you together can accomplish more than apart, but girl, you need to *accomplish*. Quit fucking around. Understand?"

"Yes." I nodded vigorously, terrified. "I understand."

"Good," she said. "I trust you will act accordingly." She eyed the parade filing by to visit the pandas. "What do you think? When humans have not only destroyed the panda's habitat but their own, should we maintain such a shrine to their precarious survival? Keep a few breeding pairs alive even when their world is totally fucked? Would that be a *gift*?" She looked coldly back toward the gift shop, the windows plastered with stuffed pandas tight as ticks, then back to me. "I can't decide. What do you think? Who would line up to see them besides me?"

I didn't think the goddess really cared what I thought. Why should she? "I'm not sure how to proceed," I said, not making excuses. It was true.

"Humans, as you see, are easily bewitched by animals, who will be only too glad to assist you."

"In dreams or in reality?"

"Both, I should think."

"Who are you?" I blurted out, knowing they don't like questions, especially that one, but *Who am I?* which she's asked on several occasions, always gets something useless, like *Who do you* believe *you are?* or her favorite, *Wrong question, Kristi.* This question too apparently. She was gone. You could see it immediately, the moment she was a kid again. The goddess was gone.

"I'm Rosa Waters," the girl said sweetly. "I'm in the fifth grade. We're going to see the pandas. Is that why you're here?"

"I'm waiting for my husband. We have to get to work."

Rosa stood, lingered, probably trying to figure out what just happened, why she left her place in line to sit down beside a stranger. "I have to go. This is my class. You just looked so sad sitting here all alone."

"You're very kind. I'm always a little sad these days, no matter how happy I am. Do you study ecology in fifth?"

Rosa smiled the smile of a bright student asked about her studies. "We do. My teacher says the planet is like a single living thing—like a cell. Isn't that wonderful?"

"Yes, it is. Sounds like you've got a good teacher."

"She's the best. Bye. I hope your husband comes soon." And Rosa was off to see the pandas.

That's when Danny showed up, I led him away, and we still haven't seen the damn pandas, though I've hit the panda cam a time or two. We had to get started. Once I convinced Danny that I had indeed conversed with a goddess (or alien or faery or wtf) he quite agreed. But I had to clear the air about *one last thing*.

He bursts out laughing. He calls me The Witch Of Many Secrets, likes to tease me with each time I told him a little bit more as comic episodes, playing me somewhere between my sexy self and Columbo, saying *one last thing*. This time I really mean it. You have to wait till a person's ready, or otherwise you might as well be talking to yourself. This started out a love story. All stories do. Now it's something else. It's grown. Even lovers need a habitat. There's no land east of Eden to escape the mess we're in. We've got to make this place work.

"Sooth, did you ever ask yourself when your power to experience others' futures began, what the triggering event was, exactly?"

"I figured it was a result of the trauma, the total scrambling of my brain."

"By trauma, you mean smacking into that tree?"

"Precisely."

"And that's why you can *experience* moments of other people's futures for them—especially the ones they *need* to see? The *tree* did it? That's your Scientific Explanation? Wrong, Sooth. You got the gift *before*. It was at the apex, when you saw the conflagration below, and it spread to the horizon. Remember that part? You were seeing the future.

Freed from the rush of time, you were perfectly still, perfectly alive, perfectly aware, a witness to the planet's death—you were one with the *goddess*, Sooth. It's *her* future you saw, looking at her fucked over planet. That's why she gave you your gift—so you can help change it, not because some clever pine was having a good day."

He's silent for a moment, gives a wry smile. "Don't knock my pine. Maybe it was part of the effort. One of the guys who peeled me out of it said it caught me like a baseball in a glove, boughs wrapped around me every which way. You have me believing stranger things. Ents are easy. But back to the goddess thing. Is this like Mother Earth? Are you saying the *planet* is like a conscious being with agency?"

"I'm saying consciousness is a feature of the whole fucking universe, Sooth. You think we're *it*? Clever apes can manage it, even tiny rodents, octopi, but something as complex as the whole fucking planet is just a big dumb rock? It must be chaos if *we* can't perceive the order? That's some science you got there. How do you guys get anything done with those big blinders on? Yes! That's exactly what I'm saying. Our "known" universe keeps getting bigger, billions of galaxies, but humans never scale down their high opinion of themselves."

He ponders that one all day, and I believe I've made a convert. It was only a matter of time. I'm irresistible.

Then he wakes me up at 3 A.M. To talk: "I've always had this feeling that I'm this way for a reason, that there's something I'm *supposed* to see someday, and I need to keep an eye out for it. Crazy thinking, like I'm chosen or something. And now you're telling me, I already *saw* it, a goddess's eye view of the planet dying, and *that's* why I'm still alive in the first place?"

"That's right. I'm sure there's a few dozen doctors who put you back together again who would argue the point, but without her, you would've been dead on contact. And you *are*—'chosen or something.'"

"By the goddess."

"Yeah."

"For her memory of the future."

"Exactly. You dream the accident all the time. I've been learning it from you."

"My dream? How?"

"Next time you dream it, you'll see a crow perched atop the tree. That's me."

"Why?"

"So that *everyone* can have it."

"You can do that?"

"Not yet. Not by myself, but that's the plan. I'm building a power grid, you might say. Speaking of which, would you like to learn a new skill?"

"Do I have a choice?"

"Always. I'm all about Free Will. It's the laying on of hands. You know how you touch people to receive their experiences? I'm saying it's a two-way street. You can *give* them experiences too."

"Like what?"

"Lots of things. Healing. In your case to share your vision with others."

"Meaning the goddess's vision."

"Any vision, but that's the one we're after. I can see things, but you experience them bone deep. With this skill you can pass it on to another. I plan to put it in a dream and give it to everyone on the planet. Give me your hands."

"We're doing it now?"

"Who woke who up? Must mean you're ready. Empty your mind."
We work on it till the sun comes up. He's a natural.

So here's the short version. In order to save the planet and the human species, the species has to change its behavior rather miraculously in a ridiculously short period of time. It's too late for modest measures, due process, dithering about the economy, tra-la-la-la-la. Hybrids and recycling ain't going to get the job done. Time for a little witchcraft. If it works, there will still be a shitstorm—there's no stopping that—but life goes on, even for the needy greedy species that appointed itself caretaker, then got us all into this mess in the first place. If it doesn't work, say good-bye to life on Earth. The extinction event to end all earthly extinction events. Literally.

How do you start to sway the whole world in a weekend? You make a movie, of course, starring the biggest star in the world, a goddess in her own right. Who better to tell a goddess's story, get that imagery out there, get everyone dreaming on the same page, on the same night? You could change the world in a single revolution. That's the theory anyway. Movie first.

Langer's idea that caught Michael's fancy, that movies are virtual dreams? Dead-on. There's a bit of a feedback loop in that. Movies often provide the language for our dreams. I'm into visualizations, dreams, spirit animals.

I have a plan, sort of. Step one: Crank up the Dream Machine.

El's place up in the mountains, where she and Michael live when they're not making a movie, has been transformed into a cozy home. I haven't seen her since they left Richmond. I've missed her like crazy. We haven't really cleared the air. When you almost die, people just let a lot of things go. El never confronted me about any of the shit I put her through. I hid behind my recovery, then Danny, then my business. Case you haven't noticed, I use people. Maybe for a good reason, but nobody likes to be used, especially by someone who claims to be their best friend.

Danny and Michael go off to talk business and smoke weed. Danny's going to walk him through the whole thing. The valley of the shadow of death. Then the farfetched, overgrown, winding trail out with me as guide, only someone else will play me, and Elissa will play the goddess. Maybe the weed will help. It's a hell of a pitch.

Gwen's reading left them all feeling hopeful that something was afoot, that I wasn't done working magic on them yet, making their lives inordinately interesting, when they could otherwise have sat around like everyone else and waited for the end, hoping they might miss it, at least the grisly parts, though it's already begun. Can't you sense it? Even those who claim not to believe a word of it, *act* as if it were true, that this whole house of cards is about to come crashing down. The scientific plans are all desperately scary fixes. All potential lifeboats won't be cheap and plentiful and most are likely to go under.

So it's down to me. Magic. Back to that Tree of Knowledge. Forbidden fruit, all you can eat. Plant an orchard in a parking lot and put your knowledge to use.

El opens a bottle of wine and pours. We're still standing in the kitchen, and she cuts right to the chase. "I'm sorry I almost killed you. I've never had the chance to say it. Danny told me you knew I was there. I almost did it. I had you in my sights. I was so pissed."

I shake my head. "You weren't even close. Give me some credit. Yourself too. You wouldn't shoot your best friend like I was Evil Dictator."

"How would you know if I had? You were having the world's loudest orgasm."

"Orgasms only heighten my powers of perception."

"Bullshit."

"I've missed you, El."

"I've missed you, too, Kris. Is the sex still that good? If I'd shot you two, it would've been out of sheer envy."

"It's better, closer, but maybe that's partly because we're on a mission, and there's not much time."

We hug and get sniffly, and everything's okay between us. Still, we talk about it. El's more incredulous than angry at the deal I made with the goddess to win Danny. Life is an ongoing deal with the goddess. So why not ask for what I want? Someone to work magic with who would never doubt me because he loves me, and never doubt my magic because that's why he fell for me in the first place. He didn't have to do it for love. He had plenty of reasons without that. I didn't have to love him, but I fell for him anyway. Hard and certain.

I tell El all this, and she's happy for me, happy for herself. She and Michael are perfect for each other. She doesn't ask if magic had anything to do with that, and I don't raise the subject. This is a milestone on the El and Kris journey—both deliriously happy at the same time—with great sex on a regular basis, an unprecedented alignment of the stars. Nobody needs consoling, not for our usual petty little bullshit anyway. We've got bigger tears to cry. Surely our friendship can endure the strain. This gives us the giggles and hugs, and we're past the bad stretch. We may never speak of it again. Now we need to make good time to the horizon. The sunset's coming.

"So how do you like being a star?" I ask her when we've settled down and smoked a little weed ourselves.

"A Star. The Star, just like you always said, and I never believed it. I like it," El says. "I didn't think I would at first, because here it was again, all this *stuff* coming at me, and it just seemed so crazy—all that money. So I figured out to give it away. Michael and I don't need that much really. We live here. We give mostly to support affordable housing, public education, food issues. I can raise millions just by doing a dozen lines looking fierce and blue in some awful space adventure. That's a few houses, a tutoring program, a community garden. And I also get to make movies I want to, and even the independent movies Michael and I make make money so I help finance new films, wonderful films. It's like magic. Is it your doing?"

"Maybe I helped set things in motion." I pantomime tapping an imaginary beach ball with my fingertips, though it was more like shoulder to boulder as big as a house filled to the rafters with El's stuff Vincent couldn't haul away—the stuff in her head.

"Well thanks, Kris. I've never been happy like this my whole life. I'm glad I didn't kill you."

"Me too. Happier you're glad. Don't think I did all this. I just opened up a way. You did the rest. You're so damn *good!*"

"I grew up in my own little world, in my own little head, making movies of my life, complete with songs and costumes. It comes natural. Pretending. Now I've got real cameras and real people watching, and everything I say or do matters way more than it should."

"You're a multi-talented genius, haven't you heard?"

"Genius don't pay the rent, as Mom would say, but that's no excuse to make hopeless movies about the apocalypse like we just can't fucking wait. Gwen did our cards, said you might have an offer for us, gave me time to think about it. Answer's yes. Always."

She smiles her warm smile, and I'm wiping tears as Danny and Michael return from the den. Michael's holding a contract. He looks like he's just seen the end of the world, which is exactly what he's done. I've seen it quite a few times now. It leaves an impression. His hands are shaking. He's still adjusting to being here now, knowing. This will take a few days or the rest of his life to process. Some report the smell never leaves them, that it haunts them day and night. Michael fixes his gaze on El, a wise choice, and smiles at her, his eyes a mix of terror and delight. "We have a deal!" he says. "We have a deal!"

Amen.

Chapter Twenty-One

Matinee

The "dreamed reality" on the screen can move forward and backward because it is really an eternal and ubiquitous virtual present. The action of drama goes inexorably forward because it creates a future, a Destiny; the dream mode is an endless Now.

—Suzanne Langer, *A Note on the Film*

El hears the pitch, and Michael tells her what he saw, what he experienced, what this has all been about. El holds out her hands to Danny. "Show me," she says.

He clasps her hands, and she weeps for days. Weeps as she writes *Gaia* from Kris's rough outline, with some Michael ideas, but mostly her own. Sometimes as she writes, she feels her there, the goddess, peering over her shoulder at the screen, her breath at her ear, whispering inspiration.

When she gets stuck, she talks to Mom.

"So Mom," she asks her. "How does Gaia feel when she gives away her child and steals a human's? How can she bear it?"

Mom looks at first as if she hasn't heard, remembering all the times she had to leave El locked up in some dump so she could feed them both, and how every time her heart ached until she was back home. "She must've felt like she had no other choice, that it would be best for her daughter in the end. The child she stole, she would dote upon, I imagine, as comfort for her loss. I couldn't do it. Give up my true daughter for someone else."

"I know, Mom. I know," she whispers, the tears flowing through her fingertips into the script. It's the sacrifice that haunts Kris. She has to believe it, or what has this all been for? But she doesn't want to believe her own mother would use her so. El pours all her love for Kris into the script, into the goddess she will play, breaking her heart to heal the world.

By the time it's done, Kris and Danny have assembled a cast who knows, thanks to Danny, they aren't just making the first episode in the latest apocalyptic adventure franchise but the actual future, everything hanging by the slenderest of threads. We hold the scissors in our hands. Snip, snip. Nothing could be easier. Just squeeze. Will we set them aside, deny ourselves the triumph of our madness?

Kris spends days and nights at the servers where the digital film in dozens of languages awaits global release, working her magic. It shatters records worldwide. It has people talking—mostly talking, doing little, not enough. It's just a movie, after all. Polling shows a shift in opinion, enough to move on to the next step. Speaking truth to power.

El comes down off the mountain into town and finds the nearest screen playing *Gaia*. She can't go out in public looking like herself without prompting chaos, as if she were a real goddess, so she's made herself up as the crone, white-haired and slightly stooped. A young man holds the door for her as she enters the lobby. A larger than life cardboard flat of her as Gaia greets her. The popcorn maker fills the place with smell and sound. As a kid, El rarely went to the movies. It was a luxury they couldn't afford. She watched the dream world on cheap battered TVs with a handful of stations and shitty reception. She had to tune in the picture and adjust the tinny sound with her own imagination. Now the dreams stream their way into screens that will fit in your pocket. Still, not everyone has seen this movie or ever will, but close,

close as possible. Even this late in its run on a weekday afternoon, the auditorium is near full.

It's not a complicated plot. The daily news provides the exposition—raging wildfires, flooded cities, mass extinctions—though there are still a chorus of deniers cherishing business as usual, the holy bottom line. Bottom feeders, Kris calls them. They would've stopped this movie if they could, but ironically, it simply made too much money to be denied. El's fame is frightening. She's praised and denounced with equal passion.

She takes a seat near the back behind a woman the age she's pretending to be and a boy who's apparently her grandson by her side. The boy chatters excitedly about the movie all his friends have seen but his parents have denied him, for religious reasons apparently. His mother isn't comfortable with a female deity; the boy doesn't have a problem with it. His grandmother cautions him not to tell his parents of her indulgence. El has to smile to herself. What could be more religious, more Christian, than saving the planet? Honoring the stewardship of life on Earth Genesis proclaims?

They sit through the trailers: Cars chase one another to no apparent purpose but to crash and burn, superheroes bicker and battle foes as ridiculous as themselves in Manichean puppet shows of good v. evil that conclude with the setup for the next sequel, lovers try to love each other even though there's no happily ever after when there's no ever after, and the glories of old wars and old heroics reassure the species how wonderful we are—or once were.

The movie begins with a flock of crows flying before the rising sun, the only music the raucous chorus of their alarm. Among them is Gaia trailing clouds of glory, her face awash with tears as she gazes upon the smoldering wreckage of the Earth below and the reds and pinks of dawn are swallowed in the soot and stench of humans about their busy days.

When she alights at a busy street corner, no one seems to notice her, and she disappears into the crowd.

She holds an infant cradled in her arms. You know the rest, more or less.

The ending, some critics complain, is too ambiguous. Perhaps a sequel will explain what happens next. But there will be no sequel except the one written by the billions of earthly lives and the choices they make when Gaia returns to darkening skies.

As the credits roll, the boy is snuffling, and the grandmother is consoling him with assurances that it's only a movie, clearly regretting her choice to indulge him with this troubling movie, offering him ice cream and burgers and new games to staunch the flow of tears, but the boy isn't having any of it. He's taken the film to heart, where it belongs, where El hoped it might lodge when she wrote it, and this fills her heart with hope.

She lays her hand upon the boy's shoulder, and the boy and the old woman turn to her, the odd old crone in the back row, and El pulls the white wig from her hair, the crooked nose from her face and smiles upon him. "Don't despair," she says and squeezes his shoulder. The boy's eyes go wide with recognition, and El slips away before anyone else can see her, out into the afternoon sun shimmering from asphalt as far as the eye can see.

Unless you look hard enough, into your heart and soul, the place where all change happens. "We have to make it personal," Kris says, "like it's our own mother who lies dying." El remembers Mom abandoned at death's door for Carl, the embodiment of everything that's wrong with the world, and it's hard not to believe she didn't deserve her mother's love. But it's not a matter of deserving. The goddess loves us anyway.

As she navigates the twisting route up the mountain, she ponders the roundabout journey Kris devised for her, for them all, to bring them to this point where they could believe and do the impossible, have faith in themselves and the transformative power of love. It had to start small, in the obscure corners of their lives and dreams, like a seed buried in the Earth.

She prays that it will grow, that it will not be the last extinction.

Back on the mountain, Michael greets her with a warm embrace, and she is filled with hope.

Chapter Twenty-Two

Potus Meets The Soothsayer

Only connect! That was the whole of her sermon. Only connect the prose and the passion, and both will be exalted, and human love will be seen at its height. Live in fragments no longer. Only connect, and the beast and the monk, robbed of the isolation that is life to either, will die.

—E. M. Forster, *Howard's End*

Even with the help of the goddess, they expected it to take longer to work their way to the top. It didn't begin well. After their initial inquiries, passed along by influential clients, the White House sent fledgling staffer Kenny to make crystal clear the new president didn't take soothsayers seriously, even ones with a client list of DC movers and shakers. To double down on this message they'd sent the lowest ranking person who wasn't cleaning bathrooms to give Danny and Kristi the brush off. Kenny knew it, and Danny knew it.

Danny felt sorry for him, wasting a perfectly good weekend afternoon with some clairvoyant crank as a demonstration of how little his bosses could give a shit by sending a nobody like him when he could be hanging out with his girlfriend who thought he was somebody special.

Danny saw some sweet future moments with Kenny and the girl, Alyssa, and told him, which completely disarmed him, not their contents but that Danny should see anything at all about him. *Little old me? Why in the world would you ever see anything about me?* He's surrounded by folks who assume Danny could fill a weighty tome with prophesies about them, but imagines himself unworthy. He's in good company. Moses. Buddha. Danny. It's not a question of worthy. Nobody's *worthy*. No humans anyway. Danny can't speak for the sparrows. Humans are always looking for that key difference that makes us so special—tools, language, awareness. Danny thinks our special distinction is that we're so damn much *trouble*—a royal pain in the ass. Too smart for our own good, but not half as smart as we think we are.

Kenny sees all that. Especially as he's falling in love with the passionate, idealistic, genius Alyssa who's ready to make a change in her life. She inspires him. Smart man.

Danny used to pluck people from the rest area parking lot and rub their noses in their futures, desperate to show them moments to come, partly to help, partly just because he could. Now he's more philosophical, more strategic. There's too much at stake to spew the future out like a fire hose. But Danny figured Kenny came instead of somebody supposedly more important for a reason. Kristi pretty much has him believing everything happens for a reason. If Kenny weren't important, he wouldn't have come, and Danny wouldn't have experienced a moment of his blissful feelings for Alyssa. That Danny knew her name—when until he showed up Danny had no idea he was the one chosen for this mission made it seem like magic.

His importance, perhaps, is his very insignificance, the White House's version of the least among us. For such an outlandish story, perhaps a modest source is best if it is to be believed, with nothing to fight for but his newfound love. Danny laid his comforting hands on Kenny's shoulders and showed him the end of the world. Showed isn't right. Not just the spectacle but the experience of Earth, dead and toxic, entirely over homo fucking sapiens who take the whole planet down with them.

Maybe that's how this life business always goes. Maybe that's why we haven't found anyone else except the millions of species who live alongside us, doomed by us to extinction. If we met another sentient species out there among the stars, why would they want to have fuck-all to do with us?

You don't have to be important for the end of life to make an impression, to light a fire inside and give you a singleness of purpose. Kenny's sincere intensity soon got him to where the buck doesn't stop, frightening quite a few folks along the way, and then it was all between Danny and the Secret Service after that, arranging for his meeting with POTUS who couldn't quite believe that Kenny, a good lad, was merely crazy.

POTUS. Danny swear to God, for years he heard that term spoken on TV or wherever and didn't have a clue what it meant, never paid attention to the context. Idly wondered now and then, *Who the Hell's POTUS?* It finally dawned on him watching some assassination plot movie. "Holy shit!" he exclaimed, realizing his ignorance. Good thing he sorted that out then. That's what they all say inside the bubble. Like it's a name, when it's a role, a position. Not even that—an acronym for a position. A mantle, a disguise, a mythology. That's why they like it so much when they don't much like their boss. Nobody but POTUS wanted this meeting to happen; no good can come from it they all agreed:

POTUS Meets The Soothsayer.

In this corner, we have the notorious rest area nutcase, not so long ago nor far away—that guy who told the cop to shoot a fifteen year old kid and raved about it on TV, a bona fide looney, and don't even ask about his wives, one a witch, the other a lunatic, about whom swirl the most incredible rumors like fog shrouding a black and white cemetery. And in the opposite corner, POTUS, sitting on top of Xanadu, wondering when's a good time to cause worldwide panic, when your approval ratings are already subterranean, you couldn't pass gas in Congress, and you just want your term to end when it's only just begun, to not be so damned *important* anymore. So useless.

POTUS needs Danny it seems, knows it instinctively. Otherwise Danny wouldn't be in this caravan of dark SUVs winding up twisting narrow roads to some obscure mountain valley in Virginia that's apparently a hideaway for POTUS to disappear and unwind. It's the new moon—which Kristi took to be auspicious. It's certainly dark. Danny can't see much of anything but the Expedition ahead of him for most of the way.

POTUS's place is cozy, nestled in a leafy hollow, once you get past the soldiers and the dogs and the fleet of beefy black vehicles. Danny wonders if it's always like this, braced for attack, or whether it's all about his visit. He's the attack. They all give him the eye, no question. He wonders what they've been told about him. Their curiosity crackles in the air. Even the dogs have a hard time settling down once Danny gets out of the car, feeding off their masters' adrenalin. The headlights are still blazing. Danny looks down at his feet so as not to be blinded as they lead him to the threshold of the POTUS hideaway. There's a sign on the door. *Simplify.* Danny tries to figure out how he fits into that dictum as a decided complication in the President's life.

As he stands waiting to be let inside, one of the black-suited crew who's been minding him leans over and whispers, "So what's the deal with you? You seem harmless enough. How come we have orders not to touch you or let you touch us?"

Kenny must've delivered one scary debriefing. Danny looks into the Secret Service man's eyes. Soon, in a week or so, he'll take a bullet for POTUS, diving in front of the shooter. According to Kris there'll be a series of assassination attempts after POTUS goes public with Xanadu. POTUS miraculously survives them all, leaving several dead heroes behind. If there's a history, they'll be remembered.

"Good advice," Danny says. The man doesn't need to know his future with so little left.

The agent at the door beckons Danny inside. It's cozy, modest. Waldenesque. It smells like wood and smoke and dog and coffee. POTUS's pooch, a beefy black lab, lies sprawled in the heat. POTUS rises and, apparently unafraid of the devil's touch, shakes Danny's hand, bids him sit in a rocker, feet to the fire. POTUS pours him coffee black with no sugar, obviously well briefed. Danny sips. It's the best coffee he's ever tasted.

Danny tells his story, how he came to experience the end of the world, and has been entrusted to share that vision at the behest of the goddess so that it might not come to pass, not expecting to be believed, of course, but to give the context for what happens next, when, still unafraid, POTUS shakes Danny's hand to bid him a bemused farewell, and Danny reveals the planet's death with a firm squeeze, not to be manly, but to keep them both from falling. Witnessing the apocalypse causes many a knee to buckle.

POTUS cries out. The vision fades. They open their eyes ringed by Secret Service, weapons pointed at Danny's head. Their hands are still clasped. POTUS's dog is howling like a fleet of fire trucks has just rolled through the room. The security dogs are going nuts on the ends of their chains. "Stand down," POTUS says. "Leave us." And they do. Danny sinks to his knees, POTUS too, sobbing in each other's arms for some while.

There was a moment Danny imagined all those guns firing at once, his head exploding—the dogs slipping loose, tearing him to pieces—more additions to his stockpile of horrible futures. Not prophetic, just terrifying. He lets them go. He has to stay focused on the future as it will be—unless they can change it, change everyone, overnight.

Danny explains about the dream, when the overwhelming majority of humans on the planet will experience what the president just did in a single turn of the Earth, and how everything needs to be ready for the ensuing changes. Danny doesn't have to ask if POTUS understands the changes he means. Xanadu suggests any number of actions to be taken to possibly survive, all politically impossible.

POTUS's protectors will be livid. Avoid the hands, they said. Was that so hard? How can we protect you if you won't protect yourself? Now you've exposed yourself to the horrible truth. Some will quit over the incident, like rats leaving a sinking ship, only there's no shoreline to swim to. Kenny, who's been cooling his heels in an interrogation facility in Quantico, will soon show up at POTUS's side, as a Special Aide to the President, someone POTUS says, "who shares my vision."

Nightmares now too.

Alyssa, in case you're wondering, is there when he's set free and also has the ear of the President and puts passionate, persuasive speeches into POTUS's mouth. Kristi was giddy the first time she did Alyssa's cards, even while Kenny was still sitting in a cell.

Their meeting is over. POTUS has to return to Washington immediately. There's much to do. Danny steps out into the night. The sky is filled with stars, visible now that the headlights are extinguished. As Danny thinks this, the headlights come back on all at once by someone's command—*Let there be light!* Screw the stars and the universe. We're only interested in ourselves.

As Danny passes by, one of the security dogs lunges toward him, and he meets him halfway, burrowing his hands into his ruff, and he springs up, his handler screaming, and licks Danny's face. Danny takes a knee and pets him all over, telling him what a good boy he is, and the dog puts his paws on Danny's shoulders and wags furiously, dancing with delight. His stunned handler has dropped the lead. The other dogs are dragging their masters toward Danny with all their strength. Laughing, Danny says, "Let them go," and they join them in a play tussle on the grassy meadow, four big German Shepherds and Danny. Cassandra will go nuts when she catches a whiff of him.

This only takes a moment or two, and he's back on his feet brushing pine needles and fur off him, the handlers snaring their disobedient badass beasts, still wagging and happy. The Secret Service can't take their dazed eyes off of Danny, all wondering, *What the fuck* is *this guy?*

A dog lover, obviously.

They leave him at his vehicle in a Park and Ride at the edge of the woods and disappear into the night. From now on he can only assume he'll be followed. Some drone is hovering somewhere wondering why he doesn't start the car and just go already. Hovering must be tedious. He wonders where the operator is. Maybe in his living room with a pizza and a laptop, *60 Minutes* in one window and Danny in another. The *60 Minutes* stories tonight, not coincidentally, are all about climate change. Maybe the drone operator could care less. He just watches Danny driving home and the planet coming apart at the seams. He doesn't see a connection. All the connections. Just pixels.

Danny doesn't want to go home yet. Kristi and Les and Courtney will all want to know how it went—revealing the apocalypse to POTUS, the beginning of the endgame. After this, the magic either works or it doesn't. Danny wants a little time to take it in, what just happened, what he just started. He'll share it soon enough. For now, he'd just like to live with it.

The hardest time he's ever lived through was riding to the hospital with Les not knowing if Kristi was alive or dead in the ambulance ahead of them. Les took his right hand from the wheel, pried it open and looked at it. "She's chosen you," he said. "Never doubt your love. Never doubt her. She made this happen. Kristi is no suicide, believe me." Then he laid his hand back on the wheel and gave it a comforting squeeze. Les lay his head back and stared at the ambulance racing down Monument. "They won't let her die." At the time Danny thought "they" meant the medical professionals, but now he knows who he meant, and he was right.

At the foot of the mountain he finds a tavern still open. There are a handful of locals at the bar. They watch TV as they sip their beers waiting for a kickoff. The network has slipped in a sliver of news in the interim to kill time—Greenland melting, Miami flooding, forests blazing, the usual. The guys at the bar are glad it has nothing to do with them or the game that's about to begin. The Cowboys vs. Washington. They're impatient for the news to conclude so the battle may begin. A classic struggle of arch rivals, the announcer teases, but first there's one more story with lots of fun footage from all around the world, played with the lightest touch, a feel-good piece for animal lovers:

Crows have been behaving oddly lately. They've been migrating, mobbing in the cities, showing up in the few places where there haven't been crows before. One murder of crows—the reporter makes a big winking deal of the spooky name—even hitched a ride on a trans Atlantic crossing and wouldn't be deterred. The passengers were charmed and fed the cruise crashers morsels from the ample buffets. Crows will apparently eat anything from crab legs to chocolate cake, even sip a Piña Colada. The captain said he would miss them, that he's dreamed about them every night since they left. Known to carry away shiny objects, the crows took his watch from his bedside and dropped it in the ocean as they departed. The captain took this to be a message, though he couldn't decipher its meaning—or didn't want to say it to the bubbly reporter who loved her some quirky crows. They ended the story with a *Heckle and Jekyll* clip, apparently unaware they were magpies, not crows, and were nothing like the crows trying to stop the end of time and timekeepers.

The guys at the bar have all been riveted to this story. One says the crows around his place have been acting spooky too, and the others nod their assent. One expert tells the reporter it's likely caused by global warming—cut to a crow catching a little shade under a drink umbrella—and the guys at the bar denounce the expert roundly. This is coal country. Disbelief in climate change is an article of faith. Even when the local power plant is burning natural gas because it's cheaper, you gotta believe coal is coming back—clean this time, someway or other. Washed in the blood of the lamb. Clean coal will be the second coming.

The commercials sell cars and fossil fuels and prescription meds. Manly trucks, safe natural gas, and erectile dysfunction remedies. The essentials. The same pretty woman seems to make the rounds through these commercials, her target audience orders another pitcher.

The music plays, and the ball is kicked, and that's the end of that. For now, they forget the crow story, but they will speak of it again. It's already showing up big time on YouTube as videos from those places where crows have never lived before start going viral. Folks are delirious about them. The crows handle the adulation well.

The crows' behavior has everything to do with climate change, though not in the way the expert meant. They're in on it—the plot to save the planet from the human race who always imagine a brighter future while denying the future they're busily creating. It's going to be hard, Danny knows, letting go, stepping down from the throne. No more Crown of Creation. We've deposed ourselves. But it's good too, to be humbled, to feel closer to the Earth who made you whoever you are, in one way or another. Danny just watches and listens. This too shall pass.

Danny has what the game watchers are having except for the self-deception he envies them. He resists the urge to set them straight, give them a dose of what POTUS just had. Instead he sips on his cold beer. Let them enjoy their game. They'll have their chance soon enough. He'll see them in his dreams.

Till then he has lots of other folks to meet. POTUS, it seems, knows everyone whose hand Danny would like to shake. Kristi drew up quite an impressive list. Courtney worked out his itinerary. The irony of the Godzilla-sized carbon footprint isn't lost on him, but the goddess sees this as the last roll of the dice. If this doesn't work, she's leaving. Apparently goddesses do have other places to go.

The rest of us are earthbound. Danny's going to be a busy man, crisscrossing the planet, miles to go before he sleeps. To dream, no perchance about it. More like last chance.

Kristi tells him nothing's certain. She means this in a good way, that the Earth can survive in spite of what he's seen. But then the magic needs to work. And there's nothing certain about magic. Knowledge they can deliver, but what folks do with it is anybody's guess.

Chapter Twenty-Three

Just Like Abraham And Isaac

If we choose to let conjecture run wild, then animals, our fellow brethren in pain, diseases, death, suffering and famine—our slaves in the most laborious works, our companions in our amusements—they may partake our origin in one common ancestor— we may be all netted together.

—Charles Darwin

The crows talk to Clint, and he talks back. They dream with him at night. They see things from way up high you can't see down here on the ground. They have a different view of things. They watch the world changing, just as they always done. This time's different. This time everything dies if things keep going like they're going. They see it sharp and clear.

Clint watches TV with his parents in the evening. What they call the news. Trainwrecks and tornadoes and people lying to each other, lying to his parents, lying to anyone fool enough to listen. They call it staying informed. They have no idea what's going on, what the crows and him know.

"Clint, why you acting so peculiar?" his mother asks him, though she knows he's always been "dreamy" as she calls it. "You been hanging around that crazy woman again?" She won't even say her name. She and her friends talk about the goings-on at Gwen's, the comings and goings at all hours. The wickedness. They think it's about rich folks' problems like divorce and addiction and mental disorders.

He doesn't answer her question. He tells her, "I met Elissa Fenice the movie star," knowing she won't believe such a bald-faced lie, and she just shakes her head and walks away. She doesn't want to know what he's up to. If she did know, she'd be on her knees praying for him, and he doesn't want that for him or her either one, her so scared for him she can't sleep nights, her thinking he's so bad only God can help him—his own mother. If it come down to him or God, he knows who his folks'd choose, so he don't go there if he can help it.

Far as they're concerned it's always God's choice anyway. Just like Abraham and Isaac. Scariest story ever heard in his life. What if that ram hadn't come along, got itself stuck? You know Isaac had to ask himself that question every day for the rest of his life. Did Abraham, the chosen one, ever give it another thought? Someday Clint hopes his parents will be proud of him, but he knows that day, if it ever comes, will be a long, long ways away. If we're lucky and last that long.

He doesn't tell Mama he met a witch named Kristi, and they meet up in the woods, and she teaches him how to develop his gift, as she calls it. He likes the way she treats him, like he's all grown up. Not even Gwen who loves him like a grandma treats him like that. Not that his real grandmas ever had much use for him except pitching in when his folks warned him he'd be burning in Hellfire For All Eternity if he didn't get his head out of the clouds and get right with God. Clint told Kristi he thought Hellfire For All Eternity would be a great name for a band, and she laughed. He wishes he could tell his parents you don't have to go nowhere to burn. Just stick around. Keep doing what you're doing. In church he learned God drowned everybody in the Flood because of all the sinful children in the world, but the way he reads the story, it's the parents who had more to answer for.

He spends days with Kristi when he's supposed to be in school, talking with the crows and rats and ants—creatures with a global reach, she says. She tells him crows even talk to other animals. Before long, she says, he'll be talking to the fishes in the sea, which he finds hard to believe—he ain't much of a swimmer. But everything she's said so far has come true. When she and Gwen get together it's like a glimpse over the rainbow. He's hoping things are going to be okay. Different. But there's nothing wrong with that. He's been different his whole life.

Kristi brings along her cat Scratch who seems to know what Clint's thinking before he does. He rides around on her shoulders. Clint scratches his head, and he seems to like that, purring like a motorboat. Clint's never been around cats much. His mother doesn't like them. First time Clint talked with crows, Kristi had him hold Scratch in his arms like a baby, and the cat purred him right through it. Like he was tuning them in on the same frequency. Sometimes a crow will perch right on the tip of Kristi's finger, and Scratch and that crow will go nose to beak like they was kissing each other.

Kristi, with Scratch draped around her neck, is like a magic person out of a story, though she's no taller than Clint and cusses worse. She makes the crows laugh. He never knew crows laughed before. Now it seems pretty obvious. She's a goddess he guesses, or good as, though she's nothing like the goddess Elissa plays in the movie everybody's talking about, *Gaia*. He's seen it five times. Makes him cry every time. His parents hate that, when he cries at stuff. It scares them. It scares him they think something's wrong with tears, even the good kind of tears, like when something real good happens, or someone does something super nice. He wants to be that someone. Far as he can tell, Jesus did too, no matter what his parents say. He doesn't think he's going to Hell for caring too much or being too nice.

He hasn't been able to talk his folks into seeing the movie. They're not quite sure it's Christian, Mama says, and maybe it isn't, but he's not stupid enough to say that doesn't matter. He lets it go. All her friends are talking about it, and she'll give in sooner or later. She'll see. Everybody will.

He met Danny too. He just showed up with Kristi one day. Every bit as spooky as Clint imagined him to be when she told Clint all he could do, because he seemed so ordinary, like some guy hanging out at the café having breakfast. Clint expected him to glow or something, twitch like a dreaming dog. Instead he was super nice right up to the point he said he was sorry and clasped Clint's hands across the table. Right there in Karen's Kitchen waiting for bacon and eggs, he showed Clint the end of the world, put him in the middle of its dying.

Broke his heart so bad he couldn't stop crying for days.

When he came around, there was Kristi by his bed, holding his hand, saying she was sorry they had to do that to somebody as sensitive as him, but they thought he should know what all this was for. So he'd be motivated, committed, passionate.

That's not how he ever thought of himself, but yeah, now? That three times over. They're trying to change the future. Trying to survive. He wishes he was older and smarter. Kristi tells him the Earth's already had too much older and smarter and could use a little young and humble and good-hearted.

He hopes she's right.

It won't be long now, Kristi says. He's run away from home and is living at her big place in Georgetown. Scratch and Cassandra sleep on his bed. Gwen just came yesterday and brought Gennie and Isabel with her. The place is getting pretty full. Elissa and Michael, Kristi told him this morning, will be coming in tonight.

At night the air is thick with dreams. They practice. The one dream. The one about the end of everything. He can't wait for Elissa to dream with them. He knows she only plays a goddess in a movie, but that's close enough for him.

A few hours before dawn, with Scratch in the lead, the dogs run free through the slumbering streets padding down alleyways into other dogs' dreams. He worries about them out there in the city. What if the dog catcher gets them? Kristi assures him Scratch won't let that happen, and besides, all the dog catchers are sound asleep.

The sky's still pink when the dogs come home and chow down in the kitchen. The clanking of their dishes always wakes Clint with a smile. It's not just us humans. We're not alone. No one wants us to fail but ourselves. So we can go to Heaven, he supposes. Or Hell. No thanks to both of them. Clint's sticking it out with the Earth.

Chapter Twenty-Four

Now I Lay Me Down To Sleep

And for all this, nature is never spent;
There lives the dearest freshness deep down things;
And though the last lights off the black West went
Oh, morning, at the brown brink eastward, springs—
Because the Holy Ghost over the bent
World broods with warm breast & with ah! bright wings.
—Gerard Manley Hopkins, *God's Grandeur*

The time has come, the magic's done. I'm not expecting a visit from the goddess or any of her emissaries, so I'm startled to find a strange young woman about my age lying in my bed like Geraldine, giving me a cool, level stare like this is her room I've blundered into. Her life.

I know immediately who she is. She looks strikingly like my mother, her mother actually. Here's the child stolen at birth to be raised by her abductors, while I was the changeling left behind to break the parents' hearts and change the world. What does that make us, sisters? Nothing?

"It appears your work is almost done," she says matter-of-factly, as if she knows all my plans. Her mother—my mother?—has told her I assume. I try to imagine that, perched on the goddess's knee.

"Yes. Tonight. Why are you here? Why now?"

"You have a choice. Do you want it back? Your life?"

"We trade places again?"

"Yes."

"What about you? Do you want my life?"

The question seems to surprise her. Why would anyone wish for such a fate? "It is not my choice. It is only fair. You had no choice. You have lived as a mortal."

"Have you been watching?"

"Sometimes." She says this as if confessing to a guilty habit. She's been watching too much perhaps. Must be a helluva distraction.

"Do you ever envy me?"

She lowers her eyes examining a deep pool of memories. "Yes. But I do not envy you death."

"Death's not so bad, as long as there's love. Without love, it's all death."

"So you wish to stay?"

"Yes. Of course. Does she care?" I ask. "About me I mean?"

"More than you can possibly imagine."

"I don't know—I've got a pretty good imagination."

She smiles, the first moment I've liked her in our brief sisterhood. "What's it like, to know you will die?" she asks, "to know that life will go on without you?"

"To be a part of the Earth, you mean? It's beautiful beyond your imagining, unless life did not go on, that life itself should wink out like a spent cinder and vanish from the Earth."

She ponders this for a moment, struggling to understand mortality when she herself will never die and vanishes to wherever it is goddesses wait for mortals to decide their fate, to listen—prayers or silence? I didn't even catch her name.

We lie in a pinwheel on the floor, the eleven of us, our arms outstretched, our hands intertwined. Scratch is perched on my chest purring, Cassandra lies between Danny's legs, Gennie between Gwen's, and Isabel between Clint's. Danny and Elissa are on either side of me.

Elissa clasps Michael's hand and Gwen clasps his other and Clint's who clasps Leslie's who clasps Danny's other hand. We're sprawled on the dining room floor, emptied of furniture, the cameras rolling. An historic moment. Here's hoping we still have history when we're done.

The sun is sinking below the horizon, the shadows, long and distorted. We start to lose the shape of things, imagine ourselves plastered to the face of an enormous sphere in a boundless universe. The planet at our backs is alive, fills us with life. The room is ringed with crows atop every molding and picture frame and lamp, the windows thrown open wide.

Danny remembers the future, we all do, and the crows burst into the night to spread the nightmare, chasing the dawn around the Earth down a slender trail of hope. We listen to the wings beating for hours in our dreams, throughout the long night.

We stop where we began, awaken. The sun rises.

Everyone Has A Dream

We wake choking from the smoke, from the stench of death and lifeless-
ness. Everything is normal. It was just a dream. Clocks tick. Faucets
drip. The old dog scratches. Only outside it is oddly quiet. No cars, no
planes, no leaf blowers, no air conditioners, no jackhammers, no sirens
wailing. Just birdsong blowing in the wind, the goddess laughing, tree
limbs swaying in the wind, the shimmer of leaves.

We hear through the thin walls, our neighbors crying.

We feel in our tiny prisons our own tears flowing.

And birds singing, singing, singing. It's a little frightening, that cho-
rus, not because we don't know why they're singing but because we do.
The sun has risen, is rising. Our dream has chased the dawn around the
world, fleeing the night and the night that lies ahead. It's a revelation.
Everything's different now. Doubt is gone. Denial is impossible. We
have finally reached what now?

We open our eyes.

We rise and go out the door onto the porch, the balcony, the pasture,
the shore, the narrow alleyway, the towering wood, the cavernous street,
the mountainside, above us only sky. All our machinery is still for the
moment. The world is not. It scampers, ambles, scuttles, slithers, hops,
gallops, flutters, and walks—gathers before us, behind us, surrounds us
in fact.

Everywhere are eyes looking back at us, great and small. Thousands
upon thousands of eyes, from the hawks to the anthills. The hawks
whistle. An elephant trumpets. A rat laughs. A snake slithers in for a

closer look to make sure we understand the question, now that we have dreamt our future: What now, humans? What now?

Now. This very moment. The past is over; the future never comes.

The crows cavort above our heads, muttering their delight.

The cars, lining the streets for as far as we can see, begin the short process of rusting in the sun, but that's okay because we don't need to go anywhere but where we are. Here. Earth.

We step into the light.

Awake.

Coming Soon!

DENNIS DANVERS
LEAVING THE DEAD

Leaving the Dead is a collection of eighteen stories about the long slow dance with death and the heartbreak of life—no zombies allowed.

• When a writer runs into the ghost of his father who died of Alzheimer's, death has restored his memory, and he's eager to share.

• An unlikely couple and an abandoned-seeing eye dog find happiness after everyone else dies.

• A college freshman goes home for the holidays with her lover who claims to be a robot—and takes her to an abandoned factory on Christmas Eve where she was born.

• A cat on death's door is miraculously healed by his owner, but lives on and on and never ages.

• When the broken dream factory shuts down, its most devoted worker has to figure out how the world will get along without broken dreams.

For more information
visit: www.SpeakingVolumes.us

On Sale Now!

STEPHEN STEELE
THE TROUBLE WITH MIRACLES

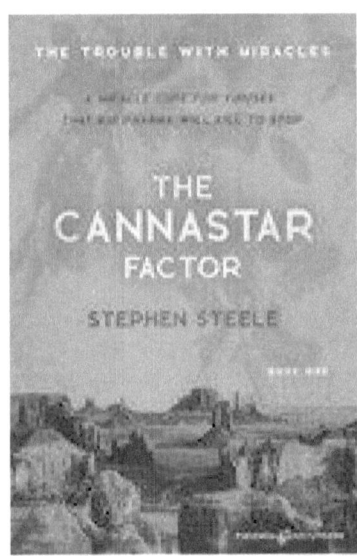 

For more information
visit: www.SpeakingVolumes.us

www.ingramcontent.com/pod-product-compliance
Lightning Source LLC
Chambersburg PA
CBHW020228260626
47156CB00002B/589